Robert Michael Ballantyne

The Settler and the Savage

A Tale of Peace and War in South Africa

Robert Michael Ballantyne

The Settler and the Savage
A Tale of Peace and War in South Africa

ISBN/EAN: 9783744756488

Printed in Europe, USA, Canada, Australia, Japan

Cover: Foto ©Andreas Hilbeck / pixelio.de

More available books at **www.hansebooks.com**

ATTACKED BY AN OSTRICH.—*Frontispiece.*—PAGE 189.

The SETTLER & the SAVAGE

A TALE.

THE

SETTLER AND THE SAVAGE

A Tale of Peace and War in South Africa

BY

R. M. BALLANTYNE,

AUTHOR OF "UNDER THE WAVES, OR DIVING IN DEEP WATERS;" "RIVERS OF ICE: A TALE ILLUSTRATIVE OF ALPINE ADVENTURE AND GLACIER ACTION;" "BLACK IVORY;" "THE PIRATE CITY ;" "THE NORSEMEN IN THE WEST;" "THE IRON HORSE;" "THE FLOATING LIGHT OF THE GOODWIN SANDS ;" "ERLING THE BOLD;" "FIGHTING THE FLAMES;" "SHIFTING WINDS;" "DEEP DOWN;" "THE LIGHTHOUSE;" "THE LIFE-BOAT;" "GASCOYNE;" "THE GOLDEN DREAM," ETC. ETC.

With Illustrations.

LONDON:

JAMES NISBET & CO., LIMITED

21 BERNERS STREET

PREFACE.

In this tale I have endeavoured to give a truth-
ful, though unavoidably slight, outline of the stirring
incidents of a most important period in the history
of the Colony of the Cape of Good Hope.

I take this opportunity to return my hearty
thanks to those kind and hospitable friends in the
Colony who aided me, during my sojourn among
them, in acquiring information about men and
things at "the Cape."

R. M. BALLANTYNE.

EDINBURGH, 1877.

CONTENTS.

                                                                    PAGE

CHAP. I.—THE WILD KARROO, ...   1

II.—INTRODUCES A CAPE-DUTCHMAN AND HIS FAMILY, AND
       SHOWS THE UNCERTAINTY OF HUMAN PLANS, .   .   23

III.—DESCRIBES THE SOMEWHAT CURIOUS BEGINNING OF
       SETTLER-LIFE IN SOUTH AFRICA,   .   .   .   38

IV.—FURTHER PARTICULARS OF "SETTLERS' TOWN," AND
       A START MADE FOR THE PROMISED LAND,   .   53

V. ADVENTURES AND INCIDENTS OF THE FIRST NIGHT IN
       THE "BUSH,"   63

VI. SPREADING OVER THE LAND,   .   .   .   77

VII. THE "LOCATION,"   89

VIII. SHOWS THE PLEASURES, PAINS, AND PENALTIES OF
       HOUSEKEEPING IN THE BUSH,   .   .   108

IX. OFF TO THE HIGHLANDS AND BLACK SNAKES IN THE
       BUSH, ...   123

X. THE LOCATION ON THE RIVER OF BABOONS, .   139

XI.—EXPLORATIONS AND HUNTING EXPERIENCES,   .   158

XII.—GIVES SOME ACCOUNT OF A GREAT LION-HUNT,   .   174

XIII.—ADVENTURE WITH AN OSTRICH, .   .   .   186

XIV. THE BERGENAARS, ...   194

XV.—TREATS OF THE ZUURVELD AGAIN, AND ONE OR TWO
       SURPRISING INCIDENTS, ...   211

CONTENTS.

PAGE

XVI.—THE GREAT FLOODS OF 1823, . 227

XVII.—TREATS OF HOPES, FEARS, AND PROSPECTS, BESIDES
DESCRIBING A PECULIAR BATTLE, . 240

XVIII.—FAIRS, FIGHTS, FREE-TRADE, FACTIONS, AND OTHER
MATTERS, ... 256

XIX.—DESCRIBES A SERIES OF EARLY RISINGS, 267

XX.—TREATS OF THE DELIGHTS, DANGERS, AND DISTRESSES
OF THE WILDERNESS, . . . 284

XXI.—TELLS OF MATTERS TOO NUMEROUS AND STIRRING TO
BE BRIEFLY REFERRED TO, . 298

XXII.—DARK AND THREATENING CLOUDS, 318

XXIII.—WAR, ... 327

XXIV.—SHOWS WHAT BEFELL A TRADER AND AN EMIGRANT
BAND, ... 348

XXV.—TREATS OF VARIOUS STRANGE INCIDENTS, SOME
INTERESTING MATTERS, AND A RESCUE, . . 365

XXVI.—RELATES INCIDENTS OF THE WAR AND A GREAT DELIVER-
ANCE, ... 375

XXVII.—THE FATE OF THE PARAMOUNT CHIEF OF KAFIRLAND, 391

XXVIII.—RESULTS OF WAR, ... 398

XXIX.—THE LAST, ... 410

LIST OF ILLUSTRATIONS.

ATTACKED BY AN OSTRICH (p. 189), . . *Frontispice*

ILLUSTRATED TITLE-PAGE.

ROUND THE CAMP-FIRES, ... *page* 64

JUNKIE COLLARS A SNAKE, . . . 215

A FIGHT WITH LOCUSTS, . . . 250

A "CAPE TIGER" SIGHTS BREAKFAST, . . . 274

THE SETTLER AND THE SAVAGE.

CHAPTER I.

THE WILD KARROO.

A SOLITARY horseman—a youth in early manhood —riding at a snail's pace over the great plains, or karroo, of South Africa. His chin on his breast; his hands in the pockets of an old shooting-coat; his legs in ragged trousers, and his feet in worn-out boots. Regardless of stirrups, the last are dangling. The reins hang on the neck of his steed, whose head may be said to dangle from its shoulders, so nearly does its nose approach the ground. A felt hat covers the youth's curly black head, and a double-barrelled gun is slung across his broad shoulders.

We present this picture to the reader as a subject of contemplation.

It was in the first quarter of the present century that the youth referred to—Charlie Considine by

name—rode thus meditatively over that South
African karroo. His depression was evidently not
due to lack of spirit, for, when he suddenly awoke
from his reverie, drew himself up and shook back
his hair, his dark eyes opened with something like a
flash. They lost some of their fire, however, as he
gazed round on the hot plain which undulated like
the great ocean to the horizon, where a line of blue
indicated mountains.

The truth is that Charlie Considine was lost—
utterly lost on the karroo! That his horse was in
the same lost condition became apparent from its
stopping without orders and looking round languidly
with a sigh.

"Come, Rob Roy," said the youth, gathering up
the reins and patting the steed's neck, "this will
never do. You and I must not give in to our first
misfortune. No doubt the want of water for two
days is hard to bear, but we are strong and young
both of us. Come, let's try at least for a sheltering
bush to sleep under before the sun goes down."

Animated by the cheering voice if not by th
words of its rider, the horse responded to the exhorta
tion by breaking into a shuffling canter.

After a short time the youth came in sight o
what appeared to be a herd of cattle in the fa
distance. In eager expectation he galloped toward
them and found that his conjectures were correct

⌐ were cattle in charge of one of that lowest
⌐e human race, a Bushman. The diminutive,
k-skinned, and monkey-faced creature was nearly
· d. He carried a sheepskin kaross, or blanket,
:is left shoulder, and a knobbed stick, or "kerrie,"
is right hand.

Can you speak English?" asked Considine as he
rode up.

The Bushman looked vacant and made no reply.

"Where is your master's house?" asked the
youth.

A stare was the only answer.

"Can't you speak, you dried-up essence of stupidity!" exclaimed Charlie with impatience.

At this the Bushman uttered something with so
many klicks, klucks, and gurgles in it that his in-
terrogator at once relinquished the use of the tongue,
and took to signs, but with no better success, his
efforts having only the effect of causing the mouth
of the Bushman to expand from ear to ear. Uttering
a few more klicks and gurgles, he pointed in the
direction of the setting sun. As Considine could
elicit no fuller information he bade him a contemptuous farewell and rode away in the direction
indicated.

He had not gone far when a dark speck became
visible on the horizon directly in front.

"Ho! Rob," he exclaimed, "that looks like something—a bush, is it? If so, we may find water there, who knows—eh? No, it can't be a bush, for it moves," he added in a tone of disappointment. "Why, I do believe it's an ostrich! Well, if we can't find anything to drink, I'll try to get something to eat."

Urging his jaded steed into a gallop, the youth soon drew near enough to discover that the object was neither bush nor ostrich, but a horseman.

The times of which we write were unsettled. Considine, although "lost," was sufficiently aware of his whereabouts to understand that he was near the north-eastern frontier of Cape Colony. He deemed it prudent, therefore, to unsling his gun. On drawing nearer he became convinced from the appearance of the stranger that he could not be a Kafir. When close enough to perceive that he was a white man, mounted and armed much like himself, he re-slung his gun, waved his cap in token of friendship, and galloped forward with the confidence of youth.

The stranger proved to be a young man of about his own age—a little over twenty—but much taller and more massive in frame. He was, indeed, a young giant, and bestrode a horse suitable to his weight. He was clad in the rough woollen and leathern garments worn by the frontier farmers, or boers, of that period, and carried one of those long heavy flint-lock guns, or "roers," which the Dutch-

African colonist then deemed the most effective weapon in the universe.

"Well met!" exclaimed Considine heartily, as he rode up.

"Humph! that depends on whether we meet as friends or foes," replied the stranger, with a smile on his cheerful countenance that accorded ill with the caution of his words.

"Well met, I say again, whether we be friends or foes," returned Considine still more heartily, "for if we be friends we shall fraternise; if we be foes we shall fight, and I would rather fight you for love, hate, or fun, than die of starvation in the karroo."

"What is your name, and where do you come from?" demanded the stranger.

"One question at a time, if you please," answered the youth. "My name is Charles Considine. What is yours?"

"Hans Marais."

"Well, Mr. Marais, I come from England, which is my native home. In the coming I managed to get wrecked in Table Bay, landed at Capetown, joined a frontier farmer, and came up here—a long and roughish journey, as probably you know, and as my garments testify. On the way I lost my comrades, and in trying to find them lost myself. For two days nothing in the shape of meat or drink has passed my lips, and my poor horse has fared little

better in the way of drink, though the karroo-bush
has furnished him with food enough to keep his
bones together. So now, you have my biography in
brief, and if you be a man possessed of any powers
of sympathy, you will know what to do."

The young Dutchman held out his huge hand,
which Considine grasped and shook warmly.

" Come," he said, while a slight smile played on
his bronzed countenance ; " I have nothing here to
give you, but if you will come with me to yon koppie
you shall have both meat and drink."

The koppie to which he referred was a scarce
discernible knoll on the horizon.

Hans Marais seemed to be a man of few words,
for he turned and galloped away, without for some
time uttering another syllable to his companion.
As for Considine, the thought of once more feasting
on any sort of meat and drink was so fascinating,
in his then ravenous condition, that he cared for
nought else, and followed his guide in silence.

Soon the herbage on the plain became more luxuriant, and in half an hour the two horsemen found
themselves riding among scattered groups of mimosa
bushes, the thorns of which were from three to five
inches long, while their sweet fragrance scented the
whole atmosphere.

On reaching the ridge of one of the undulations
of the plain, Hans Marais drew rein and gazed

intently towards the distant horizon. At the same time Considine's horse pricked up its ears, pawed the ground, and exhibited unwonted signs of a desire to advance.

"Hallo, Rob!" exclaimed its master, "what's wrong with you?"

"Your horse has been gifted by his Maker with a power," said Hans, "which has been denied to man. He scents water. But before he shall taste it he must help me to procure fresh meat. Do you see the boks on that koppie?"

"Do you mean those white specks like ostrich eggs on the hillock to the right of the big bush?"

"The same. These are spring-boks. Ride away down by that hollow till you get somewhat in their rear, and then drive them in the direction of that clump of bushes on our left, just under the sun."

Without waiting for a reply Hans rode off at a gallop, and Considine proceeded to obey orders.

A few minutes sufficed to bring him close to the spring-boks, which beautiful antelopes no sooner observed him than, after one brief gaze of surprise, they bounded away in the direction of the bushes indicated by Hans,—conscious apparently of their superior fleetness, for they seemed in no great haste, but leaped about as if half in play, one and another taking an occasional spring of six feet or more into the air. As they passed the bushes

towards which Considine drove them, a white puff
was seen to burst from them, and the huge roer of
Hans Marais sent forth its bellowing report. It
seemed as if the entire flock of boks had received an
electric shock, so high did they spring into the air.
Then they dashed off at full speed, leaving one of
their number dead upon the plain.

When Considine came up he found that Hans had
already disembowelled the spring-bok, and was in the
act of fastening the carcase on his horse behind the
saddle. Remounting immediately, the hunter galloped
towards a mound, on the top of which the bushes
formed a dense brake. Skirting this till he reached
the other side, he pulled up, exclaiming—

"There, you'll find good water in the hollow; go
drink, while I prepare supper on the koppie."

Considine went off at once. Indeed, he could
not have done otherwise, for his impatient horse
took the bit in its mouth and galloped towards a
small pool of water, which was so yellow with mud
that it resembled thin pea-soup.

Thirsty though he was, the youth could not help
smiling at his new friend's idea of "good" water,
but he was not in a condition to be fastidious.
Jumping out of the saddle, he lay down on his
breast, dipped his lips into the muddy liquid, and
drank with as much enjoyment as if the beverage
had been nectar—or Bass. Rob Roy also stood, in

a state of perfect bliss, in the middle of the pool, sucking the water in with unwearied vigour. It seemed as if man and horse had laid a wager as to who should drink most. At last, the point of utmost capacity in both was reached, and they retired with a sigh of contentment, Rob Roy to browse on the plain, and his master to betake himself to the encampment on the knoll, where Hans Marais quickly supplied him with glorious steaks of spring-bok venison.

"Isn't it an enjoyable thing to eat when one is hungry, eh?" said Considine, after half an hour's silent devotion to the duty in hand.—"Why, where got you that?"

He referred to an ostrich egg which his companion had taken from a saddle-bag, and in one end of which he was busy boring a hole.

"Found it in the sand just before I found you," said Hans. "Did you ever eat one?"

"No, never."

"Well then, you shall do so now, and I'll show you how the niggers here make an omelet."

He planted the huge egg in the hot ashes as he spoke, and kept stirring its contents with a piece of stick until sufficiently cooked.

"Not bad—eh?"

"Glorious!" exclaimed Considine, smacking his lips.

Both youths continued to smack their lips over

the egg until it was finished, after which Charlie pronounced it not only a glorious but a satisfying morsel. This was doubtless true, for an ostrich egg is considered equal to twenty-four hen's eggs.

Returning to the spring-bok steaks, the half-starved youth continued his repast, while Hans Marais, having finished, extended his huge frame beside the camp-fire, leaned upon his saddle, and smoked his pipe in benignant contemplation of his companion.

"This is pleasant!" said Charlie, pausing, with a sigh, and looking up.

"Ja, it is pleasant," replied Hans.

"Ja?" repeated Charlie, quoting the Dutch "Yes" of the other; "are you a Dutchman?"

"I am; at least I am a Cape colonist descended from Dutchmen. Why are you surprised?"

"Because," replied his companion, while he prepared another steak over the embers, "you speak English so well that I could not have known it. How came you to learn the language so perfectly?"

"My father, being wiser than some of his friends and neighbours," said Hans, "sent me to Capetown to be educated. I suppose that is the reason. We dwelt in the western part of the colony then, and I was the eldest of the family. When a number of us Dutchmen left that part of the country—being disgusted with the Government,—and came·up here,

my brothers and sister had to be taken from school.
This was a pity, for education taught me to know that
education is an inestimable blessing—the want of it
a heavy misfortune."

"True," remarked Considine. But being still too
busy with the steaks to pursue the subject he merely
added—

"Does your father live near this?"

"About seven hours' ride, which, as I daresay you
know, is forty-two miles. You shall go home with
me to-morrow."

"How many are there of you?" asked Considine,
looking at the young Dutchman over a bone. "Excuse
my being so impolite," he added, "but, d' you know,
one feels horribly like a tiger after a two days' fast."

"Don't stand on ceremony," said the other, with a
laugh. "When you are satisfied we can converse.—
There are fifteen of us: father, mother, sister, and
eleven boys besides myself. I'll tell you about them
all after supper; meanwhile I'll go fetch the horses,
for there are lions about, as I daresay you know, and
some of them are nearly as ravenous as yourself."

Hans rose, put his pipe in the band of his
broad-brimmed hat, and sauntered heavily out of the
thicket.

In a few minutes he returned, leading the horses,
and then busied himself in surrounding the camp
with an almost impenetrable wall of mimosa-thorn

branches, the spikes of which were so tremendous that it seemed as if nothing smaller than an elephant could force its way through. This done, he sat down and quietly refilled his pipe, while Considine, having at last finished his meal, drew the embers of the fire together, disposed his limbs comfortably on the ground, lay back on his saddle, and prepared to enjoy a contemplative gaze at the cheering blaze and an interrogative conversation with his new friend.

"Do you smoke?" asked Hans.

"No."

"Why?"

"Because it makes me sick, and I don't like it."

Hans looked surprised. This was a new idea to him, and he sat for some time pondering it; indeed, we may say with truth that he "smoked it." In a few minutes he looked earnestly at the youth, and asked why he came to the Cape.

"To make my fortune," answered Considine.

"Fortunes are not easily made at the Cape," was the grave reply. "My father has been making his fortune for the last quarter of a century, and it's not made yet.—Why did you choose the Cape?"

"I didn't choose it."

"No?" said the Dutchman, with a look of surprise.

"No," responded the Englishman; "my coming here was not a matter of choice; it was necessity

Come, I will make a confidant of you and relate my history. Don't be alarmed, I won't keep you up all night with prosy details. My life, as you may see, has not yet been a long one, and until this year it has been comparatively uneventful."

He paused a few moments as if to recall the past, while his companion, picking his pipe with a mimosa thorn, settled himself to listen.

"Father, mother, brothers, and sisters I have none," began Considine as he whittled a stick—a pastime, by the way, which is erroneously supposed to be an exclusively American privilege. "Neither have I grandfathers, grandmothers, aunts, nephews, nieces, or anything else of the sort. They all died either before or soon after I was born. My only living relation is an uncle, who was my guardian. He is a sea-captain, and a good man, but tough. I bear him no ill-will. I would not speak disrespectfully of him; but—he is tough, and, I incline to think, no better than he should be. Infancy and boyhood with squalling and schooling I pass over. My uncle ordered me to study for the medical profession, and I obeyed. Wishing to see a little of the world before finishing my course, I sailed in a vessel bound for Australia. We touched at Table Bay in passing. Obtaining leave, I went ashore at Capetown. The ship also went ashore—without leave—in company with six other ships, during a terrific gale which sprang up in the night. Our vessel became a total wreck. The crew were saved, but my effects went with the cargo to the bottom. Fortunately, however, I had carried ashore with me the little cash I possessed.

"I found the Capetown people very kind. One of them took me by the hand and offered me employment, but I preferred to proceed into the interior with a trader and work or shoot my way, in order to save my money. No trader being about to start at that time, I was obliged to accept the offer of a frontier farmer, who, for a small sum, agreed to allow me to accompany his waggons, on condition that I should make myself generally useful. I grudged the cash, but closed with the offer, and next day started on our journey of six hundred miles—such being the distance we had to go, according to my employer or comrade, Jan Smit."

"Who?" exclaimed Hans, with sudden energy.

"Jan Smit," repeated Considine. "Do you know him?"

"Ja—but go on," said Hans, with a nod and a smile.

"Well, I soon found that my Dutch comrade—"

"He's only half Dutch," interrupted Hans. "His mother was Dutch, but his father is English."

"Well, Dutch or English, he is the most unmitigated scoundrel I ever met."

("Ja," muttered Hans, "he is.")

"And I soon found that my trip of pleasure became a trip of torment. It is true we shot plenty of game—lions among the rest—but in camp the man was so unbearable that disgust counterbalanced all the pleasure of the trip. I tried hard to get the better of him by good-humour and jollity, but he became so insolent at last that I could not stand it. Three days ago when I asked him how far we were from his farm, he growled that it wasn't far off now; whereupon I could not refrain from saying that I was glad to hear it, as we should soon have the pleasure of parting company. This put him in a rage. He kicked over the pot containing part of our breakfast, and told me I might part company then and there if I pleased. My temper does not easily go, but it went at last. I jumped up, saddled my horse, mounted, and rode away. Of course I lost myself immediately, and for two days have been trying to find myself, without success, mourning over my fate and folly, and fasting from necessity. But for my opportune meeting with you, Mr. Marais, it might have gone hard with me and my poor horse, for the want of water had well-nigh floored us both."

"You'll never make your fortune by doctoring on the frontier," said Hans, after a few minutes' silence. "Nobody gets ill in this splendid climate —besides, we couldn't afford to waste time in that way. People here usually live to a great age, and then go off without the assistance of a doctor. What else can you turn your hand to ?"

"Anything," replied Considine, with the over-weening confidence of youth.

"Which means nothing, I suspect," said the Dutchman, "for Jack-of-all-trades is proverbially master of none."

"It may be so," retorted the other, "nevertheless, without boasting, I may venture to assert—because I can prove it—that I am able to make tables, chairs, chests, and such-like things, besides knowing something of the blacksmith's trade. In regard to doctoring, I am not entitled to practise for fees, not yet being full-flédged—only a third-year student—but I may do a little in that way for love, you know. If you have a leg, for instance, that wants amputating, I can manage it for you with a good carving-knife and a cross-cut saw. Or, should a grinder give you annoyance, any sort of pincers, small enough to enter your mouth, will enable me to relieve you."

At this Hans smiled and dispiayed a set of brilliant "grinders," which did not appear likely to give him annoyance for some time to come.

"Can you shoot ?" asked Hans, laying his hand on his companion's double-barrelled gun, which lay on the ground between them, and which, with its delicate proportions and percussion-locks, formed a striking contrast to the battered, heavy, flint-lock weapon of the Dutchman.

"Ay, to some extent, as the lions' skins in Jan Smit's waggon can testify.—By the way," added Considine quickly, "you said that you knew Smit. Can you tell me where he lives? because I still owe him the half of the money promised for permission to accompany him on this trip, and should not like to remain his debtor."

"Ja, I know where he lives. He's a bad specimen of a Dutch farmer in every respect, except as to size. He lives quite close to our farm—more's the pity!—and is one of those men who do their best to keep up bad feeling between the frontier-men and the Kafirs. The evil deeds of men such as he are represented in England, by designing or foolish persons, as being characteristic of the whole class of frontier farmers, hence we are regarded as a savage set, while, in my humble opinion, we are no worse than the people of other colonies placed in similar circumstances—perhaps better than some of them. Do you know anything of our past history?"

"Not much," replied Considine, throwing away the remnant of the stick he had been whittling and commencing on another piece. "Of course I know that the Cape was first doubled by the Portuguese commander Bartholomew Diaz in, I

think, 1486, and after him by Vasco de Gama, and
that the Dutch formed the first settlement on it
under Van Riebeck in 1652, but beyond this my
knowledge of Cape history and dates is hazy and
confused. I know, however, that your forefathers
mismanaged the country for about a century and
a half, after which it finally came into possession
of the British in 1806."

"Humph!" ejaculated Hans, while a shade of
displeasure flitted for a moment across his broad
visage. "'Tis a pity your reading had not extended
farther, for then you would have learned that from
1806 the colony has been mismanaged by *your*
countrymen, and the last fruit of their mismanage-
ment has been a bloody war with the Kafirs, which
has only just been concluded. Peace has been
made only this year, and the frontier is now at rest.
But who will rebuild the burned homesteads of this
desolated land? who will reimburse the ruined
farmers? above all, who will restore the lost lives?"

The young Dutchman's eyes kindled, and his
stern face flushed as he spoke, for although his own
homestead had escaped the ruthless savage, friends
and kindred had suffered deeply in the irruption
referred to, which took place in 1819, and one or
two of his intimate comrades had found early graves
in the wild karroo.

Considine, sympathising with his companion's

feelings, said, "I doubt not that you have much to complain of, for there is no colony under the sun that escapes from the evil acts of occasional bad or incompetent Governors. But pray do not extend your indignation to me or to my countrymen at large, for few of us know the true merits of your case. And tell me, what was the origin of the war which has just ended ?"

The young farmer's anger had passed away as quickly as it came. Letting his bulky frame sink back into the reclining position from which he had partially risen, he replied—

"Just the old story—self-will and stupidity. That domineering fellow Lord Charles Somerset, intending to check the plundering of the colony by Kafirs, chose to enter into treaties with Gaika as paramount chief of Kafirland, although Gaika himself told him plainly that he was not paramount chief. Of course the other chiefs were indignant, and refused to recognise such treaties. They did more: they made war on Gaika, and beat him, whereupon Somerset, instead of leaving the niggers to fight their own battles, must needs send a great commando of military and burghers to "restore" Gaika to his so-called supremacy. This was done. The chief T'Slambi was driven from his villages, and no fewer than 11,000 head of cattle were handed over to Gaika. While this was going on at the eastern frontier, the Kafirs invaded the colony at other points, drove in the small military posts, ravaged the whole land, and even attacked the military headquarters at Grahamstown, where, however, they were defeated with great slaughter. After this a large force was sent to drive them out of their great stronghold, the Fish River bush. This was successfully accomplished, and then, at last, the right thing was done. The Governor met the Kafir chiefs, when it was agreed that they should evacuate the country between the Great Fish River and the Keiskamma, and that the territory so evacuated should form *neutral ground*. So matters stand at present, but I have no faith in Kafirs. It is their pride to lie, their business to make war, and their delight to plunder."

"But is it not the same with *all* savages?" asked Considine.

"Doubtless it is, therefore *no* savages ought to be trusted, as civilised men are trusted, till they cease to be savages. We trust them too much. Time will show.—By the way, I hear that a new move is about to be attempted. Rumour says that your Government is going to send out a strong party of emigrants to colonise the eastern frontier. Is this true?"

"It is," replied Considine; "I wonder that you have not heard all about it before now."

"Good reasons for that. For one thing, I have just returned from a long trip into the north-western districts, and have not been in the way of hearing news for some time. Besides, we have no news-papers in the colony. Everything comes to us by word of mouth, and that slowly. Tell me about this matter."

"There is little to tell," returned Considine, replenishing the fire with a thick branch, which sent up a magnificent display of sparks and scared away a hyena and two jackals that had been prowling round the camp-fence. "The fact is that there is a great deal of distress in England just now, and a redundant population of idlers, owing to the cessation of continental wars. This seems to have put it into the heads of some people in power to encourage emigration to the eastern part of this colony. In the House of Commons £50,000 have been voted in aid of the plan, and it seems that when the proposal was first made public, no fewer than 90,000 would-be emigrants applied for leave to come out here. Of these I believe 4000 have been selected, and twenty-three vessels chartered to con-vey them out. This is all I could learn before I left England, but I suppose we shall have more light on the subject ere many months have gone by."

"A good plan," said the Dutchman, with a grim smile, "but I pity the emigrants!"

As Considine's head drooped at this point, and his eyes winked with that owlish look which indicates the approach of irresistible sleep, Hans Marais rose, and, spreading a large kaross or blanket of leopard skin on the ground, invited his companion to lie down thereon. The youth willingly complied, stretched himself beside the Dutchman, and almost instantly fell sound asleep. Hans spread a lighter covering over himself and his comrade, and, with his head on his saddle, lay for a long time gazing tranquilly at the stars, which shone with an intensity of lustre peculiar to that region of the southern hemisphere, while the yelling cries of jackals and the funereal moaning of spotted hyenas, with an occasional distant roar from the king of beasts, formed an appropriate lullaby.

CHAPTER II.

INTRODUCES A CAPE DUTCHMAN AND HIS FAMILY, AND SHOWS THE
UNCERTAINTY OF HUMAN PLANS.

THE break of day found Charlie Considine and Hans Marais galloping lightly over the karroo towards a range of mountains which, on the previous evening, had appeared like a faint line of blue on the horizon.

The sun was just rising in a blaze of splendour, giving promise of an oppressive day, when the horsemen topped a ridge beyond which lay the primitive buildings of a frontier farm.

Considine uttered an exclamation of surprise, and looked inquiringly at his companion.

"My father's farm," said Hans, drawing rein and advancing at a foot-pace.

"A lovely spot," returned his companion, "but I cannot say much for the buildings."

"They are well suited to their purpose nevertheless," said Hans; "besides, would it be wise to build fine houses for Kafirs to burn?"

"Is being burnt by Kafirs the necessary end of all frontier farms?" asked Considine, with a smile.

"Not the necessary, but the probable end. Many a one has been burnt in times gone by, and many a one will be burnt again, if the Government and people in England do not recognise and admit the two great facts, that the interest as well as the main desire of the frontier settler is *peace*, while the chief delight as well as business of the Kafir is *war*. But I suppose that you, being an Englishman, will not believe that until conviction is forced on you by experience.—Come, I will introduce you to one of those colonists who are supposed to be such dis-contented fire-eaters; I think he will receive you hospitably."

The young farmer put spurs to his horse as he spoke, and dashed away over the plain, closely followed by his new friend, who was not sorry to drop the conversation, being almost entirely ignorant of the merits of the question raised.

The style of the group of buildings to which they drew near was not entirely unfamiliar to Considine, for he had passed one or two similar farms, belonging to Cape Dutchmen, on his trip from the sea-coast to the interior. There were about this farm, however, a few prominent points of difference. The cottages, being built of sun-dried bricks, were little better

than mud-huts, but there were more of them than
Considine had hitherto seen on such farms, and the
chief dwelling, in particular, displayed some touches
of taste which betokened superior refinement in the
inhabitants. The group lay in a hollow on the
margin of an insignificant stream, whose course
through the plain was marked by a thick belt of
beautiful mimosa-bushes. Close to the houses, these
mimosas, large enough to merit the title of trees,
formed a green setting in which the farm appeared
to nestle as if desirous of escaping the sunshine.
A few cactus shrubs and aloes were scattered about
in rear of the principal dwelling, in the midst of
which stood several mud-huts resembling gigantic
bee-hives. In these dwelt some of the Hottentot and
other servants of the farm, while, a little to the right
of them, on a high mound, were situated the kraals
or enclosures for cattle and sheep. About fifty yards
farther off, a clump of tall trees indicated the position
of a garden, whose fruit-trees were laden with the
blossoms or beginnings of a rich crop of peaches,
lemons, oranges, apricots, figs, pears, plums, apples,
pomegranates, and many other fruits and vegetables.
This bright and fruitful gem, in the midst of the
brown and apparently barren karroo, was chiefly
due to the existence of a large enclosure or dam,
which the thrifty farmer had constructed about half
a mile from the homestead, and the clear waters of

which shimmered in the centre of the picture, even
when prolonged drought had quite dried up the bed
of its parent stream. The peaceful beauty of the
scene was completed by its grand background of blue
mountains.

A tall, powerful, middle-aged man, in a coarse
cloth jacket, leathern trousers or "crackers," and a
broad-brimmed home-made hat, issued from the chief
dwelling-house as the horsemen galloped up and
drew rein. The sons of the family and a number
of barking dogs also greeted them. Hans and
Considine sprang to the ground, while two or three
of the eleven brothers, of various ages—also in
leathern crackers, but without coats or hats—came
forward, kicked the dogs, and led the horses
away.

"Let me introduce a stranger, father, whom I have
found—lost in the karroo," said Hans.

"Welcome to Eden! Come in, come in," said
Mynheer Conrad Marais heartily, as he shook his
visitor by the hand.

Considine suitably acknowledged the hospitable
greeting and followed his host into the principal
room of his residence.

There was no hall or passage to the house. The
visitor walked straight off the veldt, or plain, into the
drawing-room—if we may so style it. The house
door was also the drawing-room door, and it was

divided transversely into two halves, whereby an open window could at any moment be formed by shutting the lower half of the door. There was no ceiling to the room. You could see the ridge-pole and rafters by looking up between the beams, on one of which latter a swallow—taking advantage of the ever open door and the general hospitality of the family —had built its nest. The six-foot sons almost touched the said nest with their heads; as to the smaller youths it was beyond the reach of most of them, but had it been otherwise no one would have disturbed the lively little intruder.

The floor of the apartment was made of hard earth, without carpet. The whitewashed walls were graced with various garments, as well as implements and trophies of the chase.

From the beams hung joints of meat, masses of dried flesh, and various kinds of game, large whips—termed sjamboks (pronounced *shamboks*)—made of rhinoceros or hippopotamus hide, leopard and lion skins, ostrich eggs and feathers, dried fruit, strings of onions, and other miscellaneous objects; on the floor stood a large deal table, and chairs of the same description—all home-made,—two waggon chests, a giant churn, a large iron pot, several wooden pitchers hooped with brass, and a side-table on which were a large brass-clasped Dutch Bible, a set of Dutch tea-cups, an urn, and a brass tea-kettle heated by a chafing-dish. On the walls and in corners were several flint-lock guns, and one or two of the short light javelins used by the Kafirs for throwing in battle, named assagais.

Three small doors led into three inner rooms, in which the entire family slept. There were no other apartments, the kitchen being an outhouse. On the centre table was spread a substantial breakfast, from which the various members of the family had risen on the arrival of the horsemen.

Considine was introduced to Mynheer Marais' vrouw, a good-looking, fat, and motherly woman verging on forty,—and his daughter Bertha, a pretty little girl of eight or nine.

"What is Mynheer's name?" was the matron's first question.

Mynheer replied that it was Charles Considine.

"Was Mynheer English?"

"Yes," Mynheer was proud to acknowledge the fact.

Mrs. Marais followed up these questions with a host of others—such as, the age and profession of Mynheer, the number of his relatives, and the object of his visit to South Africa. Mynheer Marais himself, after getting a brief outline of his son's meeting with the Englishman, backed the attack of his pleasant-faced vrouw by putting a number of questions as to the political state of Europe then existing, and the chances of the British Government seriously taking into consideration the unsatisfactory condition of the Cape frontier and its relations with the Kafirs.

To all of these and a multitude of other questions Charlie Considine replied with great readiness and good-humour, as far as his knowledge enabled him, for he began quickly to appreciate the fact that these isolated farmers, who almost never saw a newspaper were thirsting for information as to the world in general, as well as with regard to himself in particular.

During this bombardment of queries the host and hostess were not forgetful to supply their young guest with the viands under which the substantial table groaned, while several of the younger members of the family, including the pretty Bertha, stood behind the rest and waited on them. With the exception of the host and hostess, none of the household spoke during the meal, all being fully occupied in listening eagerly and eating heartily.

When the Dutch fire began to slacken for want of ammunition, Considine retaliated by opening a British battery, and soon learned that Marais and his wife both claimed, and were not a little proud of, a few drops of French blood. Their progenitors on the mother's side, they said, were descended from one of the French Huguenot families which settled

in the colony after the revocation of the Edict of
Nantes.

"You see," said Mynheer Marais, with a quiet
smile of satisfaction, as he applied a boiled cob of
mealies or Indian corn to his powerful teeth, "our
family may be said to be about two-thirds Dutch
and one-third French. In fact, we have also a little
English blood in our veins, for my great-grandfather's
mother was English on the father's side and Dutch
on the mother's. Perhaps this accounts to some
extent for my tendency to adopt some English and
American ideas in the improvement of my farm,
which is not a characteristic of my Cape-Dutch
brethren."

"So I have been told, and to some extent have
seen," said Considine, with a sly glance; "in fact they
appear to be rather lazy than otherwise."

"Not lazy, young sir," returned Marais with some
emphasis. "They are easy-going and easily satisfied,
and not solicitous to add to their material comforts
beyond a certain point—in short, contented with
little, like Frenchmen, which is a praiseworthy condition of mind, commended in Holy Writ, and not
disposed to make haste to be rich, like you English."

"Ah I see," rejoined Considine, who observed a
twinkle in the eyes of some of Mynheer's stalwart
sons.

"Yes," pursued the farmer, buttering another

mealie-cob, and commencing to it with infinite gusto, "you see, the Cape Dutchmen, although as fine a set of men as ever lived, are just a *little* too contented and slow; on the other hand, young sir, you English are much too reckless and fast—"

"Just so," interrupted Considine, bowing his thanks to the hostess for a third venison-steak which she had put on his plate; "the Dutch too slow, the English too fast, so that three parts Dutch, two parts French, and one part English—like a dash of seasoning—is, it seems, the perfect Marais mixture."

This remark produced a sudden and unintentional burst of laughter from the young Maraises, not so much on account of the excess of humour contained in it, as from the fact that never before had they heard a jest of any kind fabricated at the expense of their father, of whom they stood much in awe, and for whom they had a profound respect.

Conrad Marais, however, could take a joke, although not much given to making one. He smiled blandly over the edge of his mealie-cob.

"You're right, sir,—right; the mixture is not a bad one. The Dutch element gives steadiness, the English vigour, and the French spirit.—By the way, Arend," he continued, turning to one of his stout olive-branches, "talking of spirit reminds me that you will have to go to work at that leak in the dam with more spirit than usual, for we

can't afford to lose water in this dry weather. It is
not finished, I think?"

"No, father, but we hope to get it done this after-
noon."

"That's well. How many of you are at it?"

"David and I, with six Totties. Old Sam is ill,
and none of the others can be spared to-day."

"Can't some of your brothers help?" asked the
farmer. "Losing water is as bad almost as losing
gold."

"Joseph meant to come, but he started at six this
morning to look after the cattle. We hear that the
Kafirs carried off some of Jan Smit's sheep
yesterday."

"The black scoundrels!" exclaimed Conrad Marais,
with a growl and a frown, "they are never at rest,
either in times of peace or of war."

The frown passed as quickly as it came, and the
genial smile habitual to the farmer resumed its place
on his countenance as he ran his fingers through the
thick masses of his iron-grey hair and rose from the
table.

"Come, Mr. Considine," he said, putting on his
hat, "are you disposed for a ride? I take a look
round the farm every morning to see that things are
going straight. Will you join me?"

Of course Considine gladly assented, and Hans
said he would accompany them. while the other sons

—except of course the younger ones, and the baby, who was Bertha's special charge—went out to their various avocations.

A few minutes later the three horsemen were cantering over the plain.

During the ride, Considine was again questioned closely as to his future intentions and prospects, but without anything very satisfactory being evolved. At last Conrad Marais pulled up, after a long pause in the conversation, and while they advanced at a walk, said—

"Well, I've been *thinking*, and here is the outcome. You want work, Mr. Considine, and I want a workman. You've had a good education, which I count a priceless advantage. Some of my sons have had a little, but since I came here the young ones have had none at all worth mentioning. What say you to become a schoolmaster? You stop with me and give the youngsters as much as you think fit of whatever you know, and I'll give you house-room and food, with a small salary and a hearty welcome. You need not bind yourself. If you don't like it, you can leave it. If you do like it, you are welcome to stay as long as you please, and you'll thus have an opportunity of looking about and deciding on your future plans. What say you?"

Considine received the opening sentences of this proposal with a smile, but as the farmer went on he became grave, and at length seriously entertained the idea. After having slept a night over it he finally resolved to accept the offer, and next day was fairly installed as dominie and a member of the farmer's family. School-books were ferreted out from the bottom of family chests; a Hottentot's (or Tottie's) mud-hut was converted into a schoolroom; six of the farmer's sons—beginning almost at the foot of the scale—formed a class. Reading, writing, and arithmetic were unfolded to youthful and not un-willing minds, even Latin was broached by the eldest of the six, and, during a separate hour in the evening, French was taught to Bertha. Everything, in short, was put in train, and, as Considine expressed it, "the Marais Academy was going full swing," when an event occurred which instantly sent French and Latin to the right-about and scattered the three R's to the four winds.

This was nothing less than an order from the Colonial Government to the Field Cornets on the frontier to engage waggons and oxen from the farmers, to be sent to Algoa Bay for the purpose of conveying the British immigrants—expected in a few weeks—from the coast to the various locations destined for their reception.

Among others, Conrad Marais was to send two waggons and spans of oxen, each span consisting of eighteen animals. Hans Marais was to go in charge, and Hans resolved to have Considine as a companion, for the journey down to the coast was long—about 160 miles,—and the two youths had formed so strong an attachment during their short acquaintance that Considine was as anxious to go as his friend could desire.

Conrad Marais, having no objection to this arrangement, the oxen were "inspanned," and the day following that on which the order was received they set off towards the shores of the Indian Ocean.

Having to pass the residence of Jan Smit on the way, Considine seized the opportunity to visit his former cross-grained companion and pay his debt.

Jan Smit was in a more savage humour than usual when the young man walked up to his dwelling. The farmer's back was towards him as he approached. He stood nervously switching a sjambok in his right hand, while he stormed in Dutch at three of his unfortunate people, or rather slaves. One was a sturdy Hottentot named Ruyter, one a Malay named Abdul Jemalee, both of whom had travelled with Considine on the up journey. The third was the Bushman whom he had encountered when lost on the karroo, and who, owing to his inveterate stupidity, had been named Booby.

They had all been implicated in the recent loss of cattle suffered by their savage master, who had already flogged the Bushman with the sjambok and was furiously interrogating the Hottentot. At last he gave him a tremendous cut across the shoulders, which immediately raised a dark red bar thereon.

Ruyter's black eyes flashed. He did not wince, but drew himself quickly up like a man about to retaliate. Jan Smit observing and resenting the action, at once knocked him down.

Ruyter slowly rose and staggered away just as Considine came up. The youth could not resist the inclination to exclaim "Shame!"

"Who dares—" cried Jan Smit, turning fiercely round. He paused in mute surprise at sight of his former companion.

"*I* dare!" said Considine sternly; "many a time the word has been on my lips before, and now that it has passed them it may go. I came not here, however, to bully, or be bullied, but to pay my debt to you."

He drew out a leathern purse as he spoke, and the Dutchman, whose spirit was quelled both by the manner and the matter of his visitor's remark, led the way to his domicile.

The house resembled that of Conrad Marais in form, but in nothing else. Everything in and around it was dirty and more or less dilapidated. There was no dam, no garden,—nothing, in short, but the miserable dwelling and a few surrounding huts, with the cattle kraal.

Having paid his debt, Considine did not vouchsafe another word, but returned at once to the waggons. On the way he overtook Ruyter.

"My poor fellow," he said, "have you no means of redress? Can you not complain to some one— some magistrate?"

"Complain!" exclaimed the Hottentot fiercely, "what de use of complain? No one care. Nobody listen—boh! no use complain."

The man had learnt a smattering of English. He was a short but very powerful fellow, and with a more intellectual head and countenance than is common to his race.

"Where are you going just now, Ruyter?" asked Considine, feeling that it was best to change the subject just then.

"Go for inspan de waggin. Ordered down to Algoa Bay for bring up de white men."

"Then we shall probably meet on the road," said Considine, "for I am going to the same place." As he spoke, they came to a point where the road forked. The Hottentot, with a sulky "Good-day," took that path which led towards Jan Smit's cattle kraal, while Considine followed the other and re-joined his waggons. The two friends mounted their horses, the drivers set the ox-teams in motion, and the huge waggons lumbered slowly over the karroo towards the rising sun.

CHAPTER III.

DESCRIBES THE SOMEWHAT CURIOUS BEGINNING OF SETTLER-LIFE IN SOUTH AFRICA.

LEAPING over time and space with that hilarious
mental bound which is so easy and enjoyable to
writers and readers, let us fold our wings at early
morn in the month of May, and drop down on the
heights in the vicinity of Algoa Bay.

The general aspect of the bay is sandy and sterile.
On its blue waters many large vessels lie at anchor.
Some of them are trim, with furled sails and squared
yards, as if they had been there for a considerable
time.   Others have sails and spars loose and awry,
as if they had just arrived.   From these latter many
an emigrant eye is turned wistfully on the shore.   The
rising ground on which we stand is crowned by a
little fortress, or fortified barrack, styled Fort Fred-
erick, around which are the marquees of the officers
of the 72d regiment.   Below, on the range of sandhills which fringe the beach, are pitched a multitude
of canvas tents, and among these upwards of a
thousand men, women, and children are in busy

motion. There are only one or two small wooden houses visible, and three thatched cottages. Down at the water's edge, and deep in the surf, crowds of soldiers, civilians, and half-naked natives are busy hauling on the ropes attached to the large surf-boats, which are covered to overflowing with human beings. Those in the boats, as well as those in the surf and on the beach, are in a state of high excitement, and more or less demonstrative, while the seamen from a neighbouring sloop of war, who manage the boats, shout to the people at the ropes. The replies of these are drowned, ever and anon, by the roar of falling "rollers." These rollers, or great waves, calm though the morning be, come in with giant force from the mighty sea. They are the mere termination of the ocean-swell.

Reader, the scene before you marks an epoch of vast importance in South African history. It is the "landing of the British settlers" in the year 1820. The spot is that on which now stands the flourishing commercial town of Port Elizabeth, styled, not inappropriately, by its inhabitants, the "Liverpool of South Africa."

Standing near the stern of one of the surf-boats, his strong right hand grasping the gunwale, and his grave eyes fixed on the shore, one of the exiles from Scotland lifted his voice that day and said—

"Hech, sirs! it's but a puir, ill-faur'd, outlandish

sort o' country. I wad fain hope the hieland hills
of our location inland are mair pleasant-lookin' than
this."

"Keep up your spirits, Sandy Black," observed a
sturdy Highlander who stood at his side; "those
who know the country best say that our location is
a splendid one—equal to Scotland itself, if not
superior."

"It may be so, Mr. M'Tavish," replied Sandy, in
a doubtful tone of voice, "it *may* be so."

"Hallo !" suddenly and loudly exclaimed a dapper
little man, whose voice betokened him English.

"What is 't, Jerry ?" demanded Sandy Black,
turning his eyes seaward, in which direction Jerry
was gazing.

The question needed no reply, for Sandy, and
indeed all the various people in the barge who stood
high enough on its sides or lading to be able to look
over the gunwale, observed a mighty wave coming
up behind them like a green wall.

"Haul hard !" roared the seamen in charge.

"Ay, ay," shouted the soldiers on shore.

As they spoke the billow lifted the boat as if it
had been a cork, fell under it with a deafening roar,
and bore it shoreward in a tumult of seething foam.
Next moment the wave let it down with a crash and
retired, leaving it still, however, in two or three feet
of water.

"Eh, man, but that *was* a dunt!" exclaimed Sandy, tightening his hold on the gunwale, while several of his less cautious or less powerful neighbours were sent sprawling into the bottom of the boat among terrified women and children.

All was now bustle and tenfold excitement, for the soldiers on the beach hurried waist-deep into the sea for the purpose of carrying the future settlers on shore.

Thomas Pringle, the leader of the Scotch party, and who afterwards became known as the "South African poet," had previously landed in a gig. He gave an opportune hint, in broad Scotch, to a tall corporal of the 72d Highlanders to be careful of his countrymen.

"Scotch folk, are they?" exclaimed the corporal, with a look of surprise at Pringle. "Never fear, sir, but we sal be carefu' o' *them*."

The corporal was as good as his word, for he and his comrades carried nearly the whole party ashore in safety. But there were others there who owned no allegiance to the corporal. One of these—a big sallow Hottentot—chanced to get Jerry, surnamed Goldboy, on his shoulders, and, either by mischance or design, stumbled and fell, pitching Jerry over his head, just as another billow from the Indian Ocean was rushing to the termination of its grand career. It caught Jerry up in a loving embrace as

he rose, and pitched him with a noisy welcome on
the shore.

"Weel done, Jerry!" cried Sandy Black, who had
just been overturned by the same wave from the
shoulders of a burly Englishman—a previously
landed settler—"you an' me's made an impressive
landin'. Come, let's git oot o' the bustle."

So saying the stout Lowlander seized his little
English friend by the arm and dragged him towards
the town of canvas which had within a few weeks
sprung up like mushrooms among the sandhills.

Although wet from head to foot, each forgot
his condition in the interest awakened by the
strange sights and sounds around him. Their immediate neighbourhood on the beach was crowded
with emigrants, as party after party was carried
ashore shoulder-high by the soldiers, who seemed
to regard the whole affair as a huge practical joke.

The noise was indescribable, because compound.
There was the boisterous hilarity of people who felt
their feet once more on solid ground, after a long and
weary voyage ; the shouting of sailors and bargemen
in the boats, and of soldiers and natives on the
beach ; the talking and laughing of men and women
who had struck up sudden friendships on landing, as
well as of those who had crossed the sea together ; the
gambolling and the shrieking delight of children freed
from the restraints of shipboard ; the shouts of in-

dignant Government officials who could not get their orders attended to; the querulous demands of people whose luggage had gone astray in process of debarkation; the bawling of colonial Dutch by gigantic Dutch - African farmers, in broad - brimmed hats and leathern crackers, with big tobacco-pipes in their mouths; the bellowing of oxen in reply to the pistol-shot cuts applied to their flanks by half-naked Hottentots and Bushmen, whose whips were bamboos of twenty feet or so in length, with lashes twice as long; the creaking of Cape-waggons, the barking of dogs, and, as a measured accompaniment to all, the solemn regular booming of the restless sea.

Disengaging themselves from the crowded beach, Sandy Black and Jerry Goldboy proceeded towards the town of tents among the sandhills. On their way they passed several large tarpaulin-covered depots of agricultural implements, carpenter's and blacksmith's tools, and ironware of all descriptions, which had been provided by Government to be sold to the settlers at prime cost—for this grand effort at colonisation was originated and fostered by the British Government.

"Weel, weel, did ever 'ee see the like o' that, noo?" observed Sandy Black, as he passed some sandhills covered with aloes and cactuses and rare exotics, such as one might expect to find in English greenhouses.

"Well, yes," replied Jerry Goldboy, "them *are* hodd-

lookin' wegitables. I can't say that I 've much knowledge of such-like myself, 'avin bin born an' bred in
London, as I 've often told you, but they do seem
pecooliar, even to me.—I say, look 'ere; I thought
all the people 'ere was settlers."

Sandy, who was a grave man of few words, though
not without a touch of sly humour, replied, " Weel, .
so they are—an' what than ?"

" Why, w'at are them there ?" demanded Jerry,
pointing to several marquees pitched apart among
some evergreen bushes.

" H'm ! 'ee may ask that," replied the Scot; but as
he did not add more, his companion was content to
regard his words as a confession of ignorance, and
passed on with the remark, " haristocrats."

Jerry was so far right. The marquees referred to
belonged to the higher class of settlers, who had
resolved to forsake their native land and introduce
refinement into the South African wilds. The
position chosen by them on which to pitch their
tents, and the neatness of everything around, evinced
their taste, while one or two handsome carriages
standing close by betokened wealth. Some of the
occupants, elegantly dressed, were seated in camp-
chairs, with books in their hands, while others were
rambling among the shrubbery on the little emin-
ences and looking down on the bustling beach and bay.
The tents of these, however, formed an insignificant

proportion of the canvas town in which Sandy Black and his friend soon found themselves involved.

"Settlers' Camp," as it was called, consisted of several hundred tents, pitched in parallel rows or streets, and was occupied by the middle and lower class of settlers—a motley crew, truly. There were jolly farmers and pale-visaged tradesmen from various parts of England, watermen from the Thames, fishermen from the seaports, artisans from town and country, agricultural labourers from everywhere, and ne'er-do-weels from nowhere in particular. England, Scotland, Ireland, were represented—in some cases misrepresented,—and, as character was varied, the expression of it produced infinite variety. Although the British Government had professedly favoured a *select* four thousand out of the luckless ninety thousand who had offered themselves for emigration, it is to be feared that either the selection had not been carefully made, or drunkenness and riotous conduct had been surprisingly developed on the voyage out. Charity, however, requires us to hope that much of the excitement displayed was due to the prospect of being speedily planted in rural felicity in the wilds of Africa. Conversation, at all events, ran largely on this theme, as our wanderers could easily distinguish—for people talked loudly, and all tent-doors were wide open.

After wandering for some time, Sandy Black

paused, and looking down at his little friend with what may be called a grave smile, gave it as his opinion that they had got lost "in Settlers'-toon."

" I do believe we 'ave," assented Jerry.   " What 's to be done ?"

" Gang to the best hotel," suggested Sandy.

" But where *is* the best 'otel ?"

" H'm ! 'ee may ask that."

A burst of noisy laughter just behind them caused the lost ones to turn abruptly, when they observed four tall young men of gentlemanly aspect sitting in a small military tent, and much amused apparently at their moist condition.

" Why, where did you two fellows come from ?" asked one of the youths, issuing from the tent.

" From England and Scotland," replied Jerry Goldboy promptly.

" From the sea, I should say," returned the youth, " to judge from your wet garments."

" Ay, we 've been drookit," said Sandy Black.

" Bring 'em in, Jack," shouted one of the other youths in the tent.

" Come inside," said he who was styled Jack, " and have a glass of whisky.   There 's nothing like whisky to dry a wet skin, is there, Scotty ?"

To this familiar appeal Sandy replied " m—h'm," which word, we may add for the information of foreigners, is the Scotch for " Yes."

" Sit down there on the blankets," said the hospitable Jack, " we haven't got our arm-chairs or tables
made yet. Allow me to introduce my two brothers,
James and Robert Skyd; my own name is the less
common one of John. This young man of six feet
two, with no money and less brain, is not a brother
—only a chum—named Frank Dobson. Come, fill
up and drink, else you'll catch a cold, or a South
African fever, if there is such a thing. Whom shall
I pledge ?"

"My name is Jerry Goldboy," said the Englishman ; " your health, gentlemen."

" 'Am Sandy Black," said the Scot; " here's t'ee."

" Well, Mr. Black and Mr. Coldboy "—Goldboy,
interposed Jerry—" I speak for my brothers and
friend when I wish you all success in the new land."

"Do talk less, Jack," said Robert Skyd, the
youngest brother, "and give our friends a chance of
speaking.—Have you come ashore lately ?"

" Just arrived," answered Jerry.

"I thought so. You belong to the Scotch party
that goes to Baviaans River, I suppose ?" asked
Frank Dobson.

This question led at length to a full and free
account of the circumstances and destination of each
party, with which however we will not trouble the
reader in detail.

" D'ee ken onything aboot Baviaans River ?" inquired Sandy Black, after a variety of subjects had been discussed.

"Nothing whatever," answered John Skyd, "save that it is between one and two hundred miles—more or less—inland among the mountains, and that its name, which is Dutch, means the River of Baboons, its fastnesses being filled with these gentry."

"Ay, I 've heard as much mysel'," returned Sandy, "an' they say the craters are gey fierce. Are there ony o' the big puggies in the Albany district?"

"No, none. Albany is too level for them. It lies along the sea-coast, and is said to be a splendid country, though uncomfortably near the Kafirs."

"The Kawfirs. Ay. H'm!" said Sandy, leaving his hearers to form their own judgment as to the meaning of his words.

"An' what may *your* tred be, sir?" he added, looking at John Skyd.

The three brothers laughed, and John replied—

"Trade? we have no trade. Our *profession* is that of clerks—knights of the quill; at least such was our profession in the old country. In this new land, my brother Bob's profession is fun, Jim's is jollity, and mine is a compound of both, called joviality. As to our chum Dobson, his profession may be styled remonstrance, for he is perpetually checking our levity, as he calls it; always keeping us in order and snubbing us, nevertheless we couldn't

do without him. In fact, we may be likened to a
social clock, of which Jim is the mainspring, Bob
the weight, I the striking part of the works, and
Dobson the pendulum. But we are not particular,
we are ready for anything."

"Ay, an' fit for nothin'," observed Sandy, with a
peculiar smile and shrug, meant to indicate that his
jest was more than half earnest.

The three brothers laughed again at this, and
their friend Dobson smiled. Dobson's smile was
peculiar. The corners of his mouth turned down
instead of up, thereby giving his grave countenance
an unusually arch expression.

"Why, what do you mean, you cynical Scot?"
demanded John Skyd. "Our shoulders are broad
enough, are they not? nearly as broad as your own."

"Oo' ay, yer shoothers are weel aneugh, but I
wadna gie much for yer heeds or haunds."

Reply to this was interrupted by the appearance,
in the opening of the tent, of a man whose solemn
but kindly face checked the flow of flippant conversation.

"You look serious, Orpin; has anything gone
wrong?" asked Frank Dobson.

"Our friend is dying," replied the man, sadly.
"He will soon meet his opponent in the land where
all is light, and where all disputes shall be ended in
agreement."

D

Orpin referred to two of the settlers whose careers in South Africa were destined to be cut short on the threshold. The two men had been earnestly religious, but, like all the rest of Adam's fallen race, were troubled with the effects of original sin. They had disputed hotly, and had ultimately quarrelled, on religious subjects on the voyage out. One of them died before he landed; the other was the man of whom Orpin now spoke. The sudden change in the demeanour of the brothers Skyd surprised as well as gratified Sandy Black. That sedate, and literally as well as figuratively, long-headed Scot, had felt a growing distaste to the flippant young Englishers, as he styled them, but when he saw them throw off their light character, as one might throw off a garment, and rise eagerly and sadly to question Orpin about the dying man, he felt, as mankind is often forced to feel, that a first, and especially a hasty, judgment is often incorrect.

Stephen Orpin was a mechanic and a Wesleyan, in virtue of which latter connection, and a Christian spirit, he had been made a local preacher. He was on his way to offer his services as a watcher by the bedside of the dying man.

This man and his opponent were not the only emigrants who finished their course thus abruptly Dr. Cotton, the "Head" of the "Nottingham party,"

Dr. Caldecott and some others, merely came, as it were like Moses, in sight of the promised land, and then ended their earthly career. Yet some of these left a valuable contribution, in their children, to the future colony.

While Black and his friend Jerry were observing Orpin, as he conversed with the brothers Skyd, the tall burly Englishman from whose shoulders the former had been hurled into the sea, chanced to pass, and quietly grasped the Scot by the arm.

"Here you are at last! Why, man, I've been lookin' for you ever since that unlucky accident, to offer you a change of clothes and a feed in my tent —or I should say *our* tent, for I belong to a 'party,' like every one else here. Come along."

"Thank 'ee kindly," answered Sandy, "but what between haverin' wi' thae Englishers an' drinkin' their whusky, my freen' Jerry an' me's dry aneugh already."

The Englishman, however, would not listen to any excuse. He was one of those hearty men, with superabundant animal spirits—to say nothing of physique—who are not easily persuaded to let others follow their own inclinations, and who are so good-natured that it is difficult to feel offended with their kindly roughness. He introduced himself by the name of George Dally, and insisted on Black accompanying him to his tent. Sandy being a sociable, although a quiet man, offered little resistance, and Jerry, being a worshipper of Sandy, followed with gay nonchalance.

CHAPTER IV.

**FURTHER PARTICULARS OF "SETTLERS' TOWN," AND A START MADE
FOR THE PROMISED LAND.**

THREADING his way among the streets of "Settlers'
Town," and pushing vigorously through the crowds
of excited beings who peopled it, George Dally led
his new acquaintances to a tent in the outskirts of
the camp—a suburban tent, as it were.

Entering it, and ushering in his companions, he
introduced them as the gentlemen who had been
capsized into the sea on landing, at which operation
he had had the honour to assist.

There were four individuals in the tent. A huge
German labourer named Scholtz, and his wife. Mrs.
Scholtz was a substantial woman of forty. She was
also a nurse, and, in soul, body, and spirit, was
totally absorbed in a baby boy, whose wild career
had begun four months before in a furious gale in
the Bay of Biscay. As that infant "lay, on that.
day, in the Bay of Biscay O!" the elemental strife
outside appeared to have found a lodgment in his
soul, for he burst upon the astonished passengers

with a squall which lasted longer than the gale, and was ultimately pronounced the worst that had visited the ship since she left England. Born in a storm, the infant was baptised in a stiff breeze by a Wesleyan minister, on and after which occasion he was understood to be Jabez Brook ; but one of the sailors happening to call him Junkie on the second day of his existence, his nurse, Mrs. Scholtz, leaped at the endearing name like a hungry trout at a gay fly, and " Junkie " he remained during the whole term of childhood.

Junkie's main characteristic was strength of lungs, and his chief delight to make that fact known. Six passengers changed their berths for the worse in order to avoid him. One who could not change became nearly deranged towards the end of the voyage, and one, who was sea-sick all the way out, seriously thought of suicide, but incapacity for any physical effort whatever happily saved him. In short, Junkie was the innocent cause of many dread-ful thoughts and much improper language on the unstable scene of his nativity.

Besides these three, there was in the tent a pretty, dark-eyed, refined-looking girl of about twelve. She was Gertrude Brook, sister and idolater of Junkie. Her father, Edwin Brook, and her mother, dwelt in a tent close by. Brook was a gentleman of small means, but Mrs. Brook was a very rich lady—rich in the possession of a happy temper, a loving disposition, a pretty face and figure, and a religious soul. Thus Edwin Brook, though poor, may be described as a man of inexhaustible wealth.

Gertrude had come into Dally's tent to fetch Junkie to her father when Sandy Black and his friends entered, but Junkie had just touched the hot teapot, with the contents of which Mrs. Scholtz was regaling herself and husband, and was not in an amiable humour. His outcries were deafening.

" Now *do* hold its dear little tongue, and go to its popsy," said Mrs. Scholtz tenderly. (Mrs. Scholtz was an Englishwoman.)

We need not say that Junkie declined obedience, neither would he listen to the silvery blandishments of Gertie.

" Zee chile vas born zhrieking, ant he vill die zhrieking," growled Scholtz, who disliked Junkie.

The entrance of the strangers, however, unexpectedly stopped the shrieking, and before Junkie could recover his previous train of thought Gertie bore him off in triumph, leaving the hospitable Dally and Mrs. Scholtz to entertain their visitors to small talk and tea.

While seated thus they became aware of a sudden increase of the din, whip-cracking, and ox-bellowing with which the camp of the settlers resounded.

" They seem fond o' noise here," observed Sandy

Black, handing his cup to Mrs. Scholtz to be refilled.

"I never 'eard such an 'owling before," said Jerry Goldboy; "what is it all about?"

"New arrivals from zee interior," answered Scholtz; "dere be alvays vaggins comin' ant goin'.

"The camp is a changin' one," said Dally, sipping his tea with the air of a connoisseur. "When you've been here as long as we have you'll understand how it never increases much, for although ship after ship arrives with new swarms of emigrants from the old country, waggon after waggon comes from I don't know where—somewheres inland anyhow—and every now an' then long trains of these are seen leaving camp, loaded with goods and women and children, enough to sink a small schooner, and followed by crowds of men tramping away to their new homes in the wilderness—though what these same new homes or wilderness are like is more than I can tell."

"Zee noise is great," growled Scholtz, as another burst of whip-musketry, human roars, and bovine bellows broke on their ears, "ant zee confuzion is indesgraibable."

"The gentlemen whose business it is to keep order must have a hard time of it," said Mrs. Scholtz; "I can't ever understand how they does it, what between landing parties and locating 'em, and

feeding, supplying, advising, and despatching of 'em,
to say nothing of scolding and snubbing, in the
midst of all this Babel of bubbledom, quite surpasses
my understanding.—Do *you* understand it, Mr.
Black?"

"Ay," replied Sandy, clearing his throat and
speaking somewhat oracularly. "'Ee must know,
Mrs. Scholtz, that it's the result of organisation and
gineralship. Ony serjeant or corporal can kick or
drive a few men in ony direction that's wanted, but
it takes a gineral to move an army. If 'ee was to
set a corporal to lead twunty thoosand men, he'd
gie them orders that wad thraw them into a deed
lock, an' than naethin' short o' a miracle could git
them oot o't. Mony a battle's been lost by brave
men through bad gineralship, an' mony a battle's
been won by puir enough bodies o' men because
of their leader's administrative abeelity, Mrs.
Scholtz."

"Very true, Mr. Black," replied Mrs. Scholtz, with
the assurance of one who thoroughly understands
what she hears.

"Noo," continued Sandy, with increased gravity,
"if thae Kawfir bodies we hear aboot only had
chiefs wi' powers of organisation, an' was a' united
thegither, they wad drive the haill o' this colony
into the sea like chaff before the wind. But they'll
niver do it; for, 'ee see, they want mind—an' body

withoot mind is but a puir thing after a', Mrs. Scholtz."

" I 'm not so zhure of zat," put in Scholtz, stretching his huge frame and regarding it complacently; "it vould please me better to have body vidout mint, zan mint vidout body."

" H'm ! 'ee 've reason to be pleased then," muttered Black, drily.

This compliment was either not appreciated by Scholtz, or he was prevented from acknowledging it by an interruption from without; for just at the moment a voice was heard asking a passer-by if he could tell where the tents of the Scotch party were pitched. Those in the tent rose at once, and Sandy Black, issuing out, found that the questioner was a handsome young Englishman, who would have appeared, what he really was, both stout and tall, if he had not been dwarfed by his companion, a Cape-Dutchman of unusually gigantic proportions.

" We are in search of the Scottish party," said the youth, turning to Sandy with a polite bow; " can you direct us to its whereabouts ?"

" I 'm no' sure that I can, sir, though I 'm wan o' the Scotch pairty mysel', for me an' my freen hae lost 'oorsels, but doobtless Mister Dally here can help us. May I ask what 'ee want wi' us ?"

" Certainly," replied the Englishman, with a smile. " Mr. Marais and I have been commissioned to

transport you to Baviaans river in bullock-waggons,
and we wish to see Mr. Pringle, the head of your
party, to make arrangements.—Can you guide us,
Mr. Dally?"

"Have you been to the deputy-quartermaster-
general's office?" asked Dally.

"Yes, and they directed us to a spot said to be
surrounded by evergreen bushes near this quarter
of the camp."

"*I* know it—just outside the ridge between the
camp and the Government offices.—Come along, sir,"
said Dally; "I 'll show you the way."

In a few minutes Dally led the party to a group
of seven or eight tents which were surrounded by
Scotch ploughs, cart-wheels, harrows, cooking utensils
fire-arms, and various implements of husbandry and
ironware.

"Here come the lost ones!" exclaimed Kenneth
M'Tavish, who, with his active wife and sprightly
daughter Jessie, was busy arranging the interior of
his tent, "and bringing strangers with them too!"

While Sandy Black and his friend Jerry were
explaining the cause of their absence to some of the
Scotch party, the young Englishman introduced his
friend and himself as Charles Considine and Hans
Marais, to the leader, Mr. Pringle, a gentleman
who, besides being a good poet, afterwards took a
prominent part in the first acts of that great drama

--the colonisation of the eastern frontier of South
Africa.

It is unnecessary to trouble the reader with all
that was said and done. Suffice it to say that
arrangements were soon made. The acting Governor,
Sir Rufane Donkin, arrived on the 6th of June from
a visit to Albany, the district near the sea on which
a large number of the settlers were afterwards located,
and from him Mr. Pringle learned that the whole of
the Scotch emigrants were to be located in the moun-
tainous country watered by some of the eastern
branches of the Great Fish River, close to the Kafir
frontier. The upper part of the Baviaans, or
Baboons, River had been fixed for the reception of
his particular section. It was also intended by
Government that a piece of unoccupied territory
still farther to the eastward should be settled by a
party of five hundred Highlanders, who, it was
conjectured, would prove the most effective buffer
available to meet the first shock of invasion, should
the savages ever attempt another inroad.

Mr. Pringle laid this proposed arrangement before
a council of the heads of families under his charge;
it was heartily agreed to, and preparations for an
early start were actively begun.

On the day of his arrival Sir Rufane Donkin laid
the foundation of the first house of the now wealthy
and flourishing, though not very imposing, town of

Port Elizabeth, so named after his deceased wife, to whose memory an obelisk was subsequently erected on the adjacent heights.

A week later, a train of seven waggons stood with the oxen "inspanned," or yoked, ready to leave the camp, from which many similar trains had previously set out. The length of such a train may be conceived when it is told that each waggon was drawn by twelve or sixteen oxen. These were fastened in pairs to a single trace or "trektow" of twisted thongs of bullock or buffalo hide, strong enough for a ship's cable. Each waggon had a canvas cover or "till" to protect its goods and occupants from the sun and rain, and each was driven by a tall Dutchman, who carried a bamboo whip like a salmon fishing-rod with a lash of thirty feet or more. A slave, Hottentot or Bushman, led the two front oxen of each span.

Like pistol-shots the formidable whips went off; the oxen pulled, tossed their unwieldy horns, and bellowed; the Dutchmen growled and shouted; the half-naked "Totties" and Bushmen flung their arms and legs about, glared and gasped like demons; the monstrous waggons moved; "Settlers' Town" was slowly left behind, and our adventurers, heading for the thorny jungles of the Zwartkops River, began their toilsome journey into the land of hope and promise.

"It's a queer beginning!" remarked Sandy Black, as he trudged between Hans Marais and Charlie Considine.

"I hope it will have a good ending," said Considine.

Whether that hope was fulfilled the reader shall find out in the sequel.

Meanwhile some of the English parties took their departure by the same route, and journeyed in company till points of divergence were reached where many temporary friendships were brought to a close, though some there were which, although very recently formed, withstood firmly the damaging effects of time, trial, sorrow, and separation.

CHAPTER V.

ADVENTURES AND INCIDENTS OF THE FIRST NIGHT IN THE "BUSH."

A NIGHT-BIVOUAC under the mimosa-bushes of the Zwartkops River. The Cape-waggons are drawn up in various comfortable nooks; the oxen are turned loose to graze; camp-fires are kindled. Round these men and women group themselves very much as they do in ordinary society. Classes keep by themselves, not because one class wishes to exclude the other, but because habits, sympathies, interests, and circumstances draw like to like. The ruddy glare of the camp-fires contrasts pleasantly with the cold light of the moon, which casts into deepest shadow the wild recesses of bush and brake, inducing many a furtive glance from the more timid of the settlers, who see an elephant, a buffalo, or a Cape "tiger" in every bank and stump and stone. Their suspicions are not so wild as one might suppose, for the neighbouring jungle, called the Addo Bush, swarms with these and other wild animals.

The distance travelled on this first day was not

great; the travellers were not much fatigued, but were greatly excited by novelty, which rendered them wakeful. If one had gone round to the numerous fires and played eavesdropper, what eager discussion on the new land he would have heard; what anxious speculations; what sanguine hopes; what noble plans; what ridiculous ideas; what mad anticipations!—for all were hopeful and enthusiastic.

Round one of these fires was assembled the family and retainers of our Highland farmer, Kenneth M'Tavish, among whom were Sandy Black and Jerry Goldboy. They had been joined by Charlie Considine, who felt drawn somewhat to Sandy. Quite close to these, round another fire, were grouped the three bachelor brothers Skyd, with their friend Dobson. At another, within earshot of these, were Edwin Brook and his wife, his daughter Gertrude, Scholtz and his wife, Junkie, George Dally, and Stephen Orpin, with bluff Hans Marais, who had somehow got acquainted with the Brook family, and seemed to prefer their society to that of any other.

Down in a hollow under a thick spreading mimosa-bush was the noisiest fire of all, for there were assembled some of the natives belonging to the waggons of Hans and Jan Smit. These carried on an uproarious discussion of some sort, appealing frequently to our friend Ruyter the Hottentot, who appeared to be regarded by them as an umpire or an

ROUND THE CAMP-FIRES.—Page 64.

oracle. The Hottentot race is a very inferior one, both mentally and physically, but there are among them individuals who rise much above the ordinary level. Ruyter was one of these. He had indeed the sallow visage, high cheek-bones, and dots of curly wool scattered thinly over his head, peculiar to his race, but his countenance was unusually intelligent, his frame well made and very powerful, and his expression good. He entered heartily into the fun of attempting to teach the Hottentot klick to some of the younger men among the emigrants, who were attracted to his fire by the shouts of laughter in which the swarthy slaves and others indulged. Abdul Jemalee, the Malay slave, was there; also Booby the Bushman—the former grave and silent, almost sad; the latter conducting himself like a monkey—to which animal he seemed closely related —and evoking shouts of laughter from a few youths, for whose special benefit he kept in the background and mimicked every one else.

"What a noisy set they are over there!" observed Edwin Brook, who had for some time been quietly contemplating the energetic George Dally, as he performed the duties of cook and waiter to his party.

"They are, sir," replied Dally, "like niggers in general, fond of showing their white teeth."

"Come, Gertie, your mother can spare you now; let's go over and listen to them."

E

Gertie complied with alacrity, and took her father's arm.

"Oh!" she exclaimed, with a little scream, as a thorn full five inches long gave her a wicked probe on the left shoulder.

Hans Marais sprang up and gallantly raised the branch which had touched her.

"It is only Kafirs who can run against mimosa thorns with impunity," said the handsome young Dutchman.

Gertie laughed, remarked that mimosa thorns, like South African gentlemen, were unusually long and sharp, and passed on.

Hans sat down on the ground, filled his large pipe, and gazed dreamily into the fire, with something of the sensation of a hunter when he makes a bad shot.

"Now then, Goliath," said the ever busy George Dally; "move your long legs out o' that. Don't you see the pot's about to bile over?"

Hans quietly obeyed.

"If I chanced to be alongside o' that Tottie over there just now," continued George, "I'd be inclined to stop his noise with a rap on his spotted pate."

"You'd have to make it a heavy rap, then, to produce any effect," said Hans, taking a long draw at his pipe, "for he belongs to a hard-headed race."

The truth of the young farmer's words was verified

just then in a way that was alarming as well as unexpected.

One of the heavy waggons, which had been delayed behind the others by some trifling accident, came lumbering up just as Hans spoke. There was a softish sandy spot in advance of it, into which one of the front wheels plunged. The tilt caught on part of the waggon to which Ruyter belonged. To prevent damage the active Hottentot sprang forward. In doing so he tripped and fell. At the same instant a tremendous crack of the whip and a shout produced a wrench at the waggon, the hind wheel of which went over Ruyter's head and crushed it into the ground!

A roar of consternation followed, and several eager hands carefully dug out the poor man's head. To the surprise of all, the five-ton waggon had *not* flattened it! The sand was so soft that it had not been squeezed at all—at least to any damaging extent,—a round stone having opportunely taken much of the pressure on itself, so that the Hottentot soon revived, and, beyond a headache, was little the worse of the accident. He returned to his place at the fire, but did not resume his part in the discussions, which were continued as noisily as before.

In strong contrast with the other groups were those of the Dutch-African boers who had brought the waggons to the Bay. Most of them were men of colossal stature. They sat apart smoking their huge pipes in silent complacency and comfort, amused a little at the scenes going on around them, but apparently disinclined to trouble themselves about anything in particular.

Supper produced a lull in the general hum of conversation, but when pipes were lit the storm revived and continued far into the night. At last symptoms of weariness appeared, and people began to make arrangements for going to rest.

These arrangements were as varied as the characters of the emigrants.

Charlie Considine and Hans Marais, now become inseparable comrades, cleared and levelled the ground under a mimosa-bush, and, spreading their kaross thereon, lay down to sleep. George Dally, being an adaptable man, looked at the old campaigners for a few minutes, and then imitated their example. Little Jerry Goldboy, being naturally a nervous creature, and having his imagination filled with snakes, scorpions, tarantulas, etc., would fain have slept in one of the waggons above the baggage —as did many of the women and children—if he had not been laughed out of his desire by Dally, and induced to spread his couch manfully on the bare ground.

It must not be supposed, however, that Jerry, although timid, was cowardly. On the contrary, he was bold as a lion. He could not control his sensitively-strung nervous system, but instead of running away, like the coward, he was prone to rush furiously at whatever startled him and grapple with it.

Some families pitched their tents, others, deeming curtains a needless luxury in such magnificent weather, contented themselves with the shelter of the bushes.

Mean while the Hottentot attendants replenished the fires, while the boers unslung their huge guns and placed them so as to be handy; for, although elephants and lions were not nearly so numerous as they once had been in that particular locality, there was still sufficient possibility of their presence, as well as of other nocturnal wanderers in the African wilds, to render such precaution necessary. The whole scene was most romantic, especially in the eyes of those who thus bivouacked for the first time in the wilderness. To them the great waggons; the gigantic Cape-oxen—which appeared to have been created expressly to match the waggons as well as to carry their own ponderous horns; the wild-looking Hottentots and Bushmen; the big phlegmatic Dutchmen; the bristling thorns of the mimosas, cropping ou. of comparative darkness ; the varied groups of emigrants ; the weird forms of the clumps of cactus, aloes, euphorbias, and other strange plants, lit up by the fitful glare of the camp-fires, and canopied by the star-spangled depths of a southern sky—all seemed to them the unbelievable creations of a wild vision.

Poor Jerry Goldboy, however, had sufficient faith in the reality of the vision to increase his nervous condition considerably, and he resolved to lie down with his "arms handy." These arms consisted of a flint-lock blunderbuss, an heirloom in his father's family, and a bowie-knife, which had been presented to him by an American cousin on his leaving England. Twice during that day's march had the blunderbuss exploded owing to its owner's inexperience in fire-arms. Fortunately no harm had been done, the muzzle on each occasion having been pointed to the sky, but the ire of the Dutch driver in front of Jerry had been aroused, and he was forbidden to reload the piece. Now, however, observing the preparations above referred to, he felt it to be his duty to prepare for the worst, and quietly loaded his bell-mouthed weapon with a heavy charge of buckshot.

"What's that you're after, boy?" asked George Dally, who was making some final arrangements at the fire before lying down for the night.

"Oh, nothing," replied Jerry, with a start, for he had thought himself unobserved, "only seein' to my gun before turnin' in."

"That's right," said George. "Double-load it. Nothin' like bein' ready for whatever may turn up in a wild country like this. Why, I once knew a man named Snip who said he had been attacked one night in South America by a sarpint full forty feet long, and who saved his life by means of a blunder-buss, though he didn't fire at the reptile at all."

"Indeed, how was that?" asked Jerry.

"Why, just because his weapon was bell-mouthed an' loaded a'most to the muzzle. You see, the poor fellow was awoke out of a deep sleep and couldn't well see, so that instead o' firin' *at* the brute, he fired his blunderbuss about ten yards to one side of it, but the shot scattered so powerfully that one o' the out-side bullets hit a stone, glanced off, and caught the sarpint in the eye, and though it failed to kill the brute on the spot, the wound gave it such pain that it stood up on its tail and wriggled in agony for full five minutes, sending broken twigs and dry leaves flying about like a whirlwind, so Snip he jumped up, dropped his weapon, an' bolted. He never returned to the encampment, and never saw the big snake or his blunderbuss again."

"What a pity! then he lost it?" said Jerry, looking with some anxiety at a decayed branch, to which the flickering flame gave apparent motion.

"Yes, he lost the blunderbuss, but he saved his life," replied Dally, as he lay down near his little friend and drew his blanket over him. " You 'd better put the gun between us, my boy, to be handy to both—an' if *anything* comes, the one of us that wakes first can lay hold of it and fire."

There was, we need scarcely observe, a strong spice of wickedness in George. If he had suggested a lion, or even an elephant, there would have been something definite for poor Jerry's anxious mind to lay hold of and try to reason down and defy, but that dreadful " *anything* " that might come, gave him nothing to hold by. It threw the whole zoological ferocities of South Africa open to his unanchored imagination, and for a long time banished sleep from his eyes.

He allowed the blunderbuss to remain as his friend had placed it, and hugged the naked bowie-knife to his breast. In addition to these weapons he had provided himself with a heavy piece of wood, something like the exaggerated truncheon of a policeman, for the purpose of killing snakes, should any such venture near his couch.

The wild shrieks of laughter at the neighbouring Hottentot fire helped to increase Jerry's wakefulness, and when this at last lulled, the irritation was kept up by the squalling of Master Junkie, whose tent was about three feet distant from Jerry's pillow, and who kept up a vicious piping just in proportion to the earnestness of Mrs. Scholtz's attempts to calm him.

At last, however, the child's lamentations ceased, and there broke upon the night air a sweet sound which stilled the merriment of the natives. It was the mellow voice of Stephen Orpin singing a hymn of praise, with a number of like-minded emigrants, before retiring to rest. Doubtless some of those who had already retired, and lay, perchance, watching the stars and thinking dreamily of home, were led naturally by the sweet hymn to think of the home in the "better land," which might possibly be nearer to some of them than the old home they had left for ever—ay, even than the new "locations" to which they were bound.

But, whatever the thoughts suggested, the whole camp soon afterwards sank into repose. Tent-doors were drawn and curtains of waggon-tilts let down. The boers, sticking their big pipes in their hatbands, wrapped themselves in greatcoats, and, regardless of snake or scorpion, stretched their limbs on the bare ground, while Hottentots, negroes, and Bushmen, rolling themselves in sheepskin karosses, lay coiled up like balls with their feet to the fire. Only once was the camp a little disturbed, during the early part of the night, by the mournful howl of a distant hyena. It was the first that the new-comers had heard, and most of those who were awake raised themselves on their elbows eagerly to listen.

Jerry was just dropping into slumber at the time. He sat bolt upright on hearing the cry, and when it was repeated he made a wild grasp at the blunderbuss, but Dally was beforehand. He caught up the weapon and this probably saved an explosion.

"Come, lie down, you imp!" he said, somewhat sternly.

Jerry obeyed, and his nose soon told that he had reached the land of dreams.

Dally then quietly drew the charge of shot, but left the powder and laid the piece in its former position. Turning over with the sigh of one whose active duties for the day have been completed, he then went to sleep.

Gradually the fires burned low, and gave out such flickering uncertain light, when an occasional flame leaped up ever and anon, that to unaccustomed eyes it might have seemed as though snakes were crawling everywhere, and Jerry Goldboy, had he been awake, would have beheld a complete menagerie in imagination. But Jerry was now in blessed oblivion.

When things were in this condition, that incomprehensible subtlety, the brain of Junkie Brook—or something else—so acted as to cause the urchin to give vent to a stentorian yell. Strong though it was, it did not penetrate far through the canvas tent, but being, as we have said, within a few feet of Jerry's ear, it sounded to that unhappy man like the united, and as yet unknown, shriek of all the elephants and buffaloes in Kafirland.

Starting up with a sharp cry he stretched out his hand towards the blunderbuss, but drew it back with a thrill of horror. A huge black snake lay in its place !

To seize his truncheon was the act of a moment. The next, down it came with stunning violence on the snake. The reptile instantly exploded with a bellowing roar of smoke and flame, which roused the whole camp.

"Blockhead ! what d'you mean by *that ?*" growled George Dally, turning round sleepily, but without rising, for he was well aware of the cause of the confusion.

Jerry shrank within himself like a guilty thing caught in the act, and glanced uneasily round to ascertain how much of death and destruction had been dealt out. Relieved somewhat to see no one writhing in blood, he arose, and, in much confusion, replied to the numerous eager queries as to what he had fired at. When the true state of affairs became manifest, most of the Dutchmen, who had been active enough when aroused by supposed danger, sauntered back to their couches with a good-natured chuckle ; the settlers who had " turned out " growled or chaffed, according to temperament, as they followed suit, and the natives spent half an hour in up-

roarious merriment over Booby's dramatic repre-
sentation of the whole incident, which he performed
with graphic power and much embellishment.

Thereafter the camp sank once more into repose,
and rested in peace till morning.

CHAPTER VI.

SPREADING OVER THE LAND.

WITH the dawn next morning the emigrants were up and away. The interest of the journey increased with every novel experience and each new discovery, while preconceived notions and depressions were dissipated by the improved appearance of the country.

About the same time that the Scotch "party" left the Bay, several of the other parties set out, some large and some small, each under its appointed leader, to colonise the undulating plains of the Zuurveld.

Soon the pilgrims became accustomed to the nightly serenade of hyena and jackal—also to breakneck steeps, and crashing jolts, and ugly tumbles. But they were all hopeful, and most of them were young, and all, or nearly all, were disposed to make light of difficulties.

The country they were about to colonise had been recently overrun by Kafir hordes. These had

been cleared out, and driven across the Great Fish
River by British and Colonial troops, leaving the
land a wilderness, with none to dispute possession
save the wild beasts. It extended fifty miles along
the coast from the Bushman's River to the Great
Fish River, and was backed by an irregular line of
mountains at an average distance of sixty miles
from the sea.

Leaving the Zwartkops River, not only the
Scottish party, but all the other parties, filed succes-
sively away in long trains across the Sundays River,
over the Addo Hill and the Quagga Flats and the
Bushman's River heights, until the various points of
divergence were reached, when the column broke
into divisions, which turned off to their several
locations and overspread the land.

There was "Baillie's party," which crossed Lower
Albany to the mouth of the Great Fish River, and
on the way were charmed with the aspect of the
country, which was at that time enriched and
rendered verdant by recent rains, and enlivened by
the presence of hartebeests, quaggas, springboks,
and an occasional ostrich. There was, however, a
"wash" of shadow laid on part of the pleasant
picture, to counteract the idea that the Elysian
plains had been reached, in the shape of two or
three blackened and ruined farms of the old Dutch
colonists—sad remains of the recent Kafir war—

solemn reminders of the uncertainties and possi-
bilities of the future.

Then there was the "Nottingham party." They
took possession of a lovely vale, which they named
Clumber, in honour of the Duke of Newcastle, their
patron. "Sefton's party" settled on the Assegai
Bush River and founded the village of Salem, afterwards noted as the headquarters of the Rev. William
Shaw, a Wesleyan, and one of the most able
and useful of South Africa's missionary pioneers.
Wilson's party settled between the Waay-plaats
and the Kowie Bush, across the path of the elephants,
which creatures some of the party, it is said,
attempted to shoot with fowling-pieces! Of the
smaller parties, those of Cock, Thornhill, Smith
(what series of adventurous parties ever went forth
without a "Smith's" party?), Osler, and Richardson,
located themselves behind the thicket-clad sandhills of the Kowie and Green Fountain. But space
forbids us referring, even in brief detail, to the
parties of James and Hyman and Dyson, and
Holder Mouncey, Hayhurst, Bradshaw, Southey,
and of Scott, with the Irish party, and that of
Mahoney, which at the "Clay Pits," had afterwards
to meet the first shock of every Kafir invasion of
Lower Albany. Among these and other parties
there were men of power, who left a lasting mark
on the colony, and many of them left numerous

descendants to perpetuate their names—such as Hobson, Bowker, Campbell, Ayliff, Phillips, Piggott, Greathead, Roberts, Stanley, and others too numerous to mention.

But with all these we have nothing to do just now. Our present duty is to follow those sections of the great immigrant band with the fortunes of which our tale has more particularly to do.

At the points of separation, where the long column broke up, a halt was made, while many farewells and good wishes were said.

" So you 're gaun to settle thereawa' ?" said Sandy Black to John Skyd and his brothers as they stood on an eminence commanding a magnificent view of the rich plains and woodlands of the Zuurveld.

" Even so, friend Black," replied John, " and sorry am I that our lot is not to be cast together. However, let 's hope that we may meet again ere long somewhere or other in our new land."

" It is quite romantic," observed James Skyd, " to look over this vast region and call it our own,—at least, with the right to pick and choose where we feel inclined. Isn't it, Bob ?"

To this Bob replied that it was, and that he felt quite like the children of Israel when they first came in sight of the promised land.

" I hope we won't have to fight as hard for it as they did." remarked Frank Dobson.

"It's my opeenion," said Sandy Black, "that if we haena to fight *for it*, we'll hae to fight a bit to *keep* it."

"Perhaps we may," returned John Skyd, "and if so, fighting will be more to my taste than farming—not that I'm constitutionally pugnacious, but I fear that my brothers and I shall turn out to be rather ignorant cultivators of the soil."

Honest Sandy Black admitted that he held the same opinion.

"Well, we shall try our best," said the elder Skyd, with a laugh ; "I've a great belief in that word '*try*.' —Goodbye, Sandy." He held out his hand.

The Scot shook it warmly, and the free-and-easy brothers, after bidding adieu to the rest of the Scotch party, who overtook them there, diverged to the right with their friend Frank Dobson, and walked smartly after their waggons, which had gone on in advance.

"Stoot chields they are, an' pleesant," muttered Sandy, leaning both hands on a thick cudgel which he had cut for himself out of the bush, "but wofu' ignorant o' farmin'."

"They'll make their mark on the colony for all that," said a quiet voice at Sandy's elbow.

Turning and looking up, as well as round, he encountered the hazel eyes and open countenance of Hans Marais.

"Nae doot, nae doot, they'll mak' their mark,

F

but it 'll no' be wi' the pleugh, or I'm sair mista'en.
Wull mair o' the settlers be pairtin' frae us here?"

Hans, although ignorant of the dialect in which
he was addressed, understood enough to make out
its drift.

"Yes," he replied, "several parties leave us at this
point, and here comes one of them."

As he spoke the cracking of whips announced
the approach of a team. A moment later, and a
small Hottentot came, round a bend in the road,
followed by the leading pair of oxen. It was the
train of Edwin Brook, who soon appeared, riding a
small horse. George Dally walked beside him.
Scholtz the German followed, conversing with the
owner of the waggon. In the waggon itself Mrs.
Brook, Mrs. Scholtz, and Junkie found a somewhat
uneasy resting-place, for, being new to the style of
travel, they had not learned to accommodate themselves to jolts and crashes. Gertie preferred to walk,
the pace not being more than three miles an
hour.

"Oh, father!" said Gertie, running up to the side
of her sire, with girlish vivacity, "there is the tall
Dutchman who was so polite to me when I was
pricked by the thorn bush."

"True, Gertie, and there also is the Scot who was
so free and easy in giving his opinion as to the
farming powers of the brothers Skyd."

" Your road diverges here, sir," said Hans, as
Brook rode up; " I fell behind my party to bid you
God-speed, and to express a hope that we may meet
again."

" Thanks, friend, thanks," said Brook, extending
his hand. " I am obliged for the aid you have
rendered me, and the advice given, which latter I
shall no doubt find valuable.—You are bound for the
highlands, of course," he added, turning to Sandy
Black. " We of the Albany lowlands must have a
friendly rivalry with you of the highlands, and see
who shall subdue the wilderness most quickly."

This remark sent the Scot into a rather learned
disquisition as to the merits and probable prospects
of a hill as compared with a low-lying region, during
which Hans Marais turned to Gertie. Being so
very tall, he had to stoop as well as to look down
at her pretty face, though Gertie was by no means
short for her age. Indeed, she was as tall as average
women, but, being only twelve, was slender and
girlish.

" How *very* tall you are, Mr. Marais!" she exclaimed, with a laugh, as she looked up.

" True, Gertie," said Hans, using the only name
which he had yet heard applied to the girl; " true,
we Cape-Dutchmen are big fellows as a race, and I
happen to be somewhat longer than my fellows.
I hope you don't object to me on that account?"

"Object? oh no! But it *is* so funny to have to look up so high. It's like speaking to father when he's on horseback."

"Well, Gertie, extra height has its advantages and its inconveniences. Doubtless it was given to me for some good end, just as a pretty little face and figure were given to you."

"You are very impudent, Mr. Hans."

"Am I? Then I must ask your pardon. But tell me, Gertie, what do you think of the new life that is before you?"

"How stupid you are, Hans! If the new life were behind me I might be able to answer, but how can I tell how I shall like what I don't know anything about?"

"Nay, but you know something of the beginning of it," returned the young Dutchman, with an amused smile, "and you have heard much of what is yet to come. What do you think of the *prospect* before you?"

"Think of the prospect?" repeated Gertie, knitting her brows and looking down with a pretended air of profound thought; "let me see : the prospect, as I've heard father say to mother,—which was just a repetition of what I had heard him previously say to these queer brothers Skyd—is a life in the bush—by which I suppose he means the bushes— in which we shall have to cut down the trees, plough up the new soil, build our cottages, rear our sheep and cattle, milk our cows, make our butter, grow our food, and sometimes hunt it, fashion our clothing, and protect our homes.   Is that right ?"

"Well, that's just about it," was the answer; "how do you like that prospect ?"

"I delight in it," cried the girl, with a flash in her brilliant black eyes, while she half laughed at her own sudden burst of enthusiasm. "Only fancy ! mother milking the cows, and me making butter, and Scholtz ploughing, and Dally planting, and nurse tending Junkie and making all sorts of garments, while father goes out with his gun to shoot food and protect us from the Kafirs."

"'Tis a pleasant picture," returned Hans, with a bland smile, "and I hope may be soon realised.—I must bid you goodbye now, Gertie, we separate here."

"Do you go far away ?" asked the girl, with a touch of sadness, as she put her little hand into that of the young giant.

"A goodish bit.   Some six or eight days' journey from here,—according to the weather."

"You'll come and see us some day, won't you, Hans ?"

"Ja—I will," replied Hans, with emphasis.

The whips cracked again, the oxen strained, the lumbering waggons groaned as they moved away, and while the Scotch band passed over the Zuurbergen range and headed in the direction of the Winterberg mountains, their English friends spread themselves over the fertile plains of Albany.

A few days of slow but pleasant journeying and romantic night-bivouacking brought the latter to their locations on the Kowie and Great Fish River.

On the way, the party to which Edwin Brook belonged passed the ground already occupied by the large band of settlers known as "Chapman's party," which had left Algoa Bay a few weeks before them in an imposing procession of ninety-six waggons. They had been accompanied to their future home by a small detachment of the Cape Corps, the officer in command of which gave them the suggestive advice, on bidding them goodbye, never to leave their guns behind them when they went out to plough! Although so short a time located, this party had produced a marvellous change in the appearance of the wilderness, and gave the settlers who passed farther eastward, an idea of what lay before themselves. Fields had already been marked out; the virgin soil broken up; timber cut, and bush cleared; while fragile cottages and huts were springing up here and there to supplant the tents which had given the first encampments a somewhat military aspect. Grotesque dwellings these, many of them, with mats

and rugs for doors, and white calico or empty space
for windows. It was interesting, in these first locations, to mark the development of character among
the settlers. Those who were practical examined the
" lie " of the land and the nature of the soil, with a
view to their future residence. Timid souls chose
their sites with reference to defence. Men of sentiment had regard to the picturesque, and careless
fellows "squatted " in the first convenient spot that
presented itself. Of course errors of judgment had
to be corrected afterwards on all hands, but the
power to choose and change was happily great at
first, as well as easy.

As Brook's party advanced, portions of it dropped
off or turned aside, until at last Edwin found himself
reduced to one family besides his own. Even this
he parted from on a ridge of land which overlooked
his own " location," and about noon of the same day
his waggons came to a halt on a grassy mound, which
was just sufficiently elevated to command a magnificent view of the surrounding country.

"Your location," said his Dutch waggon-driver,
with a curious smile, as though he should say, " I
wonder what you 'll do with yourselves."

But the Dutchman made no further remark. He
was one of the taciturn specimens of his class, and
began at once to unload the waggon. With the able
assistance of Brook and his men, and the feeble aid

of the "Tottie," or Hottentot leader of the "span" of oxen, the boxes, ploughs, barrels, bags, cases, etc., which constituted the worldly wealth of the settlers, were soon placed on the green sward.   Then the Dutchman said "goeden-dag," or farewell, shook hands all round, cracked his long whip, and went off into the unknown wilderness, leaving the Brook family to its reflections.

CHAPTER VII.

THE "LOCATION."

In the midst of the confused heap of their property, Edwin Brook sat down on a large chest beside
his wife and daughter, and gazed for some time in
silence on his new estate and home.

To say truth, it was in many respects a pleasant
prospect.   A bright blue sky overhead, a verdant
earth around.   Grassy hills and undulations of rich
pasture-land swept away from their feet like a green
sea, until stopped in the far distance by the great
blue sea itself.   These were dotted everywhere with
copses of the yellow-flowered mimosa-bush, through
openings in which the glitter of a stream could be
seen, while to the left and behind lay the dark masses
of a dense jungle filled with arboreous and succulent
plants, acacias and evergreens, wild-looking aloes,
tall euphorbias, quaint cactuses, and a great variety
of flowering shrubs—filled also, as was very soon
discovered, with antelopes, snakes, jackals, hyenas,
leopards, and other wild creatures.   The only familiar

objects which broke the wild beauty of the scene
were the distant white specks which they knew to
be the tents just put up by those settlers who chanced
to be their " next neighbours."

" May God protect and bless us in our new home!"
said Edwin Brook, breaking the silence, and rever-
ently taking off his cap.

A heartfelt " Amen" was murmured by Mrs.
Brook and Gertie, but a strange though not unpleasant feeling of loneliness had crept over their spirits,
inducing them to relapse into silence, for they could
not avoid realising strongly that at last they were
fairly left alone to fight the great battle of life.
Edwin Brook in particular, on seeing the long team
of his Dutch driver disappear over a distant ridge,
was for the first time deeply impressed with, as it
were, the forsaken condition of himself and his
family.   It was plain that he must take root there
and grow—or die. There was no neighbouring town
or village from which help could be obtained in any
case of emergency; no cart or other means of con-
veyance to remove their goods from the spot on which
they had been left; no doctor in case of sickness;
no minister in cases either of joy or sorrow—except
indeed (and it was a blessed exception) Him who
came to our world "not to be ministered unto, but
to minister."

Strong in the comfort that this assurance gave,

Edwin Brook shook off the lethargy that had been stealing over him, and set about the duties of the present hour. The tent had to be pitched, the trunks and boxes conveyed into it, a fire kindled, the kettle boiled, the goods and chattels piled and secured from the weather, firewood cut to prepare for the night-bivouac, etc.

Much of this work was already in progress, for George Dally,—with that ready resource and quiet capacity of adaptation to circumstances which he had displayed on the voyage out and on the journey to the location,—had already kindled a fire, sent Scholtz to cut firewood, and was busy erecting the tent when Brook joined him.

"That's right, George," he said, seizing a tent-peg and mallet; "we have plenty to do here, and no time to waste."

"Very true, sir," replied George, touching his cap, for George was an innately respectful man—respectful to *all*, though with a strong tendency to humorous impudence; "very true, sir; that's just what I thought when I see you a-meditatin', so I went to work at once without wastin' any time."

"Is zat enough?" asked Scholtz, staggering up at the moment with a heavy load of firewood, which he threw on the ground.

The question was put to George, for whom the big German had a special regard, and whose orders he consequently obeyed with unquestioning alacrity, although George had no special right to command.

"Enough !" exclaimed George, with a look of surprise, "why, *zat* is not enough to scare a weasel with, much less a elephant or a—a platzicumroggijoo."

George was ignorant of South African zoology, and possessed inventive powers.

"Bring ten times as much," he added; "we shall have to keep a blazin' bonfire agoin' all night."

Scholtz re-shouldered his axe, and went off to the jungle with a broad grin on his broader countenance.

He was a man who did not spare himself, yet of a temperament that kicked at useless labour, and of a size that forbade the idea of compulsion, but George Dally could have led him with a packthread to do anything.

Before he had reached the jungle, and while the smile was yet on his visage, his blood was curdled and his face elongated by a most appalling yell ! It was not exactly a war-whoop, nor was it a cry of pain, though it partook of both, and filled the entire family with horror as they rushed to the tent on the mound from which the cry had issued.

The yell had been given by Junkie, who had been bitten or stung by something, and who, under the combined influence of surprise, agony, and wrath, had out-Junkied himself in the fervour and ferocity of his indignant protest.

The poor child was not only horrified, but inconsolable. He wriggled like an eel, and delivered a prolonged howl with intermittent bursts for full half an hour, while his distracted nurse and mother almost tore the garments off his back in their haste to discover the bite or the brute that had done it.

"It *must* have bin a serpent!" cried the nurse, agonising over a knotted string.

"Perhaps a tarantula," suggested Gertie, who only clasped her hands and looked horrified.

"Quick!" exclaimed Mrs. Brook, breaking the unmanageable tape.

"Ze chile' is growing black and vill bust!" murmured Scholtz in real alarm.

It did seem as if there were some likelihood of such a catastrophe, for Junkie's passion and struggles had rendered him blue in the face; but it was found that the bite or sting, whichever it was, had done little apparent damage, and as the child cried himself out and sobbed himself to sleep in half an hour without either blackening or bursting, the various members of the family were relieved, and resumed their suspended labours.

The shades of evening had fallen, and, among other orbs of night, the stars of that much-too-highly-complimented constellation, the "Southern

Cross," had for some time illumined the sky before these labours were completed and the wearied Brook family and household retired to rest, with weapons ready at hand and fires blazing. Wild beasts—to whose cries they were by that time accustomed—soon began their nightly serenade and carried it on till morning, but they were not wild enough to disturb the new-comers with anything more formidable than sound.

Next morning early, George Dally was the first to bestir himself. On taking a general view of surrounding nature he observed a thin column of smoke rising above the tree-tops in the direction of the stream or river to which reference has already been made.

"Perhaps it's Kafirs," thought George.

Following up that thought he returned to what we may style his lair—the place where he had spent the night—under a mimosa-bush, and there girded himself with a belt containing a long knife. He further armed himself with a fowling-piece. Thus accoutred he sallied forth with the nonchalant air of a sportsman taking his pleasure. Going down to the stream and following its course upwards he quickly came in sight of the camp-fire whose smoke had attracted his attention. A tall man in dishabille was bending over it, coaxing the flame to kindle some rather green wood over which a large

iron pot hung from a tripod. The fire was in front
of a large but not deep cavern, in the recesses of
which three slumbering figures were visible.

Drawing cautiously nearer, George discovered that
the man at the fire was John Skyd, and of course
jumped to the conclusion that the three slumbering
figures were his brothers and friend. These enter-
prising knights of the quill, having found what they
deemed a suitable spot, had selected a cave for their
residence, as being at once ready and economical.

Now, George Dally, being gifted with a reckless
as well as humorous disposition, suddenly conceived
the idea of perpetrating a practical joke. Perhaps
Junkie's performances on the previous evening suggested it. Flinging his cap on the ground, he ran
his fingers through his thick hair until it stood up
in wild confusion, and then, deliberately uttering a
hideous and quite original war-whoop, he rushed
furiously towards the cave.

The brothers Skyd and company proved themselves
equal to the occasion, for they received him at the
cavern mouth with the muzzles of four double-barrelled guns, and a stern order to halt!

Next moment the muzzles were thrown up as
they exclaimed in surprise—

"Why, Dally, is it you?"

"Didn't you hear it?" gasped George, supporting
himself on the side of the cavern.

" Hear what?"

" The war-whoop ?"

" Of course we did—at least we heard a most unearthly yell.   What was it?"

" We'd best go out and see," cried George, cocking his gun ; " if it was Kafirs the sooner we follow them up the better."

" Not so, friend George," said Frank Dobson, in a slightly sarcastic tone.   " If it was Kafirs they are far beyond our reach by this time, and if they mean us harm we are safer in our fortress here. My opinion is that we should have our breakfast without delay, and then we shall be in a fit state to face our foes—whether they be men or beasts."

Acting on this suggestion, with a laugh, the brothers leaned their guns against the wall of the cavern and set about the preparation of breakfast in good earnest.

Meanwhile George gravely assented to the wisdom of their decision, and sat down to his morning pipe, while he questioned the brothers as to their intentions.

They pointed out to him the spot where they thought of commencing agricultural operations and the site of their future dwelling—close, they said, to the cave, because that would be conveniently near the river, which would be handy for both washing, drinking, and boiling purposes.

"That's true—wery true," said George, "but it seems to me you run a risk of bein' washed away, house and all, if you fix the site so low down, for I've heard say there are floods in these parts now and again."

"Oh, no fear of that!" said Robert Skyd, who was the quietest of the three brothers; "don't you see the foundation of our future house is at least ten feet above the highest point to which the river seems to have risen in times past?"

"Ah, just so," responded George, with the air of a man not convinced.

"Besides," added John Skyd, lifting the iron pot off the fire and setting it down, "I suppose that floods are not frequent, so we don't need to trouble ourselves about 'em.—Come, Dally, you'll join us?"

"No, thank 'ee. Much obleeged all the same, but I've got to prepare breakfast for our own party. —Goin' to begin plantin' soon?"

"As soon as ever we can get the soil broken up," replied Dobson.

"Studied farmin'?" inquired George.

"Not much, but we flatter ourselves that what we do know will be of some service to us," said John.

Dally made no reply, but he greatly doubted in his own mind the capacity of the brothers for the line of life they had chosen.

His judgment in this respect was proved correct a week later, when he and Edwin Brook had occasion to visit the brothers, whom they found hard at work ploughing and sowing.

" Come, this looks business-like !" exclaimed Brook heartily, as he shook hands with the brothers; "you've evidently not been idle. I have just come to ask a favour of you, gentlemen."

"We shall grant it with pleasure, if within our powers," said Robert Skyd, who leaned on a spade with which he had been filling in a trench of about two feet deep.

" It is, that you will do me and Mrs. Brook the pleasure of coming over to our location this after-noon to dinner. It is our Gertie's birthday. She is thirteen to-day. In a rash moment we promised her a treat or surprise of some sort, but really the only surprise I can think of in such an out-of-the-way place is to have a dinner-party in her honour. Will you come ?"

The brothers at once agreed to do so, remarking, however, that they must complete the sowing of their carrot-seed before dinner if possible.

"What did you say you were sowing?" asked Brook, with a peculiar smile.

" Carrot-seed," answered Robert Skyd.

" If your carrot-seed is sown *there*," said George Dally, pointing with a broad grin to the trench, " it's

very likely to come up in England about the time it
does here,—by 'sendin' its roots right through the
world !"

"How ? what do you mean ?"

"The truth is, my dear sir," said Brook good-
humouredly, "that you've made a slight mistake in
this matter.   Carrot-seed is usually sown in trenches
less than an inch deep.   You'd better leave off work
just now and come over to my place at once.   I'll
give you some useful hints as we walk along."

The knights of the quill laughed at their mistake,
and at once threw down their implements of
husbandry.   But on going over their farm, Brook
found it necessary to correct a few more mistakes,
for he discovered that the active brothers had already
planted a large quantity of Indian corn, or " mealies,"
entire, without knocking it off the cobs, and, in
another spot of ground, a lot of young onions were
planted with the roots upwards !

"You see, Miss Gertie," said John Skyd, when
commenting modestly on these mistakes at dinner-
time, "my brothers and I have all our lives had more
to do with the planting of 'houses' and the growth of
commercial enterprise than with agricultural pro-
ducts, but we are sanguine that, with experience and
perseverance, we shall overcome all our difficulties.
Have *you* found many difficulties to overcome ?"

Gertie was not sure ; she thought she had found a

few, but none worth mentioning. Being somewhat
put out by the question, she picked up a pebble—for
the dinner was a species of picnic, served on the
turf in front of Mr. Brook's tent—and examined it
with almost geological care.

"My daughter does not like to admit the existence
of difficulties," said Mrs. Brook, coming to the rescue,
"and to say truth is seldom overcome by anything."•

"Oh, ma, how can you?" said Gertie, blushing
deeply.

"That's not true," cried Mr. Brook; "excuse me,
my dear, for so flat a contradiction, but I have seen
Gertie frequently overcome by things,—by Junkie's
obstinacy for instance, which I verily believe to be
an insurmountable difficulty, and I've seen her
thoroughly overcome, night after night, by sleep.
—Isn't that true, lass?"

"I suppose it is, father, since you say so, but of
course I cannot tell."

"Sleep!" continued Brook, with a laugh, "why,
would you believe it, Mr. Skyd, I went into what we
call the nursery-tent one morning last week, to try
to stop the howling of my little boy, and I found him
lying with his open mouth close to Gertie's cheek,
pouring the flood of his wrath straight into her ear,
and she sound asleep all the time! My nurse, Mrs.
Scholtz, told me she had been as sound as that all
night, despite several heavy squalls, and notwith-

standing a chorus of hyenas and jackals outside that might almost have awakened the dead.—By the way, that reminds me: just as I was talking with nurse that morning we heard a most unearthly shriek at some distance off. It was not the least like the cry of any wild animal I have yet heard, and for the first time since our arrival the idea of Kafirs flashed into my mind. Did any of you gentlemen happen to hear it?"

The brothers looked at each other, and at their friend Dobson, and then unitedly turned their eyes on George Dally, who—performing the combined duties of cook and waiter, at a fire on the ground, not fifteen feet to leeward of the dinner-party—could hear every word of the conversation.

"Why, yes," said John Skyd, "we did hear it, and so did your man Dally. We had thought—"

"The truth is, sir," said George, advancing with a miniature pitchfork or "tormentor" in his hand; "pardon my interrupting you, sir,—I did hear the screech, but as I couldn't say exactly for certain, you know, that it was a Kafir, not havin' seen one, I thought it best not to alarm you, sir, an' so said nothing about it."

"You looked as if you had seen one," observed Frank Dobson, drawing down the corners of his mouth with his peculiar smile.

"Did I, sir?" said George, with a simple look;

"very likely I did, for I'm timersome by nature an' easily frightened."

"You did not act with your wonted wisdom, George, in concealing this," said Edwin Brook gravely.

"I'm afraid I didn't, sir," returned George meekly.

"In future, be sure to let me know every symptom of danger you may discover, no matter how trifling," said Brook.

"Yes, sir."

"It was a very tremendous yell, wasn't it, Dally?' asked John Skyd slily, as the waiter-cook was turning to resume his duties at the fire.

"Wery, sir."

"And alarmed us all dreadfully, didn't it?"

"Oh! dreadfully, sir—'specially me; though I must in dooty say that you four gentleman was as bold as brass. It quite relieved me when I saw your tall figurs standin' at the mouth o' your cavern, an' the muzzles o' your four double-guns—that's eight shots—with your glaring eyes an' pale cheeks behind them!"

"Ha!" exclaimed John Skyd, with a grim smile—"but after all it might only have been the shriek of a baboon."

"I think not, sir," replied George, with a smile of intelligence.

"Perhaps then it was the cry of a zebra or quagga," returned John Skyd, "or a South African ass of some sort."

"Wery likely, sir," retorted George. "I shouldn't wonder if it was—which is wery consolin' to my feelin's, for I 'd sooner be terrified out o' my wits by asses of any kind than fall in with these long-legged savages that dwell in caves."

With an appearace of great humility George returned to his work at the fire.

It was either owing to a sort of righteous retribution, or a touch of that fortune which favours the brave, that George Dally was in reality the first, of this particular party of settlers, to encounter the black and naked inhabitant of South Africa in his native jungle. It was on this wise.

George was fond of sport, when not detained at home by the claims of duty. But these claims were so constant that he found it impossible to indulge his taste, save, as he was wont to say, "in the early morn and late at eve."

One morning about daybreak, shouldering his gun and buckling on his hunting-knife, he marched into the jungle in quest of an antelope. Experience had taught him that the best plan was to seat himself at a certain opening or pass which lay on the route to a pool of water, and there bide his time.

Seating himself on a moss-covered stone, he put

his gun in position on his knee, with the forefinger on the trigger, and remained for some time so motionless that a North American Indian might have envied his powers of self-restraint. Suddenly a twig was heard to snap in the thicket before him. Next moment the striped black and yellow skin of a leopard, or Cape tiger, appeared in the opening where he had expected to behold a deer. Dally's gun flew to his shoulder. At the same instant the leopard skin was thrown back, and the right arm of a tall athletic Kafir was bared. The hand grasped a light assagai, or darting spear. Both men were taken by surprise, and for one instant they glared at each other. The distance between them was so short that death to each seemed imminent, for the white man's weapon was a deadly one, and the cast of the lithe savage would doubtless have been swift and sure.

In that instant of uncertainty the white man's innate spirit of forbearance acted almost involuntarily. Dally had hitherto been a man of peace. The thought of shedding human blood was intensely repulsive to him. He lowered the butt of his gun, and held up his right hand in token of amity.

The savage possessed apparently some of the good qualities of the white man, for he also at once let the butt of his assagai drop to the ground, although he knew, what Dally was not aware of, that considering the nature of their weapons, he placed himself at a tremendous disadvantage in doing so—the act of throwing forward and discharging the deadly fire-arm being much quicker than that of poising and hurling an assagai.

Without a moment's hesitation George Dally advanced and held out his right hand with a bland smile.

Although unfamiliar with Kafir customs, he had heard enough from the Dutch farmers who drove the ox-teams to know that only chiefs were entitled to wear the leopard skin as a robe. The tall form and dignified bearing of the savage also convinced him that he had encountered no ordinary savage. He also knew that the exhibition of a trustful spirit goes a long way to create good-will. That his judgment was correct appeared from the fact of the Kafir holding out his hand and allowing George to grasp and shake it.

But what to do next was a question that puzzled the white man sorely, although he maintained on his good-natured countenance an expression of easy nonchalance.

Of course he made a vain attempt at conversation in English, to which the Kafir chief replied, with dignified condescension, by a brief sentence in his own tongue.

As George Dally looked in his black face, thoughts flashed through his brain with the speed of light.

Should he kill him outright? That would be simple murder, in the circumstances, and George objected to murder, on principle. Should he suddenly seize and throw him down? He felt quite strong enough to do so, but after such a display of friendship it would be mean. Should he quietly bid him good morning and walk away? This, he felt, would be ridiculous. At that moment tobacco occurred to his mind. He quietly rested his gun against a tree, and drew forth a small roll of tobacco, from which he cut at least a foot and handed it to the chief. The dignity of the savage at once gave way before the beloved weed. He smiled—that is, he grinned in a ghastly way, for his face, besides being black, was streaked with lines of red ochre—and graciously accepted the gift. Then George made an elaborate speech in dumb-show with hands, fingers, arms, and eyes, to the effect that he desired the Kafir to accompany him to his location, but the chief gravely shook his head, pointed in another direction and to the sun, as though to say that time was on the wing; then, throwing his leopard-skin robe over his right shoulder with the air of a Spanish grandee, he turned aside and strode into the jungle.

George, glad to be thus easily rid of him, also turned and hurried home.

This time he was not slow to let his employer know that he had met with a native.

"It behoves us to keep a sharp look-out, George," said Brook. "I heard yesterday from young Merton that some of the settlers not far from his place have had a visit from the black fellows, who came in the night, and while they slept carried off some of the sheep they had recently purchased from an up-country county Dutchman. We will watch for a few nights while rumours of this kind are afloat. When all seems quiet we can take it easy. Let Scholtz take the first watch. You will succeed him, and I will mount guard from the small hours onward."

For some days this precaution was continued, but as nothing more was heard of black marauders the Brook family gradually ceased to feel anxious, and the nightly watch was given up.

CHAPTER VIII.

SHOWS THE PLEASURES, PAINS, AND PENALTIES OF HOUSEKEEPING
IN THE BUSH.

"DON'T you think this a charming life?" asked
Mrs. Brook of Mrs. Merton, who had been her guest
for a week.

Mrs. Merton was about thirty years of age, and
opinionated, if not strong-minded, also rather pretty.
She had married young, and her eldest son, a lad of
twelve, had brought her from her husband's farm,
some three miles distant from that of Edwin
Brook.

"No, Mrs. Brook, I don't like it at all," was Mrs.
Merton's emphatic reply.

"Indeed!" said Mrs. Brook, in some surprise.

She said nothing more after this for some time,
but continued to ply her needle busily, while Mrs.
Scholtz, who by some piece of unusual good fortune
had got Junkie to sleep, plied her scissors in cutting
out and shaping raw material.

The two dames, with the nurse and Gertie, had

agreed to unite their powers that day in a resolute effort to overtake the household repairs. They were in a cottage now, of the style familiarly known as "wattle and dab," which was rather picturesque than permanent, and suggestive of simplicity. They sat on rude chairs, made by Scholtz, round a rough table by the same artist. Mrs. Brook was busy with the rends in a blue pilot-cloth jacket, a dilapidated remnant of the "old England" wardrobe. The nurse was forming a sheep skin into a pair of those unmentionables which were known among the Cape-colonists of that period by the name of "crackers." Mrs. Merton was busy with a pair of the same, the knees of which had passed into a state of nonentity, while other parts were approaching the same condition. Gertie was engaged on a pair of socks, whose original formation was overlaid by and nearly lost in subsequent deposits.

"Why do you like this sort of life, Mrs. Brook?" asked Mrs. Merton suddenly.

"Because it is so new, so busy, so healthy, so thoroughly practical. Such a constant necessity for doing something useful, and a constant supply of something useful to do, and then such a pleasant feeling of rest when at last you do get your head on a pillow."

"Oh! it's delightful!" interpolated Gertie in a low voice.

Sl
r

Well, now, that is strange. Everything depends on how one looks at things.—What do *you* think, Mrs. Scholtz?" asked Mrs. Merton.

"I 've got no time to think, ma'am," replied the nurse, giving the embryo crackers a slice that bespoke the bold fearless touch of a thorough artist. "When Junkie's not asleep he keeps body and brain fully employed, and when he is asleep I 'm glad to let body and brain alone."

"What is your objection to this life, Mrs. Merton?" asked Mrs. Brook, with a smile.

"Oh! I 've no special objection, only I hate it altogether. How is it possible to like living in a wilderness, with no conveniences around one, no society to chat with, no books to read, and, above all, no shops to go to, where one is obliged to drudge at menial work from morning till night, and one's boys and girls get into rags and tatters, and one's husband becomes little better than a navvy, to say nothing of snakes and scorpions in one's bed and boots, and the howling of wild beasts all night? I declare, one might as well live in a menagerie."

"But you must remember that things are in a transition state just now," rejoined Mrs. Brook. "As we spread and multiply over the land, things will fall more into shape. We shall have tailors and dressmakers to take the heavy part of our work in *this* way, and the wild beasts will retire

before the rifle and the plough of civilised man; hⁿ
doubt, also, shops will come in due course."

"And what of the Kafirs?" cried Mrs. Merton
sternly. "Do you flatter yourself that either the
plough- or the rifle will stop their thievish propensities? Have we not learned, when too late—
for here we are, and here we must bide,—that the
black wretches have been at loggerheads with the
white men ever since this was a colony, and is it not
clear that gentle treatment and harsh have alike
failed to improve them?"

"Wise treatment has yet to be tried," said Mrs.
Brook.

"Fiddlesticks!" returned Mrs. Merton impatiently.
"What do you call wise treatment?"

"Gospel treatment," replied Mrs. Brook.

"Oh! come now, you know that *that* has also
been tried, and has signally failed. Have we not
heard how many hundreds of so-called black con-
verts in this and in other colonies are arrant
hypocrites, or at all events give way before the
simplest temptations?"

"I have also heard," returned Mrs. Brook, "of
many hundreds of so-called white Christians, whose
lives prove them to be the enemies of our Saviour,
and who do not even condescend to hypocrisy, for
they will plainly tell you that they 'make no
pretence to be religious,' though they call them·

selves Christians. But that does not prove gospel treatment among the English to have been a failure. You have heard, I daresay, of the Hottentot robber Africaner, who was long the terror and scourge of the district where he lived, but who, under the teaching of our missionary Mr. Moffat, or rather, I should say, under the influence of God's Holy Spirit, has led a righteous, peaceful, Christian life for many years. He is alive still to prove the truth of what I say."

"I'll believe it when I see it," returned Mrs. Merton, with a decisive compression of her lips.

"Well, many people have testified to the truth of this, and some of these people have seen Africaner and have believed."

"Humph!" returned Mrs. Merton.

This being an unanswerable argument, Mrs. Brook smiled by way of reply, and turned a sleeve inside out, the better to get at its dilapidations. Changing the subject, she desired Gertie to go and prepare dinner, as it was approaching noon.

"What shall I prepare, mother?" asked Gertie, laying down her work.

"You'd better make a hash of the remains of yesterday's leg of mutton, dear; it will be more quickly done than the roasting of another leg, and we can't spare time on cookery to-day. I daresay Mrs. Merton will excuse—"

"Mrs. Brook," interrupted Mrs. Merton, with that Spartan-like self-denial to which she frequently laid claim, without, however, the slightest shadow of a title, "I can eat anything on a emergency. Have the hash by all means."

"And I'm afraid, Mrs. Merton," continued Mrs. Brook, in an apologetic tone, "that we shall have to dine without bread to-day—we have run short of flour. My husband having heard that the Thomases have recently got a large supply, has gone to their farm to procure some, but their place is twelve miles off, so he can't be back till night. You won't mind, I trust?"

Mrs. Merton vowed that she didn't mind, became more and more Spartanic in her expression and sentiments, and plied her needle with increased decision.

Just then Gertie re-entered the cottage with a face expressive of concern.

"Mother, there's no meat in the larder."

"No meat, child? You must be mistaken. We ate only a small part of yesterday's leg."

"Oh! ma'am," exclaimed the nurse, dropping the scissors suddenly, and looking somewhat guilty, "I quite forgot, ma'am, to say that master, before he left this morning, and while you was asleep, ma'am, ordered me to give all the meat we had in the house to Scholtz, as he was to be away four or

five days, and would require it all, so I gave him
the leg that was hanging up in the larder, and
master himself took the remains of yesterday's leg,
bidding me be sure to tell George to kill a sheep
and have meat ready for dinner."

"Oh, well, it doesn't matter," said Mrs. Brook;
"we shall just have to wait a little longer."

Nurse looked strangely remorseful.

"But, ma'am—" she said, and paused.

"Well, nurse?"

"I forgot, ma'am—indeed I did—to tell George
to kill a sheep."

Mrs. Brook's hands and work fell on her lap,
and she looked from Mrs. Scholtz to her visitor,
and from her to the anxious Gertie, without speaking.

"Why, what's the matter?" asked Mrs. Merton.

"My dear," replied Mrs. Brook, with a touch of
solemnity, "George Dally, our man, asked me this
morning if he might go into the bush to cut rafters
for the new kitchen, and I gave him leave, knowing
nothing of what arrangements had been made before
—and—and—in short, there's not a man on the
place, and—there's nothing to eat."

The four females looked at each other in blank
silence for a few seconds, as the full significance of
their circumstances became quite clear to them.

Mrs. Merton was the first to recover.

"Now," said she, while the Spartanic elements of her nature became intensified, "we must rise to this occasion like true women ; we must prove ourselves to be not altogether dependent on man; we must face the difficulty, sink the natural tenderness of our sex, and—and—kill a sheep !"

She laid down the crackers on the table with an air of resolution, and rose to put her fell intent in execution.

But the carrying out of her plan was not so easy as the good lady had, at the first blush of the thing, imagined it would be.   In the first place, like other heroes and heroines, she experienced the enervating effects of opposition and vacillating purpose in others.

"You must all help me," she said, with the air of a commander-in-chief.

"Help you to kill a sheep, ma'am ?" said Mrs. Scholtz, with a shudder, "I'll die first ! I couldn't do it, and I wouldn't, for my weight in gold."

Notwithstanding the vehemence of her protestation, the nurse stood by and listened while the other conspirators talked in subdued tones, and with horrified looks, of the details of the contemplated murder.

"I never even saw the dreadful deed done," said Mrs. Brook, becoming pale as she thought of it.

"Oh, mamma! much better go without meat; we could dine on cakes," suggested Gertie.

"But, my love, there is not a cake or an ounce of flour in the house."

"Women!" exclaimed Mrs. Merton severely, "we must rise to the occasion. I am hungry *now*, and it is not yet noon; what will be our condition if we wait till night for our dinner?"

This was a home-thrust. The conspirators shuddered and agreed to do the deed. Gertie, in virtue of her youth, was exempted from taking any active part, but an unaccountable fascination constrained her to follow and be a witness—in short, an accomplice.

"Do you know where—where—the *knife* is kept?" asked Mrs. Merton.

Mrs. Scholtz knew, and brought it from the kitchen.

It was a keen serviceable knife, with a viciously sharp point. Mrs. Merton received it, coughed, and hurried out to the sheep-fold, followed by her accomplices.

To catch a sheep was not difficult, for the animals were all more or less tame and accustomed to gentle treatment by the females, but to hold it was quite another thing. Mrs. Merton secured it by the head, Mrs. Scholtz laid hold of the tail, and Mrs. Brook fastened her fingers in the wool of its back. Each female individually was incapable of holding the animal, though a very small one had been purposely selected, but collectively they were more than a match for it. After a short struggle it was laid on its side, and its feet were somewhat imperfectly secured with a pocket-hand-kerchief.

"Now, ma'am," cried Mrs. Scholtz, holding tight to the tail and shutting her eyes, "do be quick."

Mrs. Merton, also shutting her eyes, struck feebly with the knife. The others having likewise shut their eyes waited a few seconds in a state of inde-scribable horror, and then opened them to find that the Spartan lady had missed her mark and planted her weapon in the ground! So feeble, however, had been the stroke that it had barely penetrated an inch of the soil.

"Oh, Mrs. Merton!" exclaimed Mrs. Brook remon-stratively.

Mrs. Merton tried again more carefully, and hit the mark, but still without success.

"It *won't* go in!" she gasped, as, on opening her eyes a second time, she found only a few drops of blood trickling from a mere scratch in the sheep's neck; "I—I *can't* do it!"

At that moment the unfortunate animal suddenly freed its head from the Spartan matron's grasp. A sharp wriggle freed its tail and feet, and in another

moment it burst away from its captors and made for
a shallow pond formed by Edwin Brook for a colony
of household ducks.

Roused to excessive indignation by the weakness
and boastfulness of Mrs. Merton, Mrs. Scholtz sprang
to her feet and gave chase. The others joined.
Hunger, shame, determination, disappointment, combined to give them energy of purpose. The sheep
rushed into the pond. Mrs. Scholtz recklessly
followed—up to the knees—caught it by the horns,
and dragged it forth.

"Give me the knife!" she shouted.

Mrs. Merton hurriedly obeyed, and the nurse,
shutting her eyes, plunged it downwards with a
wild hysterical shriek.

There was no mistake this time. Letting the
animal go, she fled, red-handed, into the innermost
recess of the cottage, followed by her horrified
friends.

"Oh! what *have* I done?" groaned Mrs. Scholtz,
burying her face in her hands.

Mrs. Brook and the others—all shuddering—
sought to soothe her, and in a short time they
regained sufficient composure to permit of their
returning to the victim, which they found lying
dead upon the ground.

Having thus got over the terrible first step, the
ladies hardened themselves to the subsequent pro-

cesses, and these they also found more difficult than they had anticipated. The skinning of a sheep they did not understand. Of the cutting up they were equally ignorant, and a terrible mess they made of the poor carcass in their varied efforts. In despair Mrs. Brook suggested to Mrs. Scholtz, who was now the chief and acknowledged operator, that they had better cut it up without skinning, and singe off the wool and skin together; but on attempting this Mrs. Scholtz found that she could not find the joints, and being possessed of no saw could not cut the bones, whereupon Mrs. Merton suggested that she should cut out four slices from any part that would admit of being penetrated by a knife, and leave the rest of the operation to be performed by Dally on his return. This proposal was acted on. Four fat slices were cut from the flanks and carried by Gertie to the kitchen, where they were duly cooked, and afterwards eaten with more relish than might have been expected, considering the preliminaries to the feast.

This was one of those difficulties that did not occur to them again. It was a preventable difficulty, to be avoided in future by the exercise of forethought; but there were difficulties and troubles in store against which forethought was of little avail.

While they were yet in the enjoyment of the

chops which had caused them so much mental and physical pain, they were alarmed by a sudden cry from Junkie. Looking round they saw that urchin on his knees holding on to the side of his home-made crib, and gazing in blank amazement at the hole in the wall which served for a window. And well might he gaze, for he saw the painted face of a black savage looking in at that window!

On beholding him Mrs. Merton uttered a scream and Mrs. Brook an exclamation. Mrs. Scholtz and Gertie seemed bereft of power to move or cry.

Perhaps the Kafir took this for the British mode of welcoming a stranger. At all events, he left the window and entered by the door. Being quite naked, with the exception of the partial covering afforded by a leopard-skin robe, his appearance was naturally alarming to females who had never before seen a native of South Africa in his war-paint. They remained perfectly still, however, and quite silent, while he went through the cottage appropriating whatever things took his fancy. He was the native whom we have already introduced as having been met by George Dally, though of course the Brook household were not aware of this.

A few other savages entered the cottage soon after, and were about to follow the example of their chief and help themselves, but he sternly ordered them to quit, and they submissively obeyed.

When he had gone out, without having condescended to notice any of the household, Master Junkie gave vent to a long-suspended howl, and claimed the undivided attention of Mrs. Scholtz, whose touching blandishments utterly failed in quieting him. The good nurse was unexpectedly aided, however, by the savage chief, who on repassing the window, looked in and made his black face supernaturally hideous by glaring at the refractory child. Junkie was petrified on the spot, and remained "good" till forgetfulness and sleep overpowered him.

Meanwhile Mrs. Merton swooned into a chair—or appeared to do so—and Mrs. Brook, recovering from her first alarm, went out with Gertie to see what the black marauders were about.

They were just in time to see the last tail of their small flock of sheep, and their still smaller herd of cattle, disappear into the jungle, driven by apparently a score of black, lithe, and naked devils, so ugly and unearthly did the Kafirs seem on this their first visit to the unfortunate settlers.

It was a peculiarly bitter trial to the Brooks, for the herd and flock just referred to had been acquired, after much bargaining, from a Dutch farmer only a few days before, and Edwin Brook was rather proud of his acquisition, seeing that few if any of the settlers had at that time become possessors of live stock to any great extent. It was, however, a salutary lesson, and the master of Mount Hope—so he had named his location—never again left his wife and family unguarded for a single hour during these first years of the infant colory

CHAPTER IX.

OFF TO THE HIGHLANDS AND BLACK SNAKES IN THE BUSH.

WHILE the settlers of this section were thus scattering far and wide, in more or less numerous groups, over the fertile plains of Lower Albany, the Scotch party was slowly, laboriously, toiling on over hill and dale, jungle and plain, towards the highlands of the interior.

The country through which the long line of waggons passed was as varied as can well be imagined, being one of the wildest and least inhabited tracts of the frontier districts. The features of the landscape changed continually from dark jungle to rich park-like scenery, embellished with graceful clumps of evergreens, and from that again to the sterility of savage mountains or parched and desert plains. Sometimes they plodded wearily over the karroo for twenty miles or more at a stretch without seeing a drop of water. At other times they came to a wretched mud hovel, the farm-house of a boer, near a permanent spring of water. Again, they were entangled among the rugged, roadless gorges and precipices of a mountain range, through which no vehicle of European construction could have passed without absolute demolition, and up parts of which the Cape-waggons were sometimes compelled to go by means of two teams,—that is, from twenty to thirty or more oxen,—being attached to each. At other times they had to descend and re-ascend the precipitous banks of rivers whose beds were sometimes quite dry and paved with mighty boulders.

"It's an unco rough country," observed Sandy Black to Charlie Considine, as they stood watching the efforts of a double team to haul one of their waggons up a slope so rugged and steep that the mere attempt appeared absolute madness in their eyes.

Considine assented, but was too much interested in the process to indulge in further remark.

"Gin the rope brek," continued Sandy, "I wadna gie muckle for the waggon. It'll come rowin' an' stottin' doon the hill like a bairn's ba'."

"No fear of the rope," said Hans Marais, as he passed at the moment to render assistance to Ruyter, Jemalee, Booby, and some others, who were shouting at the pitch of their voices, and plying the long waggon-whips, or the short sjamboks, with unmerciful vigour.

Hans was right. The powerful "trektow" stood the enormous strain, and the equally powerful waggon groaned and jolted up the stony steep until it had nearly gained the top, when an unfortunate drop of the right front wheel into a deep hollow, combined with an unlucky and simultaneous elevation of the left back wheel by a stone, turned the vehicle completely over on its side. The hoops of the tilt were broken, and much of the lading was deposited in a hollow beside the waggon, but a few of the lighter and smaller articles went hopping, or, according to Sandy Black, "stottin'" down the slope, and were smashed to atoms at the bottom.

Ruyter, Booby, and Jemalee turned towards Hans Marais with a shrinking action, as if they expected to feel the sjambok on their shoulders, for their own cruel master was wont on occasions of mischance such as this to visit his men with summary punishment; but Hans was a good specimen of another, and, we believe, much more numerous class of Cape-Dutchmen. After the first short frown of annoyance had passed, he went actively to work, to set the example of unloading the waggon and repairing the damage, administering at the same time, however, a pretty sharp rebuke to the drivers for their carelessness in not taking better note of the form of the ground.

That night, in talking over the incident with Ruyter, Considine ventured again to comment on the wrongs which the former endured, and the possibility of redress being obtained from the proper authorities.

"For I am told," he said, "that the laws of the colony do not now permit masters to lash and maltreat their slaves as they once did."

Ruyter, though by nature a good-humoured, easy-going fellow, was possessed of an unusually high spirit for one of his race, and could never listen to any reference to the wrongs of the Hottentots without a dark frown of indignation. In general he avoided the subject, but on the night in question either his wonted reticence had fled, or he felt disposed to confide in the kindly youth, from whom on the previous journey from Capetown he had experienced many marks of sympathy and good-will.

"Dere be no way to make tings better," he replied fiercely. "I knows noting 'bout your laws. Only knows dey don't work somehow. Allers de same wid *me* anyhow, kick and cuff and lash w'en I's wrong —sometimes w'en I's right—and nebber git tanks for noting."

"But that is because your master is an unusually bad fellow," replied Considine. "Few Cape farmers are so bad as he. You have yourself had experience of Hans Marais, now, who is kind to every one."

"Ja, he is good master—an' so's him's fadder, an' all him's peepil—but what good dat doos to me?" returned the Hottentot gloomily. "It is true your laws do not allow us to be bought and sold like de slaves, but dat very ting makes de masters hate us and hurt us more dan de slaves."

This was to some extent true. At the time we write of, slavery, being still permitted in the British colonies, the Dutch, and other Cape colonists, possessed great numbers of negro slaves, whom it was their interest to treat well, as being valuable "property," and whom most of them probably did treat well, as a man will treat a useful horse or ox, though of course there were—as there always must be in the circumstances—many instances of cruelty, by passionate and brutal owners. But the Hottentots, or original natives of the South African soil, having been declared unsaleable, and therefore not "property," were in many cases treated with greater degradation by their masters than the slaves, were made to work like them, but not cared for or fed like them, because not so valuable. At the same time, although not absolute slaves, the Hottentots were practically in a state of servitude, in which the freedom accorded to them by Government had, by one subterfuge or another, been rendered inoperative. Not long before this period the colonists possessed absolute power over the Hottentots, and although recent efforts had been made to legislate in their favour, their wrongs had only been mitigated,—by no means redressed. Masters were, it is true, held

accountable by the law for the treatment of their
Hottentots, but were rarely called to account, and
the Hottentots knew too well, from sad experience,
that to make a complaint would be in many cases
worse than useless, as it would only rouse the ire of
their masters and make them doubly severe.

"You say de Hottentots are not slaves, but you
treat us all de same as slaves—anyhow, Jan Smit
doos."

"That is the sin of Jan Smit, not of the British
law," replied Considine.

Ruyter's face grew darker as he rejoined fiercely,
"What de use of your laws if dey won't work?
Besides, what right hab de white scoundril to make
slave at all—whether you call him slave or no call
him slave.   Look at Jemalee!"

The Hottentot pointed with violent action to the
Malay, who, with a calm and sad but dignified mien,
stood listening to the small-talk of Booby, while the
light of the camp-fire played fitfully on their swarthy
features.

"Well, what of Jemalee?" asked Considine.

"You know dat him's a slave—a *real* slave?"

"Yes, I know that, poor fellow."

"You never hear how him was brought up here?"

"No, never—tell me about it."

Hereupon the Hottentot related the following
brief story.

Abdul Jemalee, a year or two before, had lived in Capetown, where his owner was a man of some substance. Jemalee had a wife and several children, who were also the property of his owner. Being an expert waggon-driver, the Malay was a valuable piece of human goods. On one occasion Jan Smit happened to be in Capetown, and, hearing of the Malay's qualities, offered his master a high price for him. The offer was accepted, but in order to avoid a scene, the bargain was kept secret from the piece of property, and he was given to understand that he was going up country on his old master's business. When poor Jemalee bade his pretty wife and little ones goodbye, he comforted them with the assurance that he should be back in a few months. On arriving at Smit's place, however, the truth was told, and he found that he had been separated for ever from those he most loved on earth. For some time Abdul Jemalee gave way to sullen despair, and took every sort of abuse and cruel treatment with apparent indifference, but as time went on a change came over him. He became more like his former self, and did his work so well, that even the savage Jan Smit seldom had any excuse for finding fault. On his last journey to the Cape, Smit took the Malay with him only part of the way. He left him in charge of a friend, who agreed to look well after him until his return.

Even this crushing of Jemalee's hope that he
might meet his wife and children once more did not
appear to oppress him much, and when his master
returned from Capetown he resumed charge of one
of the waggons, and went quietly back to his home
in the karroo.

"And can you tell what brought about this
change?" asked Considine.

"Oh! ja, I knows," replied Ruyter, with a decided
nod and a deep chuckle; "Jemalee him's got a
powerful glitter in him's eye now and den—bery
powerful an' strange!"

"And what may that have to do with it?" asked
Considine.

Ruyter's visage changed from a look of deep
cunning to one of childlike simplicity as he
replied—

"Can't go for to say what de glitter of him's eye
got to do wid it. Snakes' eyes glitter sometimes—
s'pose 'cause he can't help it, or he's wicked
p'raps."

Considine smiled, but seeing that the Hottentot
did not choose to be communicative on the point he
forbore further question.

"What a funny man Jerry Goldboy is!" said
Jessie M'Tavish, as she sat that same evening sipping a pannikin of tea in her father's tent.

From the opening of the tent the fire was visible

Jerry was busy preparing his supper, while he kept up an incessant run of small-chat with Booby and Jemalee. The latter replied to him chiefly with grave smiles, the former with shouts of appreciative laughter.

"He *is* funny," asserted Mrs. M'Tavish, "and uncommonly noisy. I doubt if there is much good in him."

"More than you think, Mopsy," said Kenneth (by this irreverent name did the Highlander call his better-half); " Jerry Goldboy is a small package, but he's made of good stuff, depend upon it. No doubt he's a little nervous, but I've observed that his nerves are tried more by the suddenness with which he may be surprised than by the actual danger he may chance to encounter. On our first night out, when he roused the camp and smashed the stock of his blunderbuss, no doubt I as well as others thought he showed the white feather, but there was no lack of courage in him when he went last week straight under the tree where the tiger was growling, and shot it so dead that when it fell it was not far from his feet."

"I heard some of the men, papa," observed Jessie, "say that it was Dutch courage that made him do that. What did they mean by Dutch courage?"

Jessie, being little more than eight, was ignorant of much of the world's slang.

"Cape-smoke, my dear," answered her father, with a laugh.

" Cape-smoke ?" exclaimed Jessie, " what is that ?"

" Brandy, child, peach-brandy, much loved by some of the boers, I'm told, and still more so by the Hottentots ; but there was no more Cape-smoke in Jerry that day than in you. It was true English pluck. No doubt he could hardly fail to make a dead shot at so close a range, with such an awful weapon, loaded, as it usually is, with handfuls of slugs, buckshot, and gravel; but it was none the less plucky for all that. The old flint-lock might have missed fire, or he mightn't have killed the brute outright, and in either case he knew well enough it would have been all up with Jerry Gold-boy."

" Who's that taking my name in vain?" said Jerry himself, passing the tent at the moment, in company with Sandy Black.

"We were only praising you, Jerry," cried Jessie, with a laugh, " for the way in which you shot that tiger the other day."

"It wasn't a teeger, Miss Jessie," interposed Sandy Black, "it was only a leopard—ane o' thae wee spottit beasts that they're sac prood o' in this country as to *ca'* them teegers."

" Come, Sandy," cried Jerry Goldboy, " don't rob me of the honour that is my due. The hanimal was big enough to 'ave torn you limb from limb if 'e 'd got 'old of you."

" It may be sae, but he wasna a teeger for a' that," retorted Black.—"D 'ee know, sir," he continued, turning to M'Tavish, " that Mr. Pringle's been askin' for 'ee ?"

" No, Sandy, but now that you 've told me I 'll go to his tent."

So saying the Highlander rose and went out, to attend a council of " heads of families."

Hitherto we have directed the reader's attention chiefly to one or two individuals of the Scotch party, but there were in that party a number of families who had appointed Mr. Pringle their "head" and representative. In this capacity of chief-head, or leader, Mr. Pringle was in the habit of convening a meeting of subordinate "heads" when matters of importance had to be discussed.

While the elders of the party were thus engaged in conclave at the door of their leader's tent, and while the rest were busy round their several fires, a man with a body much blacker than the *night* was secretly gliding about the camp like a huge snake, now crouching as he passed quickly, but without noise, in rear of the thick bushes; now creeping on hands and knees among the waggons and oxen, and anon gliding almost flat on his breast up to the very verge of the light thrown by the camp-

fires. At one and another of the fires he remained
motionless like the blackened trunk of a dead tree,
with his glittering eyes fixed on the settlers, as if
listening intently to their conversation.

Whatever might be the ultimate designs of the
Kafir—for such he was—his intentions at the time
being were evidently peaceful, for he carried neither
weapon nor shield. He touched nothing belonging
to the white men, though guns and blankets and
other tempting objects were more than once within
reach of his hand. Neither did he attempt to steal
that which to the Kafir is the most coveted prize of
all—a fat ox. Gradually he melted away into the
darkness from which he had emerged. No eye in
all the emigrant band saw him come or go in his
snake-like glidings, yet his presence was known to
one of the party—to Ruyter the Hottentot.

Soon after the Kafir had taken his departure,
Ruyter left his camp-fire and sauntered into the bush
as if to meditate before lying down for the night.
As soon as he was beyond observation he quickened
his pace and walked in a straight line, like one who
has a definite end in view.

The Hottentot fancied that he had got away
unperceived, but in this he was mistaken. Hans
Marais, having heard Considine's account of his talk
with Ruyter about Jemalee, had been troubled with
suspicions about the former, which led to his paying

more than usual attention to him. These suspicions were increased when he observed that the Hottentot went frequently and uneasily into the bushes, and looked altogether like a man expecting something which does not happen or appear. When, therefore, he noticed that, after supper, Ruyter's anxious look disappeared, and that, after looking carefully round at his comrades, he sauntered into the bush with an overdone air of nonchalance, he quietly took up his heavy gun and followed him.

The youth had been trained to *observe* from earliest childhood, and, having been born and bred on the karroo, he was as well skilled in tracking the footprints of animals and men as any red savage of the North American wilderness. He took care to keep the Hottentot in sight, however, the night being too dark to see footprints. Lithe and agile as a panther, he found no difficulty in doing so.

In a few minutes he reached an open space, in which he observed that the Hottentot had met with a Kafir, and was engaged with him in earnest conversation. Much however of what they said was lost by Hans, as he found it difficult to get within ear-shot unobserved.

"And why?" he at length heard the savage demand, "why should I spare them for an hour?"

He spoke in the Kafir tongue, in which the

Hottentot replied, and with which young Marais
was partially acquainted.

"Because, Hintza," said Ruyter, naming the paramount chief of Kafirland, "the time has not yet
come. One whose opinion you value bade me tell
you so."

"What if I choose to pay no regard to the opinion
of any one?" demanded the chief haughtily.

Ruyter quietly told the savage that he would
then have to take the consequences, and urged, in
addition, that it was folly to suppose the Kafirs
were in a condition to make war on the white men
just then. It was barely a year since they had been
totally routed and driven across the Great Fish River
with great slaughter. No warrior of common sense
would think of renewing hostilities at such a time—
their young men slain, their resources exhausted.
Hintza had better bide his time. In the meanwhile
he could gratify his revenge without much risk to
himself or his young braves, by stealing in a quiet
systematic way from the white men as their herds
and flocks increased. Besides this, Ruyter, assuming
a bold look and tone which was unusual in one of
his degraded race, told Hintza firmly that he had
reasons of his own for not wishing the Scotch emigrants to be attacked at that time, and that if he
persisted in his designs he would warn them of their
danger, in which case they would certainly prove

themselves men enough to beat any number of warriors Hintza could bring against them.

Lying flat on the ground, with head raised and motionless, Hans Marais listened to these sentiments with much surprise, for he had up to that time regarded the Hottentot as a meek and long-suffering man, but now, though his long-suffering in the past could not be questioned, his meekness appeared to have totally departed.

The Kafir chief would probably have treated the latter part of Ruyter's speech with scorn, had not his remarks about sly and systematic plunder chimed in with his own sentiments, for Hintza was pre-eminently false-hearted, even among a race with whom successful lying is deemed a virtue, though, when found out, it is considered a sin. He pondered the Hottentot's advice, and apparently assented to it. After a few moments' consideration, he turned on his heel, and re-entered the thick jungle.

Well was it for Hans Marais that he had concealed himself among tall grass, for Hintza chanced to pass within two yards of the spot where he lay. The Kafir chief had resumed the weapons which, for convenience, he had left behind in the bush while prowling round the white man's camp, and now stalked along in all the panoply of a savage warrior-chief, with ox-hide shield, bundle of short sharp assagais, leopard-skin robe, and feathers. For one instant the

Dutchman, supposing it impossible to escape detection, was on the point of springing on the savage, but on second thoughts he resolved to take his chance. Even if Hintza did discover him, he felt sure of being able to leap up in time to ward off his first stab.

Fortunately the Kafir was too much engrossed with his thoughts. He passed his white enemy, and disappeared in the jungle.

Meanwhile the Hottentot returned to the camp—assuming an easy-going saunter as he approached its fires—and, soon after, Hans Marais re-entered it from an opposite direction. Resolving to keep his own counsel in the meantime, he mentioned the incident to no one, but after carefully inspecting the surrounding bushes, and stirring up the watch-fires, he sat down in front of his leader's tent, with the intention of keeping guard during the first part of the night.

CHAPTER X.

THE LOCATION ON THE RIVER OF BABOONS.

THE Scotch immigrants at last found themselves in the wild mountain-regions of the interior, after a weary but deeply interesting march of nearly two hundred miles.

They had now arrived at the mouth of the Baboons or Baviaans river, one of the affluents of the Great Fish River, and had already seen many of the wild inhabitants of its rugged glen.

Their particular location was a beautiful well-watered region among the mountains which had been forfeited by some of the frontier boers at the time of their insurrection against the English Government some years before. They had now crossed the Great Fish River, and, though still within the old boundary of the colony, were upon its utmost eastern verge. The country beyond, as we are told by Pringle, in his graphic account of the expedition,[1] "for a distance of seventy miles, to the new frontier at the Chumi

[1] See *Narrative of a Residence in South Africa*, by Thomas Pringle, late Secretary to the Anti-Slavery Society.

and Keisi rivers, had been, the preceding year, forcibly
depeopled of its native inhabitants, the Kafirs and
Ghonaquas, and now lay waste and void, 'a howling
wilderness,' occupied only by wild beasts, and haunted
occasionally by wandering banditti of the Bushman
race (Bosjesmen), who were represented as being
even more wild and savage than the beasts of prey
with whom they shared the dominion of the desert."

Just before their arrival at this point, the old
waggons, with the drivers who had accompanied them
from Algoa Bay, were exchanged for fresh teams
and men, and here Ruyter, Jemalee, and Booby left
them, to proceed over a spur of one of the mountain
ranges to Jan Smit's farm on the karroo. But Hans
Marais having taken a fancy to some of the Scotch-
men, determined to proceed with them until he had
seen them fairly established in their new homes. Of
course Charlie Considine accompanied Hans.

In a wild spot among the mountains they were
hospitably received at the solitary abode of a field-
cornet named Opperman, who said that he had orders
to assist them with an escort of armed boers over
the remaining portion of their journey, and to place
them in safety on their allotted ground. This remaining portion, he told them, was up the Baviaans
River glen, and, although little more than twenty-five
miles, would prove to be harder than any part of the
journey they had yet encountered.

Remembering some of the breakneck gorges of the Zuurberg, Jerry Goldboy said that he didn't believe it possible for any route to be worse than that over which they had already passed, to which Sandy Black replied with a "humph!" and an opinion that "the field-cornet o' the distric' was likely to know what he was speakin' aboot." But Jerry never had been, and of course never could be, convinced by reason; "Nothing," he candidly admitted, "but hard facts had the least weight with him."

"'Ee've got hard fac's noo, Jerry," said Sandy, about noon of the following day, as he threw down the axe with which he had been hewing the jungle, and pulled off his hat, from the crown of which he took a red cotton handkerchief wherewith to wipe his thickly-beaded brow.

Jerry could not deny the truth of this, for he also had been engaged since early morning with a South African axe nearly as large as himself, in assisting to cut a passage up the glen.

Not only was there no road up this mountain gorge, but in some parts it was scarcely possible to make one, so rugged was the ground, so dense the jungle. But the preliminary difficulties were as nothing compared to those which met them further up; yet it was observable that the Dutch waggoners faced them with the quiet resolution of men accustomed to the overcoming of obstacles.

"You'd go up a precipice, Hans, I do believe, if there was no way round it," said Considine, as he gazed in admiring wonder at his tall friend driving his oxen up an acclivity that threatened destruction to waggon, beasts, and men.

"At ony rate he'd try," remarked Sandy Black, with one of his grave smiles.

Hans was too busy to heed these remarks, if he heard them, for the oxen, being restive, claimed his undivided attention, and the wielding of the twenty-foot whip taxed both his arms, muscular though they were.

When the long line of emigrants had slowly defiled through the *poort*, or narrow gorge, of the mountains from which Baviaans River issues into the more open valley where it joins the Great Fish River, they came suddenly upon a very singular scene, and a still more singular man. In the middle of the *poort* they found a small farm, where tremendous precipices of naked rock towered all round, so as to leave barely sufficient space on the bank of the river for the houses and cattle-folds, with a well-stocked garden and orchard. There was also a small plot of corn-land on the margin of the stream.

"'Tis a little paradise!" exclaimed Kenneth M'Tavish, as he and Considine joined a knot of men on a knoll, whence they had a good view of the little farm.

"It's an unco rocky paradise," observed Sandy
Black, "an' the angelic appendages o' wings wadna
be unsuitable to its inhabitants, for it seems easier
to flee oot o't ower the precipices than to scramble
intil't ower the rocks an' rooten trees. I wonder
wha it belangs to."

Hans Marais, who came up at the moment, explained that it belonged to a Dutch boer named
Prinslo, who had been a leader some years before in
a rebellion, but had been pardoned and allowed to
retain his lands. "You've sometimes said you
thought me a big fellow, Considine," remarked Hans
"and I can't gainsay you, but you shall see a much
bigger fellow if Prinsolo is at home, for he's a giant
even among Cape Dutchmen. We call him Groot
Willem (Big William), for he is burly and broad as well
as tall—perhaps he is taking his noon nap," added
Hans, moving forward. "He seldom lets even a single
waggon come so near without—ah! I thought so."

As he spoke a peculiarly deep bass yawn was
heard inside the principal house of the farm to which
the party now drew near. Next moment a heavy
thump sounded, as if on the floor, and immediately
after there issued from the open door a veritable
giant in his shirt-sleeves. Groot Willem was rough,
shaggy, and rugged, as a giant ought to be. He was
also sluggish in his motions, good-humoured, and
beaming, as many of the Dutch giants are. Appro

priately enough, on beholding the settlers, he uttered a deep bass halloo, which was echoed solemnly by the mighty cliffs at his back. It was neither a shout of alarm nor surprise, for he had long been aware that this visit was pending, but a hasty summons to his household to turn out and witness the stirring and unwonted sight.

It might have been supposed that a giant, whose kindred had been deprived of their lands by the British Government, and some of whom had been executed for high treason, would have regarded the British immigrants with no favourable eye, but Groot Willem appeared to have a large heart in his huge body, for he received the advance-guard of the party with genuine hospitality. Perhaps he was of an unusually forgiving spirit; or it may be that his innate sense of justice led him to recognise the de-merit of himself and his kindred; or perchance he was touched by the leniency extended to himself; but, whatever the cause, he shook the new-comers heartily by the hand, said he regarded them as next-door-neighbours, started the echoes of the precipices —which he styled Krantzes—and horrified the nearest baboons with shouts of bass laughter at every word from himself or others which bore the remotest semblance to a joke, and insisted on as many of the strangers as could be got into his house drinking to their better acquaintance in home-made brandy. The same deadly beverage was liberally distributed to the men outside, and Groot Willem wound up his hospitalities by loading the party with vegetables, pomegranates, lemons, and other fruits from his garden as he sent them on their way rejoicing. Soon afterwards he followed them, to aid in forcing a passage up the valley.

In return, as a slight acknowledgment of gratitude, Hans supplied the giant with a little powder and lead, and Mr. Pringle gave his family a few Dutch tracts and hymn-books.

"Wonders'll niver cease in this land!" said Sandy Black to Jerry Goldboy as they left the farm.

"That's true, Sandy; it's a houtrageous country."

"To think," continued the Scot, "that we should forgather wi' Goliath amang the heeland hills o' Afriky; an' him fond o' his dram tae!—Hech, man! look there—at the puggies."

He pointed as he spoke to a part of the precipice where a group of baboons were collected, gazing indignantly and chattering furiously at the intruders on their domain.

The ursine baboon is not naturally pugnacious, but neither is he timid or destitute of the means of defence. On the contrary, he is armed with canine teeth nearly an inch long, and when driven to extremities will defend himself against the fiercest wolf-hound. He usually grapples his enemy by

K

the throat with his fore and hind paws, takes a
firm bite with his formidable tusks, and tears and
tugs till he sometimes pulls away the mouthful.
Many a stout baboon has in this manner killed
several dogs before being overpowered. It is said
that even the leopard is sometimes attacked and
worried by baboons, but it is only collectively and in
large bands that they can oppose this powerful enemy,
and baboons are never the aggressors. It is only in
defence of their young that they will assail him.

The strong attachment of these creatures to their
young is a fine trait in their character. This quality
has been shown on many occasions, especially when
the creatures have been engaged in orchard-robbing,
—for they are excessively fond of fruit and remarkably destitute of conscience. On such occasions,
when hunted back to the mountains with dogs,
the females, when separated accidentally from their
young, have been seen to return to search for them
through the very midst of their pursuers, being
utterly regardless of their own safety.

The group to which Black now directed attention
consisted of several females with a number of young
ones. They were all huddled in a cleft of the
precipice, looking down in apparent surprise at
the strangers. On a neighbouring height sat a big
old satyr-like male, who had been placed there as
a sentinel. Baboons are wise creatures, and invari-

ably place sentinels on points of vantage when the females and their young are feeding on the nutritious bulbs and roots that grow in the valleys. The old gentleman in question had done his duty on the first appearance of the human intruders. He had given a roar of warning; the forty or fifty baboons that were down near the river had scampered off precipitately, dashed through the stream, or leaped over it where narrow, hobbled awkwardly on all-fours over the little bit of level ground, and clambered with marvellous agility up the cliffs, till they had gained the ledge from which they now gazed and chattered, feeling confident in the safety of their position.

"Did iver 'ee see the like? They're almost human!" said Sandy.

"Just look at that big grandmother with the blue face and the little baby on 'er back!" exclaimed Jerry.

"How d' you know she's a grandmother?" asked Considine.

"W'y, because she's much fonder of the baby than its own mother could be."

As he spoke, one of the party below them fired, and the echoes sprang in conflict from the surrounding heights, as a bullet whizzed over their heads and hit the rocks, sending a shower of harmless chips and dust among the baboons.

With a shriek of consternation they scattered and
fled up the heights at racing speed.

A burst of laughter from the settlers,—all the more
hearty that no damage had been done,—increased
the terror inspired by the shot, and seemed to
invest the animals with invisible wings.

"Tally-ho!" shouted Considine in excitement.

"The black ane for ever!" cried Sandy.

"I'll back the grey one with the short tail," said
Kenneth M'Tavish, coming up at the moment,
"although she *has* two little ones clinging to her."

"Ten to one," cried Jerry, bending eagerly forward,
"on the blue-nosed grandmother wi' the baby on
her back!"

It did indeed seem as if Jerry's favourite was
going to reach the top of the crags before any of
the other horrified creatures, for she was powerful
as well as large, and her burden was particularly
small. The infant required no assistance, but clung
to its dam with its two little hands like a limpet,
so that she could use her limbs freely. But an
unusually long and vigorous bound chanced to
loosen the little one's grasp. It fell off with a pitiful
shriek, and, with an imploring upward look on its
miserable countenance, clasped its little hands in
mute despair.

Granny or mamma,—we know not which,—
with the quick intuition of a great general, took in

the whole position like a flash of light. She turned on the ledge she had gained and dropped her tail. Baby seized it and clambered up. Then away she went like a rocket, and before the little one had well regained its former position she had topped the ridge full two yards ahead of the whole troop!

"Well done!" cried M'Tavish.

"Huzza!" shouted Jerry.

"Brute!" exclaimed Considine, striking up the muzzle of a gun which was pointed at the grandmother and child by a panting young idiot who rushed up at the moment, "would you commit murder?"

The gun exploded and sent its ball straight to the new moon, which, early though it was, had begun to display the washed-out horns of its first quarter in the sky.

"Confound you!" cried the so-called Brute, who was by no means a coward, throwing down his gun and hitting Considine a heavy blow on the chest.

Charlie "returned" on the forehead and sent the Brute head over heels on the turf, but he sprang up instantly, and there would certainly have been a battle-royal if Groot Willem, who opportunely appeared, had not seized Considine by the arm, while Hans Marais grasped the Brute by the neck and rendered further action impossible. A moment sufficed to cool the youths, for the "Brute" was young, and they both shook hands with a laugh and a mutual apology.

Soon after leaving the giant's farm the travellers reached a point where the main stream was joined by a subsidiary rivulet. Its corresponding valley branched off to the right, about eight miles in length, containing fine pasturage and rich alluvial soil. It extended eastward behind the back of the Kahaberg, where the settlers observed the skirts of the magnificent timber forests which cover the southern fronts of that range, stretching over the summits of the hills at the head of the glen. To this valley, and the wooded hills which bound it, was given the name of Ettrick Forest, while the main valley itself was named Glen Lynden.

Not far from this point the apology for a waggon track ended altogether, and thenceforth the settlers found the route difficult and dangerous to a degree far exceeding their previous experiences or their wildest conceptions. Jerry Goldboy had now "facts" enough to overturn all his unbelief. The axe, crowbar, pick, and sledge-hammer were incessantly at work. They had literally to *hew* their path through jungles and gullies, and beds of torrents and rocky acclivities, which formed a series of obstructions that tested the power of the whole party,—Groot Willem and the allies included,—to the uttermost.

Of course the difficulties varied with the scenery. Here the vale was narrow and gorge-like, with just sufficient room for the stream to pass, while precipices of naked rock rose abruptly like rampart walls to a height of many hundred feet. These in some places seemed actually to overhang the savage-looking pass, or " poort," through which the waggons had to struggle in the very bed of the stream. Elsewhere it widened out sufficiently to leave space along the river-bank for fertile meadows, which were picturesquely sprinkled with mimosa trees and evergreen shrubs, and clothed with luxuriant pasturage up to the girths of the horses. Everywhere the mountains rose around, steep and grand, the lower declivities covered with good pasturage, the cliffs above, of freestone and trap, frowning in wild forms like embattled ramparts whose picturesque sides were sprinkled with various species of succulent plants and flowering aloes.

For five days did they struggle up this short glen; two of these days being occupied in traversing only three miles of a rugged defile, to which they gave the name of Eildon Cleugh. But " nothing is denied to well-directed labour." They smashed two waggons, damaged all the others, half-killed their oxen, skinned all their knuckles, black-and-blued all their shins, and nearly broke all their hearts, till at length they passed through the last poort of the glen and gained the summit of an elevated ridge which commanded a magnificent view to the extremity of the vale.

"And now, mynheer," said the field-cornet in charge of their escort, "there lies your country."

"At last!—thank God," said the leader of the band, looking round on their beautiful though savage home with feelings of deep gratitude for the happy termination of their long and weary travels.

The toil of journeying was now succeeded by the bustle and excitement of settling down.

Their new home was a lovely vale of about six or seven miles in length, and varying from one to two in breadth, like a vast basin surrounded on all sides by steep and sterile mountains, which rose in sharp wedge-like ridges, with snow-clad summits that towered to an estimated height of five thousand feet above the level of the sea. The contrast between the warm peaceful valley and the rugged amphitheatre of mountains was very great. The latter, dark and forbidding—yet home-like and gladdening to the eyes of Scotsmen—suggested toil and trouble, while the former, with its meandering river, verdant meadows, groves of sweet-scented mimosa-trees, and herds of antelopes, quaggas, and other animals pasturing in undisturbed quietude, filled the mind with visions of peace and plenty. Perchance God spoke to them in suggestive prophecy, for the contrast was typical of their future chequered career in these almost unknown wilds of South Africa.

Left by their escort on the following day—as their English brethren had been left in the Zuurveld of Lower Albany—to take root and grow there or perish, the heads of families assembled, and their leader addressed them.

" Here, at last," said he, " our weary travels by sea and land have come to an end. Exactly six months ago, to a day, we left the shores of bonny Scotland. Since then we have been wanderers, without any other home than the crowded cabin at sea and the narrow tent on shore. Now we have, through God's great goodness and mercy, reached the 'Promised Land' which is to be our future home, our place of rest. We have pitched our tents among the mimosa-trees on the river's margin, and our kind Dutch friends with the armed escort have left us. We are finally left to our own resources; it behoves us therefore, kindred and comrades, to proceed systematically to examine our domain, and fix our several locations. For this purpose I propose that an armed party should sally forth to explore, while the rest shall remain to take care of the women and children, and guard the camp."

Acting on this advice, an exploration party was at once organised, and set forth on foot, as they had at that time no horses or live stock of any kind—

save one dog, which had been purchased by the
"Brute" (whose proper name, by the way, was
Andrew Rivers) from Groot Willem on the way up.

They found the region most desirable in all
respects. Open grassy pastures were interspersed
everywhere with clumps and groves of mimosa-trees,
while the river, a gurgling mountain-brook, mean-
dered musically through the meadows. From grove
and thicket sprang the hartebeest and duiker.
From their lairs among the reeds and sedges of the
river rushed the reitbok and wild hog; while troops
of quaggas appeared trotting on the lower declivities
of the hills.

"A magnificent region truly!" remarked Kenneth
M'Tavish as they returned home at night.

"'Eaven upon earth!" said Jerry Goldboy, with
quiet enthusiasm.

"What splendid scenery!" exclaimed Charlie Considine,—who was addicted to the pencil.

"What glorious sport!" cried his former antagon-
ist, Rivers,—who was fond of the rod and gun.

"And what aboot the Kawfirs and Bushmen?"
asked Sandy Black, who, to use his own language,
"could aye objec'."

"Time enough to think of them when they appear,"
said Rivers.

"I don't believe they're half so bad as people say,"
cried Goldboy stoutly.

"Maybe no," rejoined Black. "The place is paradise to-day, as you sagaciously remarked, Jerry, but if the Kawfirs come it'll be pandemonium to-morry. It's my opinion that we should get oursel's into a defensible camp as soon as we can, an' than gae aboot our wark wi' easy minds. Ye mind what Goliath and Hans Marais said before they left us, aboot keepin' a sharp look-oot."

As no one replied to this, the Scot changed the subject by asking Considine when he meant to leave.

"Not till Hans Marais comes over the hills to fetch me," was the reply. "He has taken upon himself to give me extended leave of absence. You know, Sandy, that I fill the office of Professor in his father's house, and of course the Marais sprouts are languishing for want of water while the schoolmaster is abroad, so I could not take it on myself to remain longer away, if Hans had not promised to take the blame on his own shoulders. Besides, rain in Africa is so infrequent, that the sprouts won't suffer much from a week, more or less, of drought. Your leader wishes me to stay for a few days, and I am anxious to see how you get on. I'll be able to help a bit, and take part in the night-watches, which I heard Mr. Pringle say he intends to institute immediately."

On the day following a site was fixed for the

commencement of the infant colony, and the tents,
etc., were removed to it. The day after being Sun-
day, it was unanimously agreed to "rest" from
labour, and to " keep it holy."

It was an interesting and noteworthy occasion, the
assembling of the Scotch emigrants on that Sabbath
day to worship God for the first time in Glen Lynden. Their church was under the shade of a vener-
able acacia-tree, close to the margin of the stream,
which murmured round the camp. On one side sat
the patriarch of the party with silvery locks, the
Bible on his knee, and his family seated round him,
—the type of a grave Scottish husbandman. Near
to him sat a widow, who had " seen better days," with
four stalwart sons to work for and guard her. Beside these were delicate females of gentle blood, near
to whom sat the younger brother of a Scotch laird,
who wisely preferred independence in the southern
wilds of Africa to dependence " at home." Besides
these there were youths and maidens, of rougher
though not less honest mould—some grave, others gay,
but all at that time orderly and attentive, while their
leader gave forth the beautiful hymn which begins,

> " O God of Bethel! by whose hand
> Thy people still are fed,"

and followed it with a selection of prayers from the
English Liturgy, and a discourse from a volume of
sermons.

While they were singing the last Psalm a beautiful antelope, which had wandered down the valley,—all ignorant of the mighty change that had taken place in the prospects of its mountain home,—came suddenly in sight of the party, and stood on the opposite side of the river gazing at them in blank amazement.

Andrew Rivers, who sat meekly singing a fine bass, chanced to raise his head at the time. Immediately his eyes opened to their full extent, and the fine bass stopped short, though the mouth did not close. With the irresistible impulse of a true sportsman he half rose, but Sandy Black, who sat near, caught him by the coat-tails and forced him firmly though softly down.

"Whist, man; keep a calm sough!"

The young man, becoming instantly aware of the impropriety of his action, resigned himself to fate and Sandy, and recovered self-possession in time to close the interrupted line with two or three of the deepest notes in the bass clef.

The innocent antelope continued to listen and gaze its fill, and was finally permitted to retire unmolested into its native jungle.

CHAPTER XI.

EXPLORATIONS AND HUNTING EXPERIENCES.

Oh they were happy times, these first days of the infant colony, when every man felt himself to be a real Robinson Crusoe,—with the trifling difference of being cast on heights of the mainland, instead of an islet of the sea, and with the pleasant addition of kindred company!

So rich and lovely was their domain that some of the facetious spirits, in looking about for sites for future dwellings, affected a rollicking indifference to situations that would have been prized by any nobleman in making choice of a spot for a shooting-box.

"Come now, M'Tavish," said Considine, on one of their exploring expeditions, "you are too particular. Yonder is a spot that's seems to have been made on purpose for you—a green meadow for the cattle and sheep, when you get 'em; stones scattered here and there, of a shape that will suit admirably for building purposes without quarrying or dressing; a clump of mimosa-trees to shelter your cottage from winds that may blow down the valley, and a gentle green slope to break those that blow up; a superb acacia standing by itself on a ready-made lawn where your front door will be, under which you may have a rustic seat and table to retire to at eventide with Mrs. M' Tavish and lovely young Jessie, to smoke your pipe and sip your tea."

"Or toddy," suggested Sandy Black.

"Or toddy," assented Considine.

"Besides all this, you have the river making a graceful bend in front of your future drawing-room windows, and a vista of the valley away to the left, with a rocky eminence on the right, whence baboons can descend to rob your future orchard at night, and sit chuckling at you in safety during the day, with a grand background of wooded gorges,—or corries, as you Scotch have it, or kloofs, according to the boers —and a noble range of snow-clad mountains to complete the picture !"

"Not a bad description for so young a man," said M'Tavish, surveying the spot with a critical eye; "quite in our poetical leader's style. You should go over it again in his hearing, and ask him to throw it into verse."

"No ; I cannot afford to give away the valuable produce of my brain. I will keep and sell it some day in England. But our leader has already fore-

stalled me, I fear.   He read to me something last
night which he has just composed, and which bears
some resemblance to it.   Listen :—

    " ' Now we raise the eye to range
       O' er prospect wild, grotesque, and strange ;
       Sterile mountains, rough and steep,
       That bound abrupt the valley deep,
       Heaving to the clear blue sky
       Their ribs of granite bare and dry,
       And ridges, by the torrents worn,
       Thinly streaked with scraggy thorn,
       Which fringes Nature's savage dress,
       Yet scarce relieves her nakedness.
        But where the Vale winds deep below,
       The landscape hath a warmer glow :
       There the spekboom spreads its bowers
       Of light green leaves and lilac flowers ;
       And the aloe rears her crimson crest,
       Like stately queen for gala drest ;
       And the bright-blossomed bean-tree shakes
       Its coral tufts above the brakes,
       Brilliant as the glancing plumes
       Of sugar-birds among its blooms,
       With the deep-green verdure blending
       In the stream of light descending.'

  " Something or other follows, I forget what, and
then :—

    " ' With shattered rocks besprinkled o'er,
       Behind ascends the mountain hoar,
       Where the grim satyr-faced baboon
       Sits gibbering to the rising moon,
       Or chides with hoarse or angry cry
       Th' intruder as he wanders by.'

"There—I can't remember the rest of it," said Considine, "and I'm not even sure that what I've quoted is correct, but you see Mr. Pringle's mind has jumped before mine,—and higher."

"Man, it's no' that bad," observed Black, with emphasis. "Depend on't—though I mak' nae pretence to the gift o' prophecy—he'll come oot as a bard yet--the bard o' Glen Lynden maybe, or Sooth Afriky.—Hech, sirs!" added Sandy, pointing with a look of surprise to a tree, many of the pendent branches of which had peculiar round-shaped birds'-nests attached to them, "what's goin' on there, think 'ee?"

The tree to which the Scot directed attention overhung the stream, and down one of its branches a snake was seen twining itself with caution. It evidently meant to rob one of the nests, for the little owner, with some of its companions, was shrieking and fluttering round the would-be robber. This kind of bird has been gifted with special wisdom to guard its home from snakes. It forms the entrance to its pendent nest at the bottom instead of the top, and hangs the nest itself at the extreme point of the finest twigs, so that the snake is compelled to wriggle downwards perpendicularly, and at last has to extend part of its body past the nest, in order to be able to turn its head upwards into the hole. Great, unquestionably, is a snake's capacity to hold

L

on by its tail, but this holding on as it were to
next-to-nothing is usually too much for it. While
the explorers were watching, the snake turned its
head upwards for the final dive into the nest, but its
coils slipped, and it fell into the water amid trium-
phant shrieks from the little birds. Nothing
daunted, however, the snake swam ashore and made
another attempt—with the same result. Again it
made the trial; a third time it failed, and then, in
evident disgust, went off to attack some easier prey.

While Considine and his companions were thus
out in search of good localities on which to plant
future homesteads, the greater part of the settlers
were engaged, at a spot which they had named
Clifton, in erecting temporary huts of the wattle-and-
dab order. Mr. Pringle himself, with a bold fellow
named Rennie, remained to guard the camp, as they
had reason to fear a surprise from Bushmen
marauders, known at that time to be roaming the
neighbourhood. More than once the sentinels were
tempted to fire into a band of baboons, whom they
not unnaturally mistook for Bushmen!

Other parties were sent out to cut wood and reeds,
which they had to carry into camp, sometimes two
or three miles, on their shoulders, while some were
despatched into the kloofs to hunt, provisions having
by that time grown scarce. Not being a sportsman
himself, and not feeling sure of the power of his

men, who were at that time unaccustomed to the gun, Mr. Pringle wisely sent two of the party to the nearest station—about forty miles distant—to inquire about a supply of provisions and a few horses, which were expected from the Government-farm of Somerset.

The first hunting party sent out was not a select one, the people generally being too eager about examining and determining their immediate locations to care about sport. It consisted of young Rivers and Jerry Goldboy. The former was appointed, or rather allowed, to go, more because of his sporting enthusiasm than because of any evidence he had yet given of his powers, and the latter merely because he desired to go. For the same reason he was permitted to arm himself with his blunderbuss. Rivers carried a heavy double-barrelled fowling-piece. He was a stout active impulsive young fellow, with the look of a capable Nimrod.

" You 'd have been better with a fowling-piece, or even a Dutch roer," said Rivers, casting a doubtful look at the blunderbuss as they entered the jungle and began to ascend one of the nearest subsidiary glens or kloofs.

" Well now, sir," said Jerry respectfully, " I don't agree with you. A man who goes a-shootin' with a fowlin'-piece or a Dutch gun must 'ave some sort o' capacity for shootin'—mustn't 'e, sir ?"

" Well, I suppose he must."

" W'ereas," continued Jerry, " a man who goes a-shootin' with a blunderbuss don't require no such qualification—*that's* w'ere it is, sir."

" D' you mean to say that you can't shoot ?" asked Rivers, with a look of surprise.

" No more, sir," replied Jerry with emphasis, "than the weathercock of a Dutch Reformed Church. Of course I know 'ow to load—powder first, ball or shot arterwards ; it's usually gravel with me, that bein', so to speak, 'andy and cheap. An' I knows w'ich end o' the piece to putt to my shoulder, like-wise 'ow to pull the trigger, but of more than that I'm hinnocent as the babe unborn. Ah ! you may laugh, sir, but after all I'm a pretty sure shot. Indeed I seldom miss, because I putt in such a 'eavy charge, and the 'buss scatters so fearfully that it's all but impossible to miss—unless you fairly turn your back on the game and fires in the opposite direction."

" You're a pleasant hunting companion !" said Rivers. " Do you know the importance of always keeping the muzzle of your gun *away* from the unfortunate fellow you chance to be shooting with ?"

" Ho, yes, sir. The dangerous natur' of my weapon is so great that I've adopted the plan of always walking, as you see, with what the milingtary call ' shouldered arms,' which endangers nothin' but the sky—includin' the planetory system—except w'en I 'appens to fall, w'en, of course, it's every man look-out for hisself. But there's one consolation for you, sir,—my blunderbuss don't go off easy. It takes two pulls of the trigger, mostly, to bring fire out o' the flint, and as I often forget to prime—there's a third safeguard in that, so to speak."

Further converse was interrupted by the sudden bursting of a duiker, or large antelope, from a thicket close beside them. Both sportsmen levelled their pieces, but, the jungle there being dense, the animal vanished before either could fire. With the eager haste of tyros, however, they ran stumbling after it until they came to an open stretch of ground which led them to the edge of a small plain. Here they simultaneously discovered that no duiker was to be seen, though they observed a troop of quaggas far out of range, and a hartebeest in the distance. The former, observing them, kicked up their heels, and dashed away into the mountains. The latter, a handsome creature, the size of an average pony and fleet as a stag, bounded into the jungle.

"No use going after these," said Rivers, with a wistful gaze.

"No, sir,—none w'atever."

"Better keep to the jungle and be ready next time," said the young sportsman. "We mustn't talk, Jerry."

"No, sir; mum's the word. But 'ow if we should meet witl a lion?"

"Shoot it of course. But there is no such luck in store for us."

After this the hunters proceeded with greater caution. As they kept in the thick bush, they frequently startled animals, which they heard leaping up and bursting through the underwood, but seldom got a glimpse, and never a shot.

"Tantalising, ain't it, sir?"

"Hush!"

They issued on another open space at this point, and, seeing a thick bed of sedges near the margin of a stream, proceeded towards it, separating from each other a few yards in order to cover the ground.

There was a sudden and violent shaking in the sedges on their approach, as if some large animal had been aroused from sleep, but the tall reeds prevented its being seen.

"Look out, Jerry, and keep more on the other side —there—Hallo!

As he spoke, a creature called by the Dutch colonists a reit-vark, or reed-swine, whose quick starts and sharp stoppages betrayed its indecision, at length made up its mind and rushed out of the reeds in wild alarm close to Rivers, who, although ready, was incapable of restraining himself, and fired in haste. The ball nevertheless slightly grazed the animal's side.

With a shriek of intense agony, such as only a brute of the porcine tribe can utter, the reit-vark swerved aside and ran straight, though unintentionally, at Jerry Goldboy.

Self-control not being Jerry's forte, he uttered a great cry, presented the blunderbuss with both hands, shut his eyes, and fired. The butt of his piece came back on his chest and floored him, and the half-pound of gravel charge went into the forehead of the reit-vark, which dropped with a final groan, whose clear import was—"no earthly use in struggling after *that!*" Recovering himself, Jerry was jubilant over his success. Rivers was almost envious.

They proceeded, but killed nothing more afterwards, though they saw much. Among other things, they saw a footprint in the sand which filled them with interest and awe.

It was that of a lion! During the journey up from the coast they had seen much game, large and small, of every kind, except the Cape "tiger" and the lion. They had indeed, once or twice, *heard* the peculiar growl or *gurr* of the former, but until this day none of the party had seen even the footprint of the king of beasts. Of course the interest and excitement was proportional. Of course, also, when the subject was discussed round the camp-fires that night, there was a good deal of "chaffing" among the younger men about the probability of a mistake as to the nature of the footprints by such unaccustomed sportsmen; but Rivers was so confident in his statements, and Jerry was so contemptuous in his manner of demanding whether there was any difference between the paw of a cat and a lion, except in size, and whether he was not perfectly familiar with a cat's paw, that no room for scepticism remained.

It had been a threatening day. Muttered thunder had been heard at intervals, and occasional showers, —the first that had assailed them since their arrival in the glen. The night became tempestuous, cold, and very dark, so that soon all were glad to seek the shelter of the tents or of the half-finished wattle-and-dab huts, except the sentinels. Of these, two were appointed for every watch. Masters and servants shared this disagreeable duty equally. Particularly disagreeable it was that night, for the rain came down in such torrents that it was difficult to keep the fires alight, despite a good supply of firewood.

About midnight the sleeping camp was aroused by the roar of a lion close to the tents. It was so loud and so tremendous that some of the sleepy-heads thought for a moment a thunderstorm had burst upon them. Every one was up in a second—the men with guns, pistols, swords, and knives. There was no mistaking the *expression* of the roar—the voice of fury as well as of power.

"Whereaboots *is* the brute?" cried Sandy Black,

who, roused to unwonted excitement by the royal voice, issued from his tent in a red nightcap and drawers, with a gun in one hand and a carving-knife in the other.

"Here!" "There!" "In this direction!" "No, it isn't!" "I say it is!" and similar exclamations, burst from every one. The uncertainty was probably occasioned partly by the mode the animal has of sometimes putting his mouth close to the ground when he roars, so that the voice rolls along like a billow; partly also by the echo from a mountain-rock which rose abruptly on the opposite bank of the river. Finding it impossible to decide the question of direction, the party fired volleys and threw firebrands in all directions, and this they did with such vigour that his kingship retired without uttering another sound.

It was a grand, a royal, almost a humorous mode of breaking a spell—the spell of unbelief in lions,—which some of the party had been under up to that moment. They remained under it no longer!

As if to confirm and fix the impression thus made, this lion,—or another,—gave some of the party a daylight interview. George Rennie, M'Tavish, Considine, Black, and others, had gone up the river to cut reeds in the bed of the stream. While they were busily engaged with their sickles, up rose a majestic lion in their very midst!

"Preserve us a'!" exclaimed Black, who was nearest to him.

Jerry Goldboy turned to seize his blunderbuss. The lion leaped upon the bank of the river, turned round and gazed upon the men.

"Let go!" exclaimed Jerry in a hoarse whisper, endeavouring to shake off the vice-like grip that Black had laid on his arm.

"Keep quiet, man," growled Black sternly.

The rest of the party were wise enough not to interfere with the lion. They were at that time inexperienced. To have wounded him would have brought disaster, perhaps death, on some of them. George Rennie (who afterwards became a celebrated lion-hunter) was emphatic in advising caution. After gazing in quiet surprise on the intruders for a minute or so, he turned and retired; first slowly, and then, after getting some distance off, at a good round trot.

This was the first sight they had of the royal beast. Afterwards, during the winter and spring, they had frequent visits from lions, but did not suffer actual damage from them. They also, in course of time, dared to "beard the lion in his den," —but of that more anon.

The labour of the settlers at this time—before oxen and horses were procured—was very severe. Of course this had the effect of weeding the little company of some of its chaff in the shape of lazy and dis-contented men. One said that he "had not been engaged to work by day, and watch by night, as well as living in constant fear of being scalped by savages or devoured by wild beasts." The observation being true and unanswerable, he was "graciously permitted to retire from the service," and returned to Algoa Bay. But on the whole there was little murmuring, and no rebellion. By degrees difficulties were smoothed down. A squatter on one of the forfeited farms, about eight miles off, who with his family lived solely on flesh and milk, was engaged to lend a hand with his waggon and oxen to "flit" the families to their various locations. He also sold the settlers a few sheep In time, more sheep and oxen were pur-chased from the Dutch farmers on the Tarka, a river on the other side of the mountains. Hottentots came from Somerset with flour. Thatched huts replaced the tents. A few horses were obtained. Gardens were cleared and enclosed. Trenches for irrigation were cut. Trees were rooted out, and ploughs were set to work. Ten armed Hottentots were sent by the magistrates of the district to which they belonged, to guard and relieve them of night-watches, and with these came the news that ten of their friend Opperman's cattle, and seven belonging to their neighbour the squatter, had been carried off by Bushmen.

At this point Sandy Black aroused the admiration
of the ten Hottentots by setting to work one morning in September—the beginning of spring in South
Africa—with a Scotch plough, which was guided
entirely by himself, and drawn by only two oxen.
His dark-skinned admirers had never seen any
other plough than the enormous unwieldy imple-
ment then in use among the Dutch, which had only
one handle, no coulter, was usually drawn by ten or
twelve oxen, and managed by three or four men and
boys.

By degrees those of the party who were good
linguists began to pick up Dutch. Mr. Pringle,
especially, soon became familiar enough with it to
be able to hold a Dutch service on Sundays, in addition to the English, for the benefit of the Hottentot
guards. He also added a slight knowledge of
medicine to his other qualifications, and was thus
enabled to minister to the wants of body and soul,
at a time when the people had no regular physician
or professional minister of the Gospel.

The arrival of horses gave the settlers opportunities
of making more extended and more thorough explorations of their own domain, and the daily routine of
life was varied and enlivened by an occasional visit
from the Tarka boers, whom they found good-natured
and hospitable—also very shrewd at a bargain!

Thus they took root and began to grow.

But before many of these things occurred Hans Marais came over the mountains, according to promise, and "Professor" Considine was fain to bid the Scotch settlers farewell, promising, however, to return and visit them on some future day.

CHAPTER XII.

GIVES SOME ACCOUNT OF A GREAT LION-HUNT.

ALTHOUGH the lion's roar had been frequently heard by the settlers of Glen Lynden, some months elapsed before they came into actual conflict with his majesty. By that time the little colony had taken firm root. It had also been strengthened by a few families of half-castes or mulattos.

One morning it was discovered that a horse had been carried off by a lion, and as his track was clearly traceable into a neighbouring kloof, the boldest men of the settlement, as well as some Dutchmen who chanced to be there at the time, were speedily assembled for a regular hunt after the audacious thief.

It was a great occasion, and some of the men who became noted for prowess in after years began their career on that day. George Rennie, who ultimately acquired the title of the Lion-hunter, came to the rendezvous with a large elephant-gun on his shoulder; also his brother John, fearless and daring as himself. Then followed the brothers Diederik and Christian Muller,—frank, free, generous-hearted Dutchmen, who were already known as among the most intrepid lion-hunters of South Africa; and Arend Coetzer of Eland's-drift; and Lucas Van Dyk, a tall dark muscular man of about six feet two, with a bushy black beard, and an eye like an eagle's, carrying a gun almost as long and unwieldy as himself; and Slinger, Allie, and Dikkop, their sturdy Hottentot servants, with Dugal, a half-tamed Bushman, the special charge of Mr. Pringle. These and several others were all armed with gun and spear and knife.

Soon our friend Sandy Black, who had been summoned from work in his garden, joined them with a rusty old flint-lock gun. He was followed by young Rivers, with a double-barrelled percussion of large calibre, and by Kenneth M'Tavish, accompanied by his wife and Jessie, both imploring him earnestly "not to be rash, and to keep well out of danger!"

"Oh! Kenneth," entreated Mrs. M., "*do* be careful. A lion is *such* a fearful thing!"

"My dear, it's *not* a 'thing,' it's an *animal*," growled Kenneth, trying to induce his wife to go home.

"Yes, but it *is* so dangerous, and only think, if it should get hold of you—and I *know* your headstrong courage will make you do something foolhardy— what is to become of me and Jessie?"

It was evident from the tone of M'Tavish's reply

that he did not care much what should become of
either wife or daughter just then, for he saw that
his male friends were laughing at him, but he was
fortunately relieved by Jerry Goldboy coming up at
the moment—with the blunderbuss on his shoulder
—and informing Mrs. M'Tavish that her "pet," a
lamb which had been recently purchased from one
of the Tarka boers, was at large, with two or three
hungry dogs looking earnestly at it!

The good lady at once forsook the old goat, and
ran back with Jessie to the rescue of the pet lamb.

"What have 'ee putt i' the 'buss?" asked Sandy
Black of Jerry, with a sly look, as the latter joined
the group of hunters.

"Well, d' you know, I ain't quite sure," replied
Jerry in some confusion; "I—I was called out so
suddenly that I 'ad scarce time to think."

".Think!" repeated Black; "it doesna tak' muckle
time to think hoo to load a gun, but to be sure
your gun is a pecooliar ane."

"Well, you see," returned Jerry, with the troubled
look still on his countenance, "it *does* require a little
consideration, because it would be useless to load
with my ordinary charge of gravel for a lion. Then
I feared to put in large stones, lest they should jam
in the barrel an' bu'st the *h*old thing. So I collected
a lot of *h*old buttons and a few nails, besides two or
three thimbles, but—"

"Weel," said Black, as his friend paused, "thae sort o' slugs wull at least gie the lion a peppery sort o' feeling, if naethin' waur."

"Yes, but, d'you see," continued Jerry, "there was a silver tea-spoon on the table when I made the collection of things, and after I had loaded I—I couldn't find the tea-spoon, and I fear—"

Just at that moment Groot Willem galloped upon the scene and was received with a hearty cheer.

The Hottentots were now sent on in advance to trace out the "spoor"—in other words, the track of the lion.

On the way one of the Dutchmen entertained those of the settlers who were inexperienced with an account of the mode in which lion-hunts should be conducted. The right way to go to work, he said, was to set the dogs into the cover and drive the lion into the open, when the whole band of hunters should march forward together and fire either singly or in volleys. If he did not fall, but should grow furious and advance upon his assailants, then they should stand close in a circle and turn their horses with their heads from the foe, horses being usually much frightened at the sight of a lion. Some should hold the bridles, while others should kneel and take careful aim at the approaching enemy, which would crouch now and then as if to measure his distance and calculate the power of his

spring. When he crouched, *that* was the time to
shoot him fair in the head. If they should miss,
which was not unlikely, or only wound the lion,
and the horses should get frantic with terror at his
roars, and break loose, there was reason to fear that
serious mischief might follow.

No Red Indian of the backwoods ever followed
the "trail" of beast or foe more unerringly than
these Hottentots and mulattos tracked that lion
through brushwood and brake, over grass and gravel,
where in many places, to an unskilled eye, there
was no visible mark at all. Their perseverance was
rewarded: they came upon the enemy sooner than
had been expected. At the distance of about a mile
from the spot where he had killed the horse they
found him in a straggling thicket.

From this point of vantage he would by no means
come out. The dogs were sent in, and they barked
furiously enough, but the lion would not condescend
to show fight. After some hours spent in thus
vainly beating about the bush, George Rennie became
impatient and resolved to "storm" the stronghold!
In company with his brother John and another man
named Ekron he prepared to enter the thicket
where the lion was concealed, and persuaded three
of the mulattos to follow in rear and be ready to
fire if their assault should prove abortive.

It was of no use that Lucas, Van Dyk, and the

Mullers, and other experienced Dutchmen, tried to dissuade them from their enterprise by assuring them that it was a ridiculous as well as reckless mode of attack, and would be almost certainly attended with fatal consequences. The brothers Rennie, as yet inexperienced, were obstinate. They were bent on attacking the lion in his den.

While this arrangement was being made the soul of Jerry Goldboy became unfortunately inflated with a desire to distinguish himself. Spiritually brave, though physically nervous, he made a sudden resolve to shoot that lion or die in the attempt! Without uttering a word he cocked his blunderbuss, and, before any one could prevent him, made a bold dash into the jungle at a point where the hounds were clamouring loudest.

"Save us a', the body's gane gyte!" exclaimed Sandy Black, promptly following. "Come on, freen's, or he's a deed man."

Sandy's impulse was suddenly arrested by a roar from the lion so tremendous that it appeared to shake the solid earth. Next moment Jerry beheld a large animal bound with a crash through the brake straight at him. His heart leaped into his mouth, but he retained sufficient vitality to present and fire. A wild yell followed, as the animal fell dead at his feet, and Jerry found that he had lodged the whole collection of buttons, nails, and miscellaneous articles, along with the tea-spoon, in the head of the best hound, which had been scared by the monarch's appalling roar!

It is difficult to say whether laughter or indignant growls were loudest on the occurrence of this, but it is certain that the brothers Rennie entered the thicket immediately after, despite the almost angry remonstrances of the more knowing men, advanced to within about fifteen paces of the spot where the lion lay crouched among the gnarled roots of an evergreen bush with a small space of open ground on one side of it.

"Now then, boys," said George Rennie, casting a hasty glance over his shoulder at the mulatto supports, "steady, and take good aim after we fire."

He put the elephant-gun to his shoulder as he spoke, his brother and comrade did the same; a triple report followed, and the three heavy balls, aimed with deadly precision, struck a great block of red stone behind which the lion was lying.

With a furious growl he shot from his lair like the bolt from a cross-bow. The mulattos instinctively turned and fled without firing a shot. The three champions, with empty guns, tumbled over each other in eager haste to escape the dreaded claws— but in vain, for with one stroke he dashed John Rennie to the ground, put his paw on him, and looked round with that dignified air of grandeur which has doubtless earned for his race the royal title. The scene was at once magnificent, thrilling, and ludicrous. It was impossible for the other hunters to fire, because while one man was under the lion's paw the others were scrambling towards them in such a way as to render an aim impossible.

After gazing at them steadily for a few seconds the lion turned as if in sovereign contempt, scattered the hounds like a pack of rats, and, with a majestic bound over bushes upwards of twelve feet high, re-entered the jungle. With a feeling of indignation at such contemptuous treatment, George Rennie re-charged his gun in haste, vowing vengeance against the whole feline race—a vow which he fully redeemed in after years. His brother John, who was injured to the extent of a scratch on the back and a severe bruise on the ribs by the rough treatment he had received, arose and slowly followed his example, and Groot Willem, growling in a tone that would have done credit to the lion himself, and losing for the moment the usual wisdom of his countrymen in such encounters, strode savagely into the jungle, followed by Sandy Black and Jerry, the latter of whom appeared to labour under a sort of frenzied courage which urged him on to deeds of desperate valour. At all events he had recharged his piece of ordnance to the very muzzle with a miscellaneous compound of sand, stones, and sticks—

anything, in short, that would go down its capacious
throat,—and, pushing wildly past Groot Willem,
took the lead.

It was perhaps well for these strangely-assorted
hunters that the lion had made up his mind to quit
the jungle. A few minutes later he was seen retreat-
ing towards the mountains, and the chase was renewed, with hounds and Hottentots in full cry.
They came up with him in a short time at bay
under a mimosa-tree by the side of a streamlet.
He lashed his tail and growled fiercely as he glared
at the dogs, which barked and yelped round him,
though they took good care to keep out of reach of
his claws. While they stirred up his wrath to the
boiling point, they at the same time distracted his
attention, so that a party of Hottentots, getting
between him and the mountain side, took up a
position on a precipice which overlooked the spot
where he stood at bay. Suddenly the lion appeared
to change his mind. Turning as before, and clearing
all obstacles at a bound, he took refuge in a dense
thicket, into which a heavy fire was poured without
any effect. Again George Rennie lost patience.
He descended from the height, accompanied by a
favourite little dog, and threw two large stones into
the thicket. His challenge was accepted on the
spot. The lion leaped out with a roar, and was
on the point of making another bound, which would

certainly have been fatal to the hunter, but the little dog ran boldly up and barked in his face. The momentary interruption saved Rennie, who leaped backward, but the dog was instantly killed witn a flashing pat from the royal paw. At the same moment a volley was fired by the Hottentots from the heights. Unfortunately the position of Rennie rendered it impossible for the Mullers or any of the other expert shots to fire.

Whether the volley had taken effect was uncertain, but it at all events turned the lion from his purpose. He wheeled round, and, abandoning the bush, took to a piece of open ground, across which the hunters and dogs followed him up hotly.

The lion now took refuge in a small copse on a slight eminence. Diederik and Christian Muller were in advance, Groot Willem on his mighty charger came next. Van Dyk was running neck and neck with Jerry Goldboy, who flourished the blunderbuss over his head and yelled like a very demon. It was obvious that he was mad for the time being. The rest came up in a confused body, many of the men on foot having kept up with the horsemen.

The Rennies, having by that time become wiser, gave up their reckless proceedings, and allowed Christian Muller, who was tacitly acknowledged the leader of the party, to direct. He gave the signal to dismount when within a short distance of the copse, and ordered the horses to be tied together as the different riders came up. This was quickly done, and of course all possibility of retreat was thus cut off. The plan was to advance in a body up the slope, leaving the horses in charge of the Hottentots.

The preparations did not take long, but before they were completed a growl was heard, then a terrific roar, and the lion, who had made up his mind to act on the offensive, burst from the thicket and bore down on the party, his eyeballs glaring with rage. Being thus taken by surprise they were unprepared. His motion was so rapid that no one could take aim—except, indeed, Jerry, who discharged his piece at the sky, and, losing his balance, fell back with a wild halloo. Selecting one of the horses, the lion darted furiously at it. The affrighted animal sprang forward, and, in so doing, wheeled all the other horses violently round. The lion missed his aim, but faced about and crouched at a distance of only ten yards for another spring. It was a terrible moment! While the monster was meditating on which victim he should leap, Christian Muller was taking quick but deadly aim. If he should merely wound the brute, certain death to some one of the party would have been the instantaneous result. Most of them knew this well.

Knowing also that Muller was cool and sure, they breathlessly awaited the result. Only three or four seconds were spent in aiming, but instants become minutes in such a case. Some of the men almost gasped with anxiety. Another moment, and Christian fired. The under jaw of the lion dropped, and blood gushed from his mouth. He turned round with a view to escape, but George Rennie shot him through the spine. Turning again with a look of vengeance, he attempted to spring, but the once powerful hind-legs were now paralysed. At the same moment, Groot Willem, Van Dyk, Sandy Black, and M'Tavish put balls into different parts of his body, and a man named Stephanus put an end to his existence by shooting him through the brain.

It was a furious combat while it lasted, and a noble enemy had been subdued, for this lion, besides being magnificent of aspect even in death, measured full twelve feet from the point of his nose to the tip of his tail.

CHAPTER XIII.

ADVENTURE WITH AN OSTRICH.

TIME passed rapidly, and the settlers, both highland and lowland, struck their roots deeper and
deeper into the soil of their adoption—watched and
criticised more or less amiably by their predecessors,
the few Dutch-African farmers who up to that time
had struggled on the frontier all alone.

One day Hans Marais was riding with Charlie
Considine on the karroo, not far from the farm-house.
They had been conversing on the condition and
prospects of the land, and the trials and difficulties
of the British settlers. Suddenly they came on an
ostrich sitting on its eggs under a bush. The bird
rose and ran on seeing the horsemen.

" I daresay the cock-bird is not far off," observed
Hans, riding up to the nest, which was merely a
slight hollow scraped in the sandy soil, and contained a dozen eggs. " He is a gallant bird; guards
his wife most faithfully, and shares her duties."

" I 've sometimes thought," said Considine musingly, "that the ostrich might be tamed and bred on your farms. With such valuable feathers it would be worth while to try."

"You are not the first who has suggested that, Charlie. My own mother has more than once spoken of it."

"Stay a minute," said Considine; "I shall take one of the eggs home to her."

"Not fit to eat. Probably half hatched," said Hans.

"No matter," returned the other, dismounting.

"Well, I'll ride to the ridge and see if the papa is within hail."

Hans did but bare justice to the cock ostrich when he said he was a gallant bird. It is within the mark to say that he is not only a pattern husband, but a most exemplary father, for, besides guarding his wife and her nest most jealously by day, he relieves her at night, and sits himself on the nest, while his better-half takes food and relaxation.

While Hans rode forward a few hundred yards, the cock, which chanced to be out feeding on the plain, observed his wife running excitedly among the bushes, and at the same moment caught a glimpse of the Dutchman.

Seven-league boots could not have aided that ostrich! With mighty strides and outstretched wings the giant bird rushed in furious rage to defend

its nest. Hans saw it, and, instantly putting spurs
to his horse, also made for the nest, but the ostrich
beat him.

" Look out, Charlie!" shouted Hans.

Charlie did look out, somewhat anxiously too,
turning his head nervously from side to side, for
while the thunder of hoofs and the warning cry of
Hans assailed him on one side, a rushing and hissing
sound was heard on the other. The suspense did
not last long. A few seconds later, and the ostrich
appeared, bearing down on him with railway speed.
He raised his gun and fired, but in the haste of the
moment missed. The cap of the second barrel
snapped. He clubbed his gun, but before he could
raise it the ferocious bird was on him. Towering
high over his head, it must have been between eight
and nine feet in height. One kick of its great two-
toed foot sufficed. The ostrich kicks forward, as a
man might when he wishes to burst in a door with
his foot, and no prize-fighter can hit out with greater
celerity, no horse can kick with greater force. If
the blow had taken full effect it would probably
have been fatal, but Considine leaped back. It
reached him, however—on the chest,—and knocked
him flat on the nest, where he lay stunned amid a
wreck of eggs.

The vicious bird was about to follow up its victory
by dancing on its prostrate foe, when Hans galloped

up. The bird turned on him at once, with a hiss and a furious rush. The terrified horse reared and wheeled round with such force as almost to throw Hans, who dropped his gun in trying to keep his seat. Jumping into the air, and bringing its foot down with a resounding smack, the bird sent its two formidable nails deep into the steed's flank, from which blood flowed copiously. The horse took the bit in its teeth, and ran.

Hans Marais was very strong, but fear was stronger. The horse fairly ran off, and the ostrich pursued. Being fleeter than the horse, it not only kept up with ease, but managed ever and anon to give it another kick on flank, sides, or limbs. Hans vainly tried to grasp his assailant by the neck. If he succeeded in this he knew that he could easily have choked it, for the ostrich's weak point is its long slender neck—its strong point being its tremendous leg, the thigh of which, blue-black, and destitute of feathers, resembles a leg of mutton in shape and size.

At last Hans bethought him of his stirrup. Unbuckling it, he swung it by the leather round his head, and succeeded, after one or two attempts, in hitting his enemy on the head with the iron. The ostrich dropped at once and never rose again.

Returning to the nest with his vanquished foe strapped to his saddle, he found Considine sitting somewhat confused among the egg-débris, much of which consisted of flattened young ones, for the eggs were in an advanced state of incubation.

"Why, Charlie, are you going to try your hand at hatching?" cried Hans, laughing in spite of himself.

Considine smiled rather ruefully. "I believe my breast-bone is knocked in. Just help me ` to examine; but first catch my horse, like a good fellow."

It was found on examination that no bones were broken, and that, beyond a bruise, Considine was none the worse of his adventure.

One egg was found to have survived the general destruction. This was taken to the farm and handed to Mrs. Marais, and that amiable lady adopted and hatched it! We do not mean to assert that she sat upon it, but having discovered, from mysterious sounds inside, that the young ostrich contained in it was still alive, and, being a woman of an experimental tendency, she resolved to become a mother to it. She prepared a box, by lining it with a warm feather pillow, above which she spread several skin karosses or blankets, and into this she put the egg. Every morning and every evening she visited the nest, felt the egg to ascertain its temperature, and added or removed a blanket according to circumstances. How the good woman knew the proper temperature is a mystery which no one could explain, but certain it is that she succeeded, for in a few days the little one became so lively in its prison as to suggest the idea that it wanted out. Mrs. Marais then listened attentively to the sounds, and, having come to a decision as to which end of the egg contained the head of the bird, she cracked the shell at that point and returned it to the nest.

Thus aided, the infant ostrich, whose head and eet lay in juxtaposition, began life most appropriately with its strongest point—put its best foot foremost; drove out the end of its prison with a kick, and looked astonished. One or two more kicks and it was out. Next time its foster-mother visited the nest she found the little one free,—but subdued, as if it knew it had been naughty,—and with that " well-what-next?" expression of counten-ance which is peculiar to very young birds in general.

When born, this little creature was about the size of a small barn-door hen, but it was exceeding weak as well as long in the legs, and its first efforts at walking were a mere burlesque.

The feeding of this foundling was in keeping with its antecedents. Mrs. Marais was a thoroughgoing but incomprehensible woman. One would have thought that boiled sheep's liver, chopped fine, and hens' eggs boiled hard, were about the most violently opposed to probability in the way of food for an ostrich, old or young. Yet that is the food which she gave this baby. The manner of giving it, too, was in accordance with the gift.

Sitting down on a low stool, she placed the patient —so to speak—on its back, between her knees, and held it fast; then she rammed the liver and egg down its throat with her fingers as far as they would reach, after which she set it on its legs and left it for a few minutes to contemplation. Hitching it suddenly on its back again, she repeated the operation until it had had enough. In regard to quantity, she regulated herself by feeling its stomach. In the matter of drink she was more pronounced than a teetotaler, for she gave it none at all.

Thus she continued perseveringly to act until the young ostrich was old enough to go out in charge of a little Hottentot girl named Hreikie, who became a very sister to it, and whose life thenceforward was spent either in going to sleep under bushes, on the understanding that she was taking care of baby, or in laughing at the singular way in which her charge waltzed when in a facetious mood.

There is no doubt that this ostrich would have reached a healthy maturity if its career had not been cut short by a hyena.

Not until many years after this did "ostrich-farming" and feather-exporting become, as it still continues, one of the most important branches of commercial enterprise in the Cape Colony; but we cannot avoid the conclusion, that, as Watt gave the first impulse to the steam-engine when he sat and watched the boiling kettle, so Mrs. Marais opened the door to a great colonial industry when she held that infant ostrich between her knees, and stuffed it with minced eggs and liver.

CHAPTER XIV.

THE BERGENAARS.

"So you like the study of French?" said Charlie Considine, as he sat one morning beside Bertha Marais in the porch of her father's dwelling.

"Yes, very much," answered the girl. She said no more, but she thought, "Especially when I am taught it by such a kind, painstaking teacher as you."

"And you like to live in the wild karroo?" asked the youth.

"Of course I do," was the reply, with a look of surprise.

"Of course. It was a stupid question, Bertha; I did not think at the moment that it is *home* to you, and that you have known no other since you were a little child. But to my mind it would be a dull sort of life to live here always."

"Do you find it so dull?" asked Bertha, with a sad look.

"No, not in the least," replied the youth, quickly. "How *could* I, living as I do with such pleasant people, like one of their own kith and kin, hunting with the sons and teaching the daughters—to say nothing of scolding them and playing chess, and singing and riding. Oh no! I'm anything but dull, but I was talking *generally* of life in the karroo. If I lived alone, for instance, like poor Horley, or with a disagreeable family like that of Jan Smit— by the way, that reminds me that we have heard news of the three runaways, Ruyter, Jemalee, and Booby."

"Oh! I'm *so* glad," cried Bertha, her fair face brightening up with pleasure, "for I am very fond of Ruyter. He was so kind to me that time he found me lying near Smit's house, when my pony ran away and threw me, and I felt so miserable when I heard that his master was cruel and often beat him with a sjambok. Often and often since he ran away—and it must be nearly a year now—I have prayed God that he might come back, and that Jan Smit might become good to him.—What have you heard?"

Considine's face wore a troubled look. "I fear," he said, "the news will distress you, for what I heard was that the three men, driven to desperation by the harsh treatment received from their master, have joined one of the fiercest of these gangs of robbers, called the Bergenaars—the gang led, I believe, by Dragoener. It was Lucas Van Dyk, the hunter, who told me, and he is said to be generally correct in his statements."

Bertha's nether lip quivered, and she hid her face in her hands for a few moments in silence.

"Oh! I'm so sorry—*so* sorry," she said at length, looking up. "He was so gentle, so kind. I can't imagine Ruyter becoming one of those dreadful Bergenaars, about whose ferocious cruelty we hear so much—his nature was so different. I *can't* believe it."

"I fear," rejoined Considine gently, "that it is true. You know it is said that oppression will drive even a wise man mad, and a man will take to anything when he is mad."

"It could not drive a Christian to such a life," returned the girl sadly. "Oh! I *wish* he had become a Christian when Stephen Orpin spoke to him, but he wouldn't."

"When did Orpin speak to him, and what did he say?" asked Considine, whose own ideas as to Christianity were by no means fixed or clear.

"It was just after that time," rejoined Bertha, "when Jan Smit had had him tied to a cart-wheel and flogged so terribly that he could not walk for some days. Orpin happened to arrive at the time with his waggon—you know he has taken to going about as a trader,—and he spoke a great deal to Ruyter about his soul, and about Jesus coming to save men from sin, and enabling them to forgive their enemies; but when Ruyter heard about forgiving his enemies he wouldn't listen any more. Pointing to his wounds, he said, 'Do you think I can forgive Jan Smit?'"

"I don't wonder," said Considine; "it is too much to expect a black fellow smarting under the sjambok to forgive the man who applies it—especially when it is applied unjustly, and with savage cruelty."

Bertha was not gifted with an argumentative spirit. She looked anxiously in the face of her companion, and murmured some broken sentences about the Lord's Prayer and the Golden Rule, and wound up by saying hesitatingly, "How can we ask forgiveness if we do not forgive?"

"You are right, Bertha," was Considine's rejoinder, uttered gravely; "but, truly, a man must be more than a man to act on such principles. Think, now of the state of things at the present time with regard to the settlers. The 'rust,' as they call that strange disease which has totally ruined the first year's crop of wheat, has thrown the most of them into difficulties, and in the midst of this almost overwhelming calamity down came the Kafirs on the Albany District, and the Bergenaars, of whom we have just been speaking, not, like men, to fight openly—that were endurable,—but like sly thieves in the dead of night, to carry off sheep and cattle from many of the farms—in some cases even killing the herdsmen. Now, what think you must be the feelings of the

settlers towards these Kafirs and runaway robbers?
—can *they* forgive?"

Bertha didn't know. She thought their feelings
must be very harsh. Diverging from the question,
however, she returned to the first regret—namely,
that her friend Ruyter had joined the Bergenaars.

"Hallo! Considine, hi! where are you?" came
the sonorous voice of Conrad Marais in the distance,
interrupting the conversation. Next moment the
hearty countenance of the farmer followed his voice
round the corner of the house.

"Come, get your gun, my boy!" he cried in some
excitement. "These villains have been down last
night and carried off two spans of my best oxen,
besides killing and devouring several sheep."

Considine started up at once.

"We shall be off in half an hour," continued the
farmer; "Hans is away gathering one or two neighbours, and the people are almost ready."

"Do you accompany them?" asked Considine.

"Of course I do. Come along."

The youth required no urging. In a few minutes
he was armed and mounted, galloping in company
with a score of horsemen—black, brown, and white—
towards the cattle-kraals. Here was already assembled by Hans a troop of mounted men, among whom
were Jan Smit and his three sons, David, Jacob, and
Hendrik, also the hunter Van Dyk. After a brief

consultation, in which Van Dyk took a prominent part, they rode off at a smart gallop.

We change the scene now to a large and dark cavern up among the wild heights of the Winterberg mountains.

It was evening, but the sun had still a considerable distance to descend before finding its bed on the western horizon. A faint gleam of day entered the cave, which was further illuminated by three fires, over which a band of savage-looking dark-skinned men were roasting chops and marrow-bones. Abdul Jemalee the Malay slave and Booby the Bushman were there, assisting at the feast. At the inner end of the cave, seated beside two men, was Ruyter the Hottentot. He was a good deal changed from the rough but careless and jolly fellow whom we first introduced to the reader. There was a stern severity on his countenance, coupled with a touch of sadness when in repose, but when called into action, or even when conversing, the softer feeling vanished, and nothing remained but the lines indicative of a stern settled purpose. Most of the robbers around him had like himself fled from harsh masters, and become hardened in a career of crime. The expression of almost every countenance was vindictive, sensual, coarse. Ruyter's was not so. Unyielding sternness alone marked his features, which, we have elsewhere remarked, were unusually good for a

Hottentot. Being a man of superior power he ha become the leader of this robber-band. It was only one of many that existed at that time among the almost inaccessible heights of the mountain-ranges bordering on the colony. His companions recognised the difference between themselves and their captain, and did not love him for it, though they feared him. They also felt that he was irrevocably one of themselves, having imbrued his hands in white man's blood more than once, and already made his name terrible on that part of the frontier.

" They should be here by this time," said Ruyter, in Dutch, to one of the men at his side. " Why did you send them off before I returned ?"

He said this with a look of annoyance. The man replied that he had acted according to the best of his judgment, and had been particular in impressing the leader of the party that he was not to touch the flocks of old Marais, but to devote himself entirely to those of Jan Smit.

To this Ruyter observed with a growl that it was not likely they would attend to such orders if Marais' herds chanced to be handy, but the robber to whom he spoke only replied with a sly smile, showing that he was of the same opinion.

Just then a man rushed into the cave announcing the fact that their comrades were returning with plenty cattle and sheep, but that they were pursued.

Instantly the chops and marrow-bones were flung aside, and the robbers, hastily arming, mounted their horses and descended to the rescue.

The band of which Ruyter had become leader had existed some time before he joined. It was a detachment from a larger band who acknowledged as their chief a desperado named Dragoener. This Bushman had been in the service of Diederik Muller, but, on being severely flogged by a hot-tempered kinsman of his master, had fled to the mountains, vowing vengeance against all white men. It is thus that one white scoundrel can sometimes not only turn a whole tribe of savages into bitter foes of the white men in general, but can bring discredit on his fellows in the eyes of Christian people at a distance, who have not the means of knowing the true state of the case. Be this as it may, however, Dragoener with his banditti soon took ample revenge on the colonists for the sjamboking he had received.

Not long previous to the period of which we write he had been reinforced by Ruyter, Jemalee, Booby, and several other runaway slaves, besides some "wild Bushmen,"—men who had never been in service, and were so called to distinguish them from men who had been caught, like our friend Booby, and "tamed." A few deserters from the Cape Corps, who possessed fire-arms, had also joined him.

Thus reinforced, Dragoener and his lieutenant had

become bolder than ever in their depredations. One
of his bands had recently carried off a large number
of cattle and horses from the Tarka boers, who had
called out a commando and gone in pursuit. Driven
into a forest ravine, and finding it impossible to
retain possession of their booty, the robbers had cut
the throats of all the animals, and, scattering into
the jungle, made their escape. Another band had
frequently annoyed the Scotsmen at Baviaans River.

When therefore the band under Ruyter heard of
the approach of their comrades with booty, and of
the pursuit by colonists, they went to the rescue,
somewhat emboldened by recent successes. On
meeting their comrades, who were driving the
cattle and horses before them in frantic haste, they
were told that the pursuers were in strong force
and numbered among them several of the boldest
men and best shots on the frontier.

There was no time for holding a council of war.
Ruyter at once divided his men into two bands.
With the larger, well armed, and having two or three
deserters with muskets, he crept into the woods to
lay an ambush for the enemy. The other band was
ordered to continue driving the cattle with utmost
speed, and, in the event of being overtaken, to cut
the animals' throats and each man look out for
himself.

If Ruyter's men had been as bold and cool as

himself they might have checked the pursuit, but when the hunter Van Dyk, who knew their ways, advanced in front of his comrades by a path known to himself, discovered their ambush and sent a bullet through the head of one of their number, they awaited no further orders. but rose *en masse*, fled through the jungle, and made for the mountains.

Van Dyk, reloading in hot haste, followed swiftly, but he had not taken three steps when Charlie Considine was at his heels. He had dismounted and followed Van Dyk. The other pursuers made a détour on horseback to cut off the robbers as they passed over some open ground in advance. In attempting this they came on a spot where the ground was strewn with the dead or dying cattle. With a yell of rage they pushed on, but utterly failed, for the bandits had headed in another direction and gained the cliffs, where pursuit on horseback was impossible. Knowing that it would have been equally fruitless to continue the chase on foot, they returned to the point where Van Dyk and Considine had entered the jungle, fully expecting to find them there, as it would have been madness, they thought, for two unsupported men to follow up the flying band. To their surprise they found no one there.

"We must follow their spoor, boys," said Conrad Marais, with an anxious look; "they cannot be far off, but we must not leave them unsupported in the jungle with such a lot of black villains flying about."

Action was at once taken. The most experienced men dismounted and traced the spoor, with the unerring certainty of bloodhounds. But they shouted and searched in vain till night compelled them to desist.

Meanwhile Van Dyk and Considine had been captured by the Bergenaars.

When Charlie overtook the hunter, as already described, his ardent spirit and strong supple limbs enabled him to outrun his more massive though not less enthusiastic companion. A short run soon convinced the hunter that there was no chance of a clothed white man overtaking a more than half-naked native in a thorny jungle. Indeed, he was already well convinced by former experience of this fact, and had intended to engage in pursuit for only a short time, in order if possible to obtain a flying shot at one or two of the robbers, but his young comrade's resolute continuance of the chase forced him to hold on longer than he desired.

"Stop! stop! young fellow," he shouted with stentorian voice; "stop, I say! You'll only waste your breath for no good," he shouted.

But Considine heard him not. He had caught sight of one of the bandits who seemed to be losing strength, and, being himself sound in wind and limb, he recklessly determined to push on.

" I'll leave you to your fate," roared Van Dyk, "if you don't stop."

He might as well have roared to a mad buffalo. Considine heeded or heard not.

" It won't do," growled the hunter in a stern soliloquy as he stopped a moment to tighten his belt. " Well, well, I little thought, Van Dyk, that you'd be brought to such a miserable fix as this, in such a stupid way too. But he mustn't be left to the Bushmen's tender mercies."

The hunter's swart countenance grew darker as he spoke, for he well knew the extremity of danger into which the reckless youth was compelling him to run, but he did not hesitate. Instead, however, of following in the steps of one who was fleeter of foot than himself, he made a détour to the right. In an hour he reached a cliff under which, he knew, from the form of the valley up which the pursuit had been conducted, his young companion must needs pass. The route he had taken was a short cut. He had headed Considine and saw him, a few minutes later, in the gorge below in full pursuit of the robber.

" H'm !" grunted Van Dyk, as he sat down on a rock and examined the priming of his great elephant-gun, " I thought as much ! The black scoundrel is just playing with him—decoying the young idiot on till he gets him surrounded by his comrades; but I'll spoil his game, though it's like to be the last shot I'll ever fire."

A low quiet sigh escaped from the hunter as he watched the two men and awaited the proper moment.

He was evidently right in his conjecture, for, as they drew near the cliff, the black man looked over his shoulder once or twice and slackened his pace. The next moment he gave a shout which proved to be a signal, for two of the robbers sprang out from the bushes and seized Considine almost before he had seen them. Vigorously he struggled, and would perhaps have thrown off both, had not the man he had been chasing turned and run to aid the others.

Quickly but steadily Van Dyk raised his gun and covered this man. Next moment the muzzle was struck aside, the ball flew harmlessly into the jungle, and the hunter was pinioned, overthrown, and rendered helpless by four of the robbers, who had been watching his motions all the time.

Van Dyk was not taken much by surprise. He knew that such danger was probable, and had done his best to avoid it. With that self-command which a life of constant danger in the woods had taught him, he bowed to the inevitable, and quietly submitted to be bound and led away.

Meanwhile Ruyter, for it was he who had been chased, came up in time to assist in securing his victim.

"What, Ruyter, is it you?" exclaimed Considine in amazement.

When the robber-chief became aware who he had captured, an expression of deep annoyance or regret crossed his face, but it quickly passed into one of stern almost sulky determination, as he ordered the two men, in Dutch, to make the bonds secure. He deigned no reply to the prisoner's question. He did not even appear to recognise him, but strode on in front, while the two robbers drove the youth up into the rocky fastnesses of the mountains.

That night our hero found himself seated in the deepest recesses of a cavern by the side of his comrade Van Dyk. The arms of both were firmly bound behind their backs, but their legs were free, their captors knowing well that a scramble among such giddy and rugged heights without the use of the hands was impossible. In the centre of the cavern sat the robbers round a small fire on which some of them were cooking a few scraps of meat.

"A pretty mess you've led yourself and me into, young fellow!" said the hunter sternly.

"Indeed I have," replied Considine, with a very penitent air, "and I would give or do anything to undo the mischief."

"Ja—always the same with wild-caps like you,"
returned the other,—"ready to give anything when
you've got nothing, and to do anything when you're
helpless.   How much easier it would have been to
have given a little heed and done a little common
sense when you had the chance!"

There was a touch of bitterness, almost fierceness,
in the hunter's tone, which, knowing the man's
kindly nature, Considine could not quite understand.

"Do you know what them reptiles there are saying?" continued Van Dyk after a brief pause.

"No, their language is mere gibberish to me."

"They're discussin' the best method of puttin' us
out of existence," said the hunter, with a grim smile.
"Some of 'em want to cut our throats at once and
have done with it; some would like to torture us
first; others are in favour of hangin', but all agree
that we must be killed to prevent our tellin' the
whereabouts of their hiding-place up here,—all except
one, the one you gave chase to this afternoon. *He*
advises 'em to let us go, but he don't seem very
earnest about it."

"I think I know the reason of his favouring us,"
said Considine, with a look of hope.

"Indeed?"

"Yes; he once journeyed with me from Capetown
to the karroo, and probably he feels a touch of
regard for his old travelling companion."

"H'm! I wouldn't give much for his regard," growled Van Dyk. "The reed is slender, but it's the only one we have to lean on now. However, we've got a reprieve, for I heard 'em say just now that they'll delay executing us till to-morrow, after reaching one of their other and safer retreats in the mountains."

The prisoners were put into a smaller cave, close to the large one, that night. Their bonds were made more secure, and, as an additional precaution, their legs were tied. Two men were also appointed to guard the entrance of their prison.

About midnight the camp was perfectly still, and the only sounds that broke the silence were the tinkling of a neighbouring rill and the footfall of the sentinels. Van Dyk and Considine were lying uneasily on the bare ground, and thinking of the tragic fate that awaited them on the morrow, when they observed the dim figure of a man approaching from the innermost end of the cavern with a drawn knife in his right hand. Both started up and leant on their elbows; more than this they could not do. They felt some alarm, it is true, but both came to the same conclusion—that it is foolish to cry out before you are hurt.

The figure bent over Van Dyk, and whispered in his ear. Next moment the hunter stood on his feet with his limbs free.

"You were right, young sir," he said to Considine
as he stooped over him and cut his bonds; "there *is*
a touch of humanity in the rascally Hottentot after
all. Come; he bids us follow him. Knows a secret
passage out o' the cave, no doubt."

The black-bearded huntsman turned as he spoke,
and followed the dim figure, which melted into the
depths of the cavern as if it had been a spirit. A
few minutes' gliding through darkness tangible, and
they found themselves in the open air among thick
bushes. Though the night was very dark there was
sufficient light to enable Considine to see the glittering of white teeth close to his face, as a voice whispered in broken English—

"You's better tink twice when you try for to chase
a Tottie next time! Go; Van Dyk, him's old hand
in de bush, will guide you safe."

Before morning Considine was back in Conrad
Marais' parlour, relating his adventures among the
Bergenaars with a half-belief that the whole affair
was nothing more than a romantic dream.

CHAPTER XV.

TREATS OF THE ZUURVELD AGAIN, AND ONE OR TWO SURPRISING
INCIDENTS.

SEATED one evening at the door of their dug-out hut or cavern on the banks of the river, the three brothers Skyd discussed the affairs of the colony and smoked their pipes.

"Never knew such a country," said John Skyd, "never!"

"Abominable!" observed James.

"Detestable!" remarked Robert.

"Why don't you Skyd-addle then?" cried Frank Dobson. "If I thought it as bad as you do, I'd leave it at once. But you are unjust."

"Unjust!" echoed John Skyd; "that were impossible. What could be worse? Here have we been for three years, digging and ploughing, raking and hoeing, carting and milking, churning and—and—and what the better are we now? Barely able to keep body and soul together, with the rust ruining our wheat, and an occasional Kafir-raid depriving us of our cattle, while we live in a hole on the river's bank like rabbits; with this disadvantage over these facetious creatures, that we have more numerous wants and fewer supplies."

"That's so," said Bob; "if we could only content ourselves with a few bulbous roots and grass all would be well, but, Frank, we sometimes want a little tea and sugar; occasionally we run short of tobacco; now and then we long for literature; coffee sometimes recurs to memory; at rare intervals, especially when domestic affairs go wrong, the thought of woman, as of a long-forgotten being of angelic mould, *will* come over us. Ah! Frank, it is all very well for you to smile, you who have been away enjoying yourself for months past hunting elephants and other small game in the interior, but you have no notion how severely our failures are telling on our spirits. Why, Jim there tried to make a joke the other day, and it was so bad that Jack immediately went to bed with a sick-headache."

"True," said Jack solemnly, "quite true, and I couldn't cure that headache for a whole day, though I took a good deal of Cape-smoke before it came on, as well as afterwards."

"But, my dear chums," remonstrated Dobson, "is it not—"

"Now don't ask 'Is it not your own fault?' with that wiseacre look of yours," said John Skyd, testily tapping the bowl of his pipe on a stone preparatory to refilling it. "We are quite aware that we are not faultless; that we once or twice have planted things upside down, or a yard too deep, besides other little eccentricities of ignorance; but such errors are things of the past, and though we now drive our drills as straight as once, heigho! we ruled our account-books, things don't and won't improve."

"If you had not interrupted me, Jack, you might have spared much breath and feeling. I was about to say, Is it not a fact that many of the other settlers are beginning to overcome their difficulties though you are not? True, it has now been found that the wheat crops, on which we at first expected almost entirely to depend, have for three seasons proved an entire failure, and sheep do not thrive on our sour grass pasturage, though they seem to have done admirably with the Scotch at Baviaans River; but have not many of those around us been successful in raising rye, barley, oats, and Indian corn? have they not many herds of healthy cattle? are not pumpkins and potatoes thriving pretty well, and gardens beginning to flourish? Our roasted barley makes very fair coffee, and honey is not a bad substitute for sugar."

"You have made a successful bag this trip, I see, by your taking such a healthy view of our circumstances," said Bob.

"Yes, I've done very well," returned Dobson;

"and I find the hunter's life so congenial, and withal so profitable, that I'm really thinking of adopting it as a profession. And that brings me to the object of my visit here to-night. The fact is, my dear fellows, that men of your genius are not fit for farmers. It takes quiet-going men of sense to cultivate the soil. If you three were to live and dig to the age of Methuselah you'd never make a living out of it."

"That's plain speaking," said John, with a nod, "and I agree with you entirely."

"I mean to speak plainly," rejoined Dobson, "and now what I propose is, that you should give it up and join me in the ivory business. It will pay, I assure you."

Here their friend entered into a minute and elaborate account of his recent hunting expedition, and imparted to John Skyd some of his own enthusiasm, but James and Robert shook their heads. Leaving them to think over his proposal, their friend went to make a call on the Brooks of Mount Hope.

"Drat that boy! he's escaped again, and after mischief I'll be bound!" was the first sound that saluted him as he walked towards the house. It was Mrs. Scholtz's voice, on the other side of the hedge with which the garden was surrounded. The remark was immediately followed by a piercing shriek from the nurse, who repeated it again and

JUNKIE COLLARS A SNAKE.—Page 215.

again. Dobson could see her through an opening
in the branches, standing helpless, with her hands
clasped and eyeballs glaring. Thoroughly alarmed,
he dashed towards the gate. At the same moment
the voice of a child was heard :—

"Oh, look!—look 'ere, nuss, ain't I cotched a
pritty ting—*such* a pritty ting!"

Springing through the gate, Dobson beheld Master
Junkie, staggering up the track like a drunken man,
with one hand clasped tight round the throat of a
snake whose body and tail were twining round the
chubby arm of its captor in a vain effort at freedom,
while its forked tongue darted out viciously. It was
at once recognised as one of the most deadly snakes
in the country.

"Ain't it a booty?" cried Junkie, confronting
Dobson, and holding up his prize like the infant
Hercules, whom he very much resembled in all
respects.

Dobson, seizing the child's hand in his own left,
compressed it still tighter, drew his hunting-knife,
and sliced off the reptile's head, just as Edwin
Brook with his wife and daughter, attracted by
the nurse's outcry, rushed from the cottage to the
rescue. Scholtz and George Dally at the same time
ran out respectively from stable and kitchen.

Mrs. Scholtz had gone into a hysterical fit of per-
sistent shrieking and laughter, which she maintained

until she saw that her darling was saved; then, finishing off with a prolonged wail, she fell flat on the
grass in a dead faint.

Junkie at the same moment, as it were, took up
the cry. To be thus robbed of his new-found pet
would have tried a better temper than his. Without
a moment's hesitation he rushed at Frank Dobson
and commenced violently to kick his shins, while he
soundly belaboured his knees with the still wriggling
tail of the poor snake.

"What a blessing!" exclaimed Mrs. Brook, grasping Dobson gratefully by the hand.

"What a mercy!" murmured Gertie, catching up
the infant Hercules and taking him off to the
cottage.

"What a rumpus!" growled Dally, taking himself
off to the kitchen.

Scholtz gave no immediate expression to his feelings, but, lifting his better-half from the grass, he
tucked her under one of his great arms, and, with
the muttered commentary, "zhe zhriecks like von
mad zow," carried her off to his own apartment,
where he deluged her with cold water and abuse till
she recovered.

"Your arrival has created quite a sensation,
Dobson," said Edwin Brook, with a smile, as they
walked up to the house.

"Say, rather, it was opportune," said Mrs. Brook;

' but for your prompt way of using the knife our darling might have been bitten. Oh! I do dread these
snakes, they go about in such a sneaking way, and are
so very deadly. I often wonder that accidents are
not more frequent, considering the numbers of them
that are about."

"So do I, Mrs. Brook," returned Dobson; "but I
suppose it is owing to the fact that snakes are
always most anxious to keep out of man's way, and
few men are as bold as your Junkie. I never heard
of one being collared before, though a friend of mine
whom I met on my last visit to the karroo used
sometimes to catch hold of a snake by the tail,
whirl it round his head, and dash its brains out
against a tree."

"You'll stay with us to-day, Dobson?" said
Brook.

Frank, involuntarily casting a glance at the
pretty face of Gertie—who had by that time attained to the grace of early womanhood,—accepted
the invitation, and that day at dinner entertained
the family with graphic accounts of his experiences
among the wild beasts of the Great Fish River
jungles, and dilated on his prospects of making a
fortune by trading in ivory. "If that foolish law,'
he said, "had not been made by our Governor, pro-
hibiting traffic with the Kafirs, I could get waggon-
loads of elephants' tusks from them for an old song.

As it is, I must knock over the elephants for myself
—at least until the laws in question are rescinded."

"The Governor seems to have a special aptitude,"
said Brook, with a clouded brow, "not only for fram-
ing foolish laws, but for abrogating good ones."

The Governor referred to was Lord Charles
Somerset, who did more to retard the progress of the
new settlements on the frontiers of Kafirland than
any who have succeeded him. Having complicated
the relations of the colonists and Kafirs, and confused as well as disgusted, not to say astonished, the
natives during his first term of office, he went to
England on leave of absence, leaving Sir Rufane
Shaw Donkin to act as Governor in his place.

Lord Charles seems to have been a resentful as
well as an incapable man, for immediately after his
return to the colony in 1821 he overturned the policy
of the acting Governor, simply because he and Sir
Rufane were at personal enmity. The colony at
that time, and the Home Government afterwards,
approved of the wise measures of the latter. He
had arranged the military forces on the frontier so
as to afford the new settlers the greatest possible
amount of protection; the Cape corps men had been
partly placed at their disposal, both to assist and
defend; those who found their allotted farms too
small had them increased to the extent of the farms
of their Dutch neighbours; acceptable public officers

were appointed; provisions were supplied on credit, and everything, in short, had been done to cheer and encourage the settlers during the period of gloom which followed their first great calamity, the failure of the wheat-crops. All this was upset on the return of Lord Charles Somerset. With a degree of tyranny and want of judgment worthy of a mere " Jack-in-office," he immediately removed from the magistracy of the British Settlement of Albany a favourite and able man, to make room for one of his own protégés and supporters. He withdrew troops from one of the most important frontier villages (in a strategic point of view), and stopped the formation of a road to it, thus compelling the settlers to desert it and leave their standing crops to the surprised but pleased Kafirs, who were perplexed as well as emboldened by the vacillating policy of white Governors! In addition to this he gave permission to the savage chief Macomo to occupy the land so vacated, thus paving the way for future wars. Instead of encouraging traffic with the Kafirs he rendered it illegal. He issued a proclamation forbidding all public meetings for political purposes; he thwarted the philanthropic and literary Pringle and Fairbairn in their attempts to establish a newspaper, and drove the former from the colony. But why proceed? We cite these facts merely to account for the cloud on Edwin Brook's brow, and for the fact that at this time many of the British settlers, who would gallantly have faced the "rust" and other troubles and difficulties sent to them by Providence, could not bear the oppression which "driveth a wise man mad," but, throwing up all their hopes and privileges as settlers, scattered themselves far and wide over the colony. This, as it happened, was much to the advantage of themselves and the old Dutch settlers with whom they mingled.

Those of them who remained behind, however, continued to fight the battle against oppression and circumstances most manfully.

Long and patiently did Mrs. Brook listen to her visitor and husband while they indignantly discussed these subjects.

"But why," said she, at last giving vent to her feelings, "why does the Government at home not remove such an incapable and wicked Governor and give us a better?"

"Because, my dear," replied Edwin, with a smile, "the incapable and wicked Governor happens to possess almost despotic *power*, and can gain the ear of men in high places at home, so that they are deceived by him, while all who venture to approach them, except through this Governor, are regarded with suspicion, being described as malcontents. And yet," continued Brook, growing warm at the thought of his wrongs, "we do not complain of those at home, or of the natural disadvantages of the country to which we have been sent. We settlers are actuated by one undivided feeling of respect and gratitude to the British Government, which future reverses will never efface; but it is peculiarly hard to have been sent to this remote and inaccessible corner of the globe, and to be left to the control of one individual, who misrepresents us and debars us the right to express our collective sentiments. Why, we might as well be living under the dominion of the Turk. But a word in your ear, Frank Dobson; meetings *have* been held, private ones, while you were away in the bush, and our case *has* been properly represented at last, and a Royal Commission of Inquiry is to be sent out to put things right. So there's hope for us yet! The clouds which have been so long lowering are, I think, beginning to clear away."

While the sanguine settler was thus referring to the clouds of adversity which had for more than two years hovered over the young settlement, the natural clouds were accumulating overhead in an unusually threatening manner. Long periods of drought are frequently followed in South Africa by terrible thunderstorms. One of these seemed to be brewing just then.

"I fear Hans and Considine will get wet jackets before they arrive," said Frank Dobson, rising and going to the window.

" Hans and Considine !" exclaimed Gertie, with a flush ; " are *they* here ?"

" Ay, they came with me as far as Grahamstown on business of some sort.—By the way, what a big place that is becoming, quite a town ! When we saw it first, you remember, it was a mere hamlet— the headquarters of the troops."

" It will be a city some day," prophesied Brook as he put on an old overcoat that had hitherto survived the ravages of time ; " you see all our comrades who have discovered that farming is not their vocation are hiving off into it, and many of them, being first-rate mechanics, they have taken to their trades, while those with mercantile tendencies have opened stores. You shall see that things will shake into their proper places, and right themselves in time, and this will be- come a flourishing colony, for the most of us are young and full of British pluck, while the climate, despite a few trifling disadvantages, is really splendid."

Edwin Brook spoke heartily, as he clapped his hat firmly on, preparatory to going out to make things secure against the expected storm.

At the same moment the South African storm- fiend (an unusually large though not frequently obtrusive one) laughed in a voice of thunder and nearly dashed in the windows with a tempest of wind and rain ! As if his voice had called up spirits from the "vasty deep," two horsemen suddenly appeared approaching at full speed. One of them was of unusual size.

"Here they come! just in time!" exclaimed, Gertie, clapping her hands in excitement.

The *girl* spoke and acted there. Then she blushed for the *woman* interfered!

Hans Marias reached the quince hedge first and sprang off his steed. Charlie Considine came second. With a wild whoop he caused his steed to leap the garden gate and dismounted at the cottage door. Then there was a hearty welcoming and inquiring, and shaking of hands, while the travellers were congratulated on having just escaped the storm.

While this was going on at Mount Hope, the Skyds were actively engaged in gathering in their cattle and otherwise making their place secure. They had more than once been warned that their position was one of danger, but being young, athletic, and rollicking, they had not cared hitherto to remove their humble dwelling. It was time enough to do that, they said, when " lovely woman" should come on the scene and render improvement in domicile necessary. Bob Skyd had more than once attempted to induce a "lovely woman " to invade the land and enlighten the cave, but somehow without success!

" We shall have it stiff," said John, as the three brothers approached their burrow.

" And heavy," added Bob.

James made no remark, but opened the door. It was growing dark at the time, and inside their cavern only a dim light prevailed.

"Why—what's—hallo! I say—"

Jim leaped back with a look of alarm. The brothers gazed in and saw, in the region of their bed (which held three easily), a pair of glaring eyeballs.

The brothers, although not superstitious, were by no means free from human weakness. At the same time they were gifted with a large share of animal courage. With beating heart John struck a light, and held up a flaming brimstone match. This caused the eyes to glare with fearful intensity, and revealed a distinct pair of horns. At that moment the match went out. With anxious trepidation another light was struck, and then it was discovered that a recently purchased goat had, under a wrong impression, taken possession of the family bed.

Laughing at this, they lit a tallow candle, which was stuck into that most convenient of candlesticks —an empty bottle.

The brothers, although not proficients, were mechanical in their way. One had set up the household bed; another had constructed a table, which had broken down only six times since their arrival; and the third had contrived a sofa. This last was Jim's work. It was a masterpiece in its way, of simplicity, and consisted of two rough planks laid on two mounds of earth, the whole being covered with a piece of chintz which fell in a curtain to the floor. This curtain, like love, covered a multitude of improprieties, in the shape of old boots, dirty linen, miscellaneous articles, and a sea-chest.

Sitting down on the sofa, John Skyd laughed long and heartily at the scene with the goat. His laugh suddenly ceased, and was replaced by an exclamation and a look of anxious surprise. "Something" had moved under the sofa! Snakes occurred to their minds at once, and the deadly character of South African snakes was well known.

"Look out, boys," cried John, leaping on the sofa, and seizing a sword which hung on a peg just above it.—"Fetch the light."

Bob quickly obeyed and revealed the tail of a large cobra disappearing among the improprieties. Jim ran to a rude cupboard where pistols and ammunition were kept, and began to load with small shot.

"This way! hold it closer to the wall," said John, in an earnest voice; "I see one of his coils at the back of the sofa. Now then, steady—there!"

He made a deadly thrust as he spoke and pinned the snake to the ground, but evidently by the wrong coil, for in a moment its angry head was seen twining up towards the handle of the sword.

"Quick, Jim—the pistol!"

Jim was ready and Bob raised the curtain of the sofa, while John stood in readiness to let go the sword and bolt if the reptile should prove to be capable of reaching his hand.

"Fire, Jim, fire! look sharp!" cried John Skyd.

Jim took aim and fired. The candle was put out by the concussion.

In the dark John could risk the danger no longer. He let go the sword and sprang with a shout upon the bed. Bob and Jim made for the same place of refuge, and, tumbling over each other, broke the pint bottle and the candle. Securing a fragment of the latter they proceeded once more to strike a light, with quaking hearts, while a horrible hissing and lashing was heard under the sofa. At last light was again thrown on the scene, and when the curtain was cautiously raised the cobra was seen to be writhing in its death-agonies—riddled with shot, and still pinned with the sword.

This scene closed most appropriately with a flash of lightning and a tremendous clap of thunder, —followed, immediately, by cataracts of rain.

CHAPTER XVI.

THE GREAT FLOODS OF 1823.

ALL that night and all next day rain came down on the land in continuous floods. The settlers had previously been visited with occasional storms, which had roused some alarm among the timid and done a little damage, but nothing like this had yet befallen them. The water appeared to descend in sheets, and not only did the great rivers wax alarmingly, but every rill and watercourse became a brawling river.

The Skyds, and one or two others who like themselves had built too near the edge of streams, were the first to suffer.

" This won't do," said John Skyd, on the evening of the second day, as he and his brothers sat in front of their cavern gazing at the turbid river, which, thick and yellow as pea-soup, was hurrying trees, bushes, and wrack in formidable masses to the sea. " We must shift our abode. Come along."

Without a word more the brothers entered their

cave, and began to carry out their goods and chattels. They were strong and active, but they had miscalculated the rapidity of the flood. Fortunately most of their valuables were removed to higher ground in time, but before all was got out a sudden increase in the rushing river sent a huge wave curling round the entire piece of ground on which their farm lay. It came on with devastating force, bearing produce, fences, fruit-trees, piggeries, and every movable thing on its foaming crest. The brothers dropped their loads and ran. Next moment the cavern was hollowed out to twice its former size, and the sofa, the rude cupboard, the sea-chest, and family bed were seen, with all the miscellaneous improprieties, careering madly down the yellow flood.

In their trousers and shirt-sleeves—for they had thrown off their coats, as all active men do in an emergency—the brothers watched the demolition of their possessions and hopes in solemn silence.

"I think," said John at length, with a sigh, "I've made up my mind to join Frank Dobson now."

Bob and Jim smiled grimly, but said never a word.

Meanwhile the settlers of Mount Hope farm were not idle. Although not fully alive to the danger of the storm, they saw enough to induce a course of rapid action. Goods and cattle were removed from low-lying buildings to higher ground, but the dwelling-house, being on the highest point in the neighbourhood—with the exception of the hills themselves—was deemed safe.

In these arrangements the family were ably assisted by the unexpected accession of their friends. Hans, Considine, and Dobson taxed their activity and strength to the utmost, so that things were soon put in a state of security. Dobson did, indeed, think once or twice of his old chums on the river, but a feeling of gallantry prevented his deserting the ladies in the midst of danger, and besides, he argued, the Skyds are well able to look after themselves.

Just as this thought passed through his mind the chums in question appeared upon the scene, announcing the fact that their entire farm had been swept away, and that *the water was still rising*.

"Well, it can't rise much higher now," said Edwin Brook, after condoling with his young friends on their misfortunes, "and the moment it begins to abate we shall go down to save all we can of your property. You know, my poor fellows, that I shall be only too glad to help you to the utmost of my power in such a sad extremity as this."

The brothers thanked their neighbour, and meanwhile aided the others in removing the farm-produce and implements to higher ground

Night at length settled down on the scene, and
the wearied party returned to the cottage for food
and rest.

"Do you think, Mr. Marais," said Gertie, looking
up timidly at the handsome young Dutchman, "that
the worst of it is over?"

Hans, who felt somewhat surprised and chilled
by the "Mister," replied that he hoped it was.

But Hans was wrong. Late that night, after they
had all lain down to rest, Edwin Brook, feeling
sleepless and uneasy, rose to look out at the window.
All was comparatively still, and very dark. There
was something grey on the ground, he thought,
but judged it to be mist. The noise of the storm,
with the exception of rushing streams, had gone
down, and though it still rained there was nothing
very unusual to cause alarm. He lay down again
and tried to sleep, but in vain. Then he thought
he heard the sound of the river louder than before.
At the same time there was a noise that resembled
the lapping of water round the frame of the house.

Jumping up, he ran to his door, opened it, discovered that the supposed mist was water, and that
his dwelling was an island in a great sea.

To shout and rouse the household was the work
of an instant. His guests were men of promptitude.
They had merely thrown themselves down in their
clothes, and appeared in an instant. Mrs. Brook

and Gertie were also ready, but Mrs. Scholtz, being fond of comfort, had partially undressed, and was distracted between a wild effort to fasten certain garments and restrain Junkie, who, startled by the shout, was roaring lustily.

"Not a moment to lose!" said Brook, running hastily into the room, where all were now assembled. "Everything is lost. We must think only of life. Lend a helping hand to the women, friends—mind the boy.—Come, wife."

Brook was sharp, cool, and decisive in his manner. Seizing his wife round the waist, he hurried her out into the dark night, stepping as he did so above the ankles in rising water.

Dobson, Considine, and the three brothers turned with a mutual impulse towards Gertie, but Hans Marais had already taken possession of her, and, almost carrying her in his powerful arms, followed her father.

"Come, my howlin' toolip," said George Dally, "you're my special and *precious* charge. Shut up, will you?"

He seized the child and bore him away with such violence that the howling was abruptly checked; while Scholtz, quietly gathering his still half-clad spouse under an arm, followed with heavy stride.

The others, each seizing the object that in his eyes appeared to be most valuable—such as a desk

or workbox,—sprang after the household and left
the house to its fate.   They first made for the cattle-
kraals, but these were already flooded and the cattle
gone.   Then they tried a barn which stood a little
higher, but it was evidently no place of refuge, for
the stream just there was strong, and broke against
it with violence.

"To the hills!" shouted Hans, lifting Gertie off
the ground altogether, as if she had been a little
child.

There was no time for ceremony.   Edwin Brook
lifted his wife in the same manner, for the water was
deepening at every step, and the current strengthen-
ing.   The darkness, which had appeared dense at first,
seemed to lighten as they became accustomed to it,
and soon a terrible state of things became apparent.
Turbid water was surging among the trees and
bushes everywhere, and rushing like a mill-race in
hollows.   One such hollow had to be crossed before
the safety of the hills could be gained.   The water
reached Edwin's waist as he waded through.   To
prevent accident, John Skyd and Considine waded
alongside and supported him.   James Skyd performed the same office for Hans, and Bob waded
just below Scholtz and his burden—which latter,
in a paroxysm of alarm, still tried frantically to
complete her toilet.

The hills were reached at last, and the whole party

was safe—as far, at least, as the flood was concerned; but a terrible prospect lay before them. The valley of Mount Hope was by that time a sea of tumultuous water, which seemed in the darkness of the night to be sweeping away and tearing up trees, bushes, and houses. Behind and around them were the hills, whose every crevice and hollow was converted into a wild watercourse. Above was the black sky, pouring down torrents of rain incessantly, so that the very ground seemed to be turning into mud and slipping away from beneath their feet. Fortunately there was no wind.

"To spend the night here will be death to the women and child," said Edwin Brook, as they gathered under a thick bush which formed only a partial shelter; "yet I see no way of escape. Soaked as they are, a cavern, even if we can find one, will not be of much service, for our matches are hopelessly wet."

"We must try to reach Widow Merton's farm," said John Skyd. "It is only three miles off, and stands on highish ground."

"It's a bad enough road by daylight in fine weather," said George Dally, on whose broad shoulder Junkie had fallen sound asleep, quite regardless of damp or danger, "but in a dark night, with a universal flood, it seems to me that it would be too much for the ladies. I know a cave, now, up on

or workbox.₃, not far off, which is deep, an' like to be
the house ·
kraals, dver do," interrupted Hans Marais, to whose
gona Gertie clung with a feeling that it was her only
hnope; "they'd die of cold before morning. We
must keep moving."

"Yes, let us try to reach the widow's farm," said
poor Mrs. Brook anxiously, "I feel stronger, I think;
I can walk now"

"Zee vidow ₃ our only chanze.—Hold up, mein
vrow," said Scholtz, taking a firmer grasp of his
wife, who, having leisure to think and look about
her now, felt her heart begin to fail. "I know
zee road vell," continued Scholtz. "It is bad, but
I have zeen vurse. Ve must carry zee vimen. Zey
could not valk."

As the women made no objection, those who had
carried them from the house again raised them in
their arms—Mrs. Scholtz insisting, however, on
being treated a little less like a sack of old clothes
—and the march along the hill-side was begun.

George Dally, knowing the way best, was set in
advance to take the responsibility of guide as well
as the risk of being swept away while fording the
torrents. The brothers Skyd, being free from precious
burdens, marched next, to be ready to support the
guide in case of accident, and to watch as well as
guard the passage of dangerous places by those in

rear. Then followed in succession Mr. Brook with his wife, Charlie Considine, Hans with Gertie, and Scholtz with his vrow, the procession closing with Frank Dobson and Junkie, the latter having been transferred to Frank when Dally took the lead.

It was a slow as well as dangerous march on that dreary night, because every step had to be taken with care, and the rivulets, white though they were with foam, could scarcely be seen in the thick darkness. Many a fall did they get, too, and many a bruise, though fortunately no bones were broken. Once George Dally, miscalculating the depth of a savage little stream, stepped boldly in and was swept away like a flash of light. Jack Skyd made a grasp at him, lost his balance and followed. For a moment the others stopped in consternation, but they were instantly relieved by hearing a laugh from George a few yards down the stream as he assisted Skyd to land. At another time Scholtz was not careful enough to follow exactly in the footsteps of Hans, and, while crossing a torrent, he put his foot in a deep hole and went down to the armpits, thereby immersing his vrow up to her neck. A wild shriek from the lady was followed by " Zounds ! hold me op !" from the man.

Hans turned short round, stretched out his long right arm—the left being quite sufficient to support Gertie,—and, seizing the German's shaggy hair with

a mighty grip, held on till one of the Skyds returned
to the rescue.

It was also a melancholy march on that dismal
night, for poor Edwin Brook was well aware, and
fully alive to the fact, that he was a ruined man.
His labour for the previous three years was totally
lost, and his property swept entirely away. Only
life was spared,—but for that he felt so thankful
as to feel his losses slightly at the time. The
brothers Skyd were also painfully alive to the fact
that they were ruined, and as they staggered and
stumbled along, a sinking of heart unusual to their
gay and cheerful natures seemed to have the effect
of sinking their steps deeper in the soft mire through
which they waded.

Only two of the party were in any degree cheerful. Gertie, although overwhelmed by the sudden
calamity, which she had yet very imperfectly realised,
felt a degree of comfort—a sort of under-current of
peace—at being borne so safely along in such powerful arms; and Hans Marais, huge and deep-chested
though he was, felt a strange and mysterious sensation that his heart had grown too large for his body
that night. It perplexed him much at the time,
and seemed quite unaccountable!

The storm had revelled furiously round the widow
Merton's wattle-and-dab cottage, and the water had
risen to within a few feet of its foundations, but

the effect on her mind was as nothing compared with that produced by the sudden storming of her stronghold by the Mount Hope family in the dead of night, or rather in the small hours of morning. The widow was hospitable. She and her sons at once set about making the unfortunates as comfortable as the extent of their habitation and the state of their larder would admit.

But the widow Merton was not the only one of the Albany settlers who had to offer hospitality during the continuance of that terrible catastrophe of 1823, and Edwin Brook's was not the only family that was forced to accept it.

All over the land the devastating flood passed like the besom of destruction. Hundreds of those who had struggled manfully against the blight of the wheat crops, and Kafir thefts, and bandit raids, and oppression on the part of those who ought to have afforded aid and protection, were sunk to the zero of misfortune and despair by this overwhelming calamity, for in many cases the ruin was total and apparently irremediable. Everywhere standing crops, implements of husbandry, and even dwellings, were swept away, and whole families found themselves suddenly in a state of utter destitution. The evil was too wide-spread to admit of the few who were fortunate enough to escape rendering effectual assistance to the many sufferers, for it was obvious that

hundreds of pounds would not be sufficient to succour
the infant colony.

In this extremity God's opportunity was found.
The hearts of men and women far away, at Capetown,
in India, and in England, were touched by the story
of distress; generosity was awakened and purses
were opened. Men such as H. E. Rutherfoord of
Capetown, the Rev. Dr. Philip, the Rev. W. Shaw,
and others like-minded, entered heartily into the
work of charity, and eventually some ten thousand
pounds were distributed among those who had
suffered. To many this was as life from the dead.
Some who would never have recovered the blow
took heart again, braced their energies anew, and ere
long the wattle-and-dab cottages were rebuilt, the
gardens replanted, and the lands cultivated as
before.

The existence of the settlement was saved, but
its prosperity was not yet secured. The battle had
gone sorely against the valiant band of immigrants,
and very nearly had they been routed, but the
reinforcements had enabled them to rally and renew
the fight. Still, it *was a* fight, and much time had
yet to come and go before they could sit down in
the sunshine of comparative peace and enjoy the
fruits of their industry.

Meanwhile the oppressions and mismanagements
of the Colonial Government went on as before. It

were useless in a tale like this to inflict details on our readers. Suffice it to say that in the distribution of lands, in treaties with the Kafirs, in the formation of laws for the protection of Hottentots and slaves, in the treatment of the settlers, a state of things was brought about which may be described as confusion worse confounded, and the oppressed people at last demanded redress with so loud a voice that it sounded in England, and produced the Royal Commission of Investigation already referred to in a previous chapter.

The arrival of the gentlemen composing this Commission followed close on the floods of 1823. The event, long looked for and anxiously desired, was hailed with a degree of eager delight scarcely to be understood except by those who had gone through the previous years of high-handed oppression, of weary wrangling and appeal, and of that hope deferred which maketh the heart sick. Expectation was raised to the highest pitch, and when it was heard that the Commissioners had reached Capetown preparations were made in Grahamstown to give them a warm reception.

CHAPTER XVII.

TREATS OF HOPES, FEARS, AND PROSPECTS, BESIDES DESCRIBING A
PECULIAR BATTLE.

MOUNTED on a pair of sturdy ponies Hans Marais
and Charlie Considine galloped over the plains of
the Zuurveld in the direction of Grahamstown.
The brothers Skyd had preceded them, Edwin Brook
was to follow.

It was a glorious day, though this was nothing
unusual in that sunny clime, and the spirits of the
young men were high. Excitement has a tendency
to reproduce itself. Hans and his friend did not
feel particularly or personally interested in the
arrival of the Royal Commissioners, but they were
sympathetic, and could not resist surrounding influences. Everywhere they overtook or passed, or
somehow met with, cavaliers on the road—middle-
aged and young—for old men were not numerous
there at that time—all hastening to the same goal,
the "city of the settlers," and all had the same tale
to tell, the same hopes to express. "Things are

going to be put right now. The Commissioners have full powers to inquire and to act. We court investigation. The sky is brightening at last; the sun of prosperity will rise in the 'east' ere long!"

In Grahamstown itself the bustle and excitement culminated. Friends from the country were naturally stirred by meeting each other there, besides being additionally affected by the object of the meeting. Crowds gathered in the chief places of the fast rising town to discuss grievances, and friends met in the houses of friends to do the same and draw up petitions.

At last the Commissioners arrived and were welcomed by the people with wild enthusiasm.

Abel Slingsby, an impulsive youth, and a friend of Hans Marais, who had just been married to a pretty neighbour of Hans in the karroo, and was in Grahamstown on his honeymoon, declared that he would, without a moment's hesitation, throw up his farm and emigrate to Brazil, if things were not put right without delay.

" No, you wouldn't," said his pretty bride, with an arch look; "you'd take time to think well over it and consult with me first."

" Right, Lizzie, right; so I would," cried Slingsby, with a laugh. "But you must admit that we have had, and still have, great provocation. Just think," he added, with returning indignation, "of

Q

free-born British subjects being allowed no newspaper to read except one that is first revised by a
jealous, despotic Governor, and of our being obliged
to procure a 'pass' to entitle us to go about the
country, as if we were Kafirs or Hottentots—to say
nothing of the insolence of the Jacks-in-office who
grant such 'passes,' or the ridiculous laws regarding the natives—bah! I have no patience to recount
our wrongs.—Come, Hans, let's go out and see what's
doing; and don't forget, Liz, to have candles ready
for the illumination, and tell the Tottie to clean my
gun.   I must be ready to do them honour, like other
loyal subjects."

The young men sallied forth and found that the
Commissioners had been received by the authorities
with sullen courtesy.

"A clear sign that the authorities know themselves to be in the wrong," said Considine, "for
honest men always court open investigation."

"This attitude looks like rebellion against the
British Government on the part of the colonial authorities," said Hans.   "I shouldn't wonder if we were
to get a surprise from them while in such a mood."

Evening drew on apace, and crowds of people
moved about to witness the illumination and other
evidences of rejoicing, while some of the more
enthusiastic sought to express their sentiments by
firing a volley with small arms.   According to an eye-

witness,* the signal was taken up at once, and, the example spreading like wildfire, the hills soon resounded on all sides with a noise that might have been mistaken for the storming of the town. This was a demonstration the authorities could not brook. The necessary orders were given and soon the bugles of the garrison sounded the assembly at Scott's Barracks, while the trumpets of the Mounted Rifles at Fort England sent squadrons of horse thundering up Bathurst Street to assist in the terrible emergency caused by blank cartridges and joyous hurrahs! Parties of infantry patrolled the streets, making prisoners in all directions, and the people assembled in Church Square to see the illuminations were surrounded by troops. The leading men there, foreseeing the advantage that would result to their cause by such a style of repressing public opinion, advised those around them to keep quiet and be true to their principles.

Hans Marais and his friends happened to be in Church Square at the time, and at once fell in with and acted on the peaceful advice, though the impulsive Slingsby found it difficult to restrain his British spirit.

"See," he said, pointing to a gentleman who approached, "there goes the Rev. Mr. Geary.

* Rev. H. H. Dugmore, *The Reminiscences of an Albany Settler*, page 25.

Do you know him, Hans? He's a man of the true sort. Let me tell you in your ear that I heard he has got into bad odour in high quarters for refusing to have anything to do with a 'proscription list' furnished by the Governor, which contains the names of persons who are to be shunned and narrowly watched—some of these persons being the best and most loyal in the colony."

As he spoke the clergyman referred to was stopped by a friend, and they overheard him express much gratification at the arrival of the Commissioners, and a hope that abuses would soon be reformed, at the same time stating his determination not to be a party man.

Unfortunately for the clergyman there were minions of the Government within earshot at the time. His words were reported, and, shortly afterwards, he was summarily removed.

Just then some of the Cape Corps men charged part of the crowd and scattered it. At the same time various persons were arrested. Among these was the indignant Slingsby. Unable to restrain his ire he called out "Shame!" and was instantly pounced upon by a serjeant and party of infantry. Immediately becoming sensible of his folly, after a momentary struggle he suffered himself to be led quietly away, but looked over his shoulder as he was marched off to the "tronk," and said hurriedly—

"Console Lizzie, Hans!"

With a look of sympathy, Hans assured his friend that he would do so, without fail, and then, with Considine, proceeded to the house where poor Lizzie had already lit up the windows and got the gun in readiness.

"They dare not keep him long," said Hans, in his vain attempts to comfort the weeping bride, "and depend upon it that the conduct of the authorities this evening will go a long way to damage their own cause and advance that of the settlers."

Hans was right. Slingsby was liberated the following morning. The Commissioners turned out to be able men, who were not to be hoodwinked. True, a considerable period elapsed before the "report" afterwards made by them took effect, and for some time the settlers continued to suffer; but in the following year the fruits of the visit began to appear. Among other improvements was the creation of a Council to advise and assist the Governor—consisting of seven members, including himself,—whereby a wholesome check was put upon his arbitrary power. Trial by jury was also introduced, and the power of magistrates was modified. These and other more or less beneficial changes took place, so that there was reason to believe a time of real prosperity had at length dawned.

But the settlers were not yet out of the furnace.

Providence saw fit to send other troubles to try them besides unjust and foolish men in power. There was still another plague in store.

One day Charlie Considine rode towards the farm which had now for several years been his home.

The young members of the Marais family had grown learned under his care, and he was now regarded as a son by old Marais and his wife, while the children looked on him as an elder brother. Charlie had not intended to stay so long, and sometimes his conscience reproved him for having given up his profession of medicine, but the longer he stayed with those sweet-tempered Dutch-African farmers with whom his lot had been cast the more he liked them, and the more they liked him. What more natural then that he should stay on from day to day, until he became almost one of themselves? When people are happy they desire no change.

But it must not be supposed that the youth's office was a sinecure. The young Marais were numerous, and some of them were stupid,—though amiable. The trouble caused by these, however, was more than compensated by the brightness of others, the friendship of Hans, and the sunshine of Bertha. The last, by the way, had now, like Gertrude Brook, sprung into a woman, and though neither so graceful nor so sprightly as the pretty English girl, she was preeminently sweet and lovable.

Well, one day, as we have said, Charlie Considine rode towards the farm. He had been out hunting alone, and a springbok tied across the horse behind him showed that he had been successful.

Rousing himself from a reverie, he suddenly found himself in the midst of a scene of surpassing beauty. In front lay a quiet pond, whose surface was so still that it might have been a sheet of clear glass. On his left the familiar mountain-range beyond the farm appeared bluer and nearer than usual, owing to the intense heat. To the right the undulating karroo, covered with wild-flowers, and dotted with clumps of mimosa-bush, terminated abruptly in a lake which stretched away, in some places like a sea, to the horizon. Islands innumerable studded the smooth surface of this lake, and were reflected in its crystal depths. Not a breath of air ruffled its surface, and there was a warm sunny brightness, a stillness, a deep quietude, about the whole scene which were powerfully suggestive of heavenly peace and rest.

"Glorious!" exclaimed Considine, reining up to a walking pace. "How delicious while it lasts, and yet how evanescent! Does it not resemble my life here? *That* cannot last."

Charlie was not given to moralising, but somehow he could not help it that day. With an unusually profound sigh he shook the reins and cantered towards the lake. It was not the first time he had seen it, and he knew full well that it would not bar his progress. Even as he gave vent to the sigh the glassy waters trembled, undulated, retreated, and, under the influence of a puff of air, slowly melted away, leaving the waterless karroo in its place.

Truly it is no wonder that thirsty travellers in African deserts have, from time immemorial, rushed towards these phantom waters of the well-known *mirage*, to meet with bitter disappointment! The resemblance is so perfect that any one might be deceived if unacquainted with the phenomenon.*

On coming within sight of the farm, Considine observed columns of thick smoke rising from various parts of the homestead. With a vague feeling of alarm he put spurs to his horse. Drawing quickly nearer he perceived that the smoke arose from the garden, and that the people seemed to be bustling about in a state of violent activity. Stretching out at full speed, he was soon at the garden gate, and found that all the bustle, energising, and shouting went on at the end farthest from the gate. As he threw the reins over a post and sprang in he could see through the trees that every one in the establishment was engaged in a wild frantic fight, in which sticks and stones, bushes and blankets, were used indiscriminately. The smoke that rose around

---

* The author, having seen the mirage while riding on the karroo, writes from personal experience.

suggested fire on the plains, and he ran in haste to render assistance.

It was a goodly garden that he passed through. Fruit-trees of every kind were so laden with golden treasures that many of the branches, unable to bear the strain, had given way and the superabundance trailed upon the earth. Vegetables of all kinds covered the borders with luscious-looking bulbs and delicious green leaves, while grapes, currants, figs, etc., half smothered their respective bushes. Through this rich display of plenty Considine dashed, and on reaching the wall at the further end found Conrad Marais with his wife and daughter, sons, servants, and slaves, engaged in furious conflict with—locusts!

The enemy had come on them suddenly and in force. The ground was alive with them. Armies, legions, were there—not full-grown flying locusts, but young ones, styled foot-gangers, in other words, crawlers, walkers, or hoppers,—and every soul in the establishment had turned out to fight.

Even the modest Bertha was there, defending a breach in the garden wall with a big shawl, dishevelled in dress and hair, flushed in face, bold and resolute in aspect, laying about her with the vigour of an Amazon. The usually phlegmatic Conrad defended another weak point, while his at other times amiable spouse stood near him making fearful and frequent raids upon the foe with the branch of

of a thorn-tree. Hans, like Gulliver among the
Lilliputs, guarded a gate in company with four of
his brothers, and they toiled and moiled like heroes,
while perspiration rolled in streams from their
blazing faces. Elsewhere men and women, boys
and girls—black, brown, and yellow—exerted themselves to the uttermost.

Never was fortress more gallantly defended,
never were ramparts more courageously assailed.
Hundreds, thousands, tens of thousands, were slain
under that garden wall—hundreds of thousands,
millions, hopped over their comrades' backs and continued the assault with unconquerable pluck. The
heroes of ancient Greece and Rome were nothing to
them. Horses, cattle, and sheep were driven in
among them and made to prance wildly, not in the
hope of destroying the foe—as well might you
have attempted to blot out the milky way,—but
for the purpose of stemming the torrent and turning,
if possible, the leading battalions aside from the
garden. They would not turn aside. " On, hoppers,
on—straight on !" was their watchword. " Death or
victory " must have been their motto !

At one spot was a hollow trench or dry ditch
leading towards an outhouse which intervened
between the locusts and the garden. No storming
party was detailed to carry the point. Where the
numbers were so vast as to cover the whole country,

that was needless. They marched in columns, and the columns that chanced to come up to the point voluntarily and promptly undertook the duty. They swarmed into the ditch. Considine and a small Hottentot boy observed the move, and with admirable skill kept the advancing column in check until a fire was kindled in the ditch. It was roused to a pitch of fierce heat that would have satisfied Nebuchadnezzar himself, and was then left, for other points of danger in the walls claimed more vigorous attention. Onward hopped and crawled the enemy and stormed the fire. The leading files were roasted alive, those following tumbled over their dead bodies into the flames. Had the rest wished to take warning by the fate of their comrades —which they did not—they would have found it impossible to escape, for those behind pushed them on. The fire was filled with the dead, overwhelmed by the dying, fairly put out by both, and the victorious army marched over in triumph. Then the outhouse met them, but they scorned to turn aside, although there was a four-foot wall, which one might have supposed more practicable. They walked straight up the outhouse and over it, and were triumphantly descending the other side in myriads before they were discovered and met, with shrieks of vengeance, by Mrs. Marais.

"It's of no use, lads," gasped old Marais, pausing

for a moment to recover breath; "the place is doomed."

"Don't say so, father," cried Hans.—" Come on, boys! we 've nearly stopped them at this gate."

Nearly,—but not quite! A few minutes later and the strength of the garrison began to fail.

"How long—has this—lasted?" asked Considine, pausing for a moment beside Bertha and panting violently.

"Since—breakfast," gasped the exhausted girl; "we—dis—covered them—justafteryou—left us.— See! they come!"

"Hallo! this way, Hans! bring the flags!" shouted Considine, observing the tremendous body of reserves which were following up the success of the stormers of the fire.

It is a curious fact that the waving of flags had been found of more avail on that occasion than most other means. The beating of the enemy with bushes and blankets was no doubt very effective, but it killed, scattered, and confused them, so that they pressed, as it were blindly, on their fate, whereas the flag-waving appeared to touch a cord of intelligence. They saw it, were obviously affected though not killed by it, and showed a tendency to turn aside. It was however only a tendency; soon the advance was resumed in force. The human giants weer beaten—fairly overwhelmed. The wall was scaled and the garden finally entered by countless myriads of this truly formidable though individually contemptible enemy.

Thus are the strong at times confounded by things that are weak!

Had these been flying instead of pedestrian locusts they might, perhaps, have been turned aside by fires, for this is sometimes done. When a farmer sees a cloud of them coming—a cloud, it may be, of three miles in length by half a mile in breadth or more —he kindles fires round his garden and fields, raises a dense smoke, and may sometimes, though not often, succeed in preventing them from alighting. But the younger or jumping locusts, strong in the stupidity of youth, cannot be turned aside thus. Nothing, indeed, but a rushing stream will stop them; even a mighty river, if not rapid, is insufficient. Stagnant pools they cross by drowning the leading multitudes, until a bridge—not "of sighs," but —of death is formed, of size sufficient to carry them over. They even cross the great Orange River thus in places where its flow is calm. In Africa they pass in such countless swarms, both winged and wingless, that their approach is viewed with dismay, for where they rest they devour every green thing, and flocks and herds are left utterly destitute, so that starvation or change of ground is unavoidable. They usually begin their march, or flight, after sunrise, and encamp at sunset—and woe betide the luckless farmer on whose lands they chance to fix their temporary abode !

Locust-swarms are followed by a little bird— named *springhaan-vogel* or locust-bird—which comes in such dense flocks as almost to darken the air. These locust-birds are about the size of a swallow, with numerous speckles like a starling. They live exclusively on locusts—follow them, build their nests, and rear their young in the midst of, and devour, them. But this is by no means the locust's only enemy. Every animal, domestic and wild, destroys and eats him. Cattle, sheep, horses, fowls, dogs, antelopes—all may be seen devouring him with greediness. He even eats himself, the cannibal ! for if any of his comrades get hurt or meet with accidents in travelling, as they often do, the nearest fellow-travellers fall on, kill and devour the unfortunates without delay.

The only human beings who rejoice at sight of the terrible locusts are the Bushmen. These have neither herds, flocks nor crops to lose, and though the wild animals on which they subsist are by these insects driven away, the Bushmen care little, for they delight in fresh locusts, follow them up, feed on them, and preserve quantities by drying them for future use.

Before morning the splendid garden of Conrad Marais was a leafless, fruitless wilderness. Not a scrap of green or gold was left. And his case was by no means singular. The whole colony was more or less visited by this plague at that time, and thus the reviving spirits of the settlers were once again knocked down by a crushing blow.

CHAPTER XVIII.

FAIRS, FIGHTS, FREE-TRADE, FACTIONS, AND OTHER MATTERS.

In the heart of the wild mountain scenery of the frontier a grim-looking fort had been built to keep the Kafirs in check. It was named Fort Wilshire, and a truly warlike place it was, with its high walls and cannon, its red troops of the line, green rifles, and blue artillery. Lying remote from civilised men, it was a dreary enough place to the troops stationed there, though, with that ready spirit of adaptation to circumstances which characterises the British soldier, the garrison dispelled some of its *ennui* by hunting.

At one period of the year, however, the little frontier fortress thoroughly changed its silent and solitary character. The Government, yielding at last to earnest entreaties and strong representations, had agreed to permit, under certain restrictions, the opening of trade with the Kafirs. A periodical "fair" was established and appointed to be held under the guns of Fort Wilshire. The colonial traders, full of energy and thirsting for opportunity, took advantage of the "fair," and assembled in hundreds, while the Kafirs, in a species of unbelieving surprise, met them in thousands to exchange wares. It was a new idea to many of these black sons and daughters of nudity, that the horns which they used to throw away as useless were in reality valuable merchandise, and that the gum, which was to be had for the gathering, could procure for them beads and buttons, and brass-wire and cotton, with many other desirable things that caused their red mouths to water.

On the day in which we introduce the scene to the reader some of the colonial traders had already arrived at the fair. These were not all of the same calibre. Some, of small means, had commenced modestly with a shoulder-bundle and went through the new land, as peddlers and packmen in older lands had done before them. Others, with more means, had set up the horse-pack, or the cart, and all aspired, while some had attained, to the waggon. These penetrated to every part of the frontier, supplying the Dutch boers with luxuries hitherto undreamed of, which, ere long, became necessities, obtaining from them sheep and cattle in exchange, with a fair proportion of their hoarded *rix-daalers*. The traders then returned to the towns, sold their stock, purchased fresh supplies, and went back to the interior. Thus was laid the foundation of a com-

merce which was destined in future years to become of great importance not only to the colony but
to the world.

The opening of trade with the Kafirs had added
materially to the prosperity of the traders, and
those assembled at Fort Wilshire represented all the
different classes.

Among the crowds who encamped under the
fort guns, Stephen Orpin, the Wesleyan, represented
those who stood on the first round of the mercantile
ladder.   Orpin was stout of limb, broad of shoulder,
strong of heart, and empty of pocket; he therefore
carried a pack in which were to be found not only
gloves, neckerchiefs, and trinkets for the women, as
well as gaudy waistcoats, etc., for the men, but New
Testaments, tracts, and little books in the Dutch
language wherewith Stephen hoped to do good to
the souls of his customers.   Orpin had come to
the "fair" with the double view of trading and holding intercourse on spiritual things with the Kafirs.
He longed to preach Christ, the crucified Saviour, to
the heathen.   Of such men, thank God, there always
have been, and we believe always will be, many in
the world—men in regard to whom bigots are apt to
say, "Lord, forbid him, for he followeth not with us,"
but of whom the Lord said, "Forbid him not, for he
that is not against us is on our part."

Among those who had attained to the enviable

ox-waggon were our friends John Skyd and Frank
Dobson. Possessing a remnant of their means when
they gave up farming, two of the brothers, James
and Robert, established a small general store in
Grahamstown, while John and Frank set up a joint
waggon and took to hunting and trading on a large
scale. Of course they bought all their supplies of
brass-wire, beads and buttons, powder and shot, etc.,
from the Skyd store, and sold their ivory, etc., at the
same place, with mutual benefit.

It was a strange and stirring sight to behold the
long files of Kafir women, straight and graceful as
Venus in body, ugly almost as baboons in visage,
coming to the fair from all parts of the land with
enormous loads on their heads of ox-hides, horns,
gum, and elephants' tusks. Threading the narrow
bush-paths in long single files, they came from
hillside and thicket towards the great centre of
attraction. Gradually the crowd thickened. Kafir
chiefs with leopard-skins thrown over their otherwise naked bodies stalked about with an assump-
tion of quiet dignity which they found it difficult
to maintain amid the excitement and temptations of
the fair. Swarthy groups found shelter among the
trees that fringed the Kieskamma below the post—
the women resting after having gladly laid down
their burdens; their lords sitting on their heels with
knob-kerrie in hand, jealously guarding their pro-

perty. The great chief himself was there, laying seignorial taxation on his people, and even condescending to *beg* for the white man's brandy.

"Come with me," said Orpin to a newly made Dutch friend; "I'm told you understand Kafir, and I want you to interpret for me. Will you?"

The Dutchman said "Ja," and went, for Orpin had a persuasive tongue and pleasant manner which induced all sorts of men to aid him. And so they two went down into the bush among the dark-skinned crew, and Stephen preached in their wondering ears the "old old story" of the Cross—a story which is never told entirely in vain, though many a time it does seem as if the effect of it were wofully disproportioned to the efforts of those who go forth bearing the precious seed.

Meanwhile Skyd and Dobson were driving lucrative bargains in another part of the field, speaking wonderful Kafir in the midst of a Babel of Dutch and English that was eminently suggestive of the ancient "tower" itself.

Besides the difficulties of language there were troubles also in reference to trade, for Kafirs, although savage, are fastidious. The men were as particular about their necklaces as any beau could be about the cut of his coat, and the women were at times very hard to please in the matter of turban-covers and kaross back-stripes. But after much haggling the contending parties came to terms, to their mutual benefit and satisfaction.

In another part of the market there seemed to be a tendency to riot. Either bargaining was more hotly carried on there, or spirits of a pugnacious tendency were congregated. Among them was a tall powerful Kafir, who had been evidently treated to a glass of something stronger than water. He was not tipsy, he was only elevated, but the elevation roused his ire to such an extent that he began to boast loudly that he could fight *any* one, and flourished his sticks or kerries in a defiant manner. Kafirs always fight with two sticks, one to hit with, the other to guard.

A trader from the Green Isle chanced to pass this man, and to be jostled by him. Every one knows of the world's opinion of the Irishman's love for fighting. Pat became nettled.

"Arrah!" says he, "yer mighty fond o' swagger, but I'll tache you manners, you black baste! Come on!"

The big Kafir came on at once, and made a blow at Pat's head with his knob-kerrie that would have ended the fight at once if it had taken effect, but the Irishman, well trained in the art, guarded it neatly, and returned with a blow so swift and vigorous that it fell on the pate of the savage like a flail. As well might Pat have hit a rock. If there is a strong point about a black man, it is his head. The Irish-

man knew this, but had forgotten it in the first flush
of combat.   He became wiser.   Meanwhile a crowd
of excited traders and Kafirs gathered round the
combatants and backed them.

The Kafir made another wild swoop at his enemy's
skull, but the blow was easily turned aside.   Pat
returned with a feint at his foe's head, but came
down with terrible force on the inside of his right
knee.   The Kafir dropped his sticks, seized his knee
with both hands, stood on one leg, and howled in
agony.

Scorning to strike a defenceless foe, Paddy gave him
a dab on the end of his already flat nose, by way of
reminding him that he was off his guard.   The Kafir
took the hint, caught up his sticks and sprang at
his opponent with the yell of a hyena, whirling aloft
both sticks at once.   The Irishman had to leap aside,
and, as he did so, drew from the Kafir a shriek of
pain by hitting him sharply on the left shin, adding
to the effect immediately by a whack under the right
eye that might have finished an average ox.   The
Kafir fell, more, however, because of the pain of the
double blow, than because of its force, for he rolled
about bellowing for a few seconds.   Then, jumping
up, he renewed the fight.   There is no saying how
long it might have lasted had not a party of troops
chanced to pass just then, who separated the combatants and dispersed the crowd.

The "fair," however, was made use of not only as an occasion for trading, preaching, and fighting, but for plotting. Chiefs met there in peace, who might otherwise have failed to meet except in battle, and these, with chiefs of banditti from the mountains, and malcontents from all quarters, concocted and hatched designs against the well-being of individuals and of the public at large.

At this time the colonists, besides being troubled by savage thieves, were threatened with disturbance from the intertribal feuds of the savages themselves· One tremendous Zulu monster of the name of Chaka —who excelled Nero himself in cruelty—was driving other tribes of Kafirs down into the colony, and designing chiefs were beginning to think or hope that the opportunity had arrived for carrying out their favourite idea of driving the white man into the sea.

In a dark forest glade, not far from the fort, and within hearing of its bugle-calls, Stephen Orpin walked up and down with one of the malcontents.

"I tell you, Ruyter, it is in vain to join with the Kafirs," said Orpin. "If all the Hottentots in Africa were to unite with them, you would not be strong enough to crush the white man."

"Why not?" demanded the Hottentot angrily, in his broken English; "we be strong as you, and brave."

"But you are not so well armed," said Orpin.

"Fact," returned the freebooter, "but time vill make dat all squaar. Smugglers bring guns to we, an' pooder. Ver' soon be all right."

"Listen, Ruyter, you are like a child. You know nothing. The land from which the white man comes will never suffer him to be driven out of Africa. England is rich in everything, and will send men to fill the places of those who fall. Besides, I think God is on the white man's side, because the white man in the main intends and tries to do good. Just think of the 'fair.' The black man wants beads and brass wire and cotton, and many other things—the white man brings these things from over the sea. On the other hand the white man wants hides, horns, ivory—the black man can supply these things. They meet to exchange, good is done by each to the other. Why should they fight?"

"For revenge," said Ruyter darkly.

"No doubt revenge is sweet to you, but it is sinful," returned Orpin. "Besides, the sweetness does not last long; and will it, let me ask, make the black man happier or the white man more sorrowful in the long-run? You should think of others, not only of yourself, Ruyter."

"Does Jan Smit ever tink of oders—of anybody but hisself?"

"Perhaps not, but Conrad Marais does, and so do

many other men of like mind. God, the Father of all men, is a God of peace, and does not permit His children to gratify feelings of revenge. Jesus, the Saviour of lost man, is the Prince of peace; He will not deliver those who wilfully give way to revenge."

"I no want deliverance," said the robber chief sternly.

"I know that," replied Orpin, "and it was to deliver you from *that* state of mind that Jesus came. Think, Ruyter, think—"

He was interrupted at this point by the sound of an approaching ox-waggon. Ruyter, being a well-known outlaw, did not dare to show himself at the fair, although not a whit worse in any respect than most of the Kafir chiefs who walked openly there unchallenged. He shrank back into the shelter of the jungle while the trader awaited the coming up of the waggon.

"Ah, here you are, Orpin—not kept you waiting long, I hope?" said John Skyd as he followed his waggon into the glade.

"Not long," answered the trader; "but we must make the most of our time now, for the day is far spent."

"It is, but I could not manage to get away sooner. We had to lay in a supply of powder and lead for the hunt, besides many other things. Dobson will be here with the other waggon immediately—he's

not fifty yards behind,—and then we shall start fair
for the elephant-ground. You're quite sure that
you know the way, I suppose?"

"I would not undertake to guide you if I were
not sure."

In a few minutes Dobson came up with the
second waggon, and the whole party set forth on a
hunting expedition into the interior, under the
guidance of Stephen Orpin, who had already
wandered so much about the colony that he was
beginning to be pretty well acquainted with a great
extent of the border line.

About the same time that Skyd and Dobson went
off to the interior another party of hunters and explorers set out on an expedition from the Scottish
settlement of Glen Lynden. But, before touching
on this, we will turn aside to relate an incident
which affected the movements of both parties, and
has reference to a small though not unimportant
personage of our story.

CHAPTER XIX.

DESCRIBES A SERIES OF EARLY RISINGS.

ONE fine morning early, high up among the krantzes and dark jungles of a kloof, or mountain gorge, which branched off from Glen Lynden, a noble specimen of an African savage awoke from his night's repose and stretched himself.

He had spent the night among the lower branches of a mimosa-bush, the opening into which was so small that it was a wonder how his large body could have squeezed through it. Indeed, it would have been quite impossible for him to have gained the shelter of that dark retreat if he had not possessed a lithe supple frame and four powerful legs furnished with tremendous claws.

We should have mentioned, perhaps, that our noble savage was a magnificent leopard—or Cape "tiger."

As he stretched himself he laid back his head, shut his eyes, and yawned, by which act he displayed a

tremendous collection of canines and grinders, with
a pink throat of great capacity. The yawn ended
in a gasp, and then he raised his head and looked
quietly about him, gently patting the ground with
his tail, as a man might pat his bedclothes while
considering what to do next. Not unlike man, he
lay down at full length and tried to go to sleep
again, but it would not do. He had evidently had
his full allowance, and therefore got up and stretched
himself again in a standing position. In this act,
bending his deep chest to the ground, he uttered a
low *gurr* of savage satisfaction, sank his claws into
the soil, and gently tore a number of tough roots
into shreds. Sundry little creatures of various
kinds in the neighbourhood, hearing the *gurr*, presented their tails to the sky and dived into their
little holes with incredible rapidity.

The leopard now shook off dull sloth, and, lashing
his sides in a penitential manner with his tail, glided
through the opening in the mimosa-bush, bounded
into the branches of a neighbouring tree, ran nimbly
out to the end of one of them, and leaping with a
magnificent spring over a gully, alighted softly on
the turf at the other side. Trotting calmly into an
open space, he stopped to take a survey of surrounding nature.

Breakfast now naturally suggested itself. At least
we may suppose so from a certain eager look which

suddenly kindled in the leopard's eye, and a wrink-
ling of his nose as a bird flitted close over his head.
At that moment a species of rabbit, or cony, chanced
to hop round the corner of a rock. The lightning-
flash is not quicker than the spring with which the
Cape-tiger traversed the twenty feet between himself and his prey.

The result was very effectual as regarded the
cony, but it was not much to gurr about in the way
of breakfast. It was a mere whet to the appetite,
which increased the desire for more.

Advancing down the kloof with that stealthy
gliding motion peculiar to the feline race, the leopard
soon came in sight of a fine bushbok, whose sleek
sides drew from him an irrepressible snicker of
delight. But the bushbok was not within spring-
range. He was at the foot of a low precipice.
Creeping to the top of this with great caution the
leopard looked over with a view to estimate distance.
It was yet too far for a spring, so he turned at once
to seek a better way of approach. In doing so he
touched a small stone, which rolled over the krantz,
bounded from crag to cliff, and, carrying several
other stones larger than itself along with it, dashed
itself at the very feet of the bushbok, which wisely
took to its heels and went off like the wind.

Sulky beyond all conception, the leopard continued
to descend the kloof until he reached a narrow pass

from which were visible not far off the abodes of
men. Here he paused and couched in quiet contemplation.

Now there was another early waking on that fine
morning, though not quite so early as the one just
described. Master Junkie Brook, lying in a packing-
box, which served as an extempore crib, in the
cottage of Kenneth M'Tavish, opened his large
round eyes and rubbed them. Getting up, he
observed that Mrs. Scholtz was sound asleep, and
quietly dressed himself. He was a precocious child,
and had learned to dress without assistance. The
lesson was more easily learned than beings living
in civilised lands might suppose, owing to the fact
that he had only two garments—a large leather
jacket and a pair of leather trousers, one huge but-
ton in front and one behind holding the latter
securely to the former. A pair of velschoen and a
fur cap completed a costume which had been
manufactured by the joint efforts of his mother and
sister and Mrs. Scholtz. The husband of the last,
on seeing it for the first time, remarked that it "vas
more like zee garb of a man of dirty zan a boy of
dree." The garb had been made of such tough
material that it seemed impossible to wear it out,
and of such an extremely easy fit that although the
child had now lived in it upwards of two years there
were not more than six patches on it anywhere.

How Junkie got to the Baviaans River may perhaps perplex the reader. It is easily explained. Hans had invited all or any of the Brook family to visit his father's farm on the karroo. Gertie catching a cold, or in some other way becoming feeble, wanted a change of air. Her father, recalling the invitation, and happening to know that Hans was in Grahamstown at the time, drove her over with Mrs. Scholtz and Junkie to make the thing proper, and offered a visit of all three. You may be sure Hans did not refuse to take them to his home in his new cart. After spending some time there Mrs. Scholtz took a fancy that she would like to go with Hans on one of his frequent excursions to Glen Lynden, but she would not leave Junkie behind. Hans objected to Junkie at first, but finally gave in, and thus the little hero found his way to the River of Baboons.

When dressed—which was soon done, as he omitted washing—Junkie began to consider what he had best do. Mischief, of course, but of what sort? That was the question.

His room was on the ground floor, and had a lattice window which opened like a door into the back premises. He pushed the window and found that it opened. What a chance! Mrs. Scholtz was still asleep, and snoring. Absence without leave was his chief delight. In two minutes he was

deep in the jungle, panting.   Knowing from long
and bitter experience that he would be pursued by
the inveterate Mrs. Scholtz, the urchin ran up the
kloof, bent on placing the greatest possible space
between him and his natural enemy in the shortest
possible time.   In this way he was not long of
drawing near to the leopard's point of observation.

No doubt that keen-sighted animal would quickly
have observed the child, if its attention had not at
the moment been attracted by other and equally
mischievous game.   A troop of baboons came down
the kloof to pilfer the white man's fruit and vegetables.   They had evidently risen late for breakfast,
and were in a hurry to reach their breakfast parlour
before the white man should awake.   There were a
dozen or so of females, several huge males, and quite
a crowd of children of various ages, besides one or
two infants clinging to their mothers' waists.

It was pitiful to see the sad anxious faces of these
infants.   Perhaps they knew their parents' errand
and disapproved of it.   More probably they felt their
own weakness of frame, and dreaded the shocks sus-
tained when their heedless ·mothers bounded from
rock or stump like balls of india-rubber.   They were
extremely careless mothers.   Even Junkie, as he
stood paralysed with terror and surprise, could not
avoid seeing that.   The troop was led by a great
blue-faced old-man baboon with a remarkably satur-

nine expression. On reaching the top of the rock which the leopard had just vacated the old man called a halt. The others came tumbling awkwardly towards him on all-fours, with the exception of several of the youngsters, who loitered behind to play. One of these, a very small bad little boy-baboon, deliberately turned aside to explore on his own account. He came down near to the foot of the rock where the leopard had concealed himself. Catching sight of his glaring enemy, the bad boy uttered a terrified squawk. Instantly all the males, headed by the old man, rushed to the rescue. Powerful though he was, the leopard was cowardly at heart. A large troop of baboons had some time ago made mince-meat of his own grandmother. Remembering this, he sloped under a bank, glided round a corner of the cliff, bounded over a bush, and sought refuge in a thicket.

It was at this moment, while in the act of bounding, that he caught sight of Junkie, but being confused at the moment, and ashamed of having been twice foiled, he slunk away with his tail between his legs and concealed himself among the branches of an old gnarled and favourite tree.

The bad boy-baboon was the only one who had seen the leopard, the old males therefore had to content themselves with a few fierce looks round in all directions, and several defiant roars. Born and bred in the midst of alarms, however, they were soon composed enough to resume their descent on the white man's stores—to the great relief of the petrified Junkie, of whom in their alarm they took no notice, regarding him, possibly, as a badly executed statue of a baboon.

Junkie quickly recovered himself, and, seeing the baboons descend the kloof, thought it safer, as well as more in accord with his original plans, to ascend.

Gladly, hopefully, did the leopard observe his decision and watch his progress. To him the tide of fortune seemed to have taken a favourable turn, for Junkie, in the innocence of his heart, made straight for the gnarled tree.

But one of the many slips so often quoted with reference to cups and lips was at this time impending over the unfortunate leopard.

There was yet one other early riser that morning—namely Booby the Bushman. In pursuance of his calling, that ill-used and misguided son of the soil arose about daybreak with much of his native soil sticking to his person, and, with a few other desperadoes like himself, made a descent on Glen Lynden—not, by any means, the first that his fraternity had made. Not so bloodthirsty as the leopard, quite as mischievous as Junkie, and much more cunning than the baboons, Booby chanced to arrive at the gorge already mentioned just at the time when Junkie

A "CAPE TIGER" SIGHTS BREAKFAST.—Page 274.

was approaching it. There was, if you will, somewhat of a coincidence here in regard to time, but
there was no coincidence in the fact of such characters selecting the same route, because whoever
passed up or down that kloof must needs go by
the gorge.

Slowly Junkie picked his way up the rugged
path towards the gnarled tree. The leopard, scarcely
believing in his good luck, licked his lips. Rapidly
the Bushman and his men descended the same path.
They rode on horses—stolen horses, of course. The
leopard heard the clatter of hoofs and looked back.
Junkie drew nearer to the gnarled tree; the leopard
looked forward. Never was savage beast more
thoroughly perplexed. Anxiety glared in his eyes;
exasperation grinned in his teeth; indecision quivered in the muscles of his tail. Just at that
moment Booby caught sight of his spotted skin.
Had the leopard been less perturbed he would have
been too wise to allow his carcass to appear. A
poisoned arrow instantly quivered in his flank. It
acted like a spur; with an angry growl and a clear
bound of no one knows how many feet, he re-entered
the jungle and fled to the mountains.

Petrified again, Junkie remained motionless till
the Bushmen robbers rode up. Booby knew that
his leopard was safe, for a poisoned arrow is sure to
kill in time, so he did not care to hasten after it

just then, but preferred to continue his approach to the white man's habitations. Great, then, was his amazement when he all but rode over Junkie.

Amazement was quickly succeeded by alarm. His knowledge of the white man's ways and habits told him at once the state of affairs. The appearance of Junkie in the company of "tigers" and baboons, was, he knew well, a mere juvenile indiscretion. He also knew that parental instincts among white men were keèn, and thence concluded that discovery and pursuit would be immediate. His own plans were therefore not only defeated, but his own safety much endangered, as his presence was sure to be discovered by his tracks. "Let's be off instanter," was the substance of Booby's communication to his brethren. The brethren agreed, but Booby had lived among white men, and although his own particular master was a scoundrel, there were those of his household—especially among the females—who had taught him something of Christian pity. He could not leave the child to the tender mercies of wild beasts. He did not dare to convey him back to the cottage of Kenneth M'Tavish. What was he to do? Delay might be death! In these circumstances he seized the horrified Junkie by the arm, swung him on the pommel of his saddle, and galloped away up the kloof and over the mountains into the deepest recesses of Kafirland

When Mrs. Scholtz awoke that morning, rubbed her eyes, looked up and discovered that Junkie's crib was empty, she sprang from her bed, perceived the open lattice, and gave vent to an awful scream. In barbarous times and regions a shriek is never uttered in vain. The M'Tavish household was instantly in the room, some of them in deshabille— some armed—all alarmed.

"Oh my!—oh me!" cried Mrs. Scholtz, leaping back into bed with unfeminine haste, "he's gone!"

"Who's gone?" asked M'Tavish.

"Junkie!"

"What! where? when? how? why?" said Mrs. M'Tavish, Jessie, and others.

Mrs. Scholtz gasped and pointed to the lattice; at the same time she grasped her garments as a broad hint to the men. They took it hastily.

"Come, boys, search about, and one of you saddle up. Go, call Groot Willem," was the master's prompt order as he turned and left the room.

Six Hottentots, a Bushman, and a Bechuana boy obeyed, but those who searched sought in vain. Yet not altogether in vain—they found Junkie's "spoor," and traced it into the jungle. While two followed it, the others returned and "saddled up" the horses. Groot Willem chanced to be on a visit to the Highlanders at the time.

"What a pity," he said, coming out of his room

and stretching himself (it was quite an impressive sight to see such a giant stretch himself!), "that the hunters **are off.**   They might have helped us."

The giant spoke with good-humoured sarcasm, believing that the urchin would assuredly be found somewhere about the premises, and he referred to the departure of an exploring and hunting party under George Rennie, which had left Glen Lynden the previous day for the interior

But when Groot Willem with his companions had ridden a considerable way up the kloof, and found Junkie's spoor mingling with that of baboons, he became earnest.   When he came to the gnarled tree and discovered that it was joined by that of horses and Cape tigers, he became alarmed.

A diligent examination was made.   Drops of blood were found on the ground.   The leopard itself was ultimately discovered stone dead in a thicket with the poisoned arrow in its side, the horse-spoor was followed up a long way, and then it was pretty clearly seen that the child had been carried off by marauders of some sort.

Of course a thorough search was made and pursuit was immediately instituted. Groot Willem and M'Tavish pushed on promptly to follow the spoor, while men were sent back to the glen for a supply of ammunition, etc., in case of a prolonged search becoming necessary.

The search was ably planned and vigorously carried out , but all in vain. Junkie had departed *that* life as thoroughly as if he had never been, and Mrs. Scholtz remained at Glen Lynden the very personification of despair.

We shall now turn to the exploring party which had left the Baviaans River on the previous day.

About this time the rumours of war among the natives of the vast and almost unknown interior of the land had become unusually alarming. A wandering and warlike horde named the Fetcani had been for some time past driving all the other tribes before them, and were said at last to be approaching the Winterberg frontier of the colony. In order to ascertain what foundation there was for these reports, as well as to explore the land, the party under Rennie was sent out. Among those who formed this party were Charlie Considine, Hans Marais, Sandy Black and his satellite Jerry Goldboy, Andrew Rivers, Diederik and Christian Muller, and the tall black-bearded hunter Lucas Van Dyk, besides Slinger, Dikkop, and other Hottentots and Bushmen.

"This is what I call real enjoyment," said Considine, as he rode with Hans, somewhat in advance of the cavalcade ;—"splendid weather, magnificent scenery, lots of game big and little, good health and freedom. What more could a man wish ?"

"Ja," said Hans quietly; "you have reason to be thankful—yet there is more to wish for."

"What more?" asked Considine.

"That the whole world were as happy as yourself," said Hans, looking full at his friend with a bland smile.

"And so I *do* wish that," returned Considine with enthusiasm.

"Do you?" asked Hans, with a look of surprise.

"Of course I do; why do you doubt it?" asked his friend, with a perplexed look.

Hans did not reply, but continued to gaze at the mountain-range towards which the party was riding.

And, truly, it was a prospect which might well absorb the attention and admiration of men less capable of being affected by the beauties of nature than Hans Marais.

They were passing through a verdant glen at the foot of the mountains, the air of which was perfumed with wild flowers, and filled with the garrulous music of parroquets and monkeys. In front lay the grand range of the Winterberg, with its coronet of rocks, its frowning steeps, its grassy slopes, and its skirts feathered over with straggling forest,—all bathed in the rich warm glow of an African sunset.

"You have not answered me, Hans," said Considine, after a pause. "Why do you think I am indifferent to the world's happiness?"

"Because," replied the other, with an expression unusually serious on his countenance, "I do not see that you make any effort—beyond being good-natured and amiable, which you cannot help—to make the world better."

Considine looked at his friend with surprise, and replied, with a laugh—

"Why, Hans, you are displaying a new phase of character. Your remark is undoubtedly true—so true indeed that, although I object to that common-place retort,—'You're another,'—I cannot help pointing out that it applies equally to yourself."

"It is just because it applies equally to myself that I make it," rejoined Hans, with unaltered gravity. "You and I profess to be Christians, we both think that we are guided by Christian prin-ciples—and doubtless, to some extent, we are—but what have we done for the cause that we call 'good,' that *is* good? I speak for myself at all events—I have hitherto done nothing, absolutely nothing."

"My dear fellow," said Considine, with a sudden burst of candour, "I believe you are right, and I plead guilty; but then what *can* we do? We are not clergymen."

"Stephen Orpin is not a clergyman, yet see what *he* does. It was seeing what that man does, and how he lives, that first set me a-thinking on this subject. He attends to his ordinary calling quite as

well as any man of my acquaintance, and I'll e
bound makes a good thing of it, but any man w
half an eye can see that he makes it subservient
the great work of serving the Saviour, whom yo
and I profess to love. I have seen him suffer los:
rather than work on the Lord's day. More than
once I've seen him gain discredit for his so-called
fanaticism. He is an earnest man, eagerly seeking
an end which is *outside* himself, therefore he is a
happy man. To be eager in pursuit, is to be in a
great degree happy, even when the pursuit is a
trifling one ; if it be a great and good one, the result
must be greater happiness ; if the pursuit has reference to things beyond this life, and ultimate success
is hoped for in the next, it seems to me that *lasting*
as well as *highest* happiness may thus be attained.
Love of self, Charlie, is *not* a bad motive, as some
folk would falsely teach us. The Almighty put love
of self within us. It is only when love of self is a
superlative affection that it is sinful, because idola-
trous. When it is said that 'love is the fulfilling of
the law,' it is not love to God merely that is meant, I
think, but love to Him supremely, and to all created
things as well, self included, because if you can
conceive of this passion being our motive power, and
fairly balanced in our breasts—God and all created
beings and things occupying their right relative
positions,—self, although dethroned, would not be

ɜd. Depend on it, Charlie, there is something
.g *here*."

ʌhe young Dutchman smote himself heavily on
broad chest, and looked at his friend for a reply.
What that reply was we need not pause to say.
These two young men ever since their first acquaintance had regarded each other with feelings akin
to those of David and Jonathan, but they had not
up to this time opened to each other those inner
chambers of the soul, where the secret springs of life
keep working continually in the dark, whether we
regard them or not—working oftentimes harshly for
want of the oil of human intercourse and sympathy.
The floodgates were now opened, and the two friends
began to discourse on things pertaining to the soul
and the Saviour and the world to come, whereby they
found that their appreciation and enjoyment of the
good things even of this life was increased considerably. Subsequently they discovered the explanation
of this increased power of enjoyment, in that
Word which throws light on all things, where it
is written that "godliness is profitable for the life
that now is, as well as that which is to come."

CHAPTER XX.

TREATS OF THE DELIGHTS, DANGERS, AND DISTRESSES OF THE
WILDERNESS.

"AFAR in the desert,"—far beyond the frontier
settlements of the colony, far from the influences of
civilisation, in the home of the wild beast and the
savage, the explorers now ride under the blaze of the
noontide sun.

They had passed over mountain and dale into the
burning plains of the karroo, and for many hours
had travelled without water or shelter from the
scorching heat. Lucas Van Dyk, who guided them,
said he knew where water was to be got, but there
was no possibility of reaching it before evening.
This announcement was received in silence, for not
a drop of the life-giving fluid had passed the lips of
man or beast since an early hour on the previous
day, and their powers of endurance were being tried
severely. The insupportable heat not only increased
the thirst, but rendered the hunters less able to bear
it. All round them the air quivered with the radia-

tion from the glaring sand, and occasionally the *mirage* appeared with its delicious prospects of relief, but as the Dutchmen knew the ground well, none were deceived by it, though all were tantalised. Compressing their lips, and urging their wearied cattle to the utmost, they pushed steadily on, no sound breaking the stillness of the desert save the creak of a waggon-wheel or the groan of an exhausted animal.

At last Charlie Considine sought to relieve his feelings by conversation :—

"This is one of the unpleasant experiences of African travel."

Hans Marais, to whom the remark was made, replied "Ja," but as he added nothing more, and looked stern, Charlie relapsed into silence.

Ere long one of the weaker oxen fell. The party halted a few minutes, while the Hottentot drivers plied their cruel whips unmercifully, but in vain. One more merciful than the drivers was there—death came to release the poor animal. Immediately, as if by magic, vultures appeared in the burning sky. From the far-off horizon they came sailing by twos and threes, as if some invisible messenger, like death himself, had gone with lightning-speed to tell that a banquet awaited them.

No time was wasted ; a brief word from the leader sufficed. The dying ox was released from the yoke that had galled it so long, and the party proceeded. Before they were a mile off the ox was dead, its eyes were out, its carcass torn open, and the obscene birds were gorging themselves. Before night it was an empty skeleton covered with a dried hide! Not many hours would suffice to remove the hide and leave only the bleaching bones. Such remains are familiar objects on South African roadsides.

That evening, according to their leader's prophecy, water was reached. It was a thick muddy pool, but it sufficed to relieve them all, and a night of comparative comfort followed a day of suffering.

Next morning, just after breakfast, a herd of springboks was observed, and several of the more eager of the party dashed off in pursuit. Among these was Considine, Hans, Andrew Rivers, and Jerry Goldboy. The two last were always first in the mad pursuit of game, and caused their placid Dutch friends no little anxiety by the scrapes they frequently ran themselves into.

"Follow them, they'll get lost," said Van Dyk to a group of Hottentots.

Two of these, Slinger and Dikkop, obeyed the order.

The antelopes were on a distant sandhill in the plain. There were two groups of them. Rivers and Jerry made for one of these. Becoming suddenly imbued with an idea worthy of a hunter.

Jerry diverged to the right, intending to allow his companion to start the game, while he should lie in wait for it under the shelter of a bush. Unfortunately the game took the opposite direction when started, so that Jerry was thrown entirely out. As it chanced, however, this did not matter much, for Jerry's horse, becoming unmanageable, took to its heels and dashed away wildly over the plain, followed by Dikkop the Hottentot.

"Mind the ant-bear holes!" shouted Dikkop, but as he shouted in Dutch Jerry did not understand him, and devoted himself to vain endeavours to restrain the horse. At first the animal looked after itself and avoided the holes referred to, but as Jerry kept tugging furiously at the reins it became reckless, and finally put a fore-leg into a hole. Instantly it rolled over, and the hunter flew off its back, turning a complete somersault in the air.

A low shrub grows in the karroo, called the ill-tempered thorn. It resembles a mass of miniature porcupine quills, an inch or two in length, planted as thickly as possible together, with the needle-points up and bristling. On one of these shrubs poor Jerry alighted!

"Oh! 'eavens, this *is* hagony!" he groaned, jumping up and stamping, while Dikkop almost fell off his horse with laughing.

To hide his mirth he bolted off in pursuit of

Jerry's charger, which he soon caught and brought back, looking supernaturally grave.

"We will rejoin the 'unters, Dikkop," said Jerry, in the tone of a man who endeavours to conceal his sufferings.

"Ja, Mynheer," said Dikkop.

Whatever Jerry Goldboy might have said, that Hottentot would have replied "Ja, Mynheer," for he understood not a word of English.

Jerry mounted with an ill-suppressed groan and rode back to the party, leaning very much forward in the saddle, while Dikkop followed, showing the white teeth in his dirty black visage from ear to ear.

Rivers soon afterwards returned with a springbok behind him, but there was no appearance of Considine or Hans. As, however, the latter was known to be an experienced traveller, no anxiety was felt for them, and the main party proceeded on its way. When night came they found that a well, on which they had counted, was dried up, and were therefore obliged to lie down without water. Several shots were fired after dark to guide the absent ones, but no reply was made. Still, those in camp felt no anxiety, knowing that Hans was quite able to take care of himself.

And so he was, truly, but he could not take care of a hot-headed youth who was as eager as Jerry in the chase, and much more daring.

At first he and Considine ran together after the springboks ; then Hans got near enough, dismounted, and shot one. While he was busy fastening the carcass on his horse, Considine continued to pursue the others ; going at full speed, he was soon far away on the horizon. Still Hans would have been able to see him if he had not got among some scattered groups of mimosa-bushes, which were sufficiently large to conceal him. When he remounted and looked around, his friend was not to be seen. He saw a few springboks, however, racing on the horizon in the direction in which Considine had galloped and concluded somewhat hastily that they were pursued by his friend. Away he went, therefore, but soon discovered that he was mistaken. He turned then, and rode quickly back, blaming himself for not having followed the footprints of his friend's horse. This he now did, and at last came up with him, but at so late an hour, and at such a distance from the line of march, that a bivouac in the plain was inevitable.

"Oh, Hans," he said, "I'm so glad you've found me! I had no idea that one could get so easily lost in an open plain."

"You've had enough experience too, one would think, to have remembered the vastness of the karroo," said Hans, dismounting and making the fastenings of the· springbok more secure. "A man soon

T

dwindles to the size of a crow in plains like this, when you gallop away from him. Men not accus- tomed to them misjudge distances and sizes in a wonderful way. I remember once being out hunt- ing with a fellow who mistook a waggon for a spring- bok!—But come, mount; we must ride on to a better camping-place than this, and be content to sleep without blankets to-night."

"I hope the camping-place is not far off, for I'm parched with thirst," said Considine, mounting and following at a smart gallop.

"I'm sorry for you," returned Hans, "for you'll see no water this night. To-morrow we'll start early and get to the waggons by breakfast-time."

This was depressing news to Considine, for the heat of the day and exertions of the chase had, as he expressed it, almost dried him up. There was nothing for it, however, but patience.

About sunset they came to a place where were some old deserted huts. In one of these they resolved to pass the night, though, from certain holes in the side, it was evidently used at times as an abode by beasts of prey. Having flint and steel, they made a fire, and while thus engaged were serenaded by the distant and dolorous howls of a hyena and the inharmonious jabberings of a jackal.

"Pleasant company!" observed Considine as he roasted a steak over the fire.

" Ja," replied Hans, who being a more expert cook was already busy with a rib.

The melancholy hoot of an owl seemed to indicate that the animal kingdom agreed with the sentiment, and the young men laughed. They were not, however, disposed to talk much. After a silent supper they lay down and slept soundly, quite oblivious of the prowlers of the night, who came, more than once, near to the door of the hut.

It was late next day when they awoke. Hans likewise missed his way, and though he afterwards discovered his mistake, they found it impossible to regain the track of their companions before sunset. All that day they were compelled to travel without tasting a drop of water, and their poor horses became so fatigued as to be scarcely equal to more than a walking pace. As Hans knew that water was not far off, he pushed on after sunset, so as to have the shorter distance to travel to it in the morning.

" It is very tantalising," he said, drawing rein when the darkness of the night rendered travelling almost impossible, " to know that our friends cannot be far off, and yet be unable to reach them."

" Hadn't we better fire a shot ?" asked Considine.

" Not of much use, I fear, but there can be no harm in trying."

The shot was fired and was instantly replied to by a tremendous roar from a lion, apparently close to where they stood. No wood was near them to make a fire, nothing but tufts of grass; they therefore pushed on towards a range of dark mountains as fast as their jaded steeds would go.

"Halt a moment," said Hans in a low voice.

They stopped and listened. The approach of the lion in rear was distinctly heard.

"We cannot escape from him, Charlie," said Hans, as they again urged their horses onward, "and in the dark we cannot take aim at him. Our only chance is to reach yonder pass or glen that looms like a black cleft in the hills, and clamber up some precipice, whence we can pelt him with stones."

He spoke in quick, earnest tones. They soon entered the gorge and were greeted by the grunt of a baboon and the squalling of its young ones, which helped to increase the savage aspect of the towering cliffs on either side. They had not proceeded far when the lion gave another tremendous roar, which, echoing from cliff to cliff, gave the luckless hunters the feeling of having got into the very heart of a lion's den. No suitable place to scramble up being found, they pushed madly on over a track of sand and bushes, expecting every instant to see the monster bound upon them. But the defile was shorter than Hans had supposed. On issuing from it they were cheered by the moon rising bright in the east, and found that their enemy had ceased to follow them at that point. Still, though weary, and with their tongues cleaving to the roofs of their mouths, they continued their march for several hours, and lying down at last, they scarcely knew how or where, they went to sleep with a prayer for protection and deliverance on their parched lips.

The weary wanderers passed that night in a very paradise, bathing in cool streams and slaking their thirst nearly, but never *quite*, to the full. There was always a peculiar desire to drink again, and, even then, to wish for more! Heavenly music, too, sounded in their ears, and the sweet shade of green trees sheltered them.

It was daybreak when they were roused from these delights by a hyena's howl, and awoke to find that they were speechless with thirst, their eyes inflamed, and their whole frames burning.

Saddling the horses at once they rode forward, and in a couple of hours reached a hill near the top of which there was a projecting rock.

"Don't let me raise your hopes too high," said Hans, pointing to the rock, " but it is just possible that we may find water *there*."

" God grant it !" said Considine.

"Your horse is fresher than mine," said Hans, " and you are lighter than I am—go first. If

there is water, hail me—if not, I will wait your
return."

With a nod of assent the youth pushed forward,
gained the rock, and found the place, where
water had once been, a dry hole!

For a few minutes he stood gazing languidly on
the plain beyond the ridge. Despair had almost
taken possession of his breast, when his eye suddenly
brightened. He observed objects moving far away
on the plain. With bated breath he stooped and
shaded his eyes with his hand. Yes, there could be
no doubt about it—a party of horsemen and bullock-
waggons! He tried to cheer, but his dry throat
refused to act. Turning quickly, he began to descend
the hillside, and chanced to cough as he went along.
Instantly he was surrounded by almost a hundred
baboons, some of gigantic size, which came fearlessly
towards him. They grunted, grinned, and sprang
from stone to stone, protruding their mouths and
drawing back the skin of their foreheads, threatening
an instant attack. Considine's gun was loaded, but
he had lived long enough in those regions to be fully
aware of the danger of wounding one of these
creatures in such circumstances. Had he done so
he would probably have been torn to pieces in five
minutes. He therefore kept them off with the
muzzle of his gun as he continued the descent.
Some of them came so near as to touch his hat while

passing projecting rocks. At last he reached the plain, where the baboons stopped and appeared to hold a noisy council as to whether they should make a great assault or not. He turned and levelled his gun.

"Come," thought he at that moment, "don't do it, Charlie. You have escaped. Be thankful, and leave the poor brutes alone."

Obeying the orders of his conscience, he re-shouldered his gun and returned to his friend, whom he found reclining under a low bush, and informed him of what he had seen. The young Dutchman jumped up at once, and, mounting, rode round a spur of the hill and out upon the plain. In an hour they had overtaken their comrades, but great was their dismay on finding that they had long ago consumed every drop of water, and that they were suffering from thirst quite as much as themselves.

"Never mind," said Lucas Van Dyk; "let me comfort you with the assurance that we shall certainly reach water in a few hours."

The hunter was right. Some hours before sunset the oxen and horses quickened their pace of their own accord—sure sign that they had scented water from afar. Shortly after, they came in sight of a stream. The excitement of all increased as they pushed forward. They broke into a wild run on nearing the stream; and then followed a scene

which is almost indescribable. The oxen were cast
loose, the riders leaped to the ground, and the whole
party, men, oxen, and horses, ran in a promiscuous
heap into the water.

"Wow, man, Jerry, hae a care; ee'll be squizzen
atween the beasts," said Sandy Black, as the active
Jerry passed him in the race.

The Scot's warning was not without reason, for
next moment Jerry was up to the knees in the
stream between two oxen, who, closing on each other,
almost burst him. Easing off, they let him drop on
hands and knees, and he remained in that position
drinking thankfully. The whole place was quickly
stirred up into a muddy compound like pea-soup,
but neither man nor beast was particular. They
struggled forward and fell on their knees—not inappropriately—to drink. One man was pushed down
by an ox, but seemed pleased with the refreshing coolness of his position, and remained where he was
drinking. Another in his haste tumbled over the
edge of the bank and rolled down, preceded by an
impatient horse, which had tripped over him. Both
gathered themselves up, somehow, with their lips
in the water,—and drank! Young Rivers, happening to gain the stream at a point where oxen and
horses were wedged together tightly, tried to force
in between them, but, failing in this, he stooped to
crawl in below them. At that moment Slinger the

"Tottie" gave a yell in Dutch, and said that a horse was trampling on him; whom Dikkop consoled by saying that *he* was fast in the mud—and so he was, but not too fast to prevent drinking. Meanwhile the Dutchmen and the knowing ones of the party restrained themselves and sought for better positions where the water was clearer. There they, likewise, bent their tall heads and suggested—though they did not sing—the couplet :—

"Oh that a Dutchman's draught might be
As deep as the ro-o-o-ling Zuyder-Zee !"

The limit of drinking was capacity. Each man and beast drank as much as he, or it, could hold, and then unwillingly left the stream, covered with mud and dripping wet! Oh, it was a delicious refreshment, which some thought fully repaid them for the toil and suffering they had previously undergone. The aspect of the whole band may be described in the language of Sandy Black, who, beholding his friends after the fray, remarked that they were all "dirty and drookit."

CHAPTER XXI.

TREATS OF MATTERS TOO NUMEROUS AND STIRRING TO BE BRIEFLY
REFERRED TO.

Soon after this the explorers passed beyond the
level country, and their sufferings were for the time
relieved. The region through which they then passed
was varied—hilly, wooded, and beautiful, and, to
crown all, water was plentiful. Large game was
also abundant, and one day the footprints of elephants were discovered.

To some of the party that day was one of deepest
interest and excitement.

Charlie Considine, who was, as we have said, an
adept with the pencil, longed to sit down and sketch
the lordly elephant in his native haunts. Andrew
Rivers and Jerry Goldboy wanted to shoot him, so
did George Rennie and the Mullers and Lucas Van
Dyk. More moderate souls, like Sandy Black, said
they would be satisfied merely to *see* him, while
Slinger and Dikkop, with their brethren, declared
that they wanted to *eat* him

At last they came in sight of him! It was a little after mid-day. They were traversing at the time a jungle so dense that it would have been impassable but for a Kafir-path which had been kept open by wild animals. The hunters had already seen herds of quaggas, and buffaloes, and some of the larger sorts of antelopes, also one rhinoceros, but not yet elephants. Now, to their joy, the giant tracks of these monsters were discovered. Near the river, in swampy places, it was evident that some of them had been rolling luxuriously in the ooze and mud. But it was in the forests and jungles that they had left the most striking marks of their habits and mighty power, for there thorny brakes of the most impenetrable character had been trodden flat by them, and trees had been overturned. In traversing such places the great bull-elephant always marches in the van, bursting through everything by sheer force and weight, breaking off huge limbs of the larger trees with his proboscis when these obstruct his path, and overturning the smaller ones bodily, while the females and younger members of the family follow in his wake.

A little further on they came to a piece of open ground where the elephants had torn up a number of mimosa-trees and inverted them so that they might the more easily browse on the juicy roots. It was evident from appearances that the animals had used their tusks as crowbars, inserting them under the roots to loosen their hold of the earth, and it was equally clear that, like other and higher creatures, they sometimes attempted what was beyond their strength, for some of the larger trees had resisted their utmost efforts.

As these signs multiplied the hunters proceeded with increased vigilance and caution, each exhibiting the peculiarity of his character, more or less, by his look and actions. The Mullers, Van Dyk, Rennie, Hans, and other experienced men, rode along, calmly watchful, yet not so much absorbed as to prevent a humorous glance and a smile at the conduct of their less experienced comrades. Considine and Rivers showed that their spirits were deeply stirred, by the flash of their ever-roving eyes, the tight compression of their lips, the flush on their brows, and the position of readiness in which they carried their guns—elephant-guns, by the way, lent them by their Dutch friends for the occasion. Sandy Black rode with a cool, sober, sedate air, looking interested and attentive, but with that peculiar twinkle of the eyes and slightly sarcastic droop at the corners of the mouth which is often characteristic of the sceptical Scotsman. On the other hand, Jerry Goldboy went along blazing with excitement, while every now and then he uttered a suppressed exclamation, and clapped the blunderbuss to his shoulder when anything moved, or seemed to move, in the jungle.

Jerry had flatly refused to exchange his artillery for any other weapon, and having learned that small shot was useless against elephants, he had charged it with five or six large pebbles—such as David might have used in the slaying of Goliath. Mixed with these was a sprinkling of large nails, and one or two odd buttons. He was a source of constant and justifiable alarm to his friends, who usually compelled him either to ride in front, with the blunderbuss pointing forward, or in the rear, with its muzzle pointing backward.

"There go your friends at last, Jerry," said Van Dyk, curling his black moustache, with a smile, as the party emerged from a woody defile into a wide valley.

"What? where? eh! in which direction? point 'em out quick!" cried Jerry, cocking the blunderbuss violently and wheeling his steed round with such force that his haunch hit Sandy Black's leg pretty severely.

"Hoot, ye loupin' eedyit!" growled the Scot, somewhat nettled.

Jerry subdued himself with a violent effort, while the experienced hunters pointed out the elephants, and consulted as to the best plan of procedure.

There were fifty at least of the magnificent animals

scattered in groups over the bottom and sides of a valley about three miles in extent; some were browsing on the succulent spekboom, of which they are very fond. Others were digging up and feeding among the young mimosa-thorns and evergreens. The place where the hunters stood was not suitable for an attack. It was therefore resolved to move round to a better position. As they advanced some of the groups of elephants came more distinctly into view, but they seemed either not to observe or to disregard the intruders.

"Why not go at 'em at once?" asked young Rivers in an impatient whisper.

"Because we don't want to be killed," was the laconic reply from Diederik Muller.

"Don't you see," explained Van Dyk, with one of his quiet smiles, "that the ground where the nearest fellows stand is not suitable for horsemen?"

"Well, I don't see exactly, but I'll take your word for it."

While they were speaking, and riding through a meadow thickly studded over with clumps of tall evergreens, Considine observed something moving over the top of a bush close ahead of him.

"Look out there!" he exclaimed, but those in advance had already turned the corner of a bush, and found themselves within a hundred paces of a huge male elephant.

Jerry at once pointed the blunderbuss and shut his eyes, and would infallibly have pulled the trigger, if Sandy Black, who had in some measure become his keeper, had not seized his wrist and wrenched the weapon from his grasp.

" Man, ye 'll be the death o' somebody yet," he said in a low stern tone.

Jerry at once became penitent, and on giving a solemn promise that he would not fire till he obtained permission, received his weapon back.

" Een groot gruwzaam karl," whispered one of the Hottentots, in broken Dutch.

" My certie, but he *is* a great gruesome carl !" said Black, echoing in Scotch the Dutchman's expression as he gazed in admiration.

" He 's fourteen feet high if he 's an inch," observed George Rennie.

The scent and hearing of the elephant are both keen, but his sight is not very good. As the wind chanced to blow from him to the hunters he had not perceived them. This was fortunate, for it would have been highly dangerous to have attacked him in such ground. They wheeled round therefore and galloped away towards some scattered rocks, whence they could better approach him on foot. Dismounting, the leaders formed a hasty plan of operations, and immediately proceeded to put it in execution.

It may have been that their explanation of the plan was not lucid, or that Jerry Goldboy's head was not clear, but certain it is that after having been carefully told what to do, he dashed into the jungle after Sandy Black and did what seemed right in his own eyes.

Black kept close to the heels of Hans Marais, and so did Considine, but Jerry soon began to pant with excitement; then he stumbled and fell. Before recovering himself from a "wait-a-bit" thorn he had been left out of sight behind. He pushed valiantly on however and came to a small open plain, where he looked anxiously round, but his comrades were nowhere to be seen. Just then a shot was fired, it was followed quickly by another, and then was heard, above the shouting of excited Hottentots, the shrill screaming of wounded and enraged elephants. Jerry heard the tremendous sounds for the first time, and quaked in his spinal marrow.

Observing the smoke of a shot on the opposite side of the little plain, he proceeded to cross over hastily, but had barely gained the middle of the open space when the shrill screams were repeated with redoubled fury. At the same time Jerry heard cries of warning, coupled with his own name. He looked right and left in alarm, not knowing where the threatened danger was likely to come from. He was not kept long in suspense.

Behind him he heard the crackling' and crashing of branches caused by elephants bursting through the wood. Then a large female with three young, but by no means small, ones issued from the edge of the jungle and made straight at the unfortunate man. Jerry turned and ran, but he had no chance; the elephants gained on him so fast that he felt, with an awful sickening of the heart, it was not possible to reach the rocky ground beyond the meadow, where he might have been safe. With the courage of despair he faced about and fired straight in the face of the old female, which ran him down with a shriek of indignation. She had only one tusk, but with that she made a prod at Jerry that would have quickly ended his days if it had not missed the mark and gone deep into the ground. She then caught him by the middle with her trunk, threw him between her fore-feet, and attempted to tread nim to death. This she certainly would have accomplished, but that Jerry was remarkably agile and very small; the ground being soft and muddy was also in his favour. Once she set her foot on his chest, and he felt the bones bending. Of course had the creature's full weight pressed it, Jerry would have been cracked like a walnut, but the monster's foot was rounded and wet, and the poor man making a desperate wrench, it slipped into the mud; then she trod on his arm, and squeezed it into the ground

U

without snapping the bone. Thus stamping and wriggling for a few seconds, the two fought on for vengeance and for life, while George Rennie, Hans, and the two Mullers ran to the rescue and fired a volley. This caused the animal to wince and look up. Jerry, taking advantage of the pause, jumped up and dived out from below her between her hind-legs—alighting on his head and turning a complete somersault. He regained his feet just as she turned round again to seize him. At that critical moment Lucas Van Dyk put a ball in her head, and Considine sent another into the root of her trunk, which induced her to turn and join her screaming offspring in the bushes.

The hunters pursued, while Jerry, covered with mud and bruises, and scarcely able to run, made off in the opposite direction. He had scarcely reached the shelter of some broken ground, when the enormous male elephant which had been previously encountered, came running past, either to the rescue of its mate, or flying in alarm at the firing. It caught one of the Hottentots who had loitered in rear of the attacking party, carried him some distance in its trunk, and then, throwing him on the ground, brought its four feet together and trod and stamped on him for a considerable time. The unfortunate man was killed instantly. It left the corpse for a little, and then returned to it, as if to make quite sure of its deadly work, and, kneeling down, crushed and kneaded the body with its fore-legs. Then seizing it again with its trunk, carried it off and threw it into the jungle.

This delay on the elephant's part gave the hunters time to return from the destruction of the female, and with several successful shots to kill the male.

" 'Tis a heavy price to pay for our sport," said Considine sadly, as he stood with his companions gazing on the body of the Hottentot, which was trodden into a shapeless mass.

" Hunters don't go out for *mere sport*," said Lucas Van Dyk, "they do it in the way of business—for ivory and hides. Of course they must take the chances of a risky trade."

This sad incident naturally cast a gloom over the party, and they remained there only long enough to cut out the tusks of the male elephant and stow them away with choice parts of the meat in their waggon.

After quitting the valley they fell in with the party under John Skyd and Frank Dobson, and led by Stephen Orpin. They were much surprised to find with these their friends Kenneth M'Tavish and Groot Willem, who soon accounted for their unexpected appearance. They had been steadily tracing the spoor of poor Junkie, had lost and refound it several times and, during their pursuit, had crossed the waggon-tracks of Skyd and his party, whom they followed up, in the faint hope that they might have heard or seen something to guide them in their search. In this they were disappointed.

After a brief council of war it was resolved to join their forces and continue the search after Junkie.

Proceeding on their way, they fell in with a wounded Kafir. He lay dying under a bush, and made no attempt to escape, although he evidently regarded the white men as enemies. Having been reassured on this point, and comforted with a piece of tobacco, he told them that his village had been attacked by the Fetcani and completely destroyed, with all the women and children—only a few of the wounded warriors like himself having escaped, to perish in the jungle. The Fetcani he described as the most ferocious warriors ever seen. They did not use the ordinary assagai or throwing spear, but a short stabbing one, and invariably closed at once with their foes with irresistible impetuosity.

On being questioned about prisoners, and reference being made to white men's children, he said that he had heard of a white boy who was brought to a village a day's march or more from where they then were, but added that the Fetcani hordes had gone off to destroy that village just after destroying his

own, and that he had no doubt it was by that time
reduced to ashes and all its inhabitants slain.

On hearing this, and learning the direction of the
village in question, the hunters went off at full gallop,
leaving the waggons to follow their spoor.

It was nearly sunset when they came to an
eminence beyond which lay the Kafir town of which
they were in search. The first glance showed that
something unusual was going on in it—at the same
time it relieved their fears to observe that it was
not yet destroyed. The mud hovels, like huge bee-
hives, in which the Kafirs dwelt, were not yet burnt,
and the only smoke visible was that which rose
from cooking fires. But it was quite plain that the
people, who in the distance seemed to swarm in
and about the place like black ants, were in wild
excitement.

"No doubt they've heard that the Fetcani are
coming," said Groot Willem, riding to the highest
point of the ridge on which they stood. "The place
seems pretty strong. I think we might do worse
than go lend the niggers a helping hand till we've
made inquiries about the lad."

Lucas Van Dyk echoed this sentiment, and so did
Stephen Orpin, but there were others who thought
it best to let the niggers fight their own battles.

"Well, friends," said Kenneth M'Tavish, "you may
hold what opinion you like on that point, but my

business just now is to go into that town and see if I can find Junkie Brook. The sooner I do so the better, so let those who choose follow me."

He rode off at a brisk trot, and was followed by the whole party. On reaching the town they halted, and the principal chief, Eno, came out to meet them. One of the Hottentots being called to interpret, the hunters were informed that the Fetcani had threatened to attack the town, and that the inhabitants were busy putting themselves in a state of defence. They were glad, said the chief, to see the white men, and hoped they would stay to assist him.

To this Stephen Orpin replied through the interpreter. Stephen somehow fell naturally into the position of spokesman and chief of the party in positions where tact and eloquence or diplomacy were wanted, though in the hunting-field he held a very subordinate place.

He told Eno that the white men had come to seek for a white boy who had been stolen from one of the frontier settlements, and that he had heard the boy was in his, Eno's, town. That he was glad to hear it, though of course he did not suppose Eno had stolen the boy, seeing that none of his people had been yet near the colony. That he and his friends now came to claim the boy, and would be glad to aid them in defending the town, if attacked while they were in it.

In reply the chief said he knew nothing about a white boy being in his town, but would make inquiries.

While this conference was going on, a man was seen to approach, running at full speed. He, fell from exhaustion on arriving, and for some moments could not speak. Recovering, he told that he had just escaped from a band of two hundred Fetcani warriors, who were even then on their way to attack the town.

Instantly all was uproar and confusion. The warriors, seizing their shields and spears, sallied forth under their chief to meet the enemy—a few of the youngest being left behind to guard the women and children. A party of the Hottentots under Kenneth M'Tavish also remained to guard the town, while the rest set off to aid the Kafirs. They were compelled, however, to ride back a short distance to meet the waggons, and obtain a supply of ammunition. Thus a little time was lost, and before they could reach the scene of action the Kafirs had met with the Fetcani warriors, been thoroughly beaten, and put to flight.

On the appearance, however, of the horsemen the pursuers halted.

"Now, lads," cried Groot Willem, "a steady volley and a charge home will send them to the right about."

"Better fire over their heads," said Orpin earnestly. "We are not at war with these men. Let us not kill if we can help it."

"I agree with that heartily," cried Charlie Considine.

"So do I," said Hans. "Depend on't the sound will suffice for men who perhaps never saw fire-arms before."

"Quite right, Maister Marais," said Sandy Black, with grave approval, "an' if oor charge is only heeded by Groot Willem an' Jerry Goldboy, tak' my word for't thae Fit-canny craters'll flee like chaff before the wund."

"Very good," said Groot Willem, with a grin. —"Come along, Jerry."

The dauntless little man answered the summons with delight, and the whole party approached the wondering Fetcani at a trot. Halting when within about eighty yards, they fired a volley from horseback over the heads of the enemy. Then, through the smoke, they charged at full speed like thunderbolts, Groot Willem roaring like a mad buffalo-bull, Jerry Goldboy shrieking like a wounded elephant, and energising fearfully with legs, arms, reins, and blunderbuss, while the others shouted or laughed in wild excitement.

The Fetcani, as Sandy Black had prophesied, could not stand it. Turning their backs to the foe.

they fled as only panic-stricken and naked niggers *can* fly, and were soon scattered and lost in the jungle.

While this was going on far out on the plain, Kenneth M'Tavish had much ado to keep the people quiet in the town—so great was their dread of falling into the hands of the ferocious Fetcani. But when the wounded warriors began to come in, breathless, gashed, and bleeding, with the report of their disaster, he found it impossible to restrain the people. The young warriors ignominiously left the place and fled, while the women followed, carrying their children and such of their worldly goods as they were loath to leave behind. For some time M'Tavish managed to restrain the latter, but when at last the hunters came thundering back after their bloodless victory, the poor women, fancying they were the enemy, flung down goods, and even babies, and ran.

The horsemen called out to assure them they were friends, but their terror was too great to permit of their comprehending, and they continued to fly.

"Come, Charlie, we must head these poor creatures, and drive them back," said Hans, as he rode over ground which was strewn with utensils, mantles, and victuals, among which many little black and naked children were seen running, stumbling, tottering, or creeping, according to age and courage.

Followed by the other horsemen, they rode ahead of the flying multitude, and, cracking their whips menacingly in front with an occasional charge, they succeeded in staying the flight and turning the poor women back. No sooner did these comprehend how matters stood than they turned, and caught up their little ones with as much affection and thankfulness as if they had just shown a readiness to die for rather than forsake them !

Among these children was one who, although as black as the ace of spades in body and face, had light curly flaxen hair. He ran about in a wild unaccountable manner, darting hither and thither, from side to side.

M'Tavish and the others, who had by that time dismounted, and were standing at their horses' heads amused spectators of the scene, looked at this urchin in surprise, until they observed that he was endeavouring to escape from a stout young woman who did her best to catch him. She had nearly succeeded, when he suddenly doubled like a hare and bore straight down on the horsemen. Seeing this, the woman gave in, and, turning, fled to the town, while the little fellow ran and clasped the Highlander by the knees.

" Oh ! Miss 'r Tavish !" he cried, and looked up.

"Eh! why—it's Junkie!" cried the Highlander, catching the child up in his arms and hugging him, by which means he left a dark imprint of him on his own breast and face.

It was indeed Junkie—naked as on the day of his birth, greased from head to foot, and charcoaled as black as the King of Ashantee!

Although an object of the deepest interest to the white men, poor Junkie was not at that moment personally attractive. He was, however, unspeakably happy at seeing white and familiar faces once more. He was also very much subdued, and had obviously profited by the rude teaching he had undergone in Kafirland, for his obedience to orders was prompt and unquestioning.

The first important matter was to clean Junkie. This was only partially effected, and with difficulty The next was to clothe him. This was done, on the spur of the moment, with pocket-handkerchiefs, each hunter contributing one till the costume was complete. A large red cotton one formed a sort of plaid; a blue one with a hole in the middle, through which his head was thrust, served as a pretty good poncho or tippet; a green one with white spots, tied round the loins, did duty as a tunic or kilt; and one of crimson silk round the head formed a gorgeous turban.

Returning to the village, the hunters found Eno the chief, and, after expressing much satisfaction at having arrived in time to lend him effectual aid at so critical a period, they presented him with gifts of brass wire and cotton cloth from the stores in Skyd and Dobson's waggons.

The chief expressed his gratitude in glowing terms, and begged the hunters to stay with him for some time. But this they would not do, as it was important to return to the colony, and report what they had seen without delay. Notwithstanding their professions of gratitude, however, these rascals stole as many small articles from the waggons as they could lay hands on, and would doubtless have taken all that the hunters possessed, if they had not been impressed by their valour, and by the dreadful fire-arms which they carried.

This accidental skirmish was the first meeting of the colonists with the Fetcani. It was not till two years later that the Government felt constrained to take active measures against these savages.

The Fetcani, or Mantatee hordes, having been driven from their own country by the bloodthirsty Zulu chief Chaka, had been preying upon other tribes for many years, and at last, in 1827, they precipitated themselves on the Tambookies, and afterwards on the Galekas, threatening to extirpate these Kafirs altogether, or to drive them into the colony as suppliants and beggars. In this extremity the Kafir chief Hintza urgently craved assistance.

It was granted. A body of the colonists sent out by Government, under Major Dundas of the Royal Artillery, defeated the warlike Fetcani, who were afterwards utterly routed and scattered, and their dreaded power finally annihilated, near the sources of the Umtata river, by a body of troops under Colonel Somerset. Hintza's warriors were present at that affair, to the number of about twenty thousand, and they hovered about during the engagement admiringly, though without rendering assistance. But when the enemy were routed and in confused retreat, they fell upon them, and, despite the remonstrances of the white men, committed the most appalling atrocities, mutilating the dead, and cutting off the arms and legs of the living, in order the more easily to obtain their brass rings and ornaments.

This warlike episode did not, however, affect the general condition of the frontier. The settlers, having overcome the misfortunes of the first years, began to prosper and multiply, troubled a good deal, no doubt, by the thievish propensities of their ungrateful black neighbours, but on the whole enjoying the fruit of their labours in comparative peace for several years.

CHAPTER XXII.

TELLS OF DARK AND THREATENING CLOUDS, AND WAR.

THE exigencies of our somewhat acrobatic tale require, at this point, that we should make a considerable bound. We shall beg the obliging reader to leap ꞷith us into the year 1834.

Hans Marais, moustached, bearded, bronzed, and in the prime of life, sits at the door of a cottage recently built close to that of his father. Beside him sits his wife—formerly Miss Gertrude Brook, and nꞷw as sweet and pretty a young woman as you would find in a month's ride through a country where sweet pretty women were, and still are, very numerous in proportion to the population.

Whether it was that Hans was timid, or Gertie shy, we cannot tell, but somehow it is only three months since they began their united career, and Han considers himself to have married rather "late in life." Gertie, being now twenty-six, begins to think herself quite an old woman. It is evident, however, that this ancient couple wear well, and are sufficiently happy—if we may presume to judge from appearances.

"Gertie," said Hans, patting the fingers which handed him his big Dutch pipe, "I fear that my father is determined to go."

"Do you think so?" said Gertie, while a sad expression chased the sunshine from her face.

"Yes, he says he cannot stand the treatment we Cape-Dutchmen receive from the British Government, and that he means to give up his farm, take his waggons and goods and treck away to the north, with the friends who are already preparing to go, in search of free lands in the wilderness where the Union Jack does not fly."

"I must be very stupid, Hans," returned his wife, with a deprecating smile, "for although I've heard your father discussing these matters a good deal of late, I cannot quite understand them. Of course I see well enough that those men who approve of slavery must feel very much aggrieved by the abolition, but your father, like yourself and many others, is not one of these—what then does he complain of?"

"Of a great deal, Gertie," replied Hans, with an amused glance at her perplexed face, "and not only in connection with slavery, but other things. It would take hours of talk to tell you all."

"But can't you give me some sort of idea of these things in a few words?"

"Yes; at least I'll try," said Hans. "I need scarcely tell you that there has been a sort of ill-will in the Cape-Dutch mind against the British Government—more's the pity—ever since the colony passed into the possession of England, owing partly to their not understanding each other, partly to incompetent and tyrannical Governors pursuing unwise policy, partly to unprincipled or stupid men misrepresenting the truth in England, and partly to the people of England being too ready to swallow whatever they are told."

"What! is all the fault on the side of the English?" interrupted Gertie, with a laugh.

"Hear me out, wife," returned Hans—"partly owing to *foolish* Dutchmen rebelling against authority, and taking the law into their own hands, and partly to *rascally* Dutchmen doing deeds worthy of execration. Evil deeds are saddled on wrong shoulders, motives are misunderstood, actions are exaggerated, judges both here and in England are sometimes in-competent, prejudice and ignorance prevent veils from being removed, and six thousand miles of ocean, to say nothing of six hundred miles of land, inter-vene to complicate the confusion surrounding right or wrong."

"Dear me! what an incomprehensible state of things!" said Gertie, opening her blue eyes very wide.

" Rather," returned Hans, with a smile; "and yet there are sensible Englishmen and sensible Cape-Dutchmen who are pretty well agreed as to the true merits of the questions that trouble us. There is the abolition of slavery, for instance: many on both sides are convinced as to the propriety of that, but nearly all are agreed in condemning the way in which it is being gone about, believing that the consequences to many of the slaveholders will be ruinous But it is useless to go into such matters now, Gertie. Right or wrong, many of the Dutch farmers are talking seriously of going out of the colony, and my father, I grieve to say, is among the number."

" And you, Hans?"

" I will remain on the old homestead—at least for a time. If things improve we may induce father to return; if not, I will follow him into the wilderness.

" And what of Considine?" asked Gertie.

" He remains to help me to manage the farm. There is no chance for him in the present exasperated state of my father's mind. He unhappily extends his indignation against England to Englishmen, and vows that my sister Bertha shall never wed Charlie Considine."

" Is he likely to continue in that mind?'

" I think so."

" Then there is indeed no chance for poor Charlie."

was the rejoinder, "for Bertha Marais will never marry in direct opposition to her father's wishes. Heigho ! 'tis the old story about the course of true love."

"He may change—he *will* change his mind, I think," said Hans, "but in the meantime he will go off into the wilderness, carrying Bertha along with him. I would have gone with him myself without hesitation, had it not been that I cannot bear to think of tearing you away just yet from the old people, and I may perhaps do some good here in the way of saving the old home."

Hans looked round with a somewhat mournful gaze at the home of his childhood, which bore evidences of the preparations that were being made by Conrad Marais to leave it.

That evening a large party of disaffected boers arrived at the homestead of Conrad Marais, with waggons, wives, children, goods, and arms, on their way to the far north. Some of these men were sterling fellows, good husbands and fathers and masters, but with fiery independent spirits, which could not brook the restraints laid on them by a Government that had too frequently aroused their contempt or indignation. Others were cruel, selfish savages who scorned the idea that a man might not " wallop his own nigger," and were more than half pleased that the abolition of slavery and its consequences gave them a sort of reason for throwing off allegiance to the British Crown and forsaking their homes in disgust; and some there were who would have been willing to remain and suffer, but could not bear the idea of being left behind by their kindred.

Next morning Conrad completed the loading of his waggons, placed his wife and children—there was still a baby!—in them, mounted his horse with the sons who yet remained with him, and bade farewell to the old home on the karroo. He was followed by a long train of his compatriots' waggons. They all crossed the frontier into Kafirland and thenceforth deemed themselves free!

This was the first droppings of a shower—the first leak of a torrent—the first outbreak of that great exodus of the Dutch-African boers which was destined in the future to work a mighty change in the South African colony.

Hans and Gertie accompanied the party for several hours on their journey, and then, bidding them God-speed, returned to their deserted home.

But now a cloud was lowering over the land which had been imperceptibly, though surely, gathering on the horizon for years past.

We have said that hitherto the colony, despite many provocations, thefts, and occasional murders, had lived in a state of peace with the Kafirs—the only time that they took up arms for a brief space being

in their defence, at Hintza's request, against the
Fetcani.

Latterly, we have also observed, the British
settlers had toiled hard and prospered. The comforts of life they had in abundance. Trade began to
be developed, and missions were established in Kafirland. Among other things, the freedom of the press
had been granted them after a hard struggle! The
first Cape newspaper, the *South African Commercial
Advertiser*, edited by Pringle the poet and Fairbairn,
was published in 1824, and the *Grahamstown Journal*,
the first Eastern Province newspaper, was issued by
Mr. Godlonton in 1831. Schools were also established.
Wool-growing began to assume an importance which
was a premonition of the future staple of the
Eastern Provinces. Savings-banks were established,
and in short everything gave promise of the colony
—both east and west—becoming a vigorous, as it
was obviously a healthy, chip of the old block.

But amongst all this wheat there had been springing up tares. With the growing prosperity there
were growing evils. A generous and well-meant
effort on the part of Christians and philanthropists
to give full freedom and rights to the Hottentots
resulted to a large extent in vagabondism, with its
concomitant robbery. The Kafirs, emboldened by
the weak, and exasperated by the incomprehensible,
policy of the Colonial Government at that time, not

only crossed the border to aid the Hottentot thieves in their work, and carry off sheep and cattle by the hundred, but secretly prepared for war. Behind the scenes were the paramount chief Hintza, the chief Macomo, and others. The first, forgetting the deliverance wrought for him by the settlers and British troops in 1828, secretly stirred up the Kafirs, whilst the second, brooding over supposed wrongs, fanned the flame of discontent raised among the Hottentots by the proposal of a Vagrancy Act.

When all is ready for war it takes but a spark to kindle the torch. The Kafirs were ready; the British, however, were not. The settlers had been peacefully following their vocations, many of the troops which ought to have been there to guard them had been unwisely withdrawn, and only a few hundred men remained in scattered groups along the frontier. The armed Hottentots of the Kat River— sent there as a defence—became a point of weakness, and required the presence of a small force to over-awe them and prevent their joining the Kafirs. At last the electric spark went forth. A farmer (Nell) was robbed of seven horses, which were traced to the kraal of a chief on the neutral territory. Restoration was refused. A military patrol was sent to enforce restitution. Opposition was offered, and the officer in command wounded with an assagai. Hintza began to ill-treat and plunder British traders who were residing in his territory under his pledged protection, and at length a trader named Purcell was murdered near the chief's kraal and his store robbed. Then Macomo began hostilities by robbing and murdering some farmers on the lower part of the Kat River, and two days afterwards the Kafir hordes, variously estimated at from eight to fifteen thousand men, burst across the whole frontier, wrapped the eastern colony in the smoke and flames of burning homesteads, scattered the unprepared settlers, demolished the works of fourteen years' labour, penetrated to within twenty miles of Algoa Bay, and drove thousands of sheep and cattle back in triumph to Kafirland.

CHAPTER XXIII.

WAR.

It was at this juncture—the Christmas-tide of 1834, and the summer-time in South Africa—that a merry party was assembled under the shade of umbrageous trees that crowned a little knoll from which could be seen the blue smoke curling from a prosperous-looking homestead in the vale below. It was a party of settlers enjoying their Christmas festivities in the open air. Hans Marais and Charlie Considine were among them, but, feeling less inclined than was their wont to join in the hilarity of the young folks, they had sauntered into the shrubbery and conversed sadly about the departure of Conrad Marais and his family, and of the unsettled state of the frontier at that time.

While they talked, an armed band of savages had crept past them unperceived, and advanced stealthily towards the party of revellers on the knoll. Coming suddenly across the tracks of these savages, Hans cast an anxious look at his companion, and said quickly—

"Look here, Charlie—the spoor of Kafirs! Let's go—"

The sentence was cut short by a wild war-cry, which was immediately followed by shouts of men and screams of women.

Turning without another word, the two friends ran back to the knoll at full speed, drawing their hunting-knives, which were the only weapons they happened to carry at the time.

On reaching the knoll a fearful scene presented itself. The Kafirs had already killed every man of the party—having come on them unawares and thrown their assagais with fatal precision from the bushes. They were completing the work of death with shouts and yells of fierce delight. Not a woman was to be seen. They had either been dragged into the bushes and slain, or had sought refuge in flight.

With a mighty shout of rage Hans and Considine dashed into the midst of the murderers, and two instantly fell, stabbed to the heart. Seizing the assagais of these, they rushed through the midst of their foes, and, as if animated by one mind, made for the homestead below. To reach the stables and get possession of their horses and rifles was their object.

The savages, of whom there were about thirty, were so taken aback by the suddenness and success of this onset, that for a few seconds they did not

pursue. Then, probably guessing the object of the
fugitives, they uttered a furious yell and followed
them down the hill. But Hans and Considine were
active as well as strong. They kept well ahead,
gained the principal house, and secured their rifles.
Then, instead of barricading the doors and defending
themselves, they ran out again and shot the two
Kafirs who first came up.

Well did the savages know the deadly nature of
the white man's rifle, although at that time they had
not themselves become possessed of it. When their
comrades fell, and the two white men were seen to
kneel and take deliberate aim at those who followed,
the whole party scattered right and left and took
refuge in the bush.

But the friends did not fire. These were not the
days of breech-loaders. Prudently reserving their
fire, they made a rush towards the stables, "saddled
up" in a few seconds, and, mounting, rode forth at
a gallop straight back to the blood-stained hillock.
To rescue, if possible, some of the females was their
object. Regardless of several assagais that whizzed
close to them, they galloped hither and thither
among the bushes, but without success.

"Let's try yonder hollow," cried Considine, pointing as he spoke.

The words had scarce left his lips when a host of
some hundreds of Kafirs, with the shields, assagais,

and feathers of savage warriors, burst out of the
hollow referred to. They had probably been attracted by the two shots, and instantly rushed
towards the white men.

Hans Marais dismounted, kneeled to take steadier
aim, fired, and shot the foremost warrior. Then,
springing on his steed at a bound, he galloped away,
loading as he went, and closely followed by his friend.
Having reloaded, Hans pulled up and again leapt to
the ground. This time Considine, appreciating his
plan, followed his example, and both were about to
kneel and fire when they perceived by a burst of
smoke and flame that the farm-buildings had been
set on fire.

In a straight line beyond, two other columns of
dense smoke indicated the position of two neighbouring farms, and a third column, away to the
right, and further removed from the line of the
frontier, suddenly conveyed to the mind of Hans
the fact that a general rising of the Kafirs had taken
place. Instead of firing, he rose and remounted,
exclaiming—

"Home, Charlie—home!"

At the moment a shout was heard in another
direction. Turning round, they observed a body of
a dozen or so of mounted Kafirs making straight
towards them. To have killed two or four of these
would have been easy enough to first-rate shots

armed with double-barrels, but they knew that those unhurt would continue the chase. They therefore turned and fled in the direction of their own home. Their steeds were good and fresh, but their pursuers were evidently well mounted, for they did not seem to lose ground.

In the kitchen of Conrad Marais's homestead Gertie stood that day, busily employed in the construction of a plum-pudding, with which she meant to regale Hans and Charlie on their return. And very pretty and happy did Gertie look, with her white apron and her dark hair looped up in careless braids, and her face flushed with exertion, and her pretty round arms bared to the dimpled elbows and scarcely capable of being rendered whiter by the flour with which they were covered.

A young Hottentot Venus of indescribable ugliness assisted in retarding her.

"The master will be here soon," said Gertie, wiping the flour and pieces of dough off her hands; "we must be quick. Is the pot ready?"

Venus responded with a "Ja," and a grin which displayed a splendid casket of pearls.

Just then the clatter of hoofs was heard.

"Why, here they come already, and in *such* a hurry too!" said Gertie in surprise, untying her apron hastily.

Before the apron was untied, however, Hans had

pulled up at the door and shouted "Gertie!" in a voice so tremendous that his wife turned pale and can quickly to the door.

"Oh, Hans! what—"

"Come, darling, quick!"

There was no time for more. Hans held out his hand. Gertie took it mechanically.

"Your foot on my toe. Quick!"

Gertie did as she was bid, and felt herself swung to the saddle in front of her husband, who held her in his strong right arm, while in the grasp of his huge left hand he held the reins and an assagai.

Poor Gertie had time, in that brief moment, to note that Charlie Considine sat motionless on his panting horse, gazing sternly towards the karroo, and that a cloud of dust was sweeping over the plain towards them. She guessed too surely what it was, but said not a word, while her husband leaped his horse through a gap in the garden wall in order to reach the road by a short cut. Double-weighted thus, the horse did not run so well as before. Con sidine was frequently obliged to check his pace and look back.

The stern frown on the Dutchman's brow had now mingled with it a slightly troubled look.

"Go on. I'll follow immediately," said Considine as he reined in.

"Don't be foolhardy," cried Hans, with an anxious look as he shot past.

Without replying, Considine dismounted, knelt on a slight eminence on the plain, and deliberately prepared to fire.

The pursuing savages observed the act, and when within about six or seven hundred yards began to draw rein.

Charlie Considine knew his rifle well; although not sighted for such a range, it was capable of carrying the distance when sufficiently elevated, and practice had accustomed him to long-range shots. He aimed a little above the head of the foremost rider, fired, and killed his horse. With the second barrel he wounded one of the Kafirs. At the same moment he observed that his late home was wrapped in flames, and that the cattle and sheep of Conrad Marais, which had been left in charge of Hans, were being driven off by the savages towards the mountains.

This was enough. Remounting, Charlie followed his friend, and was rejoiced to find on looking back that the Kafirs had ceased their pursuit.

"Strange," he said on overtaking Hans, "that they should have given in so easily."

"It is not fear that influences them," returned his friend, with deeply knitted brows; "the reptiles know there is a pass before us, and they will surely try to cut us off. They know all the short cuts better than I do. Push on!"

Urging their horses to their utmost speed, the fugitives soon approached a more broken country, and skirted the mountain range through which the pass referred to by Hans led into level ground beyond. It was a narrow track through jungle, which was dense in some places, open in others. They were soon in it, riding furiously. At one of the open spaces they caught a glimpse of a mounted Kafir making towards a part of the pass in advance of them. Hans pulled up at once, and looked eagerly, anxiously round, while he pressed the light form of Gertie tighter to his breast.

"We must fight here, Charlie," he said, as he made for a little mound which was crowned with a few bushes. "If you and I were alone we might risk forcing a passage, but—Come; they observe our intention."

A few bounds placed them on the top of the mound, where they took shelter among the bushes. These were scarcely thick enough to cover the horses, but among them was found a hole or crevice into which Hans told his wife to creep. She had barely found refuge in this place, when several assagais whizzed over their heads. Sheltering themselves behind stones, Hans and Considine looked eagerly in the direction whence the assagais had been thrown,

and the former observed the ears of a horse just
appearing over a bush.   He fired at the spot where
he conjectured the rider must be, and a yell told
that he had not missed his mark.   At the same
moment his companion observed part of a Kafir's form
opposite to him, and, firing, brought him to the ground.

Seeing this the other savages made a rush at the
mound, supposing probably that both guns were
empty.   They had either forgotten about or were
ignorant of double-barrelled weapons.   Two more
shots killed the two leading Kafirs, and the rest
turned to fly, but a gigantic fellow shouted to them
fiercely to come on, and at the same moment leaped
on Charlie Considine with such force that, although
the latter struck him heavily with the butt of his
rifle, he was borne to the ground.   The triumph
however was momentary.   Next instant Hans
Marais seized him, stabbed him in the throat, and
hurled him back among his comrades a lifeless corpse.
Charlie, recovering himself, pointed his unloaded gun
at the savages, who recoiled, turned, and fled back to
the cover of the opposite bush.

"Now is our time," said Hans, dragging his wife
from the place of shelter.   "Mount and make a dash
before they recover."

While speaking Hans was acting.   In another
moment Gertie was in her old place, Considine in the
saddle, and the two men made a bold push for life.

It turned out as the Dutchman had conjectured. The Kafirs had left all parts of the surrounding jungle to join in the assault on the mound, and when the fugitives made a dash through them, only a few had presence of mind to throw their assagais, and these missed their mark. A few bounds carried Hans and Charlie once more in advance of their enemies, but the clatter of hoofs immediately afterwards told that they were hotly pursued.

There is no saying how the chase might have ended, if they had not met with a piece of good fortune immediately afterwards. On emerging from the other end of the pass, they almost ran into a small patrol of Cape Mounted Rifles, who, attracted by the shots and cries in the pass, were galloping to the rescue.

They did not halt to ask questions, but, with a hearty cheer and a friendly wave of the hand from the officer in command, dashed into the pass and met the pursuing savages in the very teeth.

Of course the latter turned and fled, leaving, however, several of their comrades dead on the ground.

During this early period of the war the whole defending force of the frontier consisted of only between seven and eight hundred men, composed of Cape Mounted Rifles and the 75th regiment, with a few of the Artillery and Engineers, and these had to be broken up into numerous small companies, who were sent here and there where succour was most needed.

With this little patrol, Hans, Gertie, and Considine bivouacked that night, and, travelling with them, soon afterwards reached Grahamstown.

The sight of the country as they approached was a sad one. From all quarters, men, women, children, vehicles, horses, cattle, and sheep, were crowding into the town as a place of refuge. At first the settlers nearest the eastern frontier, taken by surprise, fled to temporary rallying-points. These, however, had to be abandoned for stronger places of refuge. On entering the town they found that the greatest confusion and excitement prevailed. The church had been set aᵣ rt as an asylum for the women and children, who had to put up, however, with the undesirable accompaniments of fire-arms and gunpowder. Public meetings were being held; picquets of armed citizens were being despatched to watch the main roads. All the houses were thronged to suffocation with refugees—white, brown, and black. The streets, squares, yards, gardens, and other vacant places were crowded by night, and the surrounding hills by day, with the flocks and herds that had been saved from the invaders, while the lowing and bleating of these were mingled with the sobs and wails of the widow and fatherless.

"What misery!" exclaimed Gertie, as she rode

Y

slowly through the crowds by the side of her husband, mounted on a horse lent her by one of the patrol, "Oh, how I dread to hear the news from home!"

Gertie referred to her father's home, about the condition of which she knew nothing at the time.

"Where shall we go to seek for news?" she asked anxiously.

"To the barracks," replied Hans.

"You need not be anxious, I think," said Considine; "if anything very serious had happened, it is likely the patrol who rescued us would have heard some account of it before leaving Grahamstown. —Don't you think?" he added, turning to Hans, "that we had better inquire first at Dobson's place?"

At that moment they were passing a large store, over the door of which was a blue board with the words "Dobson, Skyd, and Co." emblazoned in large white letters thereon.

The store itself presented in its windows and interior an assortment of dry goods, so extensive and miscellaneous as to suggest the idea of one being able to procure anything in it—from a silk dress to a grindstone. It was an extremely full, prosperous-looking store, and in the midst of it were to be seen, sitting on the counters, James and Robert Skyd, both looking bluffer and stronger than

when we last met them, though scarcely a day older.
James and Robert were the managing partners of
this prosperous firm; Dobson and John Skyd were
what the latter styled the hunting partners. Robert
Skyd had recently married a pretty Grahamstown
girl, and her little boy—then about one year old—
was, so said his father, the sleeping partner of the
firm, who had been vaguely hinted at by the "Co."
long before he was born. Indeed, the "Co." had
been prudently inserted with special reference to
what might "turn up" in after years. At the time
the firm was formed, it had been suggested that it
should be styled Dobson, Skyd, and Sons, but as it
was possible nothing but daughters might fall to
the lot of any of them, "Co." was substituted as
being conveniently indefinite. Dobson took pre-
cedence in the title in virtue of his having brought
most capital into the firm. He had invested his all
in it—amounting to three pounds four and nine-
pence halfpenny. John Skyd had contributed half-
a-crown, which happened to be a bad one. James
brought nothing at all, and Robert entered it a
little in debt for tobacco.

The great waggon of the hunting partners, loaded
with hides, horns, and ivory, stood at the door of
the store, as Gertie and her protectors passed, having
just arrived from a successful trip into Kafirland,
and fortunately escaped the outbreak of the war.

Fastening their bridles to one of its wheels, Hans, Gertie, and Considine entered. The first face they saw was that of Edwin Brook, into whose arms Gertie ran with a wild cry of joy.

"Why, Hans Marais!" cried James Skyd, jumping off the counter and grasping his big friend by the hand, while Robert seized that of Considine, "where have you dropped from?—But I need scarcely ask, for all the world seems to be crowding into the town. Not hurt, I hope?" he added, observing the blood which stained his friend's dress.

"Not in person," answered Hans, with a smile, returning his cordial grasp.

"And what of property?" asked Edwin Brook, looking round.

"All gone," returned Hans sadly. "I rose this morning a reasonably wealthy man—now, I am a beggar. But tell me, what of your family, Mr. Brook?"

"All saved, thank God," was the reply. "Junkie, dear boy, who is the most active young fellow in the land, managed to—Ah! here he comes, and will speak for himself."

As he spoke a tall strapping youth of about fifteen entered, opened wide his laughing blue eyes on seeing Hans, and, after a hearty greeting, told with some hesitation that he had chanced to be out hunting on foot in the jungles of the Great Fish River when the Kafirs crossed the frontier, and had managed, being a pretty good runner, to give his father warning, so that the family had time to escape. He did *not* tell, however, that he had, in a narrow pass, kept above sixty Kafirs in check with his own hand and gun until George Dally could run to the house for his weapons and ammunition, and that then the two held a hundred of them in play long enough to permit of the whole family escaping under the care of Scholtz.

"But," said Edwin Brook, who related all this with evident satisfaction, "I am like yourself, Hans, in regard to property. Mount Hope is a blackened ruin, the farm is laid waste, and the cattle are over the borders."

"And where is Mrs. Brook?" asked Considine.

"In this house. Up-stairs. Come, Gertie is getting impatient. Let us go to see her."

"Now, friends," said Considine to the brothers Skyd, who had by that time been joined by the hunting partners, "there is a matter on which we must consult and act without delay."

Here he told of Conrad Marais's departure with the boers across the frontier, and added that if the party was to be saved at all it must be gone about instantly.

"You can't go about it to-day, Charlie," said John

Skyd, "so don't give way to impatience. For such a long trip into the enemy's country we must go well armed and supplied."

"I will brook no delay," said Considine, with flushing countenance. "If it had not been for the necessity of bringing Gertie here in safety, Hans and I would have set out at once and alone on their spoor. Is it not so?"

Hans nodded assent.

"No, friends," he said, turning to the brothers with decision, "we must be off at once."

"What! without your suppers?" exclaimed Bob Skyd; "but to be serious, it won't be possible to get things ready before to-morrow. Surely that will do, if we start at daybreak. Besides, the party with your father, Hans, is a strong one, well able to hold out against a vastly superior force of savages. Moreover, if you wait we shall get up a small body of volunteers."

Hans and Charlie were thus constrained un-willingly to delay. At grey dawn, however, they rode out of Grahamstown at the head of a small party, consisting of the entire firm of Dobson and Skyd, inclusive of Junkie, whose father granted him permission to go. His mother silently ac-quiesced. Mrs. Scholtz violently protested; and when she found that her protests were useless, she changed them into pathetic entreaties that Junkie would on no account whatever go to sleep in camp with wet feet.

As soon as the invasion took place, an express had been sent to Capetown, and the able Governor, Sir Benjamin D'Urban, took instant and energetic measures to undo, as far as possible, the mischief done by his predecessors. Colonel (afterwards Sir Harry) Smith was despatched to the frontier, and rode the distance—six hundred miles—in six days.

Arriving in Grahamstown, he took command with a firm hand, organised the whole male population into a warlike garrison, built barricades across the streets, planted cannon in commanding positions, cleared the town of flocks and herds, which were breeding a nuisance, sent them to the open country with a cattle guard, and prepared not only to defend the capital, but to carry war into the enemy's country. In short, he breathed into the people much of his own energy, and soon brought order out of confusion.

The state of affairs in the colony had indeed reached a terrible pass. From all sides news came in of murder and pillage. The unfortunate traders in Kafirland fared ill at that time. One of these, Rodgers, was murdered in the presence of his three children. A man named Cramer was savagely butchered while driving a few cattle along the road. Another, named Mahony, with his wife and son-in-

law, were intercepted while trying to escape to the
military post of Kafir Drift, and Mahony was
stretched a corpse at his wife's feet, then the son-in-
law was murdered, but Mrs. Mahony escaped into
the bush with two of her children and a Hottentot
female servant, and, after many hardships, reached
Grahamstown. A mounted patrol scouring the
country fell in with a farm-house where three
Dutchmen, in a thick clump of bushes, were defending themselves against three hundred Kafirs. Of
course the latter were put to flight, and the three
heroes—two of them badly wounded—were rescued.
Nearly everywhere the settlers, outnumbered, had
to fly, and many were slain while defending their
homes, but at the little village of Salem they held
their ground gallantly. The Wesleyan chapel, mis-
sion-house, and schoolhouse, were filled with refugees,
and although the Kafirs swooped down on it at night
in large numbers and carried off the cattle, they
failed to overcome the stout defenders. Theopolis
also held out successfully against them—and so did
the Scottish party at Baviaans River, although attacked and harassed continually.

During an attack near the latter place a Scottish
gentleman of the Pringle race had a narrow escape.
Sandy Black was with him at the time. Three or
four Kafirs suddenly attacked them. Mr. Pringle
shot one, Sandy wounded another. A third ran

forward while Pringle was loading and threw an assagai at him. It struck him with great force on the leathern bullet-pouch which hung at his belt. Sandy Black took aim at the savage with a pistol.

"Aim low, Sandy," said Pringle, continuing to load.

Sandy obeyed and shot the Kafir dead, then turning round said anxiously—

"Are 'ee stickit, sir?"

"I'm not sure, Sandy," replied Pringle, putting his hand in at the waist of his trousers, "there's blood, I see."

On examination it was found that the assagai had been arrested by the strong pouch and belt, and had only given him a trifling scratch, so that the gallant and amiable Mr. Dods Pringle lived to fight in future Kafir wars.[1]

In another place, near the Kat River, thirty men were attacked by a hundred and fifty Kafirs. The latter came on with fury, but five of the farmers brought down seven of the enemy at the first discharge, and thereafter poured into them so rapid and destructive a fire that they were seized with panic, and fled, leaving seventy-five of their number dead.

Instances of individual heroism might be endlessly

---

[1] The author had the pleasure of spending a night last year (1876) under the hospitable roof of Mr. Pringle, shortly before his death, and saw the identical assagai, which was bent by the force with which it had been hurled against him on that occasion.

multiplied, but we think this is enough to show the desperate nature of the struggle which had begun.

In the course of one fortnight the labours of fourteen years were annihilated. Forty-four persons were murdered, 369 dwellings consumed, 261 pillaged, and 172,000 head of live-stock carried off into Kafirland and irretrievably lost; and what aggravated the wickedness of the invasion was the fact that during a great part of the year the Governor had been engaged in special negotiations for a new—and to the Kafirs most advantageous—system of relations, with which all the chiefs except one had expressed themselves satisfied.

Writing on the condition of the country Colonel Smith said: " Already are seven thousand persons dependent on Government for the necessaries of life. The land is filled with the lamentations of the widow and the fatherless. The indelible impressions already made upon myself by the horrors of an irruption of savages upon a scattered population, almost exclusively engaged in the peaceful occupations of husbandry, are such as to make me look on those I have witnessed in a service of thirty years, ten of which in the most eventful period of war, as trifles to what I have now witnessed, and compel me to bring under consideration, as forcibly as I am able, the heartrending position in which a very large portion of the inhabitants of this frontier are at present placed, as well as their intense anxiety respecting their future condition."

Sir Benjamin D'Urban, arriving soon afterwards, constituted a Board of Relief to meet the necessities of the distressed; and relief committees were established in Capetown, Stellenbosch, Graaff-Reinet, and other principal towns, while subscriptions were collected in Mauritius, St. Helena, and India.

Soon after the arrival of Colonel Smith, burgher forces were collected; troops arrived with the Governor on the scene of action, and the work of expelling the invader was begun in earnest. Skirmishes by small bodies of farmers and detachments of troops took place all over the land, in which the Dutch-African colonists and English settlers with their descendants vied with each other, and with the regulars, in heroic daring. Justice requires it to be added that they had a bold enemy to deal with, for the Kafirs were physically splendid men; full of courage and daring, although armed only with light spears.

CHAPTER XXIV.

SHOWS WHAT BEFELL A TRADER AND AN EMIGRANT BAND.

STEPHEN ORPIN, with the goods of earth in his waggon and the treasures of heaven in his hand, chanced to be passing over a branch of the Amatola Mountains when the torch of war was kindled and sent its horrid glare along the frontier. Vague news of the outbreak had reached him, and he was hastening back to the village of Salem, in which was his bachelor home.

Stephen, we may remark in passing, was not a bachelor from choice. Twice had he essayed to win the affections of Jessie M'Tavish, and twice had he failed. Not being a man of extreme selfishness, he refused to die of a broken heart. He mourned indeed, deeply and silently, but he bowed his head, and continued, as far as in him lay, to fulfil the end for which he seemed to have been created. He travelled with goods far and wide throughout the eastern districts of the colony, became a walking newspaper to the farmers of the frontier, and a guide to the Better Land to whoever would grant him a hearing.

But Stephen's mercantile course, like that of his affections, did not run smooth. At the present time it became even more rugged than the mountain road which almost dislocated his waggon and nearly maddened his Hottentot drivers, for, when involved in the intricacies of a pass, he was suddenly attacked by a band of "wild" Bushman marauders. The spot chanced to be so far advantageous that a high precipice at his back rendered it impossible to attack him except in front, where the ground was pretty open.

Orpin was by no means a milksop, and, although a Christian man, did not understand Christianity to teach the absolute giving up of all one's possessions to the first scoundrel who shall demand them. The moment, therefore, that the robbers showed themselves, he stopped the waggon at the foot of the precipice, drew his ever-ready double-barrelled large-bore gun from under the tilt, and ran out in front, calling on his men to support him. Kneeling down, he prepared to take a steady aim at the Bushman in advance, a wild-looking savage in a sheepskin kaross and armed with an assagai. The robbers were evidently aware of the nature of a gun, for they halted on seeing the decided action of the trader.

"Come on !" shouted Orpin to his men, looking

back over his shoulder; but his men were nowhere
to be seen : they had deserted him at the first sight
of the robbers, and scrambled away into the jungle
like monkeys.

To resist some dozens of savages single-handed
Stephen knew would be useless, and to shed blood
unnecessarily was against his principles. He therefore made up his mind at once how to act. Rising
and turning round, he discharged his gun at the
precipice, to prevent the Bushmen from accidentally
doing mischief with it; then, sitting down on a piece
of fallen rock, he quietly took out his pipe and
began to light it.

This was not meant as a piece of bravado, but
Stephen was eccentric, and it occurred to him that
there was a "touch of nature" in a pipe which
might possibly induce the Bushmen to be less rude
to him personally than if he were to stand by
and look aggrieved while his waggons were being
pillaged.

In this conjecture he was right. The robbers
rushed towards the waggon without doing him any
harm. One of them, however, picked up the gun in
passing. Then the leader seized the long whip and
drove the waggon away, leaving its late owner to his
meditations.

Stephen would have been more than human if he
could have stood the loss of all his earthly goods

with perfect equanimity. He groaned when the oxen began to move, and then, feeling a desperate desire to relieve his feelings, and a strong tendency to fight, he suddenly shut his eyes, and began to pray that the robbers might be forgiven, and himself enabled to bear his trials in a becoming manner. Opening his eyes again, he beheld a sturdy Bushman gazing at him in open-mouthed surprise, with an uplifted assagai in his hand. Stephen judged that this was the chief of the band, who had remained behind to kill him. At all events, when he ceased to pray, and opened his eyes, the Bushman shut his mouth, and poised his assagai in a threatening manner.

Unarmed as he was, Stephen knew that he was at the man's mercy. In this dilemma, and knowing nothing of the Bushman language, he put powerful constraint on himself, and looked placidly at his wallet, in which he searched earnestly for something, quite regardless, to all appearances, of the deadly spear, whose point was within ten feet of his breast.

The Bushman's curiosity was awakened. He waited until Stephen had drawn a lump of tobacco from his pouch—which latter he took care to turn inside out to show there was nothing else in it. Rising quietly, the trader advanced with a peaceful air, holding the tobacco out to the Bushman, who looked suspicious, and distrustfully shook his assagai;

but Stephen took no heed. Stopping within a couple of yards of him, he held out the tobacco at the full length of his arm. The Bushman hesitated, but finally lowered his assagai and accepted the gift. Stephen immediately resumed his pipe, and smiled pleasantly at his foe.

The Bushman appeared to be unable to resist this. He grinned hideously ; then, turning about, made off in the direction of his comrades as fast as his naked legs could carry him.

It was Booby, the follower of Ruyter the Hottentot, who had thus robbed the unfortunate trader, and, not two hours afterwards, Ruyter himself fell in with Stephen, wending his way slowly and sadly down the glen.

Desiring his men to proceed in advance, the robber chief asked Orpin to sit down on a fallen tree beside him, and relate what had happened. When he had done so, Ruyter shook his head and said in his broken English—

" You 's bin my friend, Orpin, but I not can help you dis time. Booby not under me now, an' we 's bof b'long to Dragoener's band. I 's sorry, but not can help you."

" Never mind, Ruyter, I daresay you 'd help me if you could," said Stephen, with a sigh ; then, with an earnest look in the Hottentot's face, he continued, " I 'm not, however, much distressed about the goods.

The Lord who gave them has taken them away, and can give them back again if He has a mind to; but tell me, Ruyter, why will you not think of the things we once spoke of—that time when you were so roughly handled by Jan Smit—about your soul and the Saviour?"

"How you knows I not tink?" demanded the Hottentot sharply.

"Because any man can know a tree by its fruit," returned Orpin. "If you had become a Christian, I should not now have found you the leader of a band of thieves."

"No, I not a Christian, but I *do* tink," returned Ruyter, "only I no' can onderstan'. De black heathen—so you calls him—live in de land. White Christian—so you calls *him*—come and take de land; make slabe ob black man, and kick 'im about like pair ob ole boots—I *not* onderstan' nohow."

"Come, I will try to make you understand," returned Orpin, pulling out the New Testament which he always carried in his pocket. "*Some* white men who call themselves Christians are heathens, and *some* black men are Christians. We are all,—black and white,—born bad, and God has sent us a Saviour, and a message, so that all who will, black or white, may become good." Orpin here commenced to expound the Word, and to tell the story of the Cross, while the Hottentot listened with rapt attention, or asked

z

questions which showed that he had indeed been thinking of these things since his last meeting with the trader, many years before. He was not very communicative, however, and when the two parted he declined to make any more satisfactory promise than that he would continue to "tink."

Stephen Orpin spent the night alone in a tree, up which he had climbed to be more secure from wild beasts. While sitting there, he meditated much, and came to the conclusion that he ought in future to devote himself entirely to missionary labours. In pursuance of that idea, he made his way to one of the Wesleyan mission stations in Kafirland.

On the road thither he came to a Kafir kraal, where the men seemed to be engaged in the performance of a war-dance.

On being questioned by these Kafirs as to who he was, and where he came from, Orpin replied, in his best Kafir, that he was a trader and a missionary.

The chief looked surprised, but, on hearing the whole of Orpin's story, a cunning look twinkled in his eyes, and he professed great friendship for the missionaries, stating at the same time that he was going to one of the Wesleyan stations, and would be glad to escort Orpin thither. Thereafter he gave orders that the white man should be taken to one of his huts and supplied with a "basket" of milk!

The white man gratefully acknowledged the kind offer, and, asking the name of the friendly chief, was informed that it was Hintza. Just then a court fool or jester stepped forward, and cried aloud his announcements of the events of the day, mixed with highly complimentary praises of his master. Stephen did not understand all he said, but he gathered thus much,—that the warriors had been out to battle and had returned victorious ; that Hintza was the greatest man and most courageous warrior who had ever appeared among the Kafirs, to gladden their hearts and enrich their hands ; and that there was great work yet for the warriors to do in the way of driving certain barbarians into the sea—to which desirable deed the heroic, the valiant, the wise, the unapproachable Hintza would lead them.

Orpin feared that he understood the meaning of the last words too well, but, being aware that Hintza was regarded by the colonists as one of the friendliest of the Kafir chiefs, he hoped that he might be mistaken.

Hintza was as good as his word, and set out next day with a band of warriors, giving the white man a good horse that he might ride beside him. On the way they came on a sight which filled Orpin with sadness and anxiety. It was the ruins of a village, which from the appearance of the remains had evidently been occupied in part by white men. He observed that a gleam of satisfaction lit up Hintza's swarthy visage for a moment as he passed the place.

Dismounting, the party proceeded to examine the ruins, but found nothing. The Kafirs were very taciturn, but the chief said, on being pressed, that he believed it had been a mission station which wicked men of other tribes had burned.

On the outbreak of this war some of the missionaries remained by their people, others were compelled to leave them.

The station just passed had been deserted. At the one to which Hintza was now leading Orpin the missionaries had remained at their post. There he found them still holding out, but in deep dejection, for nearly all their people had forsaken them, and gone to the war. Even while he was talking with them, crowds of the bloodstained savages were returning from the colony, laden with the spoils of the white man, and driving thousands of his sheep and cattle before them. In these circumstances, Stephen resolved to make the best of his way back to Salem. On telling this to Hintza, that chief, from some cause that he could not understand, again offered to escort him. He would not accompany him personally, he said, but he would send with him a band of his warriors, and he trusted that on his arrival in the colony he would tell to the great white chief (the Governor) that he, Hintza, did not aid the other Kafir tribes in this war.

Stephen's eyes were opened by the last speech, and from that moment he suspected Hintza of treachery.

He had no choice, however, but to accept the escort. On the very day after they had started, they came to a spot where a terrible fight had obviously taken place. The ground was strewn with the mangled corpses of a party of white men, while the remains of waggons and other signs showed that they had formed one of the bands of Dutch emigrants which had already begun to quit the colony. The savages made ineffectual attempts to conceal their delight at what they saw, and Orpin now felt that he was in the power of enemies who merely spared his life in the hope that he might afterwards be useful to them.

The band which escorted him consisted of several hundred warriors, a few of whom were mounted on splendid horses stolen from the settlers. He himself was also mounted on a good steed, but felt that it would be madness to attempt to fly from them. On the second day they were joined—whether by arrangement or not Orpin had no means of judging —by a band of over a thousand warriors belonging to a different tribe from his escort. As the trader rode along in a dejected state of mind, one of the advance-guard or scouts came back with excited

looks, saying that a large band of Dutch farmers
was encamped down in a hollow just beyond the
rise in front of them. The chief of the Kafirs ordered
the scout sternly to be silent, at the same time
glancing at Orpin. Then he whispered to two
men, who quietly took their assagais and stationed
themselves one on either side of their white prisoner
– for such he really was.

Orpin now felt certain that the group of principal
men who drew together a little apart were concerting
the best mode of attacking the emigrant farmers,
and his heart burned within him as he thought of
them resting there in fancied security, while these
black scoundrels were plotting their destruction.
But what could he do—alone and totally unarmed ?
He thought of making a dash and giving the alarm,
but the watchful savages at his side seemed to
divine his intentions, for they grasped their assagais
with significant action.

" A desperate disease," thought Orpin, " requires a
desperate remedy. I will try it, and may succeed—
God helping me." A thought occurred just then.
Disengaging his right foot from the stirrup, he made
as if he were shortening it a little, but instead, he
detached it from the saddle, and taking one turn of
the leather round his hand, leaped his horse at the
savage nearest him and struck him full on the forehead with the stirrup-iron. Dashing on at full speed,

he bent low, and, as he had hoped, the spear of
the other savage whizzed close over his back. The
act was so sudden that he had almost gained the
ridge before the other mounted Kafirs could pursue.
He heard a loud voice, however, command them to
stop, and, looking back, saw that only one Kafir—the
leader—gave chase, but that leader was a powerful
man, armed, and on a fleeter horse than his own. A
glance showed him the camp of the emigrant
farmers in a hollow about a mile or so distant. He
made straight for it. The action of the next few
seconds was short, sharp, and decisive.

The Dutchmen, having had a previous alarm from
a small Kafir band, were prepared. They had
drawn their waggons into a compact circle, closing
the apertures between and beneath them with thorn-
bushes, which they lashed firmly with leather thongs
to the wheels and dissel-booms or waggon-poles.
Within this circle was a smaller one for the protection of the women and children.

Great was the surprise of the farmers when they
heard a loud shout, and beheld a white man flying
for his life from a solitary savage. With the
promptitude of men born and bred in the midst of
alarms, they seized their guns and issued from their
fortified enclosure to the rescue, but the Kafir was
already close to Orpin, and in the act of raising his
assagai to stab him.

Seeing the urgency of the case, Conrad Marais, who was considered a pretty good shot among his fellows, took steady aim, and, at the risk of hitting the white man, fired. The right arm of the savage dropped by his side and the assagai fell to the ground, but, plucking another from his bundle with his left hand, he made a furious thrust. Stephen Orpin, swaying aside, was only grazed by it. At the same time he whirled the stirrup once round his head, and, bringing the iron down with tremendous force on the skull of his pursuer, hurled him to the ground.

"Stephen Orpin!" exclaimed Conrad Marais in amazement, as the trader galloped up.

"You've got more pluck than I gave you credit for," growled Jan Smit.

"You'll need all your own pluck presently," retorted Orpin, who thereupon told them that hundreds of Kafirs were on the other side of the ridge, and would be down on them in a few minutes. Indeed, he had not finished speaking when the ridge in question was crossed by the black host, who came yelling on to the attack,—the few mounted men leading.

"Come, boys, let's meet them as far as possible from the waggons," cried Conrad.

The whole band of farmers, each mounted and carrying his gun, dashed forward. When quite close to the foe they halted, and, every man dismounting, knelt and fired. Nearly all the horsemen among the enemy fell to the ground at the discharge, and the riderless steeds galloped over the plain, while numbers of the footmen were also killed and wounded. But most of those savages belonged to a fierce and warlike tribe. Though checked for a moment, they soon returned to the attack more furiously than before. The Dutch farmers, remounting, galloped back a short distance, loading as they went; halting again, they dismounted and fired as before, with deadly effect.

There is no question that the white men, if sufficiently supplied with ammunition, could have thus easily overcome any number of the savages, but the waggons stopped them. On reaching these, they were obliged to stand at bay, and, being greatly outnumbered, took shelter inside of their enclosure. Of course their flocks and herds, being most of them outside, were at once driven away by a small party of the assailants, while the larger proportion, with savage yells and war-cries, made a furious attack on their position.

Closing round the circle, they endeavoured again and again to break through the line or to clamber over the waggon-tilts, and never did savage warriors earn a better title to the name of braves than on that occasion. Even the bristling four and six-inch

thorns of the mimosa-bushes would not have been able
to turn back their impetuous onset if behind these
the stout Dutchmen, fighting for wives and children,
had not stood manfully loading and firing volleys of
slugs and buckshot at arm's-length from them.
The crowded ranks of the Kafirs were ploughed
as if by cannon, while hundreds of assagais were
hurled into the enclosure, but happily with little
effect, though a few of the defenders—exposing
themselves recklessly—were wounded.

While Conrad Marais was standing close to the
hind-wheels of one of the waggons, watching for
a good shot at a Kafir outside, who was dodging
about for the double purpose of balking Conrad's
intention and thrusting an assagai into him, another
active Kafir had clambered unobserved on the tilt of
the waggon and was in the very act of leaning over
to thrust his spear into the back of the Dutchman's
neck when he was observed by Stephen Orpin, who
chanced to be reloading his gun at the moment.

With a loud roar, very unlike his usual gentle
tones, Orpin sprang forward, seized a thick piece of
wood like a four-foot rolling-pin, and therewith
felled the savage, who tumbled headlong into the
enclosure.

"Oh, father!" exclaimed a terrified voice at that
moment, while a light touch was laid on Conrad's
shoulder.

" What brings you here, Bertha?" said Conrad, with an impatient gesture. " Don't you know—"

" Come, quick, to mother !" cried the girl, interrupting.

No more was needed. In a moment Conrad was in the central enclosure, where, crowded under a rude erection of planks and boxes, were the women and children. An assagai had penetrated an unguarded crevice, and, passing under the arm of poor Mrs. Marais, had pinned her to the family trunk, against which she leaned.

" Bertha could not pull it out," said Mrs. Marais, with a faint smile on her pale face, " but I don't think I 'm much hurt."

In a moment her husband had pulled out the spear, found that it had penetrated her clothing, and only grazed her breast, took time merely to make sure of this, and then, leaving her in Bertha's hands, returned to the scene of combat.

He was not an instant too soon. A yell was uttered by the savages as they rushed at a weak point, where the thorn-bush defences had been broken down. The point appeared to be undefended. They were about to leap through in a dense mass when ten Dutchmen, who had reserved their fire, discharged a volley simultaneously into the midst of them. It was a ruse of the defenders to draw the savages to that point. Whilst the Kafirs

tumbled back over heaps of dead and dying, several
other farmers thrust masses of impenetrable mimosa-
bush into the gap and refilled it. This discomfiture
checked the assailants for a little ; they drew off and
retired behind the ridge to concert plans for a renewed and more systematic attack.

CHAPTER XXV.

TREATS OF VARIOUS STRANGE INCIDENTS, SOME INTERESTING MATTERS,
AND A RESCUE.

WHILE the emigrant farmers were thus gallantly
defending themselves, the party under Hans Marais
and Charlie Considine was hastening on their spoor
to the rescue.

Their numbers had been increased by several
volunteers, among whom were George Dally and
Scholtz, also David, Jacob, and Hendrick, the sons
of Jan Smit, who had made up their minds not to
follow the fortunes of their savage-tempered sire,
but who were at once ready to fly to his rescue on
learning that he was in danger. While passing
through the country they were further reinforced by
a band of stout burghers, and by four brothers named
Bowker. There were originally seven brothers of
this family, who afterwards played a prominent part
in the affairs of the colony. One of these Bowkers
was noted for wearing a very tall white hat, in
which, being of a literary turn of mind, he delighted
to carry old letters and newspapers. From this

circumstance his hat became known as " the post-office."

Although small, this was about as heroic a band of warriors as ever took the field—nearly every man being strong, active, a dead shot, well trained to fight with wild beasts, and acquainted with the tactics of wilder men.

Proceeding by forced marches, they soon drew near to that part of the country where the be-leaguered farmers lay.

One evening, having encamped a little earlier than usual, owing to the circumstance of their having reached a fountain of clear good water, some of the more energetic among them went off to search for game. Among these were the brothers Bowker.

" There's very likely a buffalo or something in that bush over there," said Septimus Bowker, who was the owner of the "post-office" hat. " Come, Mr. Considine, you wanted to—Where's Considine ?"

Every one looked round, but Considine and Hans were not there. One of the Skyds, however, remembered that they had fallen behind half an hour before, with the intention of procuring something fresh for supper.

" Well, we must go without him. He wanted to shoot a buffalo. Will no one else go ?"

No one else felt inclined to go except Junkie Brook, so he and the four Bowkers went off. Septimus pressing the "post-office" tightly on his brows as they galloped away.

They had not far to go, game of all kinds being abundant in that region, but instead of finding a buffalo or gnu, they discovered a lioness in a bed of rushes. The party had several dogs with them, and these went yelping into the rushes, while the brothers stationed themselves on a mound, standing in a row, one behind another.

The brother with the tall white hat stood in front. Being the eldest, he claimed the post of honour. They were all fearless men and crack shots. Junkie was ordered to stand back, and complied with a bad grace, being an ardent sportsman.

"Look out!" exclaimed the brother in front to the brothers in rear.

"Ready!" was the quiet response.

Next moment out came the lioness with a savage growl, and went straight at Septimus, who cocked his gun as coolly as if he were about to slay a sparrow.

While the enraged animal was in the act of bounding, Septimus fired straight down its throat and suddenly stooped. By so doing he saved his head. Perhaps we should say the tall white hat saved it, for the crushing slap which the lioness meant to give him on the side of the head took effect on the post-office, and scattered its contents far and wide. Spurning Septimus on the shoulders with her hind-legs as she flew past, the lioness made at the brothers. Firm as the Horatii stood the other three. Deliberate and cool was their action as they took aim. Junkie followed suit, and the whole fired a volley, which laid the lioness dead at their feet.

Gathering himself up, Septimus looked with some concern at the white hat before putting it on. Remarking that it was tough, he proceeded to pick up its literary contents, while his brothers skinned the lioness. Shortly afterwards they all returned to camp.

Passing that way an hour or so later, Hans Marais and Charlie Considine came upon the spoor of the lioness.

" I say, Charlie," called out Hans, " there must be a lion in the vley there. I 've got the spoor. Come here."

" It 's not in the vley *now*," replied Charlie; " come here yourself; I 've found blood, and, hallo ! here 's a newspaper ! Why, it must be a literary lion ! Look, Hans, can you make out the name ?—Howker, Dowker, or something o' that sort. Do lions ever go by that name ?"

" Bowker," exclaimed Hans, with a laugh. " Ah ! my boy, there 's no lion in the vley if the Bowkers have been here; and see, it 's all plain as a pikestaff.

They shot it here and skinned it there, and have dragged the carcass towards that bush; yes, here it is—a lioness. They're back to camp by this time. Come, let's follow them."

As they rode along, Hans, who had been glancing at the newspaper, turned suddenly to his companion.

"I say, Charlie, here's a strange coincidence. It's not every day that a man finds a *Times* newspaper in the wilds of Southern Africa with a message in it to himself."

"What do you mean, Hans?"

"Tell me, Charlie, about that uncle of whom you once spoke to me—long ago—in rather disrespectful tones, if not terms. Was he rich?"

"I believe so, but was never quite certain as to that."

"Did he like you?"

"I rather think not."

"Had you a male cousin or relative of the same name with yourself whom he *did* like?"

"No."

"Then allow me to congratulate you on your good fortune, and read that," said Hans, giving him the newspaper.

Charlie read :—

"If this should meet the eye of Charles Considine, formerly of Golden Square, Hotchester, he is requested to return without delay to England, or to communicate with Aggard, Ale, and Ixley, Solicitors, 23A Fitzbustaway Square, London."

"Most amazing!" exclaimed Considine, after a pause, "and there can be no doubt it refers to me, for these were my uncle's solicitors—most agreeable men—who gave me the needful to fit me out, and it was their chief clerk—a Roman-nosed jovial sort of fellow, named Rundle something or other—who accompanied me to the ship when I left, and wished me a pleasant voyage, with a tear, or a drop of rain, I'm not sure which, rolling down his Roman nose. Well, but, as I said before, isn't it an astonishing coincidence?"

"It wasn't you who said that before, it was I," returned Hans, "but we must make allowance for your state of mind. And now, as we're nearing the camp, what is it to be—silence?"

"Silence, of course," said Charlie. "There's no fear of Bowker reading the advertisements through, he has far too much literary taste for that, and even if he did, he's not likely to stumble on this one. So let's be silent."

There was anything but silence in the camp, however, when the friends reached it and reported their want of luck; for the warriors were then in the first fervour of appeasing their powerful appetites.

Next morning they started at sunrise.

Early in the day they came on the mangled remains of the emigrant farmers before referred to. At first it was supposed this must be the remnant of the band they were in search of, but a very brief examination convinced them, experienced as they were in men and signs, that it was another band. Soon after, they came in sight of the party for which they were searching, just as the Kafirs were making a renewed attack. Already a few volleys had been fired by the Dutchmen, the smoke of which hung like a white shroud over the camp, and swarms of savages were yelling round it.

"The cattle and flocks have been swept away," growled Frank Dobson.

"But the women and children must be safe as yet," said Considine, with a sigh of relief.

"Now, boys," cried Hans, who had been elected captain, "we must act together. When I give the word, halt and fire like one man, and then charge where I lead you. Don't scatter. Don't give way to impetuous feelings. Be under command, if you would save our friends."

He spoke with quick, abrupt vigour, and waited for no reply or remark, but, putting himself where he fancied a leader should be, in front of the centre of his little line, set off in the direction of the emigrants' camp at a smart gallop. As the horsemen drew near they increased their pace, and then a yell from the savages, and a cheer from their friends, told that they had been observed by the combatants on both sides. The Kafirs were seen running back to the ridge on the other side of the camp, and assembling themselves hurriedly in a dense mass.

On swept the line of stalwart burghers, over the plain and down into the hollow in dead silence. The force of their leader's character seemed to have infused military discipline into them. Most of them kept boot to boot like dragoons. Even Dally and Scholtz kept well in line, and none lagged or shot ahead. As they passed close to the camp without drawing rein, the Dutchmen gave them an enthusiastic cheer, but no reply was made, save by Junkie, who could not repress a cry of fierce delight. Down deeper into the hollow they went, and up the opposite slope,—the thunder of their tread alone breaking the stillness.

"Halt!" cried the leader in a deep loud voice.

They drew up together almost as well as they had run. Next moment every man was on the ground and down on one knee; then followed the roar of their pieces, and a yell of wild fury told that none had missed his mark. Before the smoke had risen a yard they were again in the saddle. No further order was given. Hans charged; the rest followed like a wall at racing speed, with guns and bridles grasped in their left hands and sabres drawn in their right.

The savages did not await the onset. They turned, scattered, and fled. Many were overtaken and cut down. The Dutchmen sallied from the camp and joined in the pursuit. The Kafirs were routed completely, and all the cattle and flocks were recovered.

That same day there was a hot discussion over the camp-fires as to whether the emigrant farmers should return at once to the colony or wait until they should gather together some of the other parties of emigrants which were known to have crossed the frontier. At last it was resolved to adopt the latter course, but the wives and families were to be sent back to Fort Wilshire under the escort of their deliverers, there to remain till better times should dawn.

"Charlie," said Conrad Marais, as he walked up and down with his friend, "I must stick by my party, but I can trust you and Hans. You'll be careful of the women and little ones."

"You may depend on us," replied Considine, with emphasis.

"And you needn't be afraid to speak to Bertha by the way," said Conrad, with a peculiar side glance.

Charlie looked up quickly with a flush.

"Do you mean, sir, that—that—"

"Of course I do," cried the stout farmer, grasping his friend by the hand; "I forgive your being an Englishman, Charlie, and as I can't make you a Dutchman, the next best I can do for you is to give you a Dutch wife, who is in my opinion better and prettier than any English girl that ever lived."

"Hold!" cried Considine, returning the grasp, "I will not join you in making invidious comparisons between Dutch and English; but I'll go farther than you, and say that Bertha is in my opinion the best and prettiest girl in the whole world."

"That'll do, lad, that'll do. So, now, we'll go see what the Totties have managed to toss us up for breakfast."

Before the sun set that night the emigrant farmers, united with another large ·band, were entrenched in a temporary stronghold, and the women and children, with the rescue party—strengthened by a company of hunters and traders who had been in the interior when the war broke out, were far on their way back to Fort Wilshire.

CHAPTER XXVI.

RELATES INCIDENTS OF THE WAR AND A GREAT DELIVERANCE.

On reaching the frontier fort it was found to be in a state of excitement, bustle, and preparation.

News had just been received that the treacherous chief Hintza, although professedly at peace with the colony, was secretly in league with the invading chiefs, and the Governor was convinced of the necessity of taking vigorous measures against him. The savages, flushed with success, and retiring for a time to their own land with the cattle they had carried off, found in Hintza one ready to aid them in every way. It transpired that he had not only allowed the stolen cattle to be secreted in his territory, but many of his own people were "out" with the confederate chiefs fighting against the colonists, while traders under his protection had by his orders been seized and plundered. A message had therefore been sent to Hintza requiring him at once and decidedly to declare his intentions. To this, instead of a reply, the savage chief sent one of his braves, whose speech and conduct showed that his wily master only wished to gain time by trifling diplomacy. The brave was therefore sent back with another message, to the effect that if he, Hintza, should afford any of the other chiefs shelter or protection, and did not restore the booty concealed in his territory, he would be treated as an enemy. It was also proposed that himself should come and have an interview with the Governor, but this invitation he declined. Sir Benjamin D'Urban, therefore, resolved to menace the truculent chief in his own dominions, and when Hans Marais with his band entered the square of the little fort, he found the troops on the point of setting out.

The force consisted of a body of regulars and a burgher band collected from all parts of the colony. Among them were hardy Englishmen from the Zuurveld, tough with the training of fourteen years in the wilderness, and massive Dutchmen from the karroo, splendid horsemen and deadly shots.

While the bustle was at its height a party of horsemen galloped up to the gate, headed by a giant. It turned out to be a contingent from Glen Lynden, under Groot Willem of Baviaans River, with Andrew Rivers, Jerry Goldboy, and several of the Dutch farmers of the Tarka in his train.

"Ho! here you are," cried Groot Willem in his hearty bass roar, as he leaped to the ground and

seized Hans Marais by the hand. "All well at
Eden—eh?"

"Burnt out," said Hans quietly.

The giant looked aghast for a moment. Then his
friend ran hurriedly over the main points of his story.
But there was no time for talk. While salutations
were being exchanged by the members of the various
parties thus assembled, Sir Benjamin appeared,
mounted his horse, gave orders to several of his
officers, and spoke a few words to Groot Willem and
Hans. In a few minutes the troops were marched
out of the fort, and next day reached the right bank
of the Kei River.

This was the western boundary of Hintza's particular territory. On arriving, the Governor issued
general orders to the effect that Hintza was not " to
be treated as an enemy." No kraals were to be burnt,
no gardens or fields pillaged, and no natives meddled
with, unless hostilities were first begun by them, and
that no act of violence should be committed until
due notice of the commencement of hostilities had
been given. "You see," said Sir Benjamin in a
private conversation with one of his staff, "I am
resolved to take every possible precaution to avoid
giving cause of complaint to the great chief, and to
endeavour by mild forbearance to maintain peace.
At the same time, it is essential that I should act
with vigour because undue forbearance is always

misinterpreted by savages to mean cowardice, and
only precipitates the evils we seek to avoid."

On arriving at a spot where a trader named Purcell had been plundered and murdered, the troops
were met by several "councillors" from Hintza and
from the chief Booko, who were still a day's journey
distant. To these the Governor said:—

"Go, tell the Great Chief that I request an interview with himself, because I desire that peace should
be between us, and that justice should be done. I
will not cease to advance until such interview is
obtained, and it will depend on his own conduct
whether Hintza is treated by the British Government
as a friend or a foe."

But the Great Chief was doggedly bent on meeting his fate. He returned no answer to the message,
and the troops moved on. Arriving at the mission
station of Butterworth, they found it destroyed, and
here they were met by a large body of Fingoes—
native slaves—who eagerly offered their services to
fight against their cruel masters the Kafirs. These
Fingoes—destined in after years to make a deep
impression on the colony—were the remains of eight
powerful nations, who, broken up and scattered by
the ferocious Chaka and his Zulu hordes, had taken
refuge with Hintza, by whom they were enslaved
and treated in the most brutal manner. He gave
them generally the name of Fingo, which means

dog. Their eager offer to serve under the British Chief was therefore most natural, but Sir Benjamin declined their services at the time, as war had not yet been declared.

Soon after, a detachment of thirty men was sent back to the colony with despatches, in charge of an ensign named Armstrong, who was waylaid and murdered by some of Hintza's Kafirs. The Governor, finding that his overtures were treated with studied neglect, and that hostilities were thus begun, called to him a Kafir councillor and warrior, and said—

"Your master has treated all my messages with contempt. He is in secret alliance with the chiefs who have invaded our colony. He has received and concealed cattle stolen from the white men. A British trader has been deliberately murdered in his territory, near his own residence, and under his pro-
· tection, and no steps have been taken to punish the murderers. Violence and outrage have been committed by him on British traders, and missionaries living under his safeguard have been forced to flee to the Tambookie chief to save their lives. I will no. longer treat with him. Since Hintza is resolved on war, he shall have it. I will now take the Fingoes under my special protection, make them subjects of the king of England, and severely punish any who commit violence upon them. I will also carry off

all the cattle I can find.—Go, tell your master his blood shall be on his own head."

This message, which was followed up by prompt action, the capture of considerable numbers of cattle, and a successful attack on one of his principal kraals, brought the great chief to his senses—apparently, but not really, as the sequel will show. He sent in four messengers with proposals, but the Governor refused to treat with any one except Hintza himself. Terrified at last into submission, he entered the camp with a retinue of fifty followers, and was courteously received by the commander-in-chief.

During the course of these proceedings detached parties were frequently sent hither and thither to surprise a kraal or to capture cattle, and the two parties under Groot Willem and Hans Marais, having arrived at Fort Wilshire at the same time, were allowed to act pretty much in concert.

One night they found themselves encamped in a dark mountain gorge during a thunderstorm.

"Well, well," said Jerry Goldboy to Junkie, who with Scholtz had taken refuge under the very imperfect shelter of a bush, "it's 'orrible 'ard work this campaigning; specially in bad weather, with the point of one's nose a'most cut off."

Jerry referred to a wound which an assagai aimed at his heart had that day inflicted on his nose. The wound was not severe, but it was painful, and the

sticking-plaster which held the point of his unfortunate member in its place gave his countenance an
unusually comical appearance.

"Is it very zore, boy?" asked Scholtz.

"Zore! I wish you 'ad it, an' you wouldn't 'ave to
ask," returned Jerry.

"How did you come by it?" asked Junkie, looking
grave with difficulty.

"Well, it ain't easy to say exactly. You see it was
getting dark at the time, and I was doin' my best to
drive a thief of a *h*ox down a place in the kloof
where it had to stand upright, a'most, on its front-
legs, with its tail whirlin' in the *h*air. An' I 'adn't
much time to waste neither, for I knew there was
Kafirs all about, an' the troops was gettin' a'ead of me,
an' my 'oss was tied to a yellow-wood tree at the foot
o' the kloof, an' I began to feel sort o' skeery with
the gloomy thickets all around, an' rugged precipices lookin' as if they'd tumble on me, an' the great
mountains goin' up to 'eaven—oh! I can tell you it
was—it was—"

"In short, the most horrible sight you ever saw,"
said Junkie, drawing his blanket tighter round his
shoulders, and crouching nearer to the bulky form
of Scholtz for protection from the wind which was
rising.

"Yes, Junkie, it was—the most 'orrible sight I
ever saw, for wild savageness, so I drew my sword

and gave the *h*ox a prog that sent 'im 'ead over 'eels
down the kloof w'ere 'e broke 'is back.   Just at that
werry moment—would you mind takin' your toe out
o' my neck, Junkie ? it ain't comfortable : thank you.
—Well as I was sayin', at that very moment I spied
a black fellow stealin' away in the direction of my
'oss.   He saw me too, but thought I didn't see '*im*.
Up I jumps, an' run for the 'oss.   Up 'e jumps an'
run likewise.   But I was nearer than 'im, an' a deal
faster—though I don't mean to boast—"

"An' a deal frighteneder," suggested Junkie.

"P'raps, 'owever I got to the 'oss first.   I didn't
take time to mount, but went leap-frog over 'is tail
slap into the saddle, which gave the *h*old 'oss such a
skeer that 'e bolted ! The Kafir 'e gave a yell an'
sent 'is assagai after me, an' by bad luck I looks
round just as it went past, an' all but took off the
point of my nose.   Wasn't it unlucky ?"

"Unlucky ! you ungrateful man," growled Scholtz.
"You should be ver' glad de assagai did not stick
you in de neck like von zow.—Is zat rain vich I
feels in ze back of mine head ?"

'Like enough.   There's plenty of it, anyhow,"
said Junkie, trying to peer through the gloom in the
direction of the tents occupied by a small body of
regular troops which accompanied them.

As he did so a sudden squall struck the tents,
levelling two with the ground, and entirely whisking

off one, which, after making a wild circle in the air, was launched over a precipice into thick darkness, and never more seen!

Lying under another bush, not far distant, Considine and Hans lay crouched together for the purpose at once of keeping each other warm and presenting the smallest possible amount of surface to the weather. They did not sleep at first, and being within earshot of the bush under which the brothers Skyd had sheltered themselves, found sufficient entertainment in listening to their conversation.

"We scarce counted on this sort of thing," said John Skyd, "when, fifteen years ago, we left the shores of old England for 'Afric's southern wilds.'"

"That's true, Jack," was Bob Skyd's reply, "and I sometimes think it would have been better if we had remained at home."

"Craven heart! what do you mean?" demanded James.

"Ay, what do you mean?" repeated Dobson; "will nothing convince you? It is true we made a poor job of the farming, owing to our ignorance, but since we took to merchandise have we not made a good thing of it—ain't it improving every day, and won't we rise to the very pinnacle of prosperity when this miserable war is over?"

"Supposing that we are not killed in the mean-

time," said Stephen Orpin, who formed one of the
group.

"That is a mere truism, and quite irrelevant,"
retorted Dobson.

"Talking of irrelevant matters, does any one know
why Sandy Black and M'Tavish did not come with
Groot Willem?" asked Orpin.

To this John Skyd replied that he had heard some
one say a party of the Glen Lynden men had gone off
to root out a nest of freebooters under that scoundrel
Ruyter, who, taking advantage of the times, had
become more ferocious and daring than ever.

"Yet some say," observed Dobson, "that the
Hottentot robber is becoming religious or craven-
hearted, I don't know which."

"Perhaps broken-hearted," suggested Orpin.

"Perhaps. Anyhow it is said his followers are
dissatisfied with him for some reason or other. He
does not lead them so well as he was wont to."

While the white men were thus variously engaged
in jesting over their discomforts, or holding more
serious converse, their sable enemies were preparing
for them a warm reception in the neighbouring pass.
But both parties were checked and startled by the
storm which presently burst over them. At first
the thunder-claps were distant, but by degrees they
came nearer, and burst with deafening crash, seemingly close overhead, while lightning ran along the

earth like momentary rivulets of fire. At the same
time the windows of heaven were opened, and rain
fell in waterspouts, drenching every one to the
skin.

The storm passed as suddenly as it came, and at
daybreak was entirely gone, leaving a calm clear
sky.

Sleepy, wet, covered with mud, and utterly
miserable, the party turned out of their comfortless
bivouac, and, after a hasty meal of cold provisions,
resumed their march up the kloof.

At the narrowest part of it, some of the troops
were sent in advance as skirmishers, and the ambush
was discovered. Even then they were in an awkward
position, and there can be no question that if the
natives had been possessed of fire-arms they would
have been cut off to a man. As it was, the savages
came at them with dauntless courage, throwing their
assagais when near enough, and hurling stones down
from the almost perpendicular cliffs on either side.
But nothing could resist the steady fire of men who
were, most of them, expert shots. Few of the white
men were wounded, but heaps of the Kafirs lay dead
on each other ere they gave way and retreated before
a dashing charge with the bayonet.

Oh! it was a sad sight,—sad to see men in the
vigorous health of early youth and the strong powers
of manhood's prime cast lifeless on the ground and

left to rot there for the mistaken idea on the Kafirs' part that white men were their natural enemies, when, in truth, they brought to their land the comforts of civilised life; sad to think that they had died for the mistaken notion that their country was being taken from them, when in truth they had much more country than they knew what to do with . —more than was sufficient to support themselves and all the white men who have ever gone there, and all that are likely to go for many years to come; sad to think of the stern necessity that compelled the white men to lay them low; sadder still to think of the wives and mothers, sisters and little ones, who were left to wail unavailingly for fathers and brothers lost to them for ever; and saddest of all to remember that it is not merely the naked savage in his untutored ignorance, but the civilised white man in his learned wisdom, who indulges in this silly, costly, murderous, brutal, and accursed game of war !

Returning from the fight next day with a large herd of captured cattle, the contingent found that Hintza had agreed unconditionally to all the proposals made to him by the Governor; among others that he should restore to the colonists 50,000 head of cattle and 1000 horses,—one half to be given up at once, the remainder in the course of a year.

The deceitful chief was thus ready in his acquiescence, simply because he had no intention what-

ever of fulfilling his engagements. To blind his
white enemies the more effectually, he himself offered
to remain in the camp as a hostage, with his
followers. Two other chiefs, Kreli and Booko, also
joined him. This seemingly gracious conduct won
for Hintza so much confidence that orders were immediately given to evacuate his territory. He became the guest of Colonel Smith, and the Governor presented him with numerous conciliatory gifts.
Thereafter the camp was broken up and the Governor took his departure.

No sooner was his back turned than Hintza's
people commenced a general massacre of the Fingoes.
About thirty were murdered in cold blood near to
Colonel Somerset's camp.

Full of indignation, when he heard this, the Governor summoned Hintza to his presence and related
what had occurred.

" Well, and what then ?" was the Kafir's cool reply,
" are they not my dogs ?"

Sir Benjamin met this by giving orders that
Hintza and all the people with him should be put
under guard, and held as hostages for the safety of
the Fingoes. He instantly despatched messengers
to stop the carnage, and said that if it continued
after three hours he would shoot two of Hintza's
suite for every Fingo killed. He added, moreover,
that if he found there was any subterfuge in the

message they sent—as he had discovered to have been the case in former messages—he would hang Hintza, Kreli, and Booko on the tree under which they were sitting.

In less than ten minutes the messengers of the chiefs were scampering off at full speed in different directions with orders! So potent was the power of this vigorous treatment that within the short time specified the massacre was stopped.

But the Governor knew well the character of the men with whom he had to deal. To have left the Fingoes in their hands after this would have been tantamount to condemning them to suffer the revengeful wrath of their cruel masters, who would no doubt have resumed the massacre the instant the troops were withdrawn. Sir Benjamin therefore collected them together, along with the few missionaries and other British subjects who had found temporary refuge at the station of Clarkeburg. He placed them under the care of the Rev. Mr. Ayliffe, for whom the Fingoes expressed sincere regard, and transported the whole body in safety across the Kei.

"An amazing sight," observed Charlie Considine to a knot of his comrades, as they reined up on the top of a knoll, and watched the long line of Fingoes defiling before him like an antediluvian black snake trailing its sinuous course over the land, with a little knot of red-coats in front, looking like its fiery head, and sundry groups of burghers, and other troops, here and there along its body, like parti-coloured legs and claws. The length of this mighty snake may be estimated when it is said that of the Fingo nation not fewer than 2000 men, 5600 women, and 9200 children, with 22,000 cattle, were led across the Kei into the colony at that time.

The whole scene, with its multitudinous details, was a commingling of the ludicrous, the touching, and the sublime. It was mirth-provoking to observe the wild energy of the coal-black men, as they sprang from side to side, with shield and assagai, driving in refractory cattle; the curious nature of the bundles borne by many of the women; the frolicking of the larger children and the tottering of the smaller ones, whose little black legs seemed quite unequal to the support of their rotund bodies. It was touching to see, here and there, a stalwart man pick up a tired goat and lay it on his shoulders, or relieve a weary woman of her burden—or catch up a stumbling little one that had lost its mother, and carry it along in his arms. And it was a sublime thought that this great army was being led, like the Israelites of old, out of worse than Egyptian bondage, into a Christian colony, as the adopted sons and daughters of a civilised Government.

It was, in one sense, a " nation born in a day,"

for the Fingoes were destined, in after years, to become the faithful allies of their white deliverers, and the creators of much additional wealth in the colony,—a raw native material which at that time gladdened, and still rejoices, the hearts of those missionaries who look to the Fingoes with reasonable hope, as likely to become, in time, the bearers of the Gospel to their kindred in the wilds of Central Africa.

CHAPTER XXVII.

THE FATE OF THE PARAMOUNT CHIEF OF KAFIRLAND.

MEANWHILE Hintza, not having shown sufficient readiness and alacrity in redeeming his promises, was held as a hostage in the hands of the white man. He was, however, treated with the utmost consideration, and when he proposed to accompany a division of the troops, in order to exercise to the utmost his personal influence in recovering from his people the cattle and horses due, and to apprehend the murderers, according to treaty, he was allowed to do so, not only quite free in person, but even with his weapons in his hands.

Colonel Smith, however, who commanded the force, distinctly told the chief, through an interpreter, that if he attempted to escape he would instantly be shot.

The force consisted of detachments of the Cape Mounted Rifles, the 72d regiment, and the corps of Guides—350 men in all.

Towards the afternoon of the day on which they

marched, a circumstance occurred which justified Colonel Smith's suspicions as to Hintza's sincerity. They had reached a streamlet and encamped, when one of the guides reported to him that two Kafirs, with five head of cattle, were near the camp, and that Hintza, on the plea that they would be afraid to approach, had sent one of his people to bring them in.

On being questioned, the chief declined to give any explanation on the subject, and the Kafirs not only did not come in, as they were ordered, but made off, and carried the horse of Hintza's messenger along with them! The suspicion excited by this circumstance was increased by the evasive answers given to the Colonel's repeated inquiries as to the point on which Hintza wished the troops to march.

"We are going right," was the only answer that could be elicited from the taciturn savage.

After crossing the range of the Guadan Hills, the troops bivouacked on the Guanga, and here Hintza became more communicative, said that he wished them to march towards the mouth of the Bashee, by a route which he would point out, and that they must move at midnight. This was done, and they continued to move forward till eight o'clock in the morning, observing as they went the spoor of numerous herds of cattle that had been driven in that direction quite recently.

The men, being tired, were then halted for refreshment.

At this point Hintza became particularly uneasy at the vigilance with which he was watched.

"What have the cattle done," he said testily, "that you should want them? and why should my subjects be deprived of them?"

"Why do you ask such questions, Hintza?" replied Colonel Smith; "you know well the many outrages committed on the colonists by your people, and the thousands of cattle that have been stolen. It is in redress of these wrongs that we demand them."

The chief looked stern, but made no rejoinder. He appeared to recover himself, however, after breakfast, and was in high spirits while on the march. He rode a remarkably strong horse that day, which he appeared very anxious to spare from fatigue— dismounting and leading him up every ascent.

As the party advanced the tracks of numerous cattle were still found leading onward, but the animals themselves were nowhere to be seen.

"You see," remarked the chief, with a touch of sarcasm in his tone as he rode beside the Colonel, "you see how my subjects treat me: they drive their cattle from me in spite of me."

"I do not want your *subjects'* cattle, Hintza," was the Colonel's pointed reply; "I want, and will have, the *colonial* cattle which they have stolen."

"Then," returned the chief, "allow me to send forward my councillor Umtini to tell my people I am here, that they must not drive away their cattle, and that the cattle of your nation will be alone selected."

Although it was quite evident that the chief meditated mischief it was thought best to agree to this proposal. Accordingly, the councillor, after being enjoined to return that night, which he promised to do, mounted and left the camp at full speed, accompanied by an attendant.

There was ground for uneasiness and much caution in all this, for those who knew Hintza best were wont to say that he possessed in a high degree all the vices of the savage—ingratitude, avarice, cunning, and cruelty, and his treatment of the traders and missionaries under his protection, as well as his secret encouragement of the border chiefs, fully bore out their opinion.

"Now!" exclaimed the chief in high spirits when Umtini had left, "you need not go on to the Bashee, you will have more cattle than you can drive on the Xabecca."

The path the troops were passing was a mere cattle-track leading up hill, from the bed of the Xabecca river, among tangled brushwood, and occasionally passing through a cleft in the rocks. Colonel Smith was the only member of the party who rode up the hill; Hintza and the others led their horses. On drawing near to the summit, the chief and his attendants mounted and rode silently but quickly past the Colonel into the bushes.

One of the guides observing the action called to the Colonel, who immediately shouted, " Hintza, stop !"

The savage had no intention of stopping, but, finding himself entangled in the thicket, was compelled to return to the track. He did so with such coolness and with such an ingenuous smile, that the Colonel, who had drawn a pistol, felt half ashamed of his suspicions, and allowed the chief to ride forward as before.

At the top of the steep ascent the country was quite open. The Xabecca river was seen in front with a few Kafir huts on its banks. Here the chief set off at full speed in the direction of the huts.

Colonel Smith and three of the guides pursued. The latter were quickly left behind, but the Colonel, being well mounted, kept up with the fugitive. Spurring on with violence, he soon overtook him.

" Stop, Hintza !" he shouted.

But Hintza was playing his last card. He urged his horse to greater exertion, and kept stabbing at his pursuer with an assagai.

The Colonel drew a pistol, but it snapped. A second was used with like ill success. He then

spurred close up, struck the chief with the butt-end
of the pistol, and in so doing dropped it. Hintza
looked round with a smile of derision, and the
Colonel, hurling the other pistol at him, struck him
on the back of the head. The blow was ineffectual.
Hintza rode on; the troops followed as they best
could. They were now nearing the huts. At length,
making a desperate effort, the Colonel dashed close
up to the chief. Having now no weapon, he seized
him by the collar of his kaross, or cloak, and, with
a violent effort, hurled him to the ground. Both
horses were going at racing speed. The Colonel,
unable to check his, passed on, but before he was
beyond reach the agile savage had leaped to his feet,
drawn another assagai from the bundle which he
carried, and hurled it after his enemy. So good was
the aim that the weapon passed within a few inches
of the Colonel's body.

The act afforded time to those behind to come up.
Although Hintza turned aside instantly and ran down
the steep bank of the Xabecca, the foremost of the
guides—named Southey—got within gun-shot and
shouted in the Kafir tongue to the chief to stop. No
attention being paid to the order, he fired, and Hintza fell, wounded in the left leg. Leaping up in a
moment, he resumed his flight, when Southey fired
again, and once more the chief was hit and pitched
forward, but rose instantly and gained the cover of

the thicket which lined the bank of the river. Southey leaped off his horse and gave chase, closely followed by Lieutenant Balfour of the 72d regiment. The former kept up and the latter down the stream.

They had proceeded thus in opposite directions some distance when Southey was startled by an assagai striking the cliff on which he was climbing. Turning sharply, he saw Hintza's head and his uplifted arm among the bushes within a few feet of him. The savage was in the act of hurling another assagai. Quick as thought the guide levelled his gun and fired. The shot completely shattered the upper part of Hintza's skull, and next instant a mangled corpse was all that remained of the paramount chief of Kafirland.

CHAPTER XXVIII.

THE RESULTS OF WAR.

" PEACE at last!" said Edwin Brook to George
Dally, on arriving at his ravaged and herdless farm
in the Zuurveld, whither George had preceded him.

" Peace is it, sir ? Ah, that 's well. It 's about time
too, for we 've got a deal to do—haven't we, sir ?"

George spoke quite cheerily, under the impression
that his master required comforting.

" You see, sir, we 've got to go back pretty well
to where we was in 1820, and begin it all over
again. It *is* somewhat aggrawatin' ! Might have been
avoided, too, if they 'd kep' a few more troops on
the frontier."

" Well, Jack, the treaty is signed at last," said
Robert Skyd to his brother, as he sat on his counter
in Grahamstown, drumming with his heels.

" Not too soon," replied John Skyd, taking a seat
on the same convenient lounge. " It has cost us
something: houses burnt all over the settlement,
from end to end; crops destroyed; cattle carried
off, and, worst of all, trade almost ruined—except in

the case of lucky fellows like you, Bob, who sell to the troops."

"War would not have broken out at all," returned Bob, "if the Kafirs had only been managed with a touch of ordinary common sense in times past. Our losses are tremendous. Just look at the Kafir trade, which last year I believe amounted to above £40,000, —*that's* crushed out altogether in the meantime, and won't be easily revived. Kafirs in hundreds were beginning to discard their dirty karosses, and to buy blankets, handkerchiefs, flannels, baize, cotton, knives, axes, and what not, while the traders had set up their stores everywhere in Kafirland—to say nothing of your own business, Jack, in the gum, ivory, and shooting way, and our profits thereon. We were beginning to flourish so well, too, as a colony. I believe that we've been absorbing annually somewhere about £150,000 worth of British manufactured articles—not to mention other things, and now—Oh, Jack, mankind is a monstrous idiot!"

"Peace comes too late for us, Gertie," said Hans Marais to his wife, on their return to the old homestead on the karroo, which presented nothing but a blackened heap of dry mud, bricks, and charred timbers; herds and flocks gone—dreary silence in possession—the very picture of desolation.

"Better late than never," remarked Charlie Considine sadly. "We must just set to work, re-stock and re-build. Not so difficult to do so as it might have been, however, owing to that considerate uncle of mine. We're better off than some of our poor neighbours who have nothing to fall back upon. They say that more than 3000 persons have been reduced to destitution; 500 farm-houses have been burnt and pillaged; 900 horses, 55,000 sheep and goats, and above 30,000 head of cattle carried off, only a few of which were recovered by Colonel Smith on that expedition when Hintza was killed. However, we'll keep up heart and go to work with a will—shan't we, my little wife?"

Bertha—now Bertha Considine—who leaned on Charlie's arm, spoke not with her lips, but she lifted her bright blue eyes, and with these orbs of light declared her thorough belief in the wisdom of whatever Charlie might say or do.

"They say it's all settled!" cried Jerry Goldboy, hastily entering Kenneth M'Tavish's stable.

"What's all settled?" demanded Sandy Black.

"Peace with the Kafirs," said Jerry.

"Peace wi' the Kawfirs!" echoed Sandy, in a slightly contemptuous tone. "H'm! they should never hae had war wi' them, Jerry, my man."

"But 'aving 'ad it, ain't it well that it's *hover*?" returned Jerry.

"It's cost us a bonnie penny," rejoined Black.

"Nae doot Glen Lynden has come off better than ither places, for we 've managed to haud oor ain no' that ill, but wae's me for the puir folk o' the low country! An' I 'll be bound the Imperial Treasury 'll smart for 't.* But it's an ill wind that blaws nae gude. We 've taken a gude slice o' land frae the thievin' craters, for it 's said Sir Benjamin D'Urban has annexed all the country between the Kei and the Keiskamma to the colony. A most needfu' addition, for the jungles o' the Great Fish River or the Buffalo were jist fortresses where the Kawfirs played hide-an'-seek wi' the settlers, an' it 's as plain as the nose on my face that peace wi' them is not possible till they 're driven across the Kei—that bein' a defensible boundary."

"So, they say that peace is proclaimed," said Stephen Orpin to a pretty young woman who had recently put it out of his power to talk of his "bachelor home at Salem." Jessie M'Tavish had taken pity on him at last!

"Indeed!" replied Jessie, with a half-disappointed look; "then I suppose you 'll be going off again on your long journeys into the interior, and leaving me to pine here in solitude ?"

"That depends," returned Orpin, "on how you treat me! Perhaps I may manage to find my work

* The war of 1834-6 cost the Treasury £300,000, and the colonists lost in houses. stock, etc., £288,625.

nearer home than I did in days gone by. At all events I'll not go into Kafirland just now, for it's likely to remain in an unsettled state for many a day. It has been a sad and useless war, and has cost us a heavy price. Think, Jessie, of the lives lost—forty-four of our people murdered during the invasion, and eighty-four killed and thirty wounded during the war. People will say that is nothing to speak of compared with losses in other wars; but I don't care for comparisons, I think only of the numbers of our people, and of the hundreds of wretched Kafirs, who have been cut off in their prime and sent to meet their Judge. But there has been one trophy of the war at which I look with rejoicing; 15,000 Fingoes rescued from slavery is something to be thankful for. God can bring good out of evil. It may be that He will give me employment in that direction ere long."

These various remarks, good reader, were uttered some months after the events recorded in the last chapter, for the death of the great chief of Kafirland did not immediately terminate the war. On the contrary, the treaty of peace entered into with Kreli, Hintza's son and successor, was scouted by the confederate chiefs, Tyali, Macomo, etc., who remained still unsubdued in the annexed territory, and both there and within the old frontier continued to commit murders and wide-spread depredations.

It was not until the Kafirs had been hunted by our troops into the most impregnable of their woody fortresses, and fairly brought to bay, that the chiefs sent messengers to solicit peace. It was granted. A treaty of peace was entered into, by which the Kafirs gave up all right to the country conquered, and consented to hold their lands under tenure from the British Sovereign. It was signed at Fort Wilshire in September.

Thereafter Sir Benjamin D'Urban laid down with great wisdom and ability plans for the occupation and defence of the annexed territory, so as to form a real obstruction to future raids by the lawless natives —plans which, if carried out, would no doubt have prevented future wars, and *on the strength of which* the farmers began to return to their desolated farms, and commence re-building and re-stocking with indomitable resolution. Others accepted offers of land in the new territory, and a few of the Dutch farmers, hoping for better times, and still trusting to British wisdom for protection, were prevailed on to remain in the colony at a time when many of their kindred were moving off in despair of being either protected, understood, or fairly represented.

Among these still trusting ones was Conrad Marais. Strongly urged by Hans and Considine, he consented to begin life anew in the old home, and went vigorously to work with his stout sons.

But he had barely begun to get the place into something like order when a shell was sent into the colony, which created almost as much dismay as. if it had been the precursor of another Kafir invasion.

Conrad was seated in a friend's house in Somerset when the said shell exploded. It came in the form of a newspaper paragraph. He looked surprised on reading the first line or two; then a dark frown settled on his face, which, as he read on, became pale, while his compressed lips twitched with suppressed passion.

Finishing the paragraph, he crushed the newspaper up in his hand, and, thrusting it into his pocket, hastened to the stable, where he saddled his horse. Leaping on its back as if he had been a youth of twenty, he drove the spur into its flanks and galloped away at full speed—away over the dusty road leading from Somerset to the hills; away over the ridge that separates it from the level country beyond; and away over the brown karroo, until at last, covered with dust and flecked with foam, he drew up at his own door and burst in upon the family. They were concluding their evening meal.

" Read that !" he cried, flinging down the paper, throwing himself into a chair, and bringing his fist down on the table with a crash that set cups and glasses dancing.

"There!" he added, pointing to the paragraph, as Hans took up the paper—"that despatch from Lord Glenelg—the British Colonial Secretary—at the top of the column. Read it aloud, boy."

Hans read as follows :—

"'In the conduct which was pursued towards the Kafir nation by the colonists and the public authorities of the colony, through a long series of years, the Kafirs had ample justification of the late war; they had to resent, and endeavour justly, though impotently, to avenge a series of encroachments; they had a perfect right to hazard the experiment, however hopeless, of extorting by force that redress which they could not expect otherwise to obtain, and the claim of sovereignty over the new province must be renounced. It rests upon a conquest resulting from a war in which, as far as I am at present enabled to judge, the original justice is on the side of the conquered, not of the victorious party.'"

"Mark that!" cried Conrad, starting to his feet when Hans had finished, and speaking loud, as if he were addressing the assembled colony instead of the amazed members of his own family,—"mark that: '*the claim of sovereignty over the new province must be renounced.*' So it seems that the Kafirs are not only to be patted on the back for having acted the part of cattle-lifters for years, but are to be invited back to their old haunts to begin the work over again and necessitate another war !"

He stopped abruptly, as if to check words that ought not to be uttered. There was a momentary silence in the group as they looked at each other. It was broken by Conrad saying to his youngest son, in a voice of forced calmness—

"Go, lad, get me a fresh horse. I will rouse the Dutch-African farmers all over the colony. The land is too hot to hold us. We cannot hope to find rest under the Union Jack !"

We can sympathise strongly with the violent indignation of the honest Dutchman, for, in good truth, not only he and his kindred, but all the people of the colony, were most unjustly blamed and unfairly treated by the Government of that day. Nevertheless Conrad was wrong about the Union Jack. The wisest of plans are open to the insidious entrance of error. The fairest flag may be stained, by unworthy bearers, with occasional prostitution. A Secretary of State is not the British nation, nor is he even, at all times, a true representative of British feeling. Many a deed of folly, and sometimes of darkness, has unhappily been perpetrated under the protection of the Union Jack, but that does not alter the great historical fact, that truth, justice, fair play, and freedom have flourished longer and better under its ample

folds than under any other flag that flies on the face
of the whole earth.

But Conrad Marais was not in a position to consider
this just then. The boy who is writhing under the lash
of a temporarily insane father is not in a position to
reflect that, in the main, his father is, or means to be,
just, kind, loving, and true. Conrad bolted a hasty
supper, mounted the fresh steed, and galloped away
to rouse his kindred. And he proved nearly as good
as his word. He roused many of them to join him
in his intended expatriation, and many more did not
need rousing. Some had brooded over their wrongs
until they began to smoulder, and when they were
told that the *unprovoked* raid of the Kafir thieves
was deemed justifiable by the Government which
ought to have protected their frontier, but had left
them to *protect themselves*, the fire burst into a
flame, and the great exodus began in earnest. Thus,
a second time, did Conrad and his family, with many
others, take to the wilderness. On this occasion the
party included Hans and Charlie Considine, with
their families.

There was still wanting, however, that last straw
which renders a burden intolerable. It was laid on
at the time when slavery was abolished.

The Abolition Act was carried into effect on the 1st
December 1834, at which time the accursed system
of slavery was virtually brought to an end in the

colony, though the slaves were not finally freed from
all control till 1838. But the glory of this noble
work was sullied not a little by the unjust manner
in which, during these four years, the details relative
to the payment of compensation to slave-owners were
carried out. We cannot afford space here to go into
these details. Suffice it to say that, as one of the consequences, many families in the colony were ruined,
and a powerful impulse was given to the exodus, which
had already begun. The leading Dutch-African
families in Oliphant's Hock, Gamtoos River, along the
Fish River, and Somerset, sold their farms—in many
cases at heavy loss or for merely nominal sums
—crossed the border, and bade a final adieu to the
land of their fathers. These were followed by other
bands, among whom were men of wealth and education, from Graaff-Reinet, Uitenhage, and Albany, until
a mighty host had hived off into the far north.
Through many a month of toil and trouble did this
host pass while traversing the land of the savage in
scattered bands. Many a sad reverse befell them.
Some were attacked and cut off; some defended
themselves with heroism and passed on, defying
the Kafirs to arrest their progress, until at last they
reached the distant lands on which their hearts
were set—and there they settled down to plough
and sow to reap and hunt and build, but always

with arms at hand, for the savage was ever on the watch to take them at a disadvantage or unawares.

Thus were laid the foundations of the colony of Natal, the Orange Free State, and the Transvaal Republic.

CHAPTER XXIX.

THE LAST

WITH peace came prosperity. This was not indeed very obvious at first, for it took a long time to reconcile the unfortunates of the eastern provinces to their heavy losses, and a still longer time to teach them to forget. Nevertheless, from this time forward the march of the settlers of 1820, commercially, intellectually, and religiously, became steady, regular, and rapid.

No doubt they suffered one or two grievous checks as years rolled on. Again and again they had to fight the Kafir savage and drive him back into his native jungles, and each time they had more trouble in doing so than before, because the Kafir was an apt pupil, and learned to substitute the gun for the assagai; but he did not learn to substitute enlightened vigour for blind passion, therefore the white man beat him as before.

He did more than that. He sought to disarm the savage, and, to a large extent, succeeded. He

disarmed him of ignorance by such means as the
Lovedale Missionary Institution near Alice; the Institution near Healdtown, and other seminaries,—
as well as by mission stations of French, Dutch-
Reformed, Wesleyan, English, and Scotch churches
scattered all over Kafirland; he taught the savage
that "the fear of the Lord is the beginning of
wisdom," and that industry is the high-road to prosperity. Some of the black men accepted these
truths, others rejected them. Precisely the same
may be said of white men all over the world.
Those who accepted became profitable to themselves
and the community. Those who rejected continued
slaves to themselves and a nuisance to everybody.
Again we remark that the same may be said of
white men everywhere. White unbelievers continued to pronounce the "red" Kafir an "irreclaim-
able savage," fit for nothing but coercion and the
lash. Black unbelievers continued to curse the
white man as being unworthy of any better fate
than being "driven into the sea," and, between the
two, missionaries and Christians, both black and
white, had a hard time of it; but they did not give
in, for, though greatly disheartened at times, they
remembered that they were "soldiers" of the cross,
and as such were bound to "endure hardness."

Moreover, missionaries and Christians of all colours
and kinds doubtless remembered their own sins

and errors. Being imperfect men, they had in some cases—through prejudice and ignorance, but *never* through design—helped the enemy a little; or if they did not remember these errors and sins they were pretty vigorously reminded of them by white opponents, and no doubt the thought of this humbled them to some extent, and enabled them to bow more readily to chastisement. Then they braced themselves anew for the gospel-fight—the only warfare on earth that is certain to result in blessing to both the victors and the vanquished.

If any of the missionaries held with Lord Glenelg in his unwise reversal of the good Sir Benjamin D'Urban's Kafir policy, they must have had the veil removed from their eyes when that nobleman himself confessed his error with a candour that said much for his heart; reversed his own decrees, and fell back upon that very plan which at first he had condemned in such ungenerous terms. His recantation could not, however, recall the thousands of Dutch-African farmers whom he helped to expatriate. Perhaps it was well that it should be so, for good came out of this evil,—namely, the reclamation of vast tracts of the most beautiful and fertile regions of the earth from the dominion of darkness and cruelty.

But what of those whose fortunes we have been following, during this period of peace and prosperity?

Some of them remained in the colony, helped on these blessings, and enjoyed them. Others, casting in their lot with the wanderers, fought the battles and helped to lay the foundations of the new colonies.

First, Charlie Considine. That fortunate man— having come into the possession of a considerable sum of money, through the uncle who had turned out so much "better than he should be," and having become possessed of a huge family of sons and daughters through that Bertie whom he styled the "sugar of his existence,"—settled in Natal along with his friends Hans and Conrad Marais. When that fertile and warm region was taken possession of by the British, he refused to hive off with the Marais, and continued to labour there in the interests of truth, mercy, and justice to the end of his days.

Junkie Brook, with that vigour of character which had asserted itself on the squally day of his nativity, joined Frank Dobson and John Skyd in a hunting expedition beyond the Great Orange River; and when the Orange Free State was set up by the emigrant Dutchmen, he and his friends established there a branch of the flourishing house of Dobson, Skyd, and Co. Being on the spot when South Africa was electrified by the discovery (in 1866-67) of the Diamond Fields of that region, they sent their sons, whose name was legion, to dig, and soon became diamond merchants of the first water, so that when Junkie visited his aged parents on the Zuurveld—which he often did—he usually appeared with his pockets full of precious stones!

" I 've found a diamond *this* time, nurse," he said, on the occasion of one of these visits, " which is as big —oh!—as—as an ostrich-egg! See, here it is," and he laid on the table a diamond which, if not quite as big as the egg of the giant bird, was large enough to enable him, with what he had previously earned, to retire comfortably from the business in favour of his eldest son.

The sudden acquisition of riches in this way was by no means uncommon at that time, for the " Fields" were amazingly prolific, and having been discovered at a crisis of commercial depression, were the means not only of retrieving the fortunes of South Africa, but of advancing her to a condition of hitherto unparalleled prosperity.

Mrs. Scholtz—by that time grown unreasonably fat—eyed the diamond with a look of amused contempt; she evidently did not believe in it. Patting the hand of her former charge, she looked up in his laughing face, and said, with a shake of her head—

" Ah! Junkie, I always said you was a *wonderful* child."

Sitting on a bench in front of the house—no longer domestics, but smoking their pipes there as " friends" of the family, who had raised themselves to a state of comparative affluence—George Dally and Scholtz, now aged men, commented on the same diamond.

"It'll make his fortune," said George.

"Zee boy vas alvays lucky," remarked Scholtz; "zince I began to varm for myzelf I have not zeen zo big a stone."

"Ah! Scholtz," returned his friend, "the hotel business has done very well for me, an' I don't complain, but if I was young again I'd sell off and have a slap at the 'Fields.'"

"Zat vould only prove you vas von fool," said Scholtz quietly.

"I believe it would," returned George.

In regard to the Scotch party at Glen Lynden, we have to record that they continued to persevere and prosper. Wool became one of the staple articles of colonial commerce, and the hills of the Baviaans River sent a large contingent of that article to the flourishing seaport of the eastern provinces.

Of course the people multiplied, and the sturdy sons of the South African highlands did credit to their sires, both in the matter of warring with the Kafir and farming on the hills.

Sandy Black stuck to his farm with the perseverance of a true Scot, and held his own through thick and thin. He married a wife also, and when, in later years, the native blacks made a sudden descent

on his homestead, they were repulsed by a swarm
of white Blacks, assisted by an army of M'Tavishes,
and chased over the hills with a degree of energy
that caused them almost to look blue !

Andrew Rivers, being a man of progressive and
independent mind, cast about him in a state of
uncertainty for some years, devoting himself chiefly
to hunting, until the value of ostrich feathers had
induced far-sighted men to domesticate the giant
bird, and take to "farming" ostriches—incubating
them by artificial as well as natural means. Then
Rivers became an ostrich-farmer. He was joined
in this enterprise by Jerry Goldboy, and the two
ultimately bought a farm on the karroo and settled
down. Rivers had a turn for engineering, and set
himself to form a huge dam to collect rain near his
dwelling. From this reservoir he drew forth constant supplies, not only to water flocks and herds,
but to create a garden in the karroo, which soon
glowed with golden fruit.

In this he set a good example, which has been
followed with great success by many men of enterprise in those regions; and there is no doubt, we
think, that if such dams were multiplied, Artesian
wells sunk, and railways run into the karroos, those
fine though comparatively barren regions of South
Africa would soon begin to blossom like the rose.

Thus, what between ostrich feathers, wool, horses,

cattle, and enterprise, Rivers and Goldboy made themselves comfortable. Like other men of sense, they married. Thereafter the garden had to be considerably enlarged, for the golden fruit created by the streams which had been collected and stored by Rivers, proved quite inadequate to the supply of those oceans of babies and swarms of Goldboys that flooded the karroo, and filled its solitudes with shouts and yells that would have done credit to the wildest tribe of reddest Kafirs in the land.

Some of these descendants, becoming men of energy, with roving dispositions like their sires, travelled into the far north and west, and helped to draw forth the copper ore, and to open the mines of Great Namaqua-land—thus aiding in the development of South Africa's inexhaustible treasure-house, while others of them, especially the sons of Jerry, went into the regions of the Transvaal Republic, and there proved themselves Goldboys in very truth, by successfully working the now celebrated gold-fields of that region.

Stephen Orpin did not give up trade, but he prosecuted it with less and less vigour as time went on, and at last merely continued it as a means of enabling him to prosecute the great object of his life, the preaching of the gospel, not merely to those whom men style *par excellence* the "heathen," but to every one who was willing to listen to the good news—

redemption from *sin!* Ah! there was great fervour
in Stephen Orpin's tones when he said, as he often
did—" Men and women, I do not come here to make
you *good*, which, in the estimation of more than one
half of the so-called Christian world, means *goody*.
My desire is to open your eyes to see Jesus, the
Saviour from *sin*. Who among you—except the
young—does not know the power of sin; our
inability to restrain bad and vicious habits; our
passionate desire to do what we *know* is wrong;
our frequent falling from courses that we *know* to be
right? It is not that hell frightens us; it is not that
heaven fails to attract us. These ideas trouble us
little—too little. It is *present* misery that torments.
We long and desire to have, but cannot obtain; we
fight and strive, but do not succeed, or, it may be,
we do succeed, and discover success to be failure, for
we are disappointed, and then feel a tendency
towards apathetic indifference. If, however, our
consciences be awakened, then the torment takes
another form. We are tempted powerfully and cannot resist. We cannot subdue our passions; we
cannot restrain our tempers. No wonder. Has not
God said, 'Greater is he who ruleth his own spirit,
than he who taketh a city'? The greatest con-
queror is not so great as he who conquers himself.
What then? Is there *no* deliverance from sin? Yes,
there is. 'Sin shall *not* have dominion over you.'

are the words of Him who also said, 'Come unto Me, all ye that labour and are heavy laden, and I will give you rest.'"

"Stephen Orpin," cried a sturdy sinner, in whose ears these words were preached, "do you *know* all that to be true? Can you speak from experience of this deliverance, this rest?"

"Yes," cried Stephen, starting up with a sudden impulse, "I *do* know it—partly by some deliverances that have been wrought for me, partly from some degree of rest attained to, and much, very much, from the firm assurance I have that, but for God's forbearing and restraining mercy, I should have been a lost soul long long ago. Man, wherein I have failed in obtaining deliverance and rest, it has been owing to *my* sin, not to failure in the Lord's faithfulness."

But Stephen did not travel so far or so long as had been his wont in days gone by. A wife and family, in the village of Salem, exercised an attractive influence, fastening him, as it were, to a fixed point, and converting his former erratic orbit into a circle which, with centripetal force, was always drawing nearer to its centre.

In the course of his early wanderings Orpin managed to search out Ruyter the Hottentot robber, and so influenced him as to induce him to give up his lawless career and return to the colony. Ruyter drew with him Abdul Jemalee, Booby the Bushman, and one or two others, who settled down to peaceful occupations.

The Malay in particular—slavery being by that time abolished—returned to Capetown, and there found his amiable wife and loving children ready to receive him with open arms. It is true the wife was somewhat aged, like himself, and his children were grown up—some of them even married,—but these little matters weighed nothing in his mind compared with the great, glorious fact, that he was reunited to them in a land where he might call his body his own!

If Jemalee had been a man of much observation, he might have noted that many important changes had taken place in Capetown and its surroundings during his long absence. A new South African college had been erected; a library which might now stand in the front rank of the world's libraries had been collected; the freedom of the press had been largely taken advantage of, and education generally was being prosecuted with a degree of vigour that argued well for the future of the colony—especially in Stellenbosch, Wellington, and neighbouring places. But Abdul Jemalee was not a man of observation. He did not care a straw for these things, and although we should like much to enlarge on them, as well as on other topics, we must hold our hand —for the new and eastern, not the old and western, provinces of South Africa claim our undivided attention in this tale.

There is no necessary antagonism, however, between these two—'East' and 'West.' Circumstances and men have at present thrown a few apples of discord into them, just as was the case with England and Scotland of old; with the North and South in the United States of late; but, doubtless, these apples, and every other source of discord, will be removed in the course of time, and South Africa will ere long become a united whole, with a united religious and commercial people, under one flag, animated by one desire—the advancement of truth and righteousness among themselves, as well as among surrounding savages,—and extending in one grand sweep of unbroken fertility from the Cape of Good Hope to the Equator.

THE END.

Printed by T. and A. CONSTABLE, Printers to Her Majesty, at the Edinburgh University Press.